SUSANNA KEARSLEY was a museum curator before she took the plunge and became a full-time author. The past and its bearing on the present is a familiar theme in her books. She won the prestigious Catherine Cookson Fiction Award for her novel *Mariana*, and was shortlisted for the Romantic Novel of the Year Award for *Sophia's Secret*.

www.susannakearsley.com

By Susanna Kearsley

Mariana

The Splendour Falls

The Shadowy Horses

Season of Storms

Every Secret Thing
(*previously published under the name Emma Cole*)

Sophia's Secret
(*also published as* The Winter Sea)

The Rose Garden

The Firebird

THE ROSE GARDEN

Susanna Kearsley

Allison & Busby Limited
12 Fitzroy Mews,
London W1T 6DW
www.allisonandbusby.com

Hardback published in Great Britain in 2011.
This paperback edition first published in 2012.

A CIP catalogue record for this book is available from
the British Library.

10 9 8 7 6 5 4 3 2

ISBN 978-0-7490-1047-8

Typeset in 11/16 pt Sabon by
Allison & Busby Ltd.

Paper used in this publication is from sustainably managed sources.
All of the wood used is procured from legal sources and is fully traceable.
The producing mill uses schemes such as ISO 14001
to monitor environmental impact.

Printed and bound by
CPI Group (UK) Ltd, Croydon, CR0 4YY

For my sister, who, as always,
has gone on a step ahead,
and still dances in my memory
and my heart

Let the new faces play what tricks they will
In the old rooms; night can outbalance day,
Our shadows rove the garden gravel still,
The living seem more shadowy than they.

William Butler Yeats, *The New Faces*

Chapter One

I lost my only sister in the last days of November.

It's a rotten time to lose someone, when all the world is dying too and darkness comes on earlier, and when the chill rains fall it seems the very sky is weeping. Not that there's ever a good time to lose your best friend, but it seemed somehow harder to sit there and watch in that hospital room with the white-coated specialists coming and going and see only grey clouds beyond the hard windows that offered no warmth, and no hope.

When my sister had first fallen ill, we would sometimes go out to the garden and sit side by side on the bench by the butterfly bush. We would sit a long time, saying nothing, just feeling the sun on our faces and watching the butterflies dance.

And the illness had seemed very small, then – a thing she could conquer, the way she had overcome everything else fate had flung in her path. She was famous for that, for her spirit. Directors would cast her in roles that were more often given to men than to women, the rogue hero roles, and she'd carry them off with her usual flair and the audience loved it. They loved *her*. The tabloids were camped round the house through the summer, and when she went into the hospital they came there too, standing vigil around the main entrance.

But just at the end there were only the three of us there in the room: me, my sister Katrina, and her husband, Bill.

We were holding her hands, Bill and I, with our eyes on her face because neither of us could have looked at the other. And after a time there were only the two of us left, but I couldn't let go of her hand because part of me couldn't believe she was actually gone, so I sat there in dull, hollow silence until Bill stood slowly and took the hand he was still holding and laid it with care on Katrina's heart. Gently he pressed his own hand on hers one final time, then he slipped something small off her finger and passed it to me: a gold ring, a Claddagh ring, that had belonged to our mother.

Wordlessly he held it out and wordlessly I took it, and still we couldn't meet each other's eyes. And then I saw him feel his pocket for his cigarettes and turning, he went out, and I was left alone. Entirely alone.

And at the window of the room the cold November rains slid down the glass and cast their shifting shadows in a room that could no longer hold the light.

I didn't go to her memorial service. I helped arrange it, and made sure her favourite songs were sung, her favourite verses read, but when the crowds of fans and friends turned up to pay their last respects, I wasn't there to shake their hands and listen to their well-meant words of sympathy. I know there were people who thought me a coward for that, but I couldn't. My grief was a private one, too deep for sharing. And anyway, I knew it didn't matter whether I was at the church, because Katrina wasn't there.

She wasn't anywhere.

It seemed to me incredible a light as strong as hers could be extinguished so completely without leaving some small glow behind, the way a lamp that's been switched off will sometimes dimly shine against the darkness. I'd felt certain I would feel her presence somewhere . . . but I hadn't.

There were only dead leaves round the butterfly bush in the garden, and flowerless shrubs round the porch with its empty swing, and when I started to pack up her closets there wasn't so much as a movement of air in the hallway behind me to let me believe that my sister, in some way, was there with me still.

So I went through the motions. I dealt with the small things that needed attention, and tried to get on with my life in the way everybody was saying I should, while a great hollow loneliness grew deep inside me. Then spring came, and Bill came – turned up on my doorstep one Saturday morning without calling first, looking awkward. And holding her ashes.

I hadn't seen him since November, not in person, though because he had a film just out I'd seen him fairly often on the entertainment news.

He didn't want to come inside. He cleared his throat, a bit uncomfortably. 'I thought . . .' He paused, and held more tightly to the plain oak box that held Katrina's ashes. 'She wanted me to scatter these.'

'I know.' My sister's wishes hadn't been a secret.

'I don't know where to do it. Don't know where to take them. I thought maybe you . . .' His pause this time was more a moment of decision, and he held the box toward me. 'I thought you could do a better job.'

I looked at him, and for the first time since her death our eyes met and I saw the pain in his. He coughed. 'I don't need to be there when you do it, I've said my goodbyes. I just thought you'd know better than I would where she was the happiest. Where she belongs.'

And then he pushed the box into my hands and bent to kiss my forehead before quickly turning from my door and walking off. I wouldn't see him after that, I knew. We moved in different circles, and the bond we'd had between us was reduced now to the simple box he'd handed me.

Inside, I set it on the narrow table by my window, thinking.

Where she'd been the happiest, he'd said. There were so many places, really. I tried narrowing the choices in my mind, recalling images: The morning we had stood and watched the sun rise from the brink of the Grand Canyon, and Katrina's face had radiated wonderment as she had pointed out a small white aeroplane flying far below us, and she'd said she'd never seen a place so beautiful; the time she'd made a movie in Mumbai and the director had rewarded her for days of gruelling action with a weekend in Kerala on the southern coast of India, and I had flown over to join her and we'd spent our evenings walking on the black sand beach while gorgeous sunsets flamed the sky above the blue Arabian sea, and Katrina had splashed through the waves like a child, and been happy.

But then, she'd been happy wherever she went. She had danced through her life with an air of adventure and carried that happiness with her, so trying to imagine where she might have felt it the most was a difficult task, far beyond my abilities. Finally I gave up and turned my focus to the last thing Bill had said: *Where she belongs*.

That should be easier, I knew. There should be one place that would rise above the others in my memory, so I closed my eyes and waited.

It was coming on to evening when I thought of it, and once I'd had the thought it seemed so obvious to me where that place was, where I should take her.

Where both of us, once, had belonged.

Chapter Two

Crossing the Tamar for some reason made me feel different inside. It was only a river, yet each time I crossed it I felt I had stepped through some mystical veil that divided the world that I only existed in from the one where I was meant to be living. It was, my mother always used to say, a kind of homecoming that only those with Cornish blood could feel, and since my blood was Cornish on both sides for several generations back, I felt it strongly.

I'd been born in Cornwall, in the north beyond the sweep of Bodmin Moor, where my film-directing father had been working on a darkly Gothic thriller, but both my parents themselves had been raised on this gentler south coast – du Maurier country – and after my father had settled into lecturing in Screen Studies at the University of Bristol, his more regulated schedule made it possible for us to cross the Tamar every summer and come back to spend our holidays with his old childhood friend George Hallett, who lived with his young and lively family in a marvellously draughty manor house set on a hill above the sea.

We'd come back every year, in fact, until I'd turned ten and my father's work had taken us away from England altogether, setting us down on a different shoreline in Vancouver on the western coast of Canada, where he'd become a fixture at the University of British Columbia's Centre for Cinema Studies.

I had loved it in Canada, too. And of course it had been in Vancouver that my sister, newly turned eighteen, had first begun to get her acting roles – small parts at first, then larger ones that brought enough attention from the Hollywood directors who came up to film their movies in Vancouver that they'd wanted her to come down to LA, and so she had.

I'd followed her in my own turn years later, more by accident than anything. My own career path took me into marketing, and sideways through an unexpected string of opportunities to corporate public relations, and from there, again by chance, to a PR firm that worked mainly in the entertainment industry, and so I found myself at twenty-five being transferred down from Vancouver to the office in Los Angeles.

It never was my favourite place, LA, but shortly after I'd moved down, my parents had crossed paths with a drunk driver on a rain-drenched road back home, so after that Katrina was the only family I had left, and I was loathe to leave her.

We were close. When she was shooting somewhere, I

would always find the time to visit. I was there when Bill proposed to her, and there when they were married in a private ceremony to avoid the paparazzi. And she'd hired me, of course, to represent her. Just to keep it in the family, she had said. These past two years, with her success, she had become my main account.

But I had never really settled in LA, not with apartments – I had gone through four – nor with the men I'd met and dated. I had gone through even more of those, and none had stuck, the last one fading from the picture with convenience when Katrina had grown ill.

I'd barely noticed his departure, then. I didn't miss him now. I had been all but dead myself these past six months, a walking shadow, but this morning as my First Great Western train ran rattling on its rails across the Tamar I felt something deep inside me stir to life.

I was in Cornwall. And it *was* a kind of homecoming – the swiftly passing landscape with its old stone farms and hills and hedges held a warm familiarity, and when I'd changed the big train for a smaller one that ran along the wooded valley branch line leading down towards the coast, I felt an echo of the childish sense of thrilled anticipation that had signalled each beginning of those long-lost summer holidays.

The station at the line's end was a small one, plain with whitewashed walls, a blue bench set beside it, a narrow platform with a white stripe painted at its edge, and a handful of houses stacked up the green hillside behind.

Three people waited on the platform, but I only noticed one of them. I would have known him anywhere.

The last time I had seen Mark Hallett he'd just turned

eighteen and I'd been ten, too young to catch his eye but not too young to be completely smitten with his dark good looks and laughing eyes. I'd followed him round like a puppy, never giving him peace, and he'd taken it in the same good-natured way he took everything else, neither making me feel like a bother, nor letting it go to his head. I'd adored him.

Katrina had, too, though for her it had gone a bit deeper than that. He had been her first boyfriend, her first great romance, and when we had left at the end of the summer I'd watched both their hearts break. Hers had healed. I assumed his had, too. After all, we were twenty years on and our childhoods were over, although when I stepped from the train to the platform and Mark Hallett turned from the place he'd been standing, his eyes finding mine with that shared sense of sure recognition, his smile the same as it ever was, I couldn't help feeling ten again.

'Eva.' His hug was familiar yet different. He wasn't a tall man, despite his strong West Country build, and my chin reached his shoulder, whereas in my memories I'd barely come up to his chest. But the comfort I felt in his arms hadn't changed.

'No trouble with the trains?' he asked.

'No, they were all on time.'

'A miracle.' He took my suitcase from me, though he left me with my shoulder bag, I think because he knew from what I'd told him on the phone what I'd be carrying inside it.

The station didn't even have facilities, it was so small, and the car park wasn't much more than a levelled bit of gravel with a payphone at one side. Mark's van was easily identifiable by the 'Trelowarth Roses' logo on its side, ringed round by painted vines and leaves. He noticed me looking and smiled an apology. 'I would have brought the car, but I had to run a late order to Bodmin and there wasn't time to stop back at the house.'

'That's all right.' I liked the van. It wasn't the same one his father had driven when I'd come down here as a child, but it had the same mingling of smells inside: damp earth and faintly crushed greenery and something elusive belonging to gardens that grew by the sea. And it came with a dog, too – a floppy-eared mongrel with shaggy brown fur and a feathered tail that seemed to never cease wagging, it only changed speed. It wagged crazily now as we got in the van, and the dog would have crawled right through onto the front seat and settled itself on my lap if Mark hadn't with one gentle hand pushed it back.

'This is Samson,' he told me. 'He's harmless.'

They'd always had dogs at Trelowarth. In fact they had usually had three or four running round through the fields with us children and traipsing with muddy feet through the old kitchen and out to the gardens. Mark's stepmother, Claire, had forever been washing the flagstone floors.

Scratching the dog's ears, I asked how Claire was doing.

'Much better. She's out of the plaster now, up walking round on the leg, and the doctor says give it a few weeks and she'll be as right as rain.'

'Remind me how she broke it in the first place?'

'Cleaning gutters.'

'Of course,' I said, sharing his smile because we both

knew how independent Claire was, and it was no surprise that, even now that she'd moved from the manor house into the cottage, she still tried to do all the upkeep herself.

'It's a good thing,' said Mark, 'it was only the gutters, not roof slates.' The dog pushed his way in between us again and Mark nudged him back, starting the van and reversing out onto the road.

Cornish roads were like none anywhere. Here by the coast they were narrow and twisting with steep sloping banks and high hedges that block any view of what might lie ahead. My father had shaved several years off my life every time he had driven down here, at high speeds, simply honking the horn as we came to a corner and trusting that if anyone were approaching unseen round the bend they'd get out of the way. When I'd asked him once what would have happened if somebody coming towards us had chosen to do the same thing he was doing, to honk without slowing down, Dad had just shrugged and assured me it never would happen.

And luckily for us, it never had.

Mark drove a little less recklessly, but I nonetheless needed some kind of distraction from watching the road, so I asked him, 'Is Susan still living at home?'

Susan being his sister, a little bit younger than me.

'She is.' Mark pulled a face, but he didn't convince me. I knew they were close. 'We got rid of her once. She was living up near Bristol, but that didn't stick and now she's back, with plans to start some sort of tea room or something to bring in the tourists. She's full of ideas, is Susan.'

'You don't want a tea room?' I guessed from his tone.

'Let's just say I don't think there'll be too many tourists

who want tea that badly they'd brave the hike up from the village to get it.'

He did have a point. We were entering the village now – Polgelly, with its huddled whitewashed houses and its twisting streets so narrow they were closed to all but local traffic and the taxis that each summer ferried tourists to and from the trains. Mark's van, as compact as it was, could barely squeeze between the buildings.

Polgelly had once been a fishing port of some renown, but with the tourist influx into Cornwall it had changed its face from practical to picturesque, an artist's haven full of shops that sold antiques and Celtic crafts, and Bed & Breakfast cottages with names like 'Smuggler's Rest'. The old shop near the harbour where we'd always bought our fish and chips still looked the same, as did the little fudge shop on the corner. And The Hill, of course, remained the same as ever.

From the first time I'd walked up it I had thought of it like that – *The* Hill, for surely there could be no other hill on earth that could with more perfection test the limits of endurance. It was not its height alone, nor just the angle of its slope, though both were challenging. It was that, once you started up it, there seemed not to be an end to it – the road kept rising steadily through overhanging trees on stone and earthen banks, a punishing ascent that made the muscles of your thighs begin to burn and left them shaking for some minutes when you'd finally reached the top.

Yet being children, and not knowing any better, we'd gone down it every day to play with Mark and Susan's school friends in Polgelly and to sit along the harbour wall to watch the fishermen at work, and in the cheerfully forgetful way that children have we'd pushed aside all thoughts about The Hill until the time came round again for us to climb it. Mark had actually carried me the final few steps, once, which was no doubt why I'd developed such a crush on him.

This time, we had the van, but even it seemed to approach The Hill with something like reluctance, and I could have sworn I heard the engine wheezing as we climbed.

From either side the trees, still bright with new spring green, closed over us and cast a dancing play of light and shadow on the windscreen, and I caught the swift familiar blur of periwinkle tangled with the darker green of ivy winding up along the verge. And then I looked ahead, expectantly, as I had always done, for my first glimpse of the brick chimneys of Trelowarth House.

The chimneys were the first things to be seen, between the trees and the steep bank of green that ran along the road – a Cornish hedge, they called it, built of stones stacked dry in the old fashion, herringbone, with vines and varied wildflowers binding them together and the trees arched close above. Then came a break in both the trees and hedge, and there, framed as impressively as ever by the view of rising fields and distant forests, was the house.

Trelowarth House had weathered centuries upon this hill, its solid grey stone walls an equal match to any storm the sea might throw at it. For all its size it had been plainly built, a two-storey 'L' set with its front squarely facing the line of the cliffs and the sea, while its longer side ran fairly close beside the road. In what might be viewed as a testament to the skills of its original builders, none of its long line of owners appeared to have felt the need to do a major renovation. The chimneys, dutifully repointed, were in the original style, and a few of the casement windows still had the odd pane of Elizabethan glass, through which the people who had lived here then might well have watched the sails of the Armada pass.

The house itself did not encourage such romantic fancies. It looked stern and grey, unyielding, and the only softness to it was the stubborn vine of roses that had wound their way around and over the stone frame of the front door and waited there to bloom as they had done in all the summers of my childhood.

Three-quarters of the way up The Hill, Mark took the sharp left turn into the gravelled drive that angled right again along the fifty feet or so of turf that separated house and road. The garages themselves were in the back, in the old stables at the far edge of the levelled yard, but Mark stopped where we were, beside the house, and parked the van, and in an instant we were overrun by what appeared to be a pack of wild dogs, all leaping up and barking for attention.

'Down, you beasts,' Mark told them, getting out and going round to take my suitcase from the back.

I got out carefully myself, not because I was afraid of the dogs, but because I didn't want to step on them by accident. There were only three of them, as it turned out – a black cocker spaniel, a Labrador, and something that underneath all the dirt looked a bit like a setter – and with the little brown mongrel dog, Samson, who'd jumped out behind me, the pack was quite manageable.

Once I'd patted all the heads and rumpled a few ears and scratched a side or two the leaping changed to energetic wagging, with the four dogs weaving round Mark's legs and mine as we followed the curve of the path round the corner.

At the front of the house a small level lawn had been terraced out of the hillside, with hedges around it to block some part of the wind, and below that the steep green fields tumbled and rolled to the edge of the cliffs.

I was unprepared, as always, for my first view of the sea. From this high up the view was beautiful enough to steal my breath with such a swiftness that my ribcage almost hurt. There were the green hills folding down into their valley, with the darker smudges of the woods marked here and there with paler arcs of blackthorn blossom. There, too, was the harbour of Polgelly with its steeply stacked white houses looking small so far below us, and the headlands curving out to either side, already showing the first spreading cover of sea pink that made a softer contrast to the darkly jagged rock beneath. And past all that, as far as I could see, the endless rolling blue of water stretched away until it met the clouds.

Mark stopped when I stopped, turned to watch my face, and said, 'Not quite like California, is it?'

'No.' This ocean had a very different feel than the Pacific. It seemed somehow more alive. 'No, this is better.'

I hadn't heard anyone open the front door behind us, but suddenly someone said 'Eva!' and, turning, I saw a young woman in jeans and a red sweater, her dark hair cut even shorter than Mark's. This had to be Susan, I thought, though I wouldn't have known *her* if we'd met away from

Trelowarth. She'd only been seven or eight when I'd last been here. Now she was in her late twenties, grown taller and slender, her smile wide and welcoming. 'I thought I heard the van.' Her hug was just as warm. 'Honestly Eva, you look just the same. It's incredible. Even your hair. I always envied you your hair,' she told me. 'Mine would never grow like that.'

I didn't really think much of my hair, myself. My father had liked my hair long, so I'd left it that way. It was easy enough to take care of, no styling required, and whenever it got in the way I just tied it all back.

'Short hair suits you though,' I said to Susan.

'Yes, well, it's not by choice.' She smoothed it with a hand and grinned. 'I tried to dye it red . . .'

Mark said, 'It came out purple.'

'More maroon, I'd say,' she set him straight. 'And when I tried to fix it, it got worse, so I just cut it.'

'By herself,' said Mark.

'Well, naturally.'

'I could have done as good a job as that,' he told her drily, 'with my garden shears.'

Their banter was affectionate, and utterly familiar, and I felt myself relaxing in the way one only did when in the company of friends.

Susan let Mark score that last point and shrugged as she told him, 'Just drop that suitcase here for now, Claire said to bring you both round to the cottage when you got here. She's made sandwiches.'

Mark did as he was told and then fell in behind as Susan, with the dogs bouncing round her as though they'd caught some of her energy, led the way along the front walk of the house and down the long green sweep of hill towards the sea, to the place where the old narrow coast path, trampled hard as rutted pavement by the feet of countless ramblers who came up along the clifftops from Polgelly, disappeared into the Wild Wood.

I'd given it that name the summer Claire had read me Kenneth Graeme's timeless tales of Mole and Rat and Mr Toad. A chapter a night of *The Wind in the Willows* and never again could I enter that old, sprawling tangle of woods without cocking an ear for the scurrying footsteps of small unseen creatures and feeling a touch of the magic.

I still felt it now, as I followed Mark into the dim, sudden coolness. The air changed. The light changed. The scent of the woods, dank and earthy and rich, rose around me. The wood was an old one, and where it was deepest it stretched down the hill to the edge of the cliffs, but the trees grew so thickly I lost my whole view of the sea. I was closed round in branches and leaves – oak and elder and blackthorn and ghostly pale sycamores, set amid masses of bluebells.

The coast path, which entered the woods as a narrow track, broadened a little in here so two people could walk side by side, as though those who came into these woods felt more comfortable walking that way in this place where the shadows fell thick on the ferns and the undergrowth, and the high trees had a whispering voice of their own when the wind shook their leaves. But I'd never felt fear in these woods. They were peaceful, and filled with the joyously warbling songs of the birds tending hidden nests high overhead.

Susan, leading us through, turned to tell me, 'We actually do have a badger. Claire's seen it.'

If it was anything like the reclusive Mr Badger who had ruled the Wild Wood in *The Wind and the Willows*, I didn't hold out too much hope that I'd catch a glimpse of the creature myself, but it didn't stop me looking while we walked.

I caught the sharp scent of the coal smoke from Claire's cottage chimney before we stepped into the clearing, a broad semi-circular space blown with green grass that chased to the edge of the cliff, where again I could have a clear view of the sea.

I knew better than to go towards that cliff – there was a wicked drop straight down from there, all unforgiving rock and jagged stone below – but the view itself, framed by the gap in the trees with the flowers and grass in between, and the glitter of sun on the water far out where the fishing boats bobbed, was beautiful.

And facing it, set tidily against the clearing's edge, the little cottage waited for us with its walls still painted primrose-yellow underneath a roof of sagging slates.

The cottage had been rented out to tourists when I'd come here as a child, to earn a bit of extra income for Trelowarth, but apparently Claire had decided just this past year to move into it herself with all her canvases and paints, and leave the big house for her stepchildren. I couldn't really blame her. While Trelowarth House was wonderful inside, it was an ancient house with draughts and rising damp and tricky wiring, and it took a lot of work, whereas this little cottage had been put here in the Twenties and was snugly made and comfortable.

There wasn't any need to knock. We just went in, the three of us, and all the dogs came with us, spilling through into the sitting room. Claire had been reading, but she set aside the paperback and came around to fold me into the third hug of warmth and welcome that I'd had this afternoon.

Claire Hallett was a woman who defied the rules of ageing. She looked just as fit approaching sixty as she'd looked those years ago. Her hair might be a little shorter and a paler shade of blonde now from its whitening, but she was still in jeans and giving off that same strong energy, that sense of capability. Her hug seemed to be offering to carry all my burdens. 'It's so good to have you here,' she said. 'We were so very sorry when we heard about Katrina.'

Then, because I think she knew that too much sympathy on top of my reunion with the three of them might lead to tears I wasn't ready yet to cry in front of anybody, she turned the talk to other things: the cottage and the decorating projects she had planned for it, and the next thing I knew we were all in the kitchen and sitting at the old unsteady table with its one leg shorter than the others, drinking Claire's strong tea and eating cheese and pickle sandwiches as though it had been months, not years, since we'd all been together.

Susan raised the subject of the tea room she was planning. 'Mark's against it, naturally,' she told me. 'He was never one for change.'

'It's not the change,' Mark said, with patience. 'It's the simple fact, my darling, that there's really no demand for it.'

'Well, we'd create one, wouldn't we? I've told you, if

we opened up the gardens more to tourists, we could bring them by the busload.'

'Buses can't come through Polgelly.'

'So you'd bring them in the other way, across the high road from St Non's. The tourists go there anyway, to see the well – they could come on here afterwards, for lunch.' Her tone was certain, as she turned to her stepmother. 'You're on my side, surely?'

'I'm staying out of it.' Claire leant across both of them to pour me a fresh cup of tea. 'I've given up the running of Trelowarth to the two of you, you'll have to work it out yourselves.'

Susan rolled her eyes. 'Yes, well, you say you've given up Trelowarth, but we all know you could never—'

'If you're wanting an opinion,' Claire said lightly, 'you might think of asking Eva. That's her job, you know – promoting things, and dealing with the public.'

Suddenly Susan and Mark were both looking at me, and I shook my head. 'I think I should stay out of it, too.'

Mark's amusement was obvious. 'Sorry, there's no likes of that, not with Susan about. She'll be picking your brains the whole time that you're here.'

Susan said, 'You will stay for a while, won't you? Not just the weekend?'

'We'll see.'

Claire, who'd been watching me quietly, glanced at my hand. 'That's your mother's ring, isn't it?'

'Yes.' The gold Claddagh ring that Bill had slipped from Katrina's still finger and given to me in the hospital room. It had come to my mother from her Irish grandmother who'd moved across into Cornwall and who, by tradition, had passed down this small ring of gold with its crowned heart held lovingly by two gloved hands, a reminder that love was eternal.

Claire smiled, understanding, as though she knew just what had brought me here, why I had come. Reaching over, she covered my hand with her warm one and said, 'Stay as long as you like.'

Chapter Three

When we came out of the Wild Wood by the coast path and turned up to climb the slope of field towards Trelowarth House, the sun had sunk so low it stretched our shadows long in front of us and glittered in the windows that were watching our approach.

The dogs, having patiently waited while we had our visit with Claire, were all bouncing round Susan now. 'Feeding time,' she told us, before taking the dogs round to the back of the house. That was how we'd most often gone in, through the kitchen, but Mark had left my suitcase just inside the main front door, so I went that way with him now and in through the more formal entrance with its short flight of steps and the vine trailing over the lintel.

As I followed Mark through and he switched on the light, I was happy to see that the house hadn't changed; to inhale the same scents of old polished wood and wool carpets and comforting mustiness, here in the spacious square hall. Once, this whole space had most likely been panelled in the same wine-dark wood as the sitting room door on my left and the staircase that angled up just behind that to the bedrooms upstairs, but some earlier Hallett had covered the panelling over with plaster, no doubt in an effort to make the great space seem more welcoming.

On my left and beyond the great staircase, a narrower corridor carried on back to the games room and the kitchen at the rear of the house, and off to my right lay the doors to the dining room and the big front room.

Beside me Mark waited, my suitcase in hand. 'We weren't sure if you'd want your old room, or—'

Their thoughtfulness touched me. 'Yes, please.'

He let me go first up the stairs. They were old stairs, as old as the house, running up from the hall at a perfect right angle to pause at a half-landing before doubling back on themselves for the final rise up to the first floor. The stair steps themselves were of stone, worn concave at their centres by centuries of climbing feet, and the walls of both stairway and landing were still the original panelling, wood of the same dark mahogany hue as the old doors downstairs, so that while I was climbing I couldn't help feeling I'd somehow stepped into the past.

The first floor looked rather less ancient, with carpets to cover the old floors and softly striped wallpaper brightening things. There were furnishings here that I didn't recall, but I knew my way round.

And I knew which door led to the room I had shared with Katrina. Being in the far front corner, closest to the road, it had three windows – two that looked towards the sea and one that overlooked the drive, that last one set beside the fireplace with its screen of flowered needlepoint in front.

The double bed still sat in the same place it always had, its headboard to the west wall so its footboard faced the fireplace. Katrina and I had both slept in that bed when we'd stayed here, the six years' gap between our ages making me a nuisance to her, keeping her awake by constant chattering, or stealing more than my share of the covers.

I smiled faintly at the memories, even as I felt the stabbing pain of loss. I fought it back and found my voice as Mark came up behind me in the doorway, and I said, 'You've moved the pictures. The old shepherd and his wife.'

'Oh, right.' He looked above the bed, where I was looking. 'They're in the dining room, I think.'

'It's just as well. They had those eyes that always watched you.'

Mark set the suitcase by the bed, and looked around in friendly silence for a moment. Then his gaze came round to me. 'How are you doing, really?'

I didn't meet his eyes directly. 'Fine. I'm fine.'

'You're not.'

'I will be. It takes time, I'm told.'

'Well, if you need to talk, you know I'm here.'

'I know.'

He touched my shoulder briefly as he passed. 'You know the house,' he said. 'Just make yourself at home, then.'

'Thanks.'

The door had a lock, but we'd never been allowed to lock the door as children and I didn't feel the need to do it now.

There were, in fact, three doors into this room. Trelowarth House was a proper smuggler's house, with doors that led from room to room as well as to the corridor, a feature that had made it unsurpassed for games of hide and seek. Just as the smugglers had been able to evade capture by sneaking from one room to another while the customs men were searching for them, so we children had slipped secretly between the upstairs rooms to the frustration of whoever had been 'it'.

Besides the main door to the corridor, my room had one more door further along the same wall, that connected with the bedroom just behind here on this east side of the house, a room that Claire had used for sewing, almost never giving it to guests because Uncle George's cigar smoke had often seeped in from his study beyond.

And the third door was set in the wall by the head of the bed, and led to a smaller front bedroom that had, I recalled, been used mostly for storage.

I didn't bother looking in there now. There'd be plenty of time for exploring tomorrow. Instead I sat down on the bed, making the bedsprings creak lightly as I looked around at the room from my childhood vantage point. The room looked much the same to me as it had twenty years ago. The walls were still a soft sea-green, the bedspread hobnailed, white and fringed, the curtains lace and insubstantial, lifting with the cool May breezes blowing through the partly open window. The wide-planked floor was bare, save for an old worn rug between the wardrobe on the two-doored wall and the small rocking chair set in the fireplace corner, and the same old white-framed mirror hung above the chest of drawers between the windows at the front.

In the mornings this was one of the first rooms to catch the light, but it was late now and the afternoon was fading into evening, and the room was full of shadows. I could have put a light on, but I didn't. I lay back instead, my hands behind my head.

I only meant to rest a moment, then wash up and go downstairs. But lying there, my face brushed by the soft sea breezes blowing in the window, feeling comfortably nostalgic in the dim, high-ceilinged room, my weariness began to weight my limbs until I couldn't move, and didn't really want to.

By the time the sound of Mark's sure footsteps had gone all the way downstairs and crossed the hall below, I was no longer listening.

I realised my mistake a few hours later when a restless dream brought me back wide-eyed to wakefulness, into the dark of a house that had fallen asleep. Rolling, I turned on the bedside lamp and checked my watch and found that it was nearly midnight.

'Damn.' I'd had just enough sleep that I knew I would never drift off again, no matter how much I needed the rest. And I needed it badly. The time change and long hours of travel were taking their toll and if I didn't get back to sleep now I'd pay a steep price in the morning.

I tried to resettle myself. Getting up, I changed out of my clothes into proper pyjamas, and snuggled in under the blankets and switched off the light. It was no use. The minutes ticked by.

'Damn,' I said again, and giving up I rose to rummage in my handbag.

I'd had sleeping pills prescribed for nights like these, because my doctor had assured me it was normal to do battle with insomnia from time to time while grieving. I had never had to use them, but I'd brought the pills to Cornwall just in case.

I took one pill and climbed back into bed, taking care not to pull all the covers to my side, from force of long habit, and mumbling 'Good night' to the place where my sister should be.

The first thing I thought when I woke was, I wasn't alone.

I knew where I was. My mind had already made sense of the signals and sorted them into awareness – the sound of the gulls and the scent of the air and the way that the sunlight speared into the room through the unshuttered windows. I heard voices talking quietly somewhere close by, not much above a whisper, the way that people talk when they don't want to wake someone who's sleeping. Mark and Susan, I assumed, but then I wasn't sure because both voices sounded male. I couldn't catch more than an odd word, fleeting, here and there: 'away' was one, and then, quite clear, 'impossible'.

The voices stopped. Began again, much closer to my head this time, and then I realised that they must be coming through the wall from the next room, the small front bedroom.

Workmen, probably. Old houses like Trelowarth always needed something done, and Mark had mentioned something when we'd been at Claire's about some sort of trouble with the wiring. My mind was alert enough now to be wary of having strange men in the next room, and rolling I reached with my one hand to lock the connecting door set in the wall by the head of my bed.

The door handles here were the old-fashioned kind with a thumb latch, without any keyholes, but small sliding bolts had been set just above them, and this bolt shot home with a satisfyingly sturdy click that made me feel a little more secure while I got dressed.

In the corridor outside my room I met Mark, who was coming upstairs. 'Good, you're up,' he said. 'Susan just sent me to see if you were. She's got breakfast on. How did you sleep?'

'Very well, thanks.' I gave a nod towards the closed door to the spare front room and added, 'You can tell them they don't have to be so quiet, now I'm up.'

He looked at me. 'Tell whom?'

'The workmen,' I said, 'or whoever they are. In there.'

Still looking at me strangely, he opened his mouth to reply and then shut it again, as though wanting to make very sure he was right before speaking. He turned the handle of the room beside my own and pushed the door wide enough to put his head round, then said to me, certain, 'There's nobody in here.'

I looked for myself. 'But I heard them. Two men. They were talking.'

'Then they must have been outside.'

'They didn't sound like they were outside.'

'Sound plays tricks, sometimes,' he told me, 'in old houses.'

Unconvinced, I made a final study of the empty room, then let him close the door.

He said, 'Come down for breakfast.'

Downstairs, Susan had a full cooked breakfast on the go, with sausage spitting in the pan and floured tomatoes sizzling beside them, eggs and toast and juice and coffee that smelt sharp and rich and heavenly and brought my eyes more fully open.

Susan, turning, waved a spatula towards the table. 'Have a seat, it's hardly ready.'

The kitchen had had a remodel since I'd last been here, and the table was a larger one than I remembered, but it occupied the same spot by the window that looked out across what used to be the stable yard, now greenly ringed with overhanging trees and with the former stable building now converted to a garage at its farther edge. I sat where I had always sat, my shoulder to the window wall, and looked across the yard towards the terraced gardens, sheltered by their high brick walls.

The gardens were all separately enclosed and named: the Lower Garden, closest to the house; the Middle Garden; then the largest one, the Upper Garden, and my favourite of them all, the Quiet Garden, which I'd loved best for its name.

These were the legacy of Mark and Susan's great-great-grandfather, who'd returned from the Boer War with only one leg and a mind in sore need of tranquillity. Nostalgia for a simpler time had driven him to cultivate traditional varieties of roses that were falling out of fashion with the rise of the more modern hybrids gaining popularity because they could bloom more than once a season.

Disdainful of these new hybrid perpetuals, he'd cared for his old-fashioned roses with a passion that he'd passed to his descendants, and through the hard work and investment of subsequent Halletts the business had grown into one of the country's most highly regarded producers of older historic varieties. In fact, thanks to the family's obsessive caretaking, these gardens now sheltered some roses that might have been lost altogether to time were it not for Trelowarth.

The sizzling from the cooker brought my gaze back from the window and I watched while Susan turned the sausage.

'Honestly,' I said, 'you didn't have to go to all this trouble. Cereal and milk would be enough.'

Mark, who'd been pouring the coffee, came over to hand me my mug and sat down in the place just across from me. 'It's not for you,' he assured me. 'She's trying to soften me up.'

'I am not,' was Susan's protest.

Mark said, 'So I guess it's coincidence, then, that you've set your big file of plans for the tea room out here on the table?'

'I wanted to look at them.'

'Wanted to show them to Eva, more like.'

'I did not.' Susan scraped the sausages out of the pan and crossing to the table set Mark's plate down, hard, in front of him.

Oblivious, he pointed at the folder with his fork. 'You've got the legends of Trelowarth and that sort of rubbish in there, don't you?'

Susan passed my plate across for me and, with her own in hand, sat down herself. 'Of course.'

'Good. So then you can reassure Eva we don't have a ghost.'

It was my turn to protest. 'I never said—'

'Why would she think there's a ghost?' Susan asked.

'She's been hearing men's voices upstairs.'

Susan told him, with feeling, 'I wish.'

Mark grinned. 'What, that we had men upstairs?'

'No, stupid. That we had a ghost. Now *that* would bring the tourists in.'

Mark told her that depended on the ghost.

Ignoring him, she asked me what the voices had been saying, and I shrugged.

'I couldn't hear.'

Mark said, 'Perhaps they came to give a warning.' Imitating a stern, ghostly voice, he went on, 'Do not build a tea room at Trelowarth.'

'Do you see?' asked Susan, looking to me for support. 'You see the sort of thing I have to deal with.'

'And you love me anyway.' Her brother's smile was sure.

'Yes, well, lucky for you that I do. That's the only thing keeps me from planting you in the back garden alongside your roses.'

Mark took the threat lightly, and turned his attention to me. 'So then, what are your plans for the day?'

I said, 'I don't know. I suppose I should take care of . . . what I came for.'

That sobered the mood. Mark looked down at his plate and went on eating silently, then he said quietly, 'Do you know where?'

'I was thinking,' I started, then paused for a moment, collecting myself. 'I was thinking of up by the Beacon.' He didn't react, but I still felt the need to explain, 'She would want to be somewhere where she had been happy.'

Mark gave a short nod and said, 'That's a good spot, then.' And after a moment, 'You want me to come with you?'

He offered that as though it didn't matter either way, but there was something in his tone that made me ask him, 'Would you like to?'

Pushing his half-empty plate away he told me, 'Yes, I would.'

I glanced towards the clearing sky. 'We ought to wait until the sun comes out.'

'Right.' He hadn't finished with his coffee, either, but he set that down as well, and stood. 'You let me know, then, when you're ready.' And with that he turned away and went to start his work.

Chapter Four

'He really did love her, didn't he?' Susan, standing at the sink to rinse our breakfast dishes, tipped her head to one side in a movement that was half-familiar. 'I mean, it's not as though he's been pining away all these years, or anything, and he's had girlfriends since who were serious, but your sister was special, I think.'

I pushed at a small bit of egg with my knife. 'Well, she was his first love,' I said. 'At least, that's what he told her. I know he was hers. And you never forget your first love.'

'I suppose not.' She frowned. 'I don't honestly remember what they were like as a couple, I was only seven. And you and I played together more, really. Katrina and Mark always seemed so much older.' She was filling the sink now with water and dish soap, and I would have risen to help her if she hadn't motioned me down again. 'Sit. You're a guest.'

'Not that kind of a guest. I can help.'

'No, you can't,' she insisted, and from her expression she wouldn't be budged, so I did as she told me and stayed in my seat at the table while she started washing the cutlery. 'Who was *your* first love?' she asked me, and the question broke the subtle air of sadness that had settled on us; brought the light again into the room.

I smiled. 'A boy at my school in Vancouver. He played junior hockey, I spent all my weekends in freezing cold ice rinks.' Somehow it didn't have quite the same level of romance as Mark and Katrina. 'And you?'

'I'm still waiting for mine,' Susan said. 'I'm too fussy, Mark tells me. I want what my dad and Claire had.'

'God, you'll be waiting a long time for that.' Even my parents, for all their devotion to each other, hadn't been a patch on Uncle George and Claire. The Halletts had been one of those rare couples who, between them, made a little world that no one else could touch. True soulmates.

Susan ran the dishrag round a coffee mug. 'I know. Worth waiting for, though, I think. And it doesn't mean I can't have some adventures in the meantime.'

She'd been born to have adventures. Although she'd been the youngest and the smallest of the four of us, she'd been the one most likely to explore, to push the boundaries, and she'd often had the skinned knees and the bandages to prove it. From the little I had seen now of the woman she'd grown into I suspected she still had that spirit in her, that her mind still saw beyond the limits others liked to place on things.

Which made me wonder why she had come back here,

to this quiet little corner of the country, and Trelowarth.

'Mark said you'd been living near Bristol,' I ventured.

She glanced at me. 'Did he?' I had the strong impression I had somehow touched a nerve without intending to, but Susan hid it with a shrug. 'Yes, well, I had my own catering business up there, did he tell you?'

He hadn't, but I took the opportunity to shift to safer ground. 'So then you should be able to make a success of your tea room.'

'I hope so. I mean, Mark would never complain, but I know that it hasn't been easy these past few years, since Dad's investments went—' She stopped and glanced at me and quickly looked away and would have likely changed the subject if I hadn't stopped her.

'Susan.'

'Yes?'

'Trelowarth's in financial trouble?' I could read reluctance in her eyes. I asked her, 'How bad is it?'

'Bad enough. But don't tell Mark I told you, or he'll plant *me* in the garden with the roses.'

I imagined a place this big must take a good deal of money to run. Apart from the house, there was all the land – not just the gardens themselves, but the fields where the roses were actually grown. Most of the regular work could be done by two men, but with Uncle George gone that meant Mark would have had to hire someone to help. They'd be busiest during the winter months, digging the bare-rooted roses and shipping them off to fill all of the orders that would have come in through the year, after which all the rest of the harvest still had to be potted and delivered to the garden centres that had always sold

Trelowarth roses. But even at this time of year there was much to be done. Taking care of Trelowarth, I knew, was a full-time concern.

'Anyway,' Susan said, 'that's really why I came back. To help out where I could.'

'Hence the tea room.'

'Exactly. My dad used to talk about having one someday. I thought if we put in a tea room and opened the gardens for tours, it might bring in some revenue and make more people aware of our product.' She heard her own words and smiled wryly. 'I've been swotting up on marketing, can you tell?'

'Good for you, though. That's just what you should do.' My gaze found the folder of plans she had left on the table. 'You mind if I look at these?'

'No, go ahead. Only—'

'—don't tell Mark. I know.' I reached for the folder. 'Why is he so set against your tea room?'

Susan set the final teacup on the draining board and pulled the plug to let the water out. 'I wouldn't say he's set against it, more that he's resistant, and that's just because it doesn't fit his vision of Trelowarth. Mark's a purist, like my grandfather. Change doesn't interest him.' She grinned. 'If you ask me, Mark's simply not sure about sharing our roses with strangers.'

Reading her notes while I finished my coffee, I rotated one drawing slightly to help get my bearings. 'So you'd put the tea room over there, then,' I said, pointing at an angle out the window, past the stretch of level turf that once had been the stable yard and to the tangled greenery beyond it.

'That's right, in Dad's old greenhouse. No one uses it any more, but it's still got all the plumbing in place and the glass is all good. I've been told that it wouldn't be hard to convert.' She came round beside me to study the plans. 'Claire's grandparents met in a tea room, apparently. She told us the story, it's very romantic. I'll have to ask if she remembers the name of the place. We could call ours the same, put a bit of her history here, too.'

This was the sort of project that my mother, with her passion for historical research, would have loved. If she'd been living still, she would have wasted little time in digging through the records to unearth the finer details of Trelowarth's past.

But when I said as much to Susan, she said only, 'She'd have bored herself to tears, then. They're all deadly dull, my family, and they've been here for two hundred years, at least. I keep hoping that I'll come across a smuggler or a pirate, someone infamous, to help bring in the tourists.'

'Someone famous might work just as well.' I kept my focus on the drawings and the notes as I reminded her, 'You have a famous movie star who used to spend her summers here, remember.'

'No,' she said. 'It wouldn't feel right, trading on Katrina's name. And Mark would never go for it. You know my brother.'

Yes, I did. The years might change our outer selves, but underneath it all we stayed the same, we kept our patterns, and I knew where I should look for him when I went out a short while later with the box of ashes. In the mornings, he had always started in the highest terrace and worked down from there. I found him in the Quiet Garden, pulling weeds. His boots were caked and muddy and the wind had blown his hair and he was wearing an old denim jacket not unlike the one I held a memory of him wearing when he worked among the roses.

He stopped as I came in through the old wooden door in the high stone wall, into the roofless, still space where the wind couldn't reach with its fine salty spray from the sea that could burn through the delicate petals and leaves. When Mark saw what I'd brought with me, what I was carrying, he asked me, 'Ready, then?'

'Whenever you are.'

He tugged off his gloves, set his tools away tidily into the small corner shed, and picked up a small battered rucksack he slung on his shoulder before leading me out of the garden.

The walk to the Beacon was one of the prettier walks at Trelowarth. We went down the hill to the coast path again, through the Wild Wood as if we were going to Claire's, but we passed by the cottage and right through the clearing and into the woods again, still on the coast path. We came out the other side close to the top of the cliffs, close enough to be able to hear the harsh rush of the waves as they broke on the black rocks and shingle beneath. Here we left the path, turning our backs to the sea as we came to the fence of a broad sloping pasture where several cows lazily stood with their heads to the grass, paying no heed to either of us as we climbed up and over the stile.

Mark helped me over, then went back to walking just in front of me, head down, his thoughts turned inward. I knew why.

He'd often brought Katrina up here, that last summer. This had been their special place, a place to get away from all the adults and us younger children, to be on their own together. I'd been too young then to be my sister's confidante, too young for her to tell me what they'd talked about up here. I'd only known that when she'd been with Mark up at the Beacon, she had come back shining like a lamp had been switched on inside her, stepping lightly as the butterflies that danced around my feet now as my shoes brushed through the bluebells in the windblown grass.

And Mark, I knew, was walking with the memories.

I had memories of my own to keep me company. My mother, loving history as she did, had loved the romance of the Beacon, ancient relic of the days when there had been a chain of signal fires on hilltops all along the coast of Britain, standing ready to be lit in times of trouble. They had served a double purpose, calling everyone who saw them to come out and take up arms against the enemy, while at the same time swiftly sending warning word to London of approaching danger. In Elizabethan times, this beacon at Trelowarth had been used to pass the signal when the sails of the Armada were first spotted from the shore.

In those days, the Beacon would have been a sight to see – a high stone table, higher than a man, much like the Neolithic cromlechs that one still saw perched on hillsides in this area, but with a pile of kindling wood, perhaps, stacked up on top of it in readiness. My mother's words had painted such a clear and vivid picture of it in my mind that when we'd come up here on picnics I had always felt the urge to keep a sharper watch on the horizon for a stealthy Spanish sail, and sometimes glanced from left to right along the coast to see if I could spot another beacon fire flaring in the distance.

I still felt a small tug of that same feeling now as we came to the top of the field, to the level place scattered with old weathered stones that had tumbled into a rough circle, and gave little hint of their earlier purpose, except for the stone at the centre that lay like a low table, cracked at one end.

The view from here was wide and unobstructed – I could see the whole unbroken line of coast, headland to headland, the waves beating white on the black cliffs and dark shingle beaches, and the sea deep blue today beneath a warmly glinting sun.

I set the box that held Katrina's ashes on the table stone, and looked at Mark, who looked at me.

And then he reached into the rucksack he had carried up with him and brought out three small paper cups, the kind you find near water coolers, and a dark-green bottle. 'We should do this right,' he said.

'What is that?'

'Scrumpy. When Katrina and I came up here, we always brought a bottle with us.'

'Scrumpy?'

'Cider. With a kick.' He filled a cup and set it on the wooden box, then poured two more and handed one to me, then raised his up as though to make a toast. 'Here's to . . .' he said, then faltered. 'Well, to hell with it,' he finished off, and drained the cup.

I drank mine, too, and Mark poured out the third cup on the box itself before he stepped aside and gave a nod to me. 'Go on, then.'

With uncertain hands I flipped the latch that held the

box shut. 'There was something I was going to read.'

Mark looked at me and waited.

'From *The Prophet*,' I explained. 'Kahlil Gibran's *The Prophet*. There's a passage about death that Katrina always liked. She read it at our parents' funeral.'

I had crammed the folded paper in a pocket, and I had to tug it out and spread it smooth against the blowing breeze.

'*For what is it to die*,' I read, '*but to stand naked in the wind and to melt into the sun? And what is it to cease breathing, but to . . . but to . . .*' And there my voice trailed off and would not carry on, and Mark reached over for the page and gently took it from my hand, and went on with the reading in his steady voice. I turned my face towards the sea and let my eyes be dazzled by the brightness of the water while Mark finished off the passage and came down to the last lines:

'*And when you have reached the mountaintop, then you shall begin to climb.*

And when the earth shall claim your limbs, then shall you truly dance.'

It seemed the perfect time, then, so I tipped the box and let the ashes spill.

Beside me, very quietly, Mark told them, 'Go and dance, now.'

And they caught the wind and did just that, and for that fleeting instant there were three of us again upon the wide and sunlit hill, before the ashes gathered on an upward swirl of breeze that blew them westward, out across the blue and endless sparkle of the sea.

Chapter Five

'Do you know,' I said to Mark, 'I think I'm getting drunk.'

We were still sitting on the cool ground at the summit of the hill with all the old stones of the Beacon tumbled round us, giving us some shelter from the strengthened wind that blew across the waving grass and wildflowers.

I looked down at my paper cup. 'What do you call this stuff again?'

'Scrumpy.'

'Scrumpy.' I'd have to remember that name, and avoid it in future, I thought. It came on at first like common apple cider, and then suddenly you realised you were 'Definitely getting drunk,' I said. 'You have the rest.'

Without a word he poured the bottle's dregs into his own cup and sat back and leant his elbows on the table rock, and looked as I was looking down the hillside to the sea. Like me, he seemed to be in no great hurry to go anywhere.

As if he'd read my thoughts, he asked, 'How long till you have to go back?'

'I don't, actually.' Far over the water the tiny white speck of a gull wheeled and languidly dipped and I followed its flight with my faintly blurred gaze. 'I don't have a job or apartment, I gave them both up. It's not home for me there any more, not since . . .' Letting the words trail off, I gave a shrug. 'When Bill gave me those ashes, I had to think hard, really think, about where I should scatter them. Where she belonged. And it got me to thinking where *I* belonged, now that she's gone. I have friends in LA, but not real friends, you know? Not the kind you can really depend on. And where I was living . . . well, it was all right, but it just wasn't . . . just wasn't . . .'

'Home?'

'No.' It was comforting to know he understood. 'I thought I might look round here for a property to rent. A little cottage, maybe.'

'Everything around here will be full up for the summer,' was his guess. Then when he saw my disappointment he went on, 'But come the autumn you could have your pick of properties, and meantime you can stay right where you are, with us.'

'Oh, Mark, I couldn't. That would be imposing.'

'Why? We have the room,' he pointed out. 'You always used to come and stay the summer.'

His tone had taken on a stubborn edge that I recalled enough to know I wouldn't win the argument, and so I simply told him, 'Well, you'd have to let me pay you, then.'

'The hell I would.'

'I have the money, Mark. I have more money than I need. I can't just sit here like a sponge and let you feed me and take care of me when . . .' Just in time I caught myself, remembering I wasn't meant to know about Trelowarth being in financial difficulty.

Mark glanced sideways. 'When what?'

'Nothing.'

Silence dropped between us like a stone. I felt his gaze grow keener. 'What has Susan told you?'

'Nothing.'

I had never been much good at lying and I knew it, but he didn't press the point, and after studying my face a moment longer he looked back towards the sea again and told me, 'Friends don't pay.'

There was no way of getting round that, so I took a different tack. 'Then let me pay in kind.' I paused a moment, trying through the growing haze of drink to organise my argument, both because I had only just thought of it and because all of a sudden it struck me as something that truly appealed to me, something I'd even enjoy. 'I could help Susan with her tea room project, help her get it off the ground.'

'Oh, right. That's all I need.'

'You've seen her plans?'

'You think I've had a choice?'

I said, 'I like them.'

'Do you?'

It was more a comment, really, than a question, but I answered, 'Yes. She's seems to have it all in hand, she's thought it through.'

'I don't doubt that.' His mouth curved, briefly. 'She gets

that from our mother. My dad was the one who had all the ideas, but Mum was the person who saw things got done.'

He'd remember his mother, of course. He'd been eleven when she died, whereas Susan had still been a baby and I'd just started nursery school. My earliest memories went no further back than his stepmother, Claire, and Claire had always been so wonderful I'd never given much thought to the woman who'd preceded her.

'My dad was rudderless when Mum died. It's a good thing he met Claire, she really set him on his course again.' Mark's eyes crinkled faintly with fondness. 'She's a different sort of woman than my mum was, though, is Claire.'

'Well, she's an artist.'

'That she is. So was your sister,' he informed me. 'Even back when we were young, before she ever started acting, she still had that spirit in her, same as Claire. They need the space to spread their wings. Like butterflies.' He squinted at the brightness of the sea as he looked westward, where the restless wind had blown Katrina's ashes. 'Ever try to hold a butterfly? It can't be done. You damage them,' he said. 'As gentle as you try to be, you take the powder from their wings and they won't ever fly the same. It's kinder just to let them go.'

I looked at him, and asked because I'd always wondered, 'Is that why you stopped writing to Katrina?'

'She had bigger wings than most,' he said. 'She needed room to use them, and she couldn't do that here, now, could she? Anyway, it worked out for the best. She found her husband. They seemed happy.'

'Yes, they were.'

'Then that's all right.'

We fell to silence once again, and might have gone on sitting there all afternoon if overhead the clouds had not begun to thicken and to threaten rain.

Mark stood first, more steady on his feet than me, and reached a hand to help me up. 'Come on,' he said. 'We'd best head back.'

He carried the now-empty box for me, walking a few steps ahead down the field. Getting over the stile in the pasture fence took a bit more concentration this time, I couldn't get my legs and hands to coordinate in quite the same way as before and I nearly flipped headfirst down into the dirt, but luckily Mark didn't see that. Recovering my balance, I followed him carefully into the woods.

It was cool in here, quiet with ferns and the thick press of trees, and all the little flowers that I hadn't noticed coming up, but that I noticed now since I was keeping such a close watch on my feet and where they landed. There were little white wildflowers close by the edge of the path, and I wanted to ask Mark their name, but I suspected that he'd just come back with something long and Latin, like he always used to do. Show Mark something as lovely as a tiny Star-of-Bethlehem, and he would take one look at it and without blinking say it was an *Ornithogalum umbellatum*. No, it had been my mother who had given me the names of all the grasses and the flowers I had brought back from my afternoon adventures in the woods and fields. I still remembered some of the old names she'd taught me – *tailor's needles*, *feather-bow*, *penny-cake* and *lady's smock*.

Lady's smock used to be easy to find at this time of the year. I was looking for some when we came to the clearing where Claire's cottage sat with its windows wide open and welcoming. We hadn't bothered stopping in to see her when we'd come through here the first time, on our way up to the Beacon, because what we had gone up there to do had been a private sort of pilgrimage for both of us. But it would never do to pass Claire's cottage twice and not stop long enough to say hello.

Mark went to knock, but got no answer.

'She's gone out,' I guessed.

'Most likely.' Still, he took his own keys out and stepped inside and called out from the entryway, then had a quick look round to reassure himself she wasn't lying ill or injured somewhere. 'Gone off sketching something, probably,' he gave his final verdict as he reappeared. 'She does it all the time.' Glancing up at the sky he said, 'I ought to get her windows shut before this rain starts. You go on, I'll catch you up. No need for us both to get soaked.'

The first splat of a raindrop on my shoulder helped convince me.

I moved quickly through the trees – a little too quickly, perhaps, because before I'd made it halfway through I started feeling dizzy, so I stopped and briefly closed my eyes, recovering my balance. When I opened them again the woods became a blur of green and brown and quiet shadows. Damn the Scrumpy, I thought. It was muddling my thoughts, and confusing my vision.

A tree a short distance in front of me went all unfocused, dividing in two. And there suddenly seemed to be two paths as well, one I didn't remember that angled away to the cliffs. I heard footsteps coming up behind me and I turned, expecting Mark, but there was no one there.

It must have been an echo, I decided, because here was Mark just coming into view now on the path and looking slightly blurred as well until I focused with an effort. Seeing me standing there seemed to surprise him. He turned his collar up against the damp wind shaking through the leaves and asked me, 'Something wrong?'

'No, not at all.' I stood as steadily as I was able, not wanting to let on how much the Scrumpy had affected me. 'It's just that I couldn't remember which path to take.'

He laughed at that – the first time I had heard him laugh since I'd been back, and turned me round so I could see with my own eyes the way through the trees. 'There is only the one path, you know.'

There seemed little point in arguing. I simply let him take my hand as he had done when I was small, and as we came out of the woods the rain came on in earnest and we made a breathless run for it across the rising field towards the house.

The dogs had been out in the garden as well. They sat lined up like penitents in the back corridor while Claire, with mop in hand, dealt with the criss-crossing paw tracks that muddied the floor. The corridor smelt of stone and plaster, and the rubber of old boots left drying underneath the rows of hooks that held a heaped array of well-used coats and cardigans. As Mark and I came diving in the door, wet through and stamping mud from our own feet, Claire gave us both a look.

'Not one more step,' she warned us, 'till you've taken off those boots. I'm nearly finished, I don't want to have to do this over.'

As Mark bent to his laces the dogs swarmed him happily, pleased he'd come down to their level. He fended them off as he told Claire, 'You don't need to do it at all. I'll take care of it.'

But there was no breaking the long years of habit. She twisted the mop in its bucket of hot water, wringing it out and then slapping it onto the flagstones in front of the dogs. 'And you lot,' she said, as she swished past them, 'can stay where you are, till your feet dry.'

I could have sworn the dogs snickered, the way men will nudge one another and wink when their wives tell them off. Claire had noticed it, too, and she gave them a withering look that made the setter and the Labrador lie down, pretending submission. The cocker spaniel and the little mongrel, Samson, stayed near Mark, and would have followed him in defiance of Claire's orders if he hadn't told them both to stay. They whined a token protest, but they did as they'd been told.

Mark said, good-naturedly, '*My* feet wouldn't be wet at all, if I hadn't had to stop and close your windows.'

'Did I leave them open? Sorry.' Thanking him, she glanced towards the windows just behind him as he straightened, but they both were tightly shut.

This was the part of the house that we children had passed through most often – the workaday, less showy side of Trelowarth. The section we were in now jutted furthest back into the yard – on one side of the corridor two windows and the door faced out across the yard itself, while on the other side the laundry room and office nestled side by side, their doorways all but hidden in among the hanging coats.

I left my own boots with their heels lined up against the wall, the way Claire liked them, and led the way round past the narrow back staircase that dropped like a chute from the old servants' quarters above, and then up the one uneven step to the kitchen.

Mark brought the box with him, and asked where I wanted it.

'Anywhere's fine.' It was only a box now, with nothing inside.

Claire, who'd followed behind us, asked, 'How did it go?' in a tone that, to anyone else, might have sounded as though she were asking an everyday question.

I said, 'It was perfect, thanks.'

Mark put in, 'Eva got drunk.'

'I did not.'

'Get over it, you said yourself you were.' His grin was, like his stepmother's tone of voice, designed to even out the day's emotions. 'You still are. You ought to see your eyes.'

'Well, if they're anything like yours,' I said, 'I guess I'll need some coffee.'

'Guess you will. I'll make some, shall I?' And he headed for the kettle with an amiable purpose.

I was moving much more slowly, and Claire came to take my elbow. 'What on earth were you two drinking?'

'Scrumpy.'

'Ah. Then you'll be needing to sit down, darling.'

She took me through into the big front room that we had always called the library, because of all the bookshelves, and she saw me seated next to the piano, and then Mark came, with coffee for us all, and slouched into the sofa at my side. His hair was curling as it dried, and he looked so much like the boy he'd been once that it seemed incredible to me so many years had passed since I'd last sat in here, like this. With them.

Claire's mind had been travelling on the same line. 'I feel I ought to send you straight upstairs to have a bath,' she told me.

'I don't think I'd manage the stairs at the moment.' I leant my head back on the cushions, then brought it back upright to stop it from spinning as Claire asked where we'd taken the ashes.

Mark answered. 'The Beacon.'

If Claire understood the full meaning of that, she gave no indication. She only said, 'Oh yes, it's lovely up there.'

'It was, today,' he said. 'Where's Sue?'

'I'm here,' said Susan, coming in. She stopped inside the doorway, looked from Mark to me. 'Are you all right?'

'I'm fine,' Mark said, 'but Eva's had too much to drink.'

I sighed. 'I have not. Anyway, you can talk. Look at the state of you.'

'I'm not the one seeing double, now am I?'

Claire's voice was calm. 'Children.'

Susan came all the way into the room and sat down on my other side, curious. 'Who's seeing double?'

Mark rolled his head sideways. 'Eva tried to convince me there were two paths in the Wild Wood.'

I couldn't argue that, but I could lay the blame where it belonged. 'It's his fault.'

Susan looked at me in sympathy. 'What was it, whisky?'

'Scrumpy.'

'God. How could you?' she asked Mark.

His shrug seemed a great effort. 'Before you rush to judgement, you should know that *after* drinking Scrumpy with me, Eva started thinking that your tea room was a wonderful idea.'

I elbowed him. He clutched his ribs and half-laughed, 'Ow.'

'I thought it was a wonderful idea before the Scrumpy.'

Susan, looking pleased, asked, 'Did you?'

'Yes. I was just telling Mark I'd like to help you set it up. Be your PR consultant, if that would be any use to you.'

Mark said, to Claire and Susan, 'In exchange for room and board. She'll be staying with us for the summer.'

He didn't mention anything about my plans to rent a cottage nearby when the tourist season ended in the autumn, presumably because, like me, Mark knew that Claire was generous to a fault, and had she known that I was looking for a cottage she'd have instantly insisted I take hers.

As it was, she smiled approval at me warmly from her corner while beside me Susan said, delighted, 'Are you? Eva, that's wonderful. Really, it's going to be just like old times.'

Mark shot her a sideways look over my head that I took as a silent reminder that things weren't exactly the same, with Katrina not here, and because I felt Susan's self-conscious reaction I covered the moment of awkwardness with, 'So you see, I'll have plenty of time to help out with your plans for the tea room.'

Susan gratefully said, 'I can show you the greenhouse tomorrow. Felicity's coming to help me start clearing it out. There are things stored in there that I don't think have moved since I went off to uni.'

Claire smiled. 'Very likely before that.'

I asked, 'Who's Felicity?'

'One of my friends from the village. You'll like her, I think. Won't she, Claire?'

'Yes, we all like Felicity.' Claire looked with affection at her stepson, who was sinking ever lower on the sofa. 'You'll be fast asleep, Mark, if you sit there much longer.'

'Mm.' He closed his eyes, and proved her point by drifting off immediately, breathing in a slow and even rhythm.

'Men,' said Susan, rather fondly. Then to me, 'You ought to have a nap as well, I'm sure it's been a trying day.'

It had, and she was right, except my cup of coffee had kicked in now and I wasn't feeling sleepy any more. Instead I sat with Claire and Susan, talking of small things while Mark snored on. And when we'd finished all the coffee in the pot and Claire had started thinking about what to make for supper, I felt more awake than ever.

'I can help,' I offered.

Susan shook her head. 'No, we can do it. You just stay here and relax.'

'You've only just arrived,' said Claire, and rubbed my shoulder as she passed. 'Let us take care of you.'

The sitting room was filled with things to do, except I couldn't play piano and I didn't want to turn the television on while Mark was still asleep. Instead I stood and stretched and went to make a study of the bookshelves, where I recognised the old and battered bindings of the local history books my mother had so loved to give to Uncle George and

Claire as gifts. It had been something of a passion for her, hunting down forgotten volumes in her favourite musty shops in London, antiquarian establishments with creaking floors and crowded shelves.

I chose one book and opened it: *A History of Polgelly*, written in the 1800s by a gentleman who, from his tone, had been an ardent Methodist. He disapproved quite heartily of all that had gone on here and had nothing good to say about Trelowarth, which he said had been 'a den of godless blackguards though its current owner, Mr Hallett, has done what he can to drive the devil from that place.'

Unfortunately, being such a devout man, the author of *A History of Polgelly* never did get round to mentioning exactly what it was those godless blackguards had been up to. Losing interest, I re-shelved his cheerless book and tried another one: *Polgelly Through the Ages*.

This was better. Not as preachy, and its author was a more romantic soul who started off with ancient legends and the story of the old well at St Non's, and wove his facts with bits of poetry that made the book a pleasant read.

I was halfway through by supper, and I took it upstairs afterwards to read in bed, in hopes that it would lull me off to sleep. But once again, I found myself too restless, whether from an overdose of coffee or residual emotion from our scattering the ashes, and when midnight came and went and left me staring at the walls I took another of my sleeping pills and waited for the drowsiness to claim me.

I was in that strange, floating place, well aware I was nearly asleep and past caring, when I thought I heard the same voices I'd heard before breakfast, the barest of whispers that seemed to come straight from the wall by my head.

'Oh, knock it off,' I mumbled with my face against the pillow. 'Let me sleep.'

They didn't stop. But in the end, I didn't mind, because the one voice had a very pleasant rhythm to it, and I let it soothe me into letting go my final hold on consciousness.

Chapter Six

Susan had been right. I really liked her friend Felicity.

She was, like Susan, lively and intelligent and quick to laugh, a pretty young woman with dark hair that would have come down in a cascade of curls if she hadn't kept it bound back with elastics and a clip and tied a scarf around it, gypsy style, presumably to guard against the dust that we were raising.

'I mean, honestly,' she asked us as she lifted yet another broken snooker cue, 'why would somebody keep all these?'

'You didn't know my Dad.' Susan smiled. 'He probably had plans to make them into something useful.'

'Yes, well, I've got plans for them and all.' She chucked the cue with all the others on the growing rubbish heap outside the door. The greenhouse was a fairly modern structure. According to Susan it had been built a decade ago, when Uncle George had suddenly decided he wanted to breed roses, to create new varieties instead of only cultivating existing ones, but as with so many things that Uncle George had started with enthusiasm, it had failed to hold his interest long. His passion for hybridising had waned when it proved to be trickier work than he'd thought it would be, and at some point he must have abandoned his efforts because it appeared that the greenhouse had been given over to storage for several years now.

We three had spent the last two hours since breakfast digging through the clutter and attempting to create a bit of order. It was challenging.

'The thing is,' said Felicity, 'your family doesn't seem to have thrown anything away. What is this, your first shoe?' She held a tiny trainer up, and Susan looked.

'More likely Mark's.' She'd found a treasure of her own. 'Come look at this,' she said, and spread the pages of a heavy album open so that we could see the photographs. The colours of the pictures had begun to change a bit with age, more reddish than they should have been, but still they showed some lovely views around Trelowarth gardens.

'This shouldn't be in here, it's going to get ruined.' Susan turned the pages reverently. 'Oh look, there's Claire.'

'That's quite the outfit,' said Felicity.

'Have a heart, it *was* the Eighties. Eva, look at this. Just look.'

I looked, and saw a charming picture of the Lower Garden with the roses all in bloom and beautiful. I said, 'You ought to have that one enlarged and hang it up in here.'

Susan turned toward Felicity. 'Could you do that, Fee?'

'Course I could.'

'Fee's brilliant with photography. You ought to see her pictures of the harbour,' Susan told me.

'Well, it's what the tourists want. I had some made up into notecards for the shop last summer. Couldn't keep enough of them in stock.'

I asked her, curious, 'Where is your shop?'

'Beside Penhaligon's.'

'Where Mrs Kinneck's used to be,' said Susan. 'You remember Mrs Kinneck, Eva? She had all those jars of sweets behind the counter, and she always gave us liquorice babies.'

I remembered.

'It's all changed, now,' Susan said. 'The old shops are all gone. Except the fudge shop – that's still there, thank God – but Mrs Griggs is gone, and Mr Turner's.'

I asked, 'What about the little place that sold the seashells in the baskets, near the harbour?'

'It's a tea room, now,' she told me, 'but the girl that runs it can't make scones for toffee.'

'Sue will put her out of business,' said Felicity.

Susan turned another page of photographs. 'I don't want to put anybody out of business, Fee. I'm only interested in keeping us *in* business.' She looked down at the photographs, determined. 'My father would spin in his grave if Trelowarth passed out of the family.'

Felicity held up a long piece of signboard with the name 'Trelowarth Roses' stencilled on it in blue paint. 'What's this?'

'Oh. Part of the display we used to take around to flower shows, when Dad was still keen on that sort of thing.'

I vaguely remembered the rhythm of all those shows, spread through the season from springtime to autumn, although as a child I'd been barely aware of the effort that Uncle George put into preparing for them. Looking at the neglected display, I asked, 'Doesn't Mark do shows?'

'He hasn't in years. He's a true Hallett male,' Susan said. 'You can't blast the man out of his garden unless he sees a need for it, and now he's got the Internet he rarely sees the need for being sociable. He's going to die a bachelor,' she predicted.

'Oh, I doubt it. Mark's a handsome man,' I said.

'Well, not with this hairstyle, he isn't.' Still flipping through the pages of the photograph album, she turned it so Felicity and I could see the photo of a teenaged Mark with denims and fluorescent lime-green T-shirt, with his hair blow-dried and feathered like a 1980s pop star.

Felicity laughed out loud. 'And who on earth is that, behind him?'

'That,' said Susan, 'would be Claire, again. We really should take these to show her, she'll have probably forgotten they were here.'

Felicity thought it more likely that Claire had been storing the album out here in the greenhouse on purpose, to bury the evidence. 'Who would want to be reminded of those clothes?'

But it was getting near to lunchtime and my stomach was aware of it, and Claire had made it clear she was expecting us for sandwiches and tea, which at the moment seemed a very good idea.

The same thought must have struck the dogs, for all of them fell in behind us as we walked downhill towards the coast path, bouncing playfully on one another until Susan with a whistle sent them racing on ahead. The larger three dogs vanished in the woods, but scruffy Samson circled back and snuffled happily along close by my heels as Susan and Felicity forged on ahead of us.

I'd always liked the company of dogs. I'd never had one of my own. When I was younger in Vancouver we'd had two cats that my father had said firmly were the only pets we needed, and none of my apartments in LA would have allowed a pet, but walking now with Samson I reflected on how comforting the bond could be between a person and a dog.

Apparently he liked me, too. He wagged his stumpy tail at the least word from me, and seemed content himself to let the others go ahead while he stayed close beside me on the path, so when he paused to let his nose explore a patch of undergrowth, I stopped as well and waited for him. 'What's so interesting?'

Samson couldn't tell me what he smelt, of course. He cocked his ears to catch my voice but kept his nose down, focused on the scent around the leaves. A rabbit, likely. Maybe even Susan's badger. I was going to suggest we move along when something rustled not far off, and Samson's head shot up. One sniff and he was after it, his little body plunging through the trees, and even as I drew in breath to call him back the trees themselves began to shift and move.

At least, it looked as though that's what the trees were doing. Startled by the strangeness of it, I stopped short.

The path, for some reason, appeared to have narrowed. The wind had grown suddenly warmer and sunlight was filtering down through the leaves at a new angle, dappling everything round me with shadows. And there, just in front of me, where I knew full well it hadn't been moments before, was a fork in the path.

The surprise held me motionless. That, and the uneasy knowledge that what I was looking at couldn't be real. It was only a trick of the mind. Had to be. There was only *one* path through the woods. Mark had shown me that yesterday – and anyway I'd just been looking right there, at that very spot, not half a minute earlier, and I'd seen nothing. Only trees.

The second path lay quietly in shadow, unconcerned with my refusal to believe that it was there. It curved away towards the cliffs, towards the sea, and all the ragged growth along its edges showed it hadn't just been newly made, as did the deeply sliding marks that looked like footprints left by someone walking there just after rain.

Confused, I looked along the path I knew, the only path that should have been there, but Felicity and Susan had gone on so far ahead I couldn't see them anymore. I called out to them anyway. 'Susan?'

But nobody answered.

The wind shook the branches and leaves overhead and the scenery shifted again, faintly dizzying. I closed my eyes.

Something crashed through the ferns at my side and my heart jumped straight into my throat, beating hard. Then a snuffling nose nudged my leg. Very slowly, I opened my eyes and looked down, to see Samson returned from his chasing whatever it was, with a bit of twig stuck in the fur of his fast-wagging tail.

I breathed carefully. Lifted my gaze to the trees. All was just as it should be – one path through the woods, every tree in its place, and Felicity walking with Susan ahead of me.

And when my own legs stopped trembling, I followed them.

Lunch was a blur. I remembered to eat, and to follow along with the table talk so I could nod when I needed to. I even joined in a couple of times. But I wasn't entirely there, and Claire noticed.

She wasn't the kind of a person to pry. Still, she took me in hand after lunch, when we'd moved with our biscuits and tea to the patio in the back garden. Claire's garden had a fairy-tale look to it, bordered as it was by the tall trees of the Wild Wood. Whatever grew here grew in shade. A trailing vine heaped tiny buds of honeysuckle all along the waist-high wall of stone built in the tight-fitted herringbone pattern so common in this part of Cornwall, and the back of the garden was lush with soft ferns and tall spikes of something that looked darkly tropical. Yet in defiance of the shadows, Claire had set a sundial squarely at the centre of her garden in the one place where the sunlight always reached, and with a ring of upturned earth around it, ready to be planted.

When Felicity and Susan brought out the photo album once again and started flipping through its pages, Claire said, 'Eva, come and help me plant my flowers, darling.'

She fetched me a spare pair of gardening gloves and a trowel and took me across to the sundial, beneath which a varied assortment of seedlings were waiting in small plastic pots. 'Here.' She tipped out a small spindly flower of some kind, its fragile roots bound in a pressed clump of soil, and I knelt down beside her to take it. At first we said nothing. We planted the flowers together in a rhythm I remembered – scoop, set one down, tamp, tamp, mound up a basin to keep in the rainwater, reach for the next one, then scoop, set one down, tamp, tamp . . .

The repetition soothed me, and the sunlight caught my moving hand and glinted on the little golden Claddagh ring. 'Aunt Claire.'

'Yes?'

'Can I ask you something?'

'Certainly.'

'When Uncle George died . . .' No, that wasn't right. I started over. '*After* Uncle George died, did your mind ever play tricks on you?'

'What sort of tricks?'

'Well, make you think you saw things that weren't really there.'

She stopped digging with her trowel partway in the earth and glanced up again. 'Are *you* seeing things?'

'Sometimes. And hearing them.'

'You mean the voices you heard in your room. Mark did mention that, yesterday.'

I mounded my basin with careful hands. 'What, did he think I was losing my mind?

'No, of course not.' She gently pinched a dead and wilted bloom from the next plant before she set it in its hole. 'Our bodies have a lot to deal with, darling, when we're grieving. And in answer to your question, yes, my mind played tricks when I lost George. It still does, even now. I smell his aftershave, from time to time. It's been five years this spring,' she said, 'and sometimes I still feel as though he's very near.' She looked directly at me then, and smiled a small and understanding smile. 'Be patient, Eva. It will all get easier.'

I'd reached the final flower. 'Yes, I know.' Scoop, set it down, tamp, tamp.

'There,' said Claire with satisfaction, dusting off her hands against her legs as she stood to inspect our work.

I rose too, and for the first time took a good look at the sundial. The stone base had graceful curved lines and the vane on its top face that marked the sun's passing was shaped like a butterfly pausing at rest with its wings folded upwards, set to cast its ever-moving shadows round a dial of Roman numerals raised in elegant relief. Around the whole top ran a poignant bit of poetry, in script:

The butterfly counts not months but moments,
And has time enough.

I traced the letters with one finger. Claire said, 'That's a lovely poem, don't you think? By Rabindranath Tagore, I've always liked his poetry. Felicity outdid herself, I think.'

'Felicity made this?'

'It's what she does,' said Claire. 'She's quite a brilliant sculptress.'

'Yes, she is.'

The bronze wing of the butterfly was casting its long shadow at the halfway point between the Roman numerals one and two, and Claire looked at her wristwatch to compare the times. 'Bang on,' she said. 'There's something to be said for the old ways.' A breeze swept singing through the branches of the trees that marked the edges of the woods around us, and she raised her face to it. 'I've always rather liked the Celtic view of life, that this world and the next one aren't so separate from each other. My grandmother believed that. She was Welsh, you know – a true Celt, through and through – and if you'd told *her* you'd heard whispers in your walls, she would have taken it in her stride,' she said, with certainty. 'She would have said you'd heard the voices of the people living at Trelowarth, sharing space with us, but in another time.'

I thought that was a rather lovely concept, and I said as much.

'I think so, too,' said Claire. 'So there, you see? Perhaps the voices you've been hearing aren't imagined ones at all.'

'You're only saying that to make me feel less crazy.'

'Is it working?'

'Sort of.' With a rueful smile I leant into the comfort of her one-armed hug, and told her, 'Thank you.'

'You're most welcome.'

Turning, she looked back towards the patio, where Susan and Felicity were sitting with their heads bent close together over the old photos. 'Haven't you two finished laughing at my frocks, yet?'

'Hardly.' Susan called over. 'We're choosing a few to put up in the tea room.'

'You do, and I'll take them back down.'

'Not of *you*,' Susan said with a laugh. 'Of the greenhouse. Like this one.' She hefted the album, and rose and came over to show us.

'Oh,' Claire said. 'Well yes, that one's lovely.'

Looking at the picture of the greenhouse, with Claire's

mention of her grandmother still recent in my mind, I said to Susan, 'Weren't you going to ask Claire about the tea room where her grandparents met?'

'So I was.'

Felicity, who'd come across to join us by the sundial, didn't know the story, and asked Claire, 'Your grandparents met in a tea room?'

'They did.'

Susan prompted, 'You have to tell the story, it's romantic. Especially the part where your grandfather takes off his clothes.'

Claire smiled. 'He did no such thing.'

'He did. He took off his shirt.'

'He was being a gentleman.'

Felicity found that amusing. 'That's what they all say.'

Claire went on, 'It had started to rain, and my grandmother's group – she had come down to Cornwall with some of her friends, from St Davids, in Wales – they got caught in it, soaked to the skin, so they ducked into the tea room to get warm. And my grandfather was working there that day, he was a plumber, and he saw her and was smitten.'

Susan picked up the tale. 'So he went straight over to her table and whipped off his shirt, and—'

'Nothing quite so dramatic.' Claire's wry glance was indulgent. 'He saw that she was shivering, and offered her his own dry shirt. A gentleman,' she said again. 'Although, in fairness, Gran always suspected that he only did it to show off his chest. He was a well-built man.'

'What was the name of the tea room?' asked Susan.

'The Cloutie Tree.'

Perfect for Cornwall, I thought. 'Cloutie trees' were a Celtic tradition, most often a thorn tree that grew by a holy well, on which the faithful tied 'clouts', bits of cloth they'd first dipped in the water, to take away sickness and wounds. As the cloth wore away to the elements, the ailment supposedly healed. There was one of these trees at St Non's, in fact, not all that far from here, only the pilgrims who came to the holy well there were more likely to wish for things other than health when they tied their bright strips of cloth onto the tree. I'd once wished for a pony, myself, though I'd never received one.

'The Cloutie Tree Tea Room.' Susan tried the name herself, and seemed to like it. 'I believe I'll call mine that, as well. What do you think, Claire?'

Claire looked as though her thoughts were somewhere far away. I saw her pull them back again, and find a smile. 'I think it would be lovely, Susan. Very fitting.'

She touched the sundial at her side with almost wistful fingers and then turned and went to put her tools away.

It struck me as I watched her walk across the wild back garden that Claire, like me, had lost her family young. Her grandparents, her parents – they'd have all been gone, as mine had now gone, by the time she reached her twenties, since according to my parents she had been alone when she had married Mark and Susan's father. And except for Mark and Susan, she was now alone again.

It was the way of things, I thought. We never knew what time would bring us. Looking down, I watched the shadow shift a fraction on the sundial.

Counting, not by months, but moments, as the poem said. I almost envied that bronze butterfly, content to live completely in the present, unconcerned with what had gone before. What might have been.

The memory of Claire's words of comfort rose again to fill my mind: *Be patient, Eva. It will all get easier.*

I hoped – I really hoped – that she was right.

Chapter Seven

The term 'hallucination', read the article I'd called up on the Internet, *is applied to false perceptions made by any of the senses, though the ones that are most commonly involved are sight and hearing.*

Shifting again in the chair at Mark's desk in the room that he used as his office, just off the back corridor, I settled in to keep reading. The article scrolled for what seemed like forever and slipped into language that probably only made sense to psychiatrists, but the subsection on 'Auditory Hallucinations' perfectly described the kind of voices I'd been hearing from my room. And while most people seeing things appeared to conjure non-existent people and not empty paths, it was still obvious to me that what I'd seen in the Wild Wood fit the criteria for 'Visual Hallucinations'.

The causes, the article told me, were varied. If I ruled out schizophrenia, that left a list of others that included stress, depression and fatigue. And there were several medications that apparently induced hallucinations as a side-effect. Particularly sedatives.

I rummaged in my handbag on the floor beside the chair to find the sleeping pills I'd been prescribed, and entering the name on the computer searched for side-effects. Yes, there it was – right there in black and white: *hallucinations*.

I could feel myself relax. I wasn't going mad at all, I thought, relieved. It was the pills, and nothing more. And if I didn't take them any more, then that would be the end of it, because the detailed article explained hallucinations always stopped when one removed their cause.

Outside the office in the corridor I heard the back door open and the stamp of boots and scrabbling feet of dogs. I just had time to drop the pills back in my handbag and close down my search screens, returning to the colourful display of website templates I'd been looking at before, as Mark came in and asked me, 'Any joy?'

'I don't know. Which one do you like?'

He arched an eyebrow warily. 'I thought you said the website was for Susan.'

'Well, she'll be maintaining it,' I said, 'but it's Trelowarth's image that we're putting out here, and you'll want to have some say in that. Besides,' I pointed out, 'your blog will be from the same template.'

'*My* blog?'

'You're the expert on Old Garden roses. Oh, come on.' I smiled at his expression. 'You'll have fun. You'll get to interact with all your customers.'

'I do that now. They email me their orders and I fill them.'

'Mr Sociable.'

'And what exactly am I meant to blog about?'

I gave a shrug. 'Whatever you get up to in the garden. Or the history of the roses. Or whatever strikes your fancy. It's your blog.'

'All right then, mastermind.' He hitched a chair close to my own and sat. 'You win.' He scanned the templates. 'That one's not too bad.'

'Good. That's the one that Susan liked, as well. Now, let's talk colours . . .'

Mark had always been a good sport. He endured another half an hour of website-planning torture with me before he began to fidget.

'Never mind,' I said. 'I've got enough to start with. I can have this up and running for you in a week.'

'A week.' From the way he looked around I could tell that the prospect of having me taking up half his home office for that length of time gave him pause.

I reassured him, 'I don't have to work in here, if it's a problem. I can use your extra printer and the laptop, on the kitchen table.'

'No need for that. I tell you what,' he said, 'why don't you use my dad's old study? Set the printer and the laptop up in there, and you can work in peace. You won't be tripping over all my mess.'

A good solution, really. Uncle George's study was conveniently close to my own bedroom, and well across the landing from both Mark and Susan's rooms, so I could work late if I wanted without worrying I'd keep them up. And working late was how I got myself through those first nights without the sleeping pills, which I had safely buried at the bottom of a drawer.

I was, if nothing else, productive in my work. I had the website done within a week, as promised, and when Wednesday rolled around again I'd finished with the final bits of testing, and was drifting off to sleep at night without the aid of anything, and feeling more myself.

And very ready for a change of scene. It had been raining off and on for the past week, and so I hadn't really minded being cloistered in the study, but stepping out the back door now I found the morning bright and fresh and sunny, with a clean wind off the sea that swept the calling gulls along with it and cleared my cobwebbed mind.

The dogs came bounding up to greet me and raced off again to be with Mark, wherever he was working in the gardens. I considered going after them, but knew I wouldn't be much help to Mark, I'd only slow him down. Besides, now that I had the website done, I needed to discuss the next steps in our new promotion plan, and that meant finding Susan.

She was in the greenhouse with Felicity, standing just inside the door and staring at the plumber who'd arrived a few minutes before, sent by Andrews & Son from St Non's to inspect the old plumbing and give her a quote for the work to be done. I couldn't help but stare a bit myself – he was a decidedly well-built young man, so much so that Felicity, watching him study the pipes, nudged her friend and said, 'Well done you. Recreating the past with precision, aren't you?'

Susan asked, 'What?'

'Recreating Claire's Cloutie Tree Tea Room, right down to the good-looking plumber. I'd like to see *him* take his shirt off.'

'Fee!'

'What? He can't hear us. God, will you just look at that.'

I looked too, and smiled a little as the plumber, seemingly completely unaware he had an audience, reached up to test the soundness of an overhead joint in the piping, a movement that showed off his broad muscled chest.

'What's his name?' asked Felicity.

Susan, equally awed, shook her head. 'I don't know. They just sent him.'

'Well, they've got my business.'

I smiled even more at Felicity's tone, but it didn't convince me. She'd been up to Trelowarth a few times this past week, enough for me to come to the conclusion that Felicity, for all her talk, was already quite hopelessly infatuated.

Mark, of course, had no idea. I could see how Felicity looked at him when he came into a room, and the way that she constantly watched him, the light in her smile when he spoke to her. But men could be so impossibly blind, I thought, just as the plumber was blind to the fact we were all of us watching him now.

'Perhaps I ought to see if he has any questions,' Susan said, all innocence, then spoilt it with a wink and crossed the greenhouse with a more purposely feminine walk than her usual breezy stride.

Felicity watched her friend go with approval. To me, she said, 'It's good to see her taking an interest in men again, after the last one.'

After Susan's sharp reaction to my mention of her time in Bristol, I hadn't pried further, but I felt safe in asking Felicity now, 'Was he awful?'

'Not at all. But he was older. Much older than Sue, and that made things quite difficult, sometimes. She didn't really fit in with his friends, and he didn't fit in with hers, and . . . well, they came from different generations, different worlds, and sometimes that's a gap that can't be bridged. I know she tried. It was your sister's death,' she told me, 'that decided things, I think. Sue said it made her realise life was just too short, so she came home.' She glanced at me confidingly. 'Your sister's death affected everyone round here. It was a blow.'

'To me as well.'

I liked the way Felicity accepted that, not leaping in with platitudes. 'Was she your only sister?'

'Yes.'

'I can't imagine. Me, I've got three sisters and two brothers. Breed like rabbits, we do. Every time I go home for a visit it seems that I've got a new nephew or niece.'

'Where's home?' I asked her.

'Somerset.'

It surprised me she wasn't from Cornwall. She looked Cornish enough, with her dark hair and eyes and her small, tidy figure set off to advantage in jeans and a form-fitting shirt and the gypsy-like scarf that today bound her curls in a long swinging ponytail. She'd picked up a bit of the accent as well, the distinctive and musical cadence of West Country speech, and I wouldn't have known that she wasn't a native.

'It's not all that far away, really,' she told me, 'though when I first came down here it seemed like a different world, like I had crossed some great divide.'

'You did,' I said. 'You crossed the Tamar.' And I told her

what my mother had told me about the crossing of the river Tamar and how it affected those with Cornish blood.

'Well, I must have an ancestor from Cornwall then,' she said, 'because I definitely felt it. I was on a summer holiday with friends, and I had one more year to finish uni, and all that time the only thing I thought about was how to get back here. And in the end I just packed up and came. No plans. My parents thought I'd gone completely mad. They still do,' she said, 'but they've given up trying to cure me. I've told them, it's Cornwall. There's no way to fight it.'

I knew what she meant. There was something about this remote western corner of Britain that captured the soul and refused to let go, something ancient and wild in the moors and black cliffs and the voice of the sea that spoke always of something unseen and enchanted.

Felicity tried to express it in words. 'In Cornwall,' she told me, 'one truly feels magic could actually happen.'

I thought of those words as I walked down The Hill after lunch on my way to the bank in Polgelly. There was no one but me on the road. Which was just as well, really, since there would have been little room for a car to push past me, especially once I got under the shady green canopy of the arched trees, with the steeply-banked hedges of stone, turf and tangled growth rising to block out my view of the fields at both sides. As the breeze shook the leaves overhead I remembered the strong sense of magic I'd felt here myself, as a child.

I'd been sure there were fairies concealed in the soft nodding bluebells that peered from the grass of the verge, and I'd trodden with care so as not to disturb them. Each stir of the breeze through the leaves had, to my childish ears, seemed to carry a faint lilting music, not meant for the grown-ups, that beckoned me on. I had often imagined the tunnel of trees was the doorway to fairyland, and I'd been certain that one day I'd step out the other side into some wonderful place.

It hadn't happened to me then. It didn't happen now. But still, I felt a thrilling echo of that old anticipation as I passed out of the trees and started down into Polgelly. Here, I thought, was all the magic one could need.

I felt like a child in the summer again at the first sight of the whitewashed shops and houses on the twisting streets, the rooftops stacked like toy blocks up the hills around the harbour where the gulls, drawn by the smells of fish and seaweed, circled with their plaintive cries.

The tide was out. Along the closer edges of the harbour all the smaller boats lay drunkenly tipped over on their hulls in the wet mud, still at their moorings while they waited for the sea's return.

The harbour was a classic smuggler's haven, curving like a finger inland, shielded at its entrance by the jagged rocks along the coast. If there had been no houses here to mark the spot it would have been impossible to know there was a harbour in behind those rocks, and even as it stood it took a bit of skill and luck for any tourist who tried navigating in by sailboat.

The street that ran along the harbour wall looked very much as I'd remembered it. The bank had undergone a change of name, but it still sat on the same corner, and the same strong scents of polished floors and paperwork were there to greet me as I entered. The new accounts manager, Mr Rowe, was a patient and thorough man who walked me through all the forms that I had to fill out. I had kept my British passport and was still a British citizen, which made things somewhat simpler.

'And you're living at Trelowarth, now, you said?'

'That's right.'

'I'll use that as your local address, then. And how much money would you like me to arrange to have wired over from your bank in California?'

I said, 'All of it,' and handed him the printed details of my two American accounts. He raised his eyebrows at the sum, but didn't comment. All he said was, 'Very good, I'll have this all approved and let you know when we receive your money.'

'Thank you.' With a handshake, I went out again, crossing the road to the fudge shop.

The little bell still rang as I went in, and as I crossed the threshold I felt ten years old again, transported by the sweet assault of wondrous smells too rich and varied to be numbered or identified. I bought half a pound of my old favourite flavour, mint chocolate, and took it out with me, intending to indulge in more nostalgia and enjoy it while I sat among the tourists on the sun-warmed harbour wall, but my eye was caught instead by the green chemist's sign a little further up the winding street. Felicity had said her own shop was beside the chemist's, so I tucked the rattly paper bag of fudge into my pocket and went up to have a look.

I'd expected to find it closed, since Wednesdays were Felicity's days off and she was still up helping Susan at the greenhouse, but an 'Open' sign was hanging in the front door like an invitation, so I ventured in.

The shop had a lovely, eclectic appeal, like its owner. There were notecards in delicate pen and ink, scenes of the harbour, and wind chimes of spun glass that caught the sun, sparkling. A rainbow of silk scarves and bright Celtic jewellery in silver and gold fought for space with a jumbled display of framed paintings, a few of which were Claire's – I knew the strong sweep of her brushstrokes and the boldness of her palette and the way she brought her scenes alive with light.

Felicity's sculptures were here as well, castings in bronze that showed all of the skill of the butterfly sundial, and more. My favourites were the little piskies, fairy folk of Cornwall – different versions of the same small figure, looking as though somebody had caught them in the middle of a dance.

Behind me, near the till, I heard a stool scrape and the sound of footsteps crossing the shop floor, and then a young man's voice, friendly, spoke up at my side. 'Can I help you?'

I glanced round with a shake of my head. 'I'm just looking.'

'See anything you like?' The lazy smile let me know the double meaning was intentional. He would have been about my age, nice-looking, with golden-blond hair and blue eyes that seemed oddly familiar.

I looked at him more closely and his smile grew more reproachful as he said, 'You don't remember me.'

I wasn't certain. 'Oliver?'

Surely it couldn't be Oliver, son of the woman who'd

looked after Susan and Mark when their mother had died. Having come with his mother each day to Trelowarth he'd known both the house and the grounds just as well as the rest of us did. Even after Claire had married Uncle George his mother had come up to help from time to time, and when we children came down to Polgelly we had often played with Oliver.

He folded his arms on his chest, looking pleased. 'You remembered.'

'Yes, well, you don't forget boys who throw rocks at you.'

'Once,' he said. 'I threw a pebble at you *once*, and anyway as I recall you picked it up and chucked it back. And you had better aim.'

I had. I'd hit him on the forehead. Knocked him over. 'You grew up.'

'And you.' He smiled again. 'Mark didn't say that you were coming for a visit. Are you here for long?'

'I might be,' I said. 'So you work with Felicity, then?'

He corrected me. 'Only on Wednesdays. I'm closed myself, Wednesdays.' In answer to my questioning look, he said, 'I have my own Smugglers' Museum.'

'Oh? Whereabouts?'

'Down by the harbour, between the pub and the tea room.' Oliver grinned. 'I weighed twelve stone when I started up the museum. I won't tell you what I weigh now.'

He looked fit as an athlete, to me. With his head tipped to one side, he asked, 'Do you smell chocolate?'

'It's my fudge.' I took the bag out of my pocket to show him. 'It's energy,' I told him. 'For The Hill.'

'Let's have a piece then.'

I offered the bag and he reached in and helped himself.

'What's your excuse?' I asked. 'You live down here.'

'True.' The charm was deliberate. 'But I have a feeling I'm going to be climbing The Hill fairly often myself, in the very near future.'

Chapter Eight

I cheated, in the end. I didn't climb back to Trelowarth by the road, but went around the harbour's edge and up the coast path, up the gentler slope that rose by stages to the level of the clifftop, keeping to the bottom of the fields below Trelowarth as it wound its way towards the Wild Wood.

At the side of the path, clumps of dark spiky gorse were in bloom with their deep-yellow flowers, the foxgloves were rampant, and thick drifts of sea pink spilt over the edge of the cliffs. I could hear the full roar of the sea here, the swirl of the spray crashing hard on the rocks far below where I walked, and the sullen retreat of the waves.

Most tourists avoided this stretch of the coast path. Only seasoned ramblers came this way, or people who wanted to visit the Beacon. Or those, like myself, who preferred the wilder, untouched ways, and didn't mind walking too close to the edge.

Even so, when the path reached a place where it rounded a cleft in the cliffside a little *too* closely, a quick downward glance at the white water boiling below on the rocks made me feel slightly dizzy. And when, as I straightened, the wind rose with a sudden force that rocked me on my feet, I turned my back to it and left the path for safety's sake, cutting up on a diagonal through the fields below the house.

I huddled in my jacket, head tucked down, and climbed determinedly. I'd nearly reached the house when it occurred to me that something wasn't right.

I should have reached the lawn by now. The level hedged lawn at the front of the house where we'd always played badminton. But I hadn't. I lifted my head to see how much further I had yet to go. And then I stopped dead in my tracks.

The lawn was gone.

And where it should have been, not fifteen feet from me, a man was standing with his back towards me, unaware. He seemed to be watching the road.

He wore a sleeveless coat of some rough brown material that flared below his waist, and the sleeves of the white shirt he wore underneath it were rolled to his elbows in working-man style. On his legs he wore tight-fitting brown trousers tucked into boots, also brown, that came up to his knees. And his hair – that was brown as well, worn long enough to be combed back and tied at his collar, the way I'd seen sailors wear their hair in period films.

He couldn't be real, I thought. Clearly he was nothing more than another hallucination. A good one, to be sure, and very vivid, but not real.

But it was frightening to know I'd lost control of my

own senses so completely. I could only stand there, frozen, not quite certain what to do. And I would always in my mind replay the moment when, incredibly, he turned. And saw me, too.

His eyes were not brown. They were of some lighter colour, clear in their intensity against his suntanned face.

Uneasy, I stepped backwards, and he raised one hand to calm me.

'Do not fear me. I'll not harm you.' Something struck me as familiar in the cadence of his voice – a deep voice, rough around the edges.

But I *was* afraid. It made no sense for me to be, I knew, because he wasn't real, he wasn't there. Pure instinct made me take another backwards step, and then another.

'Wait,' he said, and moved as if to follow, only something very curious began to happen then. As I moved backwards and away from him, he started to dissolve and fade, becoming like a shadow I could almost see, but not.

I thought I saw him stretch his hand towards me as though trying to reach out, to stop my leaving. And then all at once he was no longer there on the hillside, and in the same heartbeat I wasn't there, either.

Instead I was back on the coast path again, standing all by myself at the place where it rounded a cleft in the cliffside a little too closely, and watching the water boil white on the black rocks below.

Uncle George's study, where I'd worked on the computer this past week, had been my favourite room for hiding in when we'd played hide-and-seek as children. From behind the green chair I'd been able to see all three doors – the one directly opposite that led into the corridor, and both doors that connected with the rooms to either side. The old desk had a kneehole space that had been just the size for me to crouch in, and the long and heavy drapes that hung to each side of the window were the perfect length for someone small to hide behind.

I couldn't hide there now, but it was maybe no coincidence that I had sought my refuge here this afternoon. I'd been here an hour, having raced up through the fields in record time to find, to my relief, that there was no one in the house yet – they were all still out attending to their work. Which meant nobody was here to ask me why I was now surfing through the Internet for articles on mental illness and hallucinations.

What disturbed me wasn't simply that I'd slipped out of reality so quickly and so easily, but that I could have done it so completely, and that my own sense of place and time had been so badly skewed that in my mind I could believe I'd climbed the hill and seen the man in brown, when actually I'd never left the coast path.

I could no longer blame the sleeping pills – even though the articles I'd read did say withdrawal from the drugs could have the same effect as taking them, I'd only taken two pills to begin with and I'd gone a week without them, so I doubted I was going through withdrawal. And in case the cause was stress, I'd tried removing any source of that as well, even going so far as to take off my wristwatch and put it away in the drawer with my mobile phone, both former trappings of my tightly scheduled life.

I'd done everything I could do, but this obviously wasn't something I should try to diagnose myself. I'd have to find a local doctor and explain what had been happening and see if there was any way to treat it. And I had to find out how I ought to handle any episodes I might have in the meantime.

Curled in the green chair, I scrolled through the pages and carried on reading:

Sane people know they are hallucinating. Those with mental illnesses do not.

Well *that*, at least, was one small bit of comfort. I'd been very well aware, the whole time I'd been interacting with the strange man on the hill, that he had not been real. And yet, it had all felt so real. The strong wind and the sun's warmth and the hardness of the ground beneath my feet . . .

Hallucinations can involve a multitude of senses – touch and taste and smell as well as sight and hearing – to the point where it can be all but impossible to distinguish the imagined from the real. A glass of juice, the writer said, *will taste like juice, and silk will feel like silk.*

I searched on for further points on 'Seeing People', and discovered it was common to imagine human figures when hallucinating, and to hear them speak, and just as common to be able to have conversations in which they responded exactly as real people would. The articles assured me that, so long as these imagined people didn't try to tell me to do questionable things, like kill somebody, they were harmless.

Our studies have shown, one psychiatrist said, *that while ignoring these apparitions appears to have little effect, success can sometimes be achieved by simply telling them to go away.*

Moreover . . .

I broke off my reading as a movement caught the corner of my eye.

I glanced up, expecting Mark or Susan, only there was no one in the doorway to the corridor. No one . . . and yet the doorway was not empty.

The figure of a man was passing. I could see him very faintly, like a grey transparent shadow, moving past as though he'd meant to walk right by the room. But at the doorway's edge he stopped and leant back slightly, looking in as though he'd just seen something that he too considered out of place.

I closed my eyes and held my breath, not moving. Counted heartbeats. One. Two. Three. *It isn't real*, I told myself. My brain cells were misfiring, as the articles had just explained. There wasn't really anybody there.

And when I looked again, there wasn't.

It gave me a thrill of accomplishment, knowing I'd managed to control it that time. Maybe that was all it took, a short pause to remind myself that I was only seeing things. At least I would be able then to muddle through until I'd had a chance to see a doctor.

On the desk a small brass carriage clock whirred briefly and began to chime the hours: Five o'clock. The others would be coming in quite soon, I thought, which meant I should stop sitting here and try to make myself a bit more useful to my hosts by going down and finding something I could cook them all for supper.

I stood and reached to switch off the computer, but before my hand made contact, the entire desk and what was on it wavered out of focus with the room, and then dissolved.

I closed my eyes again, more firmly this time, fighting back with all I had. I heard the window rattling as though from a blast of wind, and felt a brightening of light against my eyelids that surprised me into opening my eyes.

The door connecting with the spare room next to this one was now open, too, and framed within it stood the man in brown.

At least, the man who had been wearing brown, the last time I'd imagined him. This time, in place of the jacket, he wore a wine-red dressing gown that hung unfastened so that I could see he was still fully dressed beneath it in the plain white shirt and trousers and tall boots. It should have made him less imposing, but it didn't. With the door frame for a reference he looked taller to me here. He'd have been six foot something, easily. His shoulders blocked the open space. He didn't smile.

His voice was low and quiet, carefully controlled. 'What are you?'

I was thinking just how odd a question that was for my own hallucination to be asking when his right arm shifted slightly and I saw what he was holding in his hand. I saw the knife.

It was a dagger, small and neatly made, and fit his hand so well I only really saw the blade, but that was all it took to make me feel a twinge of fear. Irrational, I knew, because this man was my creation, my own mind had called him up from somewhere, and as all the articles had said, he would be harmless. But I started to retreat, to back away as I had done before when we had faced each other on the hillside, hoping it would have the same effect. It didn't. This time, instead of disappearing, he came after me and in two strides had crossed the room to take a firm hold of my arm with his free hand.

If the contact was a shock to me it seemed to shock him more, as though he'd been expecting that his hand would pass right through me. I was much too stunned to struggle, and besides, there was no point. His grip was far too strong, and he was far too close.

He asked again, as though the answer mattered even more, 'What are you?'

Trying to remember the advice that had been in the final article I'd read, I met his gaze with all the calmness I could muster, and replied, 'I'm real. And you are not. Now, go away.'

The dressing gown he'd worn was made of heavy silk, with hand-stitched seams. I knew this because he had shrugged it off a moment earlier and given it to me, with the excuse that my own clothes appeared 'ill-suited to the weather'. It did, in fact, feel cooler in the room than it had felt before, and more damp, and the dressing gown, although it was imaginary, seemed to make a difference, so I thanked him.

After all, I reasoned, if I had to sit here with my own hallucination, who was acting like a gentleman, I could at least be courteous. I knew the situation would correct itself in time, and for the moment it was nothing short of fascinating.

Smoothing a fold of the dressing gown, I let the weight of the dark-red silk slip through my fingers and marvelled again at the power the mind had to make things seem real. It was one thing to read a psychiatrist's paper on how hallucinations could deceive a person's senses. It was quite another thing to wear a dressing gown that wasn't there – to feel the fabric plainly in my hand, and see the little imperfections in the stitches of the sleeve.

Even the chair I was sitting in couldn't be real, but I felt every bump of its low slatted back. There were two chairs, with curving arms, set facing one another by the window in this room that, while a vastly altered rendering of Uncle George's study, still appeared to be a masculine retreat. Between the two chairs was a little table of dark wood that held a tray of pipes for smoking, one of which sat on its own and clearly was a favourite. There were no shelves for books but there were books stacked on the one free-standing cabinet that appeared to have a locking door, and books again at one end of the long and narrow table set against the wall, and on the table was a bottle that the man was lifting now to fill a pewter cup with something that both looked and smelt like brandy.

'I'm not going to faint,' I promised as he set it on the table.

'I did not imagine that you were.' He took the other chair and with one elbow on the table tipped the bottle over his own cup. 'But it is clear your health has been affected by the shock of your arrival, and you would be wise to guard it.'

'I haven't arrived anywhere,' I corrected him. 'You're the one who keeps turning up, and you're not even real.'

'Am I not?'

I hadn't yet adjusted to the difference that a smile made to his face. I'd been too overwhelmed before to take much notice of his looks, beyond the broader details, but now that I'd relaxed more I was very much aware he was a very handsome man, for an illusion. His hair was not plain brown, but brown with glints of gold that caught the light. Close up, I now could see that his light-coloured eyes were green, so clear that at some angles they appeared transparent, and beneath the roughness of a day-old growth of beard his cheek and jaw were shaped with strength. A handsome man. But when he smiled he bordered on the irresistible.

I drank my brandy.

Thankfully, it had a taste. And even better, an effect. If I was going to have hallucinations, I decided, I would have to try to make them less distracting.

This one studied me with eyes that seemed to weigh the possibilities. 'You clearly are no ghost, and I do not believe in witches.'

'Well, I don't believe in *you*,' I told him. 'Go away.'

I might as well have swatted at a fly. He didn't vanish this time, either. All he did was settle back, the cup of brandy cradled in his hand, and watch me quietly a moment as though trying to decide how he should deal with me. 'Where are you from? I only ask because your speech is strange,' he said. 'Your accent is not of this place.'

'Yours isn't, either.'

'I was born and raised in London.'

'Really?'

'You do not believe me?'

'You're not real,' I reminded him. 'You can be born where you like.'

'Thank you.' Now he looked amused.

How long was this going to last, I wondered? All my previous hallucinations had been brief ones. This was going on for far too long. Maybe, I thought, if I took more charge of what was happening, controlled the situation more, I'd speed things up.

I drained my glass and told him, 'Look, I can't just sit here, I have things to do.'

He stared at me. 'You do?'

'Yes. So if you'll excuse me . . .'

As I stood, he stood as well as if by reflex, and when I went out he followed. Happily the corridor looked very much the same as in the real Trelowarth, and I headed for my bedroom door.

The man behind me asked, 'Where are you going?'

'To my room.' The old thumb-latched door handle actually fit in quite well with the age of the other things I was imagining, though the room itself looked a bit different inside when I opened the door. Unfazed, I stepped across the threshold, turned to face the man who wasn't really there, and told him, 'Look, you're being very nice, but really I just want to be alone, so *go away*.'

I put as much force as I could into those words, but as before he only stood and looked right back at me instead of disappearing as he was supposed to.

With a sigh I said, 'Oh, fine,' and closed the door between us.

There were voices in the next room.

One was now familiar to me, but the other was a stranger's who was making no great effort to be quiet. His was not a Cornish voice. It sounded Irish, and impatient.

'Have you no sense left at all? 'Tis not your battle, and you know it.'

'And whose battle is it, then?' That was the man in brown, I recognised his level tone.

'Not yours.' The Irishman was firm. 'Not mine.'

Half an hour or more had passed, or so it seemed, and I was still as deep as ever in the same hallucination, in this room that was my own, yet not my own. The walls were plaster-white, not green, and where the wardrobe should have stood there was a simple washstand with a bowl and pitcher on it. Gone, too, were the rocking chair and chest of drawers, replaced by two low trunks and a small writing desk tucked in the window alcove by the fireplace. But the fireplace was the same one, and the wide-planked floor still creaked when I set foot on it, and the bed was where it should be. Not the same bed, to be sure. This was a larger one – a tester bed with wooden headboard and high posts and railings set with rings to hold the curtains that hung drawn back to the posts at all four corners. With the canopy above it looked like something that belonged in a museum or historic home.

I was sitting on it now. I'd heard the footsteps in the next room as the man in brown went into it, and several minutes after that a different man – the Irishman, presumably – had climbed the stairs and come along the corridor, and now the two were arguing.

The Irishman went on, 'When did the flaming Duke of Ormonde ever think to do you favours? Never, that's when. Did he think to put his hand in when they had you up to Newgate? Did he come to pay you visits?'

'Fergal.'

'Did he?'

'I am bound to him by blood.'

'Well fine,' the man named Fergal said. 'Let him go spill his own, then, and leave us a bit of peace.'

A low laugh answered him. 'You will remind me not to ever cross you?'

'Sure if I'd thought you ever would, you'd have been dead before now.'

''Tis a comforting thought.'

'Jesus, you need to be thinking now. Fine if you're putting your head in a noose, that's your business. But not for those bastards.'

'I thought you were all for the king.'

'So I am. 'Tis the men he keeps around him I've no faith in. They've had nearly one full year to bring him back since Queen Anne died, and they've done nothing.' I heard footsteps cross the floor, and heard the handle of a door turn. 'Just you think on what I've said, now.'

'Do you mean to roast the squabs tonight?'

I heard the footsteps pause. 'Now what the devil does that have to do with anything?'

'I think more clearly when I'm fed.'

'Is that a fact?'

'You might do well to roast an extra bird.'

'I'll roast the flock for you,' the Irishman said drily, 'if it helps you find your sense.'

He didn't slam the door exactly, but he closed it with a force that gave his final statement emphasis. I heard his footsteps tramping down the stairs.

Now where on earth, I wondered, had I conjured *him* up from? And why was his name Fergal? I had never met a Fergal.

From the hall below, the Irishman called up the stairs, 'The constable is coming!'

Oh, terrific, I thought. *Someone else to join the party.* I'd have stayed exactly where I was, except I caught the faint sound of a horse's hooves above the wind and couldn't help but wonder if I'd actually hallucinated horses, so I rose to have a look.

I heard the floorboards in the next room creak as though somebody else were doing likewise, crossing to the window, looking out towards the road.

The horse and rider coming up The Hill had an official look – the horse a gleaming bay, the man who rode him middle-aged and wearing black clothes with a hat that slanted down to hide his face. From the next room I heard an exhaled breath that might have been annoyance, and then footfalls crossing back again, the opening and closing of the door, and steps that took the stairs by twos on their way down.

I found it strange to stand there at the window where I'd stood so often and gaze out upon a scene that looked the same yet not the same, as though an artist had gone over it again but lightly, painting trees where none had been before, erasing roofs and buildings from the village of Polgelly and retexturing the road to rutted dirt.

The rider had turned off that road now and halted his horse at the front of the house, and was shifting as though to dismount when the front door banged below me and the man in brown – still hatless, but wearing his jacket again – came in view.

With my window tight shut and the wind beating hard on the glass I heard nothing of what the men said, but they didn't shake hands, and the constable stayed in the saddle. I couldn't see anything of his face under the hat, but his gestures had an arrogance I found unpleasant, and from their body language I'd have guessed the two men didn't like each other. As the man in brown shrugged off some comment the constable made, the sun glinted on something and I saw that he'd put on more than his coat before coming outside. He had strapped on a sword belt. The sword itself hung at his left side, a deadly thing partly concealed underneath the long jacket but meant to be seen.

I was focused on that when the constable lifted his head.

He was looking up, scanning the windows. His gaze landed squarely on me and without really thinking I took a step backwards . . .

The room slowly melted.

And just as before on the coast path, I found myself back in the same place I'd been when the vision had started. This time I was standing at the desk in Uncle George's study, with my hand outstretched to switch off the computer, with the carriage clock in front of me still chiming off the hour.

The final chime fell ringing in the silence as I noted that the clock's hands were still pointed to the same position: Five o'clock.

Incredible, I thought, that the hallucination could have taken no real time at all. Yet here I was, and there the clock was, showing me the proof.

I turned off the computer and sank gratefully into the green chair, propping both elbows on the desk for support as I lowered my head to my hands. Then in sudden confusion, I stopped.

Raised my gaze again. Stared at my sleeve. Touched it, just to be sure.

The red silk of the dressing gown ran smoothly through my fingers, still as dark as wine. And somehow now as real as I was.

Chapter Nine

It was still there the following morning, when, having locked my bedroom door, I pulled the wardrobe open and drew the garment on its hanger from the very back, where I had hidden it. Not something I'd imagined, but a real, substantial dressing gown, a little faded now and frayed a bit around the seams, but still the same one I had worn while I was . . . well, that was the problem, because now I didn't know *what* I'd been doing.

All I knew was that, whatever had occurred, it must have happened in the blinking of an eye. The carriage clock on Uncle George's desk could not be argued with. Even if I'd fallen into some kind of a trance for that brief instant, and the dressing gown had been there in the study – which it hadn't, I was sure of it – I'd scarcely have had time to put it on before the clock had finished chiming.

But if that wasn't what I'd done, then that would mean

that what I had experienced was real. The man in brown was real.

I shook my head. It simply wasn't logical. I couldn't wrap my thoughts around it. Travelling through time was something people did in books or films. It didn't really happen. Yet the dressing gown here in my hands, and its obvious age, seemed to stand in denial of that line of reasoning, and I couldn't think of how else to explain it. I'd tried. I had spent the whole night trying hard to come up with another excuse for the dressing gown's being here, and I'd come up empty-handed, with nothing to show for the effort except a real headache in place of the fake one I'd used last night as an excuse to miss supper.

I would have skipped breakfast this morning as well, if there hadn't just then been a knock at my door.

'Eva?' Susan's voice.

Thrusting the dressing gown back in the wardrobe I crossed to the door and unlocked it to open it.

'Still have the headache?' she guessed when she saw me. 'Poor you. I've made tea and some toast. You can't go without eating.' She brought the tray in with her, setting it down on the bed. 'Is there anything else I can get you?'

'No, really, this—' Looking down at the tray, I deliberately dragged my mind back from my own worries, into the here and the now. 'This is perfect. And so thoughtful. Thank you. You have to stop spoiling me.'

'Well,' Susan said, 'you're our guest.' And when she saw me start to protest, she put in, 'Besides, it's not as though you're doing nothing in return. You've spent the past week building us a website.' With a smile she said, 'That's likely how you got your headache.'

'No.' But since I couldn't very well explain how I *had* got it, I took a bite of my toast instead. Then I remembered, 'It's ready, by the way. Your website.'

'Really? Can I see it?'

I was hesitant to go back into Uncle George's study after what had happened last time, but I couldn't think of any good excuse to make. My indecision must have shown on my face because she said, 'If you're not up to it this morning—'

'No, it's fine.' I squared my shoulders slightly. 'I'm fine. I'd love for you to see it.'

She insisted that I finish off my toast first, but I brought the tea along with me and sipped it for its steadying effect as we ran through the different pages of the site.

It wasn't until later, when we'd finished with the website and we'd talked about the next step of publicity – the press release – and she'd gone off to fetch some details of the gardens' history to include in it, that it suddenly occurred to me that history might be one thing I could use to help shed light on what had happened to me yesterday.

The Irishman, as I recalled, had said a name: the Duke of Ormonde.

Though it had meant nothing to me then, and didn't now, it sounded real enough. And real dukes would be mentioned in *Burke's Peerage*.

There were, in fact, two Dukes of Ormonde listed on the Internet, but since the man named Fergal had said something about Queen Anne, too, I chose the second duke, who'd lived through Queen Anne's reign.

I wished my mother had been here to give me one of her amazing history lessons, but she wasn't, so I settled for the basics, starting off in 1714 with Queen Anne's death and the dispute over who should inherit the throne – her half-brother James Stuart, who was Catholic and living in exile near France, or the properly Protestant German Prince George, a more distant relation. I read the accounts of how deeply divisive the politics were at the time, with the Tories who favoured the rights of young James locking horns with the Whigs who supported Prince George. And I read of the riots and public unrest that had followed George's coronation as the King of all Great Britain.

Which brought me to the spring of 1715, when Jacobites – the followers of James – were plotting armed rebellion, making plans to rise in arms and bring young James himself across to claim his throne.

It seemed most people's sympathies in Cornwall had been squarely with the Tories and James Stuart, and they hadn't tried to hide the fact. And so King George's parliament, controlled by Whigs, had swiftly moved to stamp out any smoulderings that might ignite the fires of a dangerous rebellion.

The Duke of Ormonde, hero of the people, had been right there in the thick of it. Three years earlier, when the mighty Duke of Marlborough had fallen out of favour, the dashing Ormonde had replaced him as commander of the British armies fighting on the Continent, and his patriotic exploits had increased his popularity to the point that the Whigs had grown uneasy. When Ormonde had taken the side of the Jacobites, the Whigs had moved against him, too. He and another leading Tory, Lord Bolingbroke, had been charged with High Treason, and though both men had managed to evade arrest and imprisonment by fleeing the country, Parliament had gone ahead and impeached them in their absence, stripped them of their rights and status, left them both as marked and wanted men.

I had his portrait on the monitor when Susan came back.

'Who is that?' she asked.

'James Butler, second Duke of Ormonde.' A man I'd never heard of until yesterday. A man who was as real as the red dressing gown. And how could I have even known his name, I wondered, if I hadn't travelled to the past?

'And who is he?' asked Susan.

I gave her a summary of his biography, adding, 'He played a big part in the Jacobite uprisings down here in Cornwall. Maybe I'll find he's connected somehow to Trelowarth. You never know.'

She frowned. 'I thought the Jacobites were Scottish.'

'So did I. But there were lots of them in England, too, apparently.'

She leant closer, studying the picture. 'Nice wig.'

'Yes, well, most men wore them back then.' I knew one man who didn't, or at least he hadn't worn one either time that I had met him, but I couldn't say that, either. Instead I looked more closely at the portrait, searching for some small resemblance to the man in brown who'd said, about the Duke, that he was 'bound to him by blood'. If they were relatives, that blood appeared to be the only thing they shared. The Duke of Ormonde's face was soft and overfed, his nose too long and large, his gaze too proud and condescending.

'What year were the uprisings?' asked Susan.

'1715.'

'Before the Halletts came here, then. Well, as you say, you never know. It would be fun to have some kind of tale to tell to tourists, and a Jacobite rebellion's always good.'

Not for the Jacobites, I thought. Things never had gone very well for them. At least the Irishman named Fergal had appeared to sense that it was not a fight worth fighting, and I couldn't help but wonder if he'd ever managed to convince the man in brown. Perhaps I'd never know.

I pushed the thought aside and settled in to work with Susan on the press release, a thing I'd done a hundred times before with other clients, so the process was predictable and calming. Susan had some good ideas.

'We should use the word "romance",' she said, 'and "lost", because they paint a sort of picture, don't they? And I think what makes Trelowarth interesting is that we have so many roses here that might otherwise have vanished, been forgotten. It makes Trelowarth like a . . .' Pausing as though searching for the proper phrase, she finished, 'Well, it's like a time machine. One step into the gardens takes you back a hundred years.' Her face grew bright. 'That might make a brilliant heading, don't you think? "Step back in time – come visit the old roses of Trelowarth".'

I kept my fingers steady on the keyboard as I typed. 'Yes, that's quite good.'

Step back in time. Step back in time. The words kept playing over in my mind and stayed there even after Susan had gone off again to see to something over at the greenhouse. *Back in time . . .*

My fingers hesitated on the keyboard. Then I opened a

new window for a search, and typed in: 'Time Travel'.

I didn't know what I'd expected. Strange stuff, I supposed. A lot of people writing, 'Hi, my name is Zog, I'm from the future.' But that wasn't what I found. Instead I found page after page of true science, with actual physicists – some of them famous – discussing the concept as though it were wholly respectable, even conducting experiments at universities.

Much of their dialogue, arguing theories and drawing those squiggly equations that filled half a page, was beyond me. They talked about space-time and wormholes and String Theory, extra dimensions and closed timelike curves. But not one of them said that it couldn't be done. Even the great Stephen Hawking was quoted as saying, in one of his lectures, that 'according to our present understanding' of the laws of physics, travel back in time was not impossible.

It all had to do, so I gathered, with Einstein's Theory of Relativity having proved that time and space were curved and changeable, not fixed and absolute as Isaac Newton had maintained.

There was a portrait of Sir Isaac Newton in his old age, painted sometime, it said, around 1710. He had a pleasant sort of face, but it was not his face I noticed; not his face that made me shrug away the shivers that chased lightly down my spine.

It was the simple fact that he was wearing the exact same style of dressing gown that hung now in my wardrobe. And the sight of it convinced me, even more than Stephen Hawking's words, that all the reading I had done on mental health and all my plans to see a doctor had been nothing but a wasted effort. Though it seemed incredible, I *had* gone back in time.

And that wasn't something a doctor could cure.

There were voices in the next room.

My eyes opened to the darkness with a wary sensibility, and waited to adjust to the faint moonlight from outside my bedroom windows. The house had always had a lonely feel this late at night, and as a child I'd hated waking up this way, surrounded by the shadows, but tonight I only felt relieved to see that everything was in its proper place – the beds, the chair, the wardrobe. I was where I was supposed to be.

Three days had gone by since I'd travelled back into the past, and in the meantime things had been so normal I might easily have slipped back into thinking I'd imagined what had happened, if there hadn't been the dressing gown as evidence.

The voices went on talking, low and quiet, from the far side of the wall behind my head. The man-in-brown's voice was familiar to me now, at least in tone, and I presumed the other speaker was the Irishman. His voice was the more animated one that rose and fell as though in argument, while through it all the other answered back with level calm.

I wasn't feeling calm, myself. I knew I'd heard the voices on their own before, when nothing else had happened, but a lot had changed since then, and now the sound of them unnerved me, made me want to put a bit of space between us. Just in case.

Forcing myself into action, I got up and went to the bathroom.

There was darkness in the corridor as well, but I had walked this route enough by night to do it with a blindfold. By the light above the mirror in the bathroom I examined my face with a frown. 'You're a coward, you know.' Which was true. But I still took my time, and I waited a good fifteen minutes before going back.

The bedroom was quiet. No more voices.

Just the whisper of the night breeze through the partly opened windows. And the sound of someone breathing from the bed.

My heart began to pound so heavily it held me to the place where I was standing just inside the door. I couldn't move.

It wasn't my bed any more. The moonlight fell on posts and curtains and the figure of a man who lay stretched out full-length on top of the blankets, his hands behind his head, still clothed in breeches and the white shirt I had seen him in before. There was light enough for me to recognise the angles of his profile. I could hear him breathing evenly, asleep.

Or so I thought.

Until his voice spoke from the shadows.

'I do confess I have forgot your name.'

He'd spoken quietly, and mindful of the fact there might be other people sleeping in the house, I answered just as low. 'You never asked it.'

His head turned till he was looking right at me, though nothing else about him moved. The moonlight gleamed behind him but I couldn't see his eyes or his expression. 'Do you have one?'

Did I have a name? I couldn't quite remember. 'Eva.'

'Eva. Is that all?'

'My name is Eva Ellen Ward.'

'A good name.' In the dark he looked at me a moment longer. 'I did fear that you had come to harm since last I saw you, Eva Ward.'

'I'm fine.'

'So I do see. And glad I am to see it, for your welfare has weighed heavy on my conscience.'

'Why is that?'

'Because I did not think to warn you not to leave the house,' he said. 'This countryside would offer little safety to a woman, and the roads around should not be lightly travelled.'

'I wasn't on the roads.'

'No?'

'No. And I didn't go outside the house.'

'So where, then . . . ? Ah,' he told me. 'You went back.'

'Yes.' I considered how to tackle this. The last time he had seen me I'd been claiming that he wasn't real, and telling him to go away. He probably already thought I was crazy. But I wanted to know. 'Am I right in thinking I've just travelled back in time?'

He didn't answer right away, but after some reflection he replied, 'That would depend entirely upon where you began.'

Which seemed a logical assumption. I could see no harm in telling him the year that I'd just come from. If he registered surprise, I didn't notice. 'Yes,' he told me then. 'You have indeed come back in time by some three centuries.'

'It's 1715?'

'It is.' That did surprise him. 'How did you know the year?'

'I did some reading.'

'You can read.' It wasn't actually a question, more a challenge, I could hear it in his voice. 'A brave accomplishment for a woman, even one who voyages through time.'

'You don't believe me?'

'On the contrary. 'Tis ghosts and walking spirits that I never have believed in, so I must confess I find your tale a singular relief.' He paused in thought. 'So, have you learnt to work this magic at your will?'

'And if I had,' I asked him, 'do you really think I would have turned up here, like this?'

'In my own chamber, do you mean, and in the middle of the night?' I sensed his smile, but was more focused on his words.

'This is your room?'

''Tis why I chose to fall asleep in it.'

I said, 'But when I came in here the last time . . . when I—'

'Told me I should go away?' His tone was openly amused.

I hoped the faint light covered my embarrassment. 'You didn't tell me this was your room, too.'

'An oversight on my part, I'll admit. Perhaps the shock of finding out that I did not, in fact, exist, after a lifetime of believing that I did, had some effect upon my manners.'

I was blushing now in earnest. 'Look, I'm sorry I was rude to you. I thought that I was seeing things.'

'I did not take offence,' he said. 'It did not trouble me to share my chamber then, no more than it does now.' He shifted round, and sat up slowly as he swung his long legs to the floor. Somehow he looked much larger that way, sitting with his white shirt gleaming ghost-like in the pale light of the moon. There was a silent moment. Then, 'You've changed your clothes,' he said, as though just noticing.

If he'd asked me at that moment I could not in truth have told him what clothes I *was* wearing. Glancing down myself at my plain T-shirt and pyjama bottoms, I said by way of explanation, 'I was sleeping, too.'

He seemed to be deciding something. 'If you are still here by day, you will need proper clothes to wear.'

I hadn't thought of that.

He stood and said, 'Wait here.' I had forgotten just how tall he was. His shoulder passed me at the level of my eyes as he went through the door connecting with the small front bedroom next to us, returning not long after with what looked to be a bulky length of fabric that he pressed into my hands. 'Take this, and wear it if you will.'

I told him, 'Thank you,' and he gave a nod, still standing in the door between the two rooms, his expression too obscured by shadows to be clearly seen. He told me, 'Sleep well, Eva Ward,' and with a backwards step he closed the door between us.

There was no way I could sleep. I didn't even try. Instead I sat and faced the window near the bed, the one that had the most familiar view, and fixed my gaze on the far place where the dark sea was met by sky, and stayed there waiting till the sun began to rise.

Its first rays came, not through that window, but the ones that faced the road and flanked the fireplace. The slanting sunlight, faint at first, chased out the shadows from the corners, falling warm across the floorboards and the surface of the writing desk that sat against the wall.

It touched the fabric that I still held in my arms as well, and I could finally see it was a dress – a bodice and a separate trailing skirt, with something like a nightgown underneath them, and a pair of shoes like slippers that fell tumbling to the floor as I rose carefully and spread the clothes out on the bed to have a better look.

The gown – for that was what it was – was plain but beautiful. The bodice had a low round neck and straight three-quarter sleeves, and was stiffened at its seams with supple boning, like a corset. The skirt was plain as well but full. It ran like silk between my fingers when I touched it, and its colour shifted in the light from blue to grey and back again.

It seemed so strange to think of wearing clothes like these, but then again, if I were truly stuck here in this time I couldn't very well walk round in my pyjamas.

And it was easier than I'd expected, sorting out how everything went on. First came the undergarment, a simple plain chemise with rounded neck and sleeves that fit quite closely to my elbows and below that widened into tiers of lace, so when I put the bodice on, that lace peeked out from underneath the bodice's three-quarter sleeves and softened the effect. I ought to have put the skirt on, really, before the bodice, but I managed to get everything adjusted – the skirt tied round my waist and the bodice smoothed down over that, so it all looked like one piece.

Both the slippers and gown fitted me well, which surprised me. I'd thought that I might be too short or not slender enough, but the skirt brushed the floor without trailing too much and the bodice, while snug, was not tight, though I found it a bit of a challenge to fasten. It closed at the front and was held not with buttons but pins, so I pricked myself painfully trying to do it, and swore out loud once in frustration. I was sliding in the last pin when the room's door was flung open and a man angrily asked, 'Who the devil are you?'

I could not have mistaken the voice of the Irishman, but his appearance surprised me. He wasn't a large man, as I had expected. He stood average height with black hair and a face that I guessed would ordinarily have been quite friendly.

It wasn't, though, just at the moment.

He glowered. 'I said, who the devil might you be?'

'I'm Eva.' It sounded inadequate, even to me, and too late I decided I shouldn't have spoken at all, since the sound of my accent had narrowed his eyes.

'Eva.' Planting himself in the doorway, he folded his arms firmly over his chest. 'Tell me, where do you come from? And how did you come to be here in this house?'

Neither question was one I could easily answer. I didn't feel safe with this man, like I had with the other one. There was anger and open distrust in his eyes, and no promise that he would behave like a gentleman. Not that I thought he would actually hurt me. I only suspected he wouldn't much care either way if he did.

I tried calming the waters. My memory raced backward in search of his name. 'Fergal. That's your name, isn't it? Fergal?'

His gaze narrowed further. 'And who told you that?'

'He did.'

'Who did?' he challenged me, moving another step into the room.

Damn, I thought. I had no clue what his name was. 'The man . . .'

'Which man would that be?'

'The man who lives here.'

He took one more step and the black eyebrows rose in a mocking expression. 'He told you my name?'

'Yes.'

''Tis odd, do you not think, that he'd tell you my name and not tell you his?'

I had no easy answer to that one, and so I said nothing while Fergal advanced.

'So he told you my name. And he gave you that gown, no doubt.'

Something in how he was looking at what I was wearing felt wrong, but I didn't know why. 'Yes.'

He spat the word, 'Liar.'

I lifted my chin. I was scared and confused but I still had my limits, and deep in me I felt the stir of rebellion. 'It isn't a lie.'

I'd surprised him with that. I saw his flash of hesitation and drew strength from it.

'You go and ask him,' I said bravely. 'Go and ask him where I got this gown. He'll tell you.'

'Will he, now?' His tone was still belligerent, but he had lost a little of the righteousness. He tipped his head to one side while he looked at me and thought. And then he said, 'All right then, if you've got a mind to test the devil, we'll go ask him, you and me together.'

'Fine.' I said it bravely, though I didn't really have a

choice. He'd taken such a firm hold on my arm that I could not have broken free of it if I'd been fool enough to try.

The whole way down the stairs he kept on muttering his certainty, as much for his own ears as mine. 'Haven't I known him these twenty long years and he's never once done a thing yet without telling me first, and he'd be burning that gown with his own hands I think before he'd let another woman wear it in his sight, you mark me . . .'

On and on the tirade went, as Fergal dragged me with him through the hall into the kitchen. He apparently expected me to show the fear appropriate for somebody about to have their lie exposed, but all I really felt as we got closer to our goal was the relief of knowing I would soon be proven right. The fact that I was growing calmer by the minute didn't help his mood.

'All right then,' he repeated, when we reached the back corridor and the door leading outside. 'We'll just see who's telling tales, now.'

He had thrust me through the heavy door ahead of him, so when I stopped abruptly on the threshold there was nothing he could do but stop as well and swear an oath, and it was luck alone that kept us both from going down like dominoes.

But I paid no attention. I was busy staring at the man who stood not far in front of me, my man in brown who looked as though he'd just been at the stone-built stables set beyond the sweep of yard. His boots were clumped with mud and there were straws still clinging to his sleeve. There was no welcome in his eyes. His gaze had locked with Fergal's past my shoulder in a wordless kind of warning.

And beside him, dressed in black as he had been before, the constable stood watching us as well. Or, more correctly, watching me.

'Well, now.' The constable's voice was as smooth as the fin of a shark slicing water. 'And who have we here?'

Chapter Ten

I'd met people in my life who were pure poison. I had learnt to know the look of them – the way their smiles came and went and never touched their eyes, those eyes that could be so intense at times and yet revealed no soul. Such people might look normal, but inside it was as though some vital part of them was missing, and whenever I saw eyes like that I'd learnt to turn and run and guard my back while I was leaving.

The instant that I looked into the cold eyes of the constable, I knew what sort of man he was. But here I couldn't turn and run. I still had Fergal standing solid at my back.

The constable came forward slowly, sizing up this new turn of events. He looked to be in his mid-forties, not a tall man but a lean and wiry one, his long face lean as well and framed by the uncompromising curls of a white-powdered wig beneath the brim of his black hat. His gaze travelled my length from my loose-hanging hair to the hem of the gown that he too seemed to recognise. The sight of it kindled a new light of interest behind the dark eyes that returned to my face as he said, in a tone that was meant to provoke, 'Butler, you do surprise me. I would not have thought you a man to waste time with a harlot.'

'Mind your tongue, sir,' said the man in brown, his voice controlled. 'You speak of Fergal's sister, come to help us keep the house.'

I felt the slight reaction of the Irishman behind me, though he barely moved at all, and for a weighted moment I was unsure whether he would play along.

The constable was unconvinced. 'Your sister?' he asked Fergal. 'I was not aware you had one.'

There was silence as the Irishman appeared to be deciding something, then he drew himself up at my back, defensive and defiant. 'I have seven of them, ay. This one's next eldest to myself, she is.'

The constable was studying my face for a resemblance. Whether he found any I didn't know, but I doubted it. 'What is your name?' he asked.

'She cannot speak,' said Fergal, and his hard grip on my arm grew tighter, warning me to silence.

'Why is that?'

'You'd have to take that up with the Almighty, for He made her. All I know is that she never learnt the way of it.' He was a brilliant liar. In his voice I heard no hint of hesitation, and I couldn't help but admire the speed at which he'd seen the danger and defused it all at once. My voice didn't fit here. Even if I'd been able to manage an Irish accent, my patterns of speech were too modern, I would have slipped up. Now he'd saved me from having to try.

The man in brown said, 'Eva, this would be Constable Creed from the village. I do not doubt that, as he is a gentleman, he'll wish to offer his apologies and bid you welcome.'

It was a daring gamble, but he stood his ground and pulled it off. The constable's disquieting gaze took in my borrowed gown one final time before he gave an unrepentant nod and said unconvincingly, 'Mistress O'Cleary, I meant no offence. You are welcome of course to Trelowarth.' He took a step back and extended his nod to the other two. 'Gentlemen.' And then he turned and went out of the yard.

He left tension behind. I could feel it in the man behind me; see it in the squaring of the shoulders of the man in brown, who hadn't moved a step from where he stood. He was wearing the clothes I remembered, the tight brown trousers ending just below the knee in boots, a full white shirt with what I thought was called a stock tied round his neck beneath the long brown jacket that he wore unbuttoned, hanging open. But he had shaved, his jawline clean and strongly drawn. It made him look more civilised.

I felt the exchange of looks over my head as he said to his friend, 'Were you wanting to see me?' The question seemed careless enough, and relaxed, but I knew from his face he was keeping his guard up, aware that the constable might still be listening.

Fergal no doubt was aware of that, too, but he had his own questions to ask, in his own way. He nudged me a half a step forward and said, 'She'd a mind to come show you the gown, and to have me tell you how she does appreciate the gesture. 'Tis most generous.'

With a glance at Fergal's hold upon my arm, the man in brown turned his attention to my clothes, and for a moment in his eyes I thought I glimpsed a fleeting darkness like the passing of a pain, but it was so swift I wasn't certain. It had vanished by the time his eyes met mine. He said to Fergal, 'Tell your sister I am pleased she finds it to her liking, for in truth it suits her well.'

I sensed a challenge had been made and answered, and with what seemed like reluctance Fergal let me go. He grumbled, 'Sure you can tell her that yourself, she's got her ears.' And without waiting, he turned on his heel. 'Come have your breakfasts, then, and perhaps one of the pair of you can tell me what the bleeding Christ is going on.'

The kitchen window had a different view than I was used to. There were no walled gardens, neatly kept and tended, to look out on – only two old apple trees that grew close by the house, both beaten by the unforgiving coastal winds into hard twisted shapes that reached towards the hill as though in search of refuge.

And the kitchen itself was a much different room. There were no fitted cupboards, no worktops, no stove, just the fireplace and stone hearth and iron hooks hung with a motley collection of pans and utensils, the purpose of most of which I didn't know.

But the table, although it was smaller and rougher, was in the same spot, pushed up under the window. And sitting there having a breakfast of dark ale and bread felt familiar enough that it calmed me a little.

Fergal had calmed a bit, too, though his face betrayed his open incredulity at what he'd just been told. He filled his tankard for a second time and said, 'So you're telling me, then, that you've come from the future.'

'That's right.' I didn't care if he believed me. My only defence was the truth.

He was looking at me strangely. He shifted his attention to the man in brown beside me, who'd been sitting back in silence while I'd talked. 'And you believe this?'

'I have seen it.' With his booted legs stretched out beneath the table and his folded arms across his chest, he said, 'I've seen her pass between the worlds. 'Tis not a trick.'

'It might be witchcraft.' But he said it without any true conviction.

'Other men than you and I believe in witches,' said the man in brown, and Fergal gave another nod.

'Ay. But if not witchcraft, what then?'

'Why not truth?'

'Because the two of us both know it is impossible.'

'And men once thought the sea had limits that could not be sailed beyond for fear of dragons,' was his friend's reply. He turned his head to look at me, his clear eyes thoughtful on my face. 'I would submit that she is her own proof that it is possible.'

Fergal set his tankard on the table. 'See now, all that this is doing is to make my head ache like the devil has a hammer to it, so if you'll both excuse me I have work

I should be seeing to.' With a scrape he pushed his chair back and went out, and left us sitting there together by the window.

It was open, and the morning winds from off the sea were coming in by gentle gusts that crossed the sill and brushed my hands, a reassuring touch. Unseen within the tangled branches of the nearest apple tree a songbird had begun to trill, a carefree sound that seemed in contrast to my troubles.

At my side the man in brown said, 'Fergal is a good man. But he does not lightly give his trust.'

'I've noticed.' I gave my arm an absent rub, remembering.

'I give you my apologies if you were roughly handled.'

'That's all right. He thought I was a thief. Besides, he's more than made it up to me, coming up with that story for your constable.'

He gave a shrug, acknowledging the truth of that, and as he turned his head away the silence started settling between us once again.

I said, 'I didn't know your name.'

His eyes came back to me. 'I beg your pardon?'

'That's why Fergal thought I was a thief,' I said. 'Because I didn't know your name.'

A moment passed, and then with the suggestion of amusement in his voice he tossed my own words from our meeting in the bedroom last night back at me. 'You never asked me.'

Two could play that game, I thought. I met his gaze with one as steady. 'Do you have one?'

No denying the amusement now. It briefly lit his eyes

inside as he said, 'Daniel Butler. At your service, mistress.'

'Thank you, Mr Butler.'

With a gallant nod he pushed his own chair back and stood and stretched and said, 'Now, by your leave, I have some work myself I must attend to. I'd advise you keep within the house, but you may have the freedom of it.'

'Thank you.'

'Oh, and Eva?'

'Yes?'

He'd stopped within the doorway. 'I should think a woman who had slept in my own bed might properly presume to call me Daniel.' With the smile still in his eyes he left, before I'd had the time to form a suitable reply.

It felt so strange to walk the rooms I knew so well and find them different.

The furniture was more austere and harder in its lines, though I could sense a woman's hand had tried to soften the décor a little, likely the woman whose gown I was wearing. There were cushions on a few chairs, and woven rush seats on some others, and long hanging curtains in calico prints at the sides of the windows. The downstairs hall hadn't yet been plastered over and the rich wood panelling made everything seem darker, but the rooms themselves were brightened by their carpets and their picture frames with lively prints of country life hung all round on the walls, and everywhere I looked were candles, set in sconces on the walls or shielded by glass chimneys on a table or a mantelpiece, all waiting to be lit against the darkness come the evening.

Some downstairs rooms were used for other purposes – the dining room from my own time was used here as a sitting room – but in the big front room I'd always known as the library there were still shelves, and books, and in the place of the piano was a cabinet full of china cups and plates and curiosities that trembled with a tinkling sound in rhythm with my footsteps on the wide-planked floor.

Intrigued, I took a closer look.

The cups and plates and saucers were a delicate design of whorls and rosebuds on an ivory background, carefully lined up in proud display. And on the shelf below were seashells, gorgeous things of varied shapes and colours. Some I recognised from my collecting days: a knobbled murex, pink and white, the iridescent rainbow lining of an abalone, and the broad flat fan of a Japanese scallop. And set in their midst was a little glass box, hinged and shaped like a scallop-shell too, and inside was a tightly wound curl of dark hair tied with blue ribbon.

Only that, and nothing more, and yet it was enough to speak to me. It told me Daniel Butler had lost someone, too, as I had.

Other footsteps shook the cabinet as they came into the room, and then they stopped, and Fergal's voice behind me said, 'You'll not find anything in there of any value, save the dishes.'

'I'm not going to steal your dishes.'

Coming up beside me, he glanced at my face with curiosity, then looked down at the little shell-shaped box that held my interest.

'That was his wife's,' he told me, in a voice turned clipped and hard.

I'd guessed as much. Just as I'd guessed the dress that I was wearing had been hers as well. I smoothed it with a hand and would have turned, but Fergal's sharp eyes had caught sight of something else with my small movement.

'That's an Irish ring,' he said, and gave a nod towards the Claddagh ring I wore. 'I've seen its like in Galway.' With a narrowed gaze he asked me, 'May I?' and I put my hand within his rough one while he turned it to the light. 'I've never seen one made so small. How did you come by it?'

'It's been passed down from my grandmother,' I told him. 'She was Irish.'

'Was she, now? And where was it she came from?'

'I'm not sure.'

'No doubt from Galway, if she had a ring like this.'

I said, 'It's called a Claddagh ring. A lot of people have them.'

Fergal raised an eyebrow slightly at the name. 'A Claddagh ring? 'Tis as unlikely a name as I've heard for a token of love. Have you been to the Claddagh? No? It is the finest place to fish in all the western shore of Ireland, and yet you'll not get near it if you come there as a stranger, for the fishermen of Claddagh are a fierce breed to themselves. They'll sink your ship as soon as look at you.'

I couldn't help it. 'So are you from Claddagh, then?' I asked him.

Fergal, not expecting that, stared down at me a moment.

Then he smiled. 'Nah. Me, I come from County Cork, where all the men are soft and mannered, don't you know.' He let me have my hand back. 'Are you hungry, Eva Ward?'

'A little.'

'Can you cook?'

'A little.'

'Well,' he said, 'then come along with me if you've the courage to. We'll put you to the test.'

Chapter Eleven

I saw a different side of Fergal in the kitchen than I'd seen before. His roughened edges smoothed a bit and what I'd seen as grumpiness revealed itself to be a dry and entertaining wit. He even smiled now and then, and from the crinkling lines that marked the outer corners of his eyes when he was smiling I imagined that he did it much more often than he'd led me to believe. On top of which, he seemed to be completely in his element in this room of the house. He cooked with skill.

'And wasn't I sent off to sea the minute I was walking,' he replied when I remarked on it, 'and I proved myself of no great use to anyone except the ship's own cook, who taught me all I know. 'Tis why I'm better stewing fish than roasting fowl, as you'll be learning to your cost.'

I didn't recognise the type of bird that he was now preparing. There were two of them, narrow and lean.

Perhaps ducks. I said, 'But you are not a ship's cook now.'

'I am at that, from time to time. Whenever Danny sails.'

'He has a ship?'

'The very best of ships.' He gave a nod. 'The *Sally*. She's away just now with Danny's brother at her helm, but when he brings her back you'll likely see her for yourself.'

I took this in. 'So who's the captain? Mr Butler or his brother?'

Fergal's sideways look said I'd amused him. 'Well now, there's a question no man yet could answer for you. 'Tis for certain sure that neither Jack nor Danny could, they've argued it for years between their own selves. Like as not the *Sally* knows, but being such a lady as she is she goes as nicely for the one as for the other.' He skewered the birds with a long spit and set them to roast on the hearth while he dusted his hands and moved on to the vegetables.

There I could help him, at least. I could peel things and chop them and toss them together into the three-footed iron kettle in which he was making what looked to be some sort of soup, richly thickened with barley.

He shot me another glance while I was working. 'You're not a woman to complain, I'll give you that.'

'And who would I complain to?'

'Fair enough.'

'Besides,' I said, 'I'll have to practise being silent, won't I, now you've got the constable convinced that I can't talk.'

'Ay, well, I'm sorry for all that,' he said, not looking in the least bit sorry. 'But 'twas all that I could think to keep him from discovering the queer way that you talk. He'd have asked questions, to be sure.'

'No, don't be sorry. It was very gallant of you.'

'Was it, now?'

'It was. And thank you.'

With his head tipped to one side he wiped the blade of his own cutting knife to clean it, while he kept his eyes on me as though deciding something. Then he set the knife down and remarked, 'I have a thirst from all this work, now. Will you have a drink of cider, Eva Ward?'

I was hesitant, remembering Mark's scrumpy, but I knew that this was more than just the offer of a drink, it was the offer of a hand in truce. I couldn't turn it down. 'Yes, thank you.'

Which was why, when Daniel Butler finally came in from whatever chores he had been doing, he took one look at my eyes – which looked far too bright even from my side – and lifted his eyebrows.

'Take your boots from under there,' said Fergal, stopping his friend from taking a seat. 'Have you no manners at all? We've a lady among us, we'll dine at the table we're meant to be dining at.'

That turned out to be in the long room beyond the pantry that in my time was a games room, but in this time had wood-panelled walls, not wallpaper, and shutters on the windows, and where Uncle George's billiard table should have been, right at the centre of the room, there stood a trestle table built of heavy oak, with ten imposing chairs.

Fergal set us three places around the one end. 'You'll pardon the dust,' he said, giving the table a wipe that whirled particles upward to dance in the light. 'We'd a girl coming up from the village to clean for us, but her da's fallen ill and she's needed at home, so we've had to make do for ourselves this last while.'

It was a big house for two men on their own. When I'd visited Trelowarth as a child there'd been a local woman, Mrs Jenner, who had done most of the housework, and even today Mark and Susan had cleaners come in every week.

Daniel Butler took the end seat with a smile and told me, 'Do not let him stir your sympathies. He charms a girl up here with regularity, and 'tis the rare occasion that one leaves without first taking up a broom.'

'You're telling secrets, now,' said Fergal, but he winked as he went out to fetch our dinner from the kitchen.

I looked at Daniel Butler's handsome face and asked him, disbelieving, 'Fergal charms the girls up here?'

'He does. He is not always so ill-natured, as you seem to have discovered for yourself.' The smile lingered in his eyes. 'What were you drinking?'

'Cider.'

'Then you have impressed him, for the cider in our cellars here was made by his own hand, and he does guard it as a dragon guards its gold. He would not offer it to anyone he did not feel was worthy.'

'Yes, well, I'm honoured but I hope he doesn't make a habit of it. Cider makes my head spin.'

'Do you have it in your own time?'

'Cider? Yes. It makes my head spin there, as well.'

'So there are some things at least that are the same for you.' Beneath the lightness of his voice I thought I caught a trace of something like a scientific interest. 'I should think it must feel strange, to step into another age and find yourself so far removed from all you know. Like being shipwrecked in a foreign land.'

It was a good analogy. 'It feels like that a bit.' I hadn't really stopped to analyse it all that much. A part of me, I knew, was still adjusting to the shock of being tossed around in time, and I could only cope with every situation as it came. But now I came to think of it, it was like being washed up on the shore of some strange country not my own. Except, 'The house is still the same,' I said. 'At least, I know my way around the rooms. That helps a little. And the fact that you believe me, that helps too.' I hadn't realised how much that last fact meant to me until I'd said the words out loud.

I looked away from him, and coughed to clear my throat, and changed the subject as I glanced around the room for inspiration. 'Have you lived here at Trelowarth long?'

'Twelve years. It was left me by an uncle who desired I should settle myself to a more honest trade.'

But before I could ask him, 'More honest than what?' Fergal came with an armful of plates heaped with food.

'There,' he said, as he set mine in front of me, 'best to enjoy that, I've nothing so fancy to serve you tomorrow. It's stirabouts now, till I'm next to the market.'

It was plain food, but flavourful. Fergal had basted the roast birds with honey, and seasoned the barley and vegetables with unknown spices and herbs that made everything sit on my stomach with comfortable warmth. I ate with knife and spoon, as both of them were doing, grateful for the light ale Daniel Butler offered me in place of cider. Although the small tin tumbler it was served in gave the ale a faint metallic taste, it was at least a drink that, slowly sipped, could leave me sober.

The men drank wine, a rich red wine they drank from tumblers like my own, of beaten tin. As Fergal poured the dregs into his own cup, he remarked, 'We'll soon be out of this as well. We've but a single case remaining in the cellar.'

Daniel Butler said, ''Tis good we've got your cider, then.'

'The devil you do. Any man will be losing his hand if he touches those kegs.'

'Do you see?' Daniel Butler directed that comment at me, with a smile. 'Did I not say he guarded his casks like a dragon?'

'Ay, and did you think to tell her why I do that, now? Did you say what your brother did the one time that I turned my back? And didn't he have all my cider on the *Sally* and away on the next tide without so much as a farewell and by-your-leave?'

'Well, that is Jack for you.'

'Ay, steal the coins right off a dead man's eyes and do it smiling, so he would.' But there was still a grudging admiration in his tone, from which I guessed he couldn't help but like the man they spoke of. Then he seemed to think of something. 'Jesus, Danny, he'll be coming back at any time now.'

'And?'

'Well, how the devil will you be explaining *her*?' This with a nod across the table towards me. 'You know as well as I do Jack can never keep his mouth shut, and he'll never be convinced she came the way she says she did.'

I watched while Daniel Butler weighed the options in his mind, and then he gave a shrug and said, 'She is your sister, come to help us keep the house. Is that not what you said to Creed? And he believed it.'

'Did he? Sure of that then, are you?'

'No.' His eyes were thoughtful on my face. 'But Jack is not as clever as the constable. And Eva, I suspect, is rather more so. Will it bother you,' he asked, 'to play a part?'

I wasn't sure, despite his faith in me, that I could pull it off. I'd never been much good at acting; never had Katrina's gift. She would have loved this whole experience, I knew, of stepping back into another age. She'd have thrown herself into the role, would have altered her accent and gestures until Daniel Butler himself would have thought she was from his own time. She'd have had an adventure.

I smiled faintly, feeling for the thousandth time the small and pulling pain of separation and the hollow ache of being left behind. I saw his eyes grow quizzical, and so I said, 'I'll try. But I'm afraid I'm not an actress.'

'It was not my intention to suggest you were. I would not so insult you.' The apology was so swift and sincere it surprised me until I remembered that actresses had once been seen as no better than prostitutes, women who offered themselves to the public for money and couldn't be classed as respectable. I thought of the actresses I'd known and worked with, the wealth and the power of some of them, and couldn't help but reflect on how far we had come in a few hundred years. But I felt much too tired at the moment to try to explain that, and all that I said was, 'I wasn't insulted.'

Fergal feigned insult on my behalf. 'Mind how you speak to my sister, now,' he warned his friend. Then, to me, 'I'd best show you the house, so you'll know where things are.'

Daniel said, 'I can do that.'

Fergal's long look assessed him, and seemed to see something he hadn't expected, because he leant back in his chair with new interest. 'All right.'

To be honest, I paid more attention to Daniel than I did to what he was telling me as I was shown through the rooms of Trelowarth. The downstairs I'd already seen, which was a good thing because all that I managed to take in down there was that Daniel had nice hands he used when he talked, and that when he smiled it carved a shallow cleft in his right cheek. All useful things, but as we climbed the stairs I tried to focus more on my surroundings, and a little less on how his shoulders moved beneath his jacket.

Only that, too, wasn't altogether pointless, as it prompted me to say, 'I'm really sorry that I didn't bring your dressing gown back with me.'

He half-turned on the landing. 'What?'

'Your dressing gown. The one you loaned me.'

'Ah.' He gave a nod. 'My banyan. It is of no consequence. I'll have another made.'

But I realised that if I returned to my own time in what I was wearing right now, in this gown that had once been his wife's, that was something he couldn't replace. And I wondered if he realised it, too.

If he did, he kept it to himself as he began to show me through the upstairs rooms. I had already seen his study, but he added, 'Should you wish something to read, you may take any book that you please from in here, or from downstairs. You saw the shelves there?'

I assured him I had. 'Thank you.'

'Nobody else in this house has much liking for books,' he said. 'Fergal has no patience for reading, and my brother Jack would rather be the author of his own adventures. This,' he said, 'is Jack's room.' He nodded to the door of the back bedroom. 'And I'll warn you, though I love my brother dearly, you'd be wisest not to venture near this door when he's at home. 'Tis not for nothing all the mothers in Polgelly lock their daughters up for safekeeping when Jack comes into harbour.'

The warning was a light one, so I answered him in kind, 'I doubt your brother will be bothered with me, seeing as I'm sleeping in your room.'

His eyes were laughing when he looked at me. 'My brother might just take that as a challenge.'

We were so close now in the corridor I had to look a long way up. A man would have to be a fool, I thought, to challenge Daniel Butler's right to anything. It wasn't just his height, or strength of build, it was the whole of him, that certain quiet sense of self-assuredness that told me he would not be on the losing side too often in a fight. Were I a man myself, I wouldn't want to test him.

I was looking at him, thinking this, when I first realised that his eyes weren't laughing any more. And then he noticed I had noticed and he let his gaze drift upwards from my own and said, 'Tomorrow I shall find you pins, so you can dress your hair.'

'I don't know how to.'

'No?' He focused on my eyes again, but briefly. 'No, of course you would not know. Well, that will be a minor thing to overcome.'

I asked, 'Where are *you* sleeping?' because suddenly it seemed like something I should know.

For an answer he crossed to the door of the room beside mine. 'Here,' he told me, as the door swung open.

This was where he and Fergal had been talking when I'd overheard them, in this narrow bedroom filled with soft light from the single window at the front. The bed here was not quite as big as the one he'd turned over to me in the room next door, but it was also high and canopied with curtains of a soft sky blue. A long-lidded blanket box sat at the foot of the bed, and a chair had been placed by the window so someone could sit looking out at the view of the green hills that rolled to the changeable sea.

It was a woman's room. I didn't need to ask whose it had been because her presence was so tangible I all but saw her sitting in the chair beside the window. I imagined he did, too.

I wondered how long she'd been dead, but didn't like to pry, and so I turned my gaze instead towards the closed door in the wall between this room and mine. He looked as well, and said, 'I do not doubt that I could find a lock to fit that latch, if it would ease your fears.'

I turned to him. 'My fears?'

'You surely have them, being far from home among strange men. And you were frightened when we met.'

'You had a knife, and you were angry,' I reminded him.

'Did it seem like anger to you? For my part, it felt like cowardice. I'd never faced a ghost.'

'Well, any ghost that saw you come at them like that would likely take off running.'

Daniel Butler smiled. He hadn't moved, and yet I felt the space between us shrinking as he said, 'But you are not a ghost.'

I shook my head.

'And I'll admit you do not seem afraid.'

I said, 'I'm not afraid at all.' The words surprised me when I said them, for I knew that they were true. I said them over, to be sure: 'I'm not afraid.'

He watched my face a moment, then he gave a nod and told me, 'Good. For that is a beginning.'

Sleeping was impossible. I rolled my face into the pillow, eyes closed tightly.

I did not belong here. This was not my room, and not my bed. And yet, a part of it felt right to me, and somewhere deep inside my mind a tiny voice kept speaking up to say that Daniel Butler had been wrong to tell me I was far from home.

It was a voice I couldn't quiet, and I rolled again and dragged the covers with me, staring out the open window at the moonlit sky shot through with stars that danced against the blackness of infinity. The sea had a voice tonight, rolling and whispering on the dark shore as though trying to give me advice. I ignored it at first, but when other sounds, equally furtive and low, rose to join it, I gave in and rolled from my bed, crossing barefoot to stand at the window.

I'd changed back into my pyjamas, and the beautiful gown was spread out on the chair in the corner to wait for tomorrow.

Tomorrow, when I would see Daniel and Fergal, I would be shown what to do with my hair so that Daniel could take me outside, as he'd promised, and give me a tour of the property.

From where I stood now at the front of the house I could see the broad slope of the hill rolling down to the cliffs and the sea, with the darkness of the Wild Wood pressing closer to the house and looking larger than my memory of it, shot through in places with the ghostly white of blackthorn still in bloom. The sounds continued, and I saw a stir of shadows in the woods.

They slipped out one by one and left the path to turn uphill and climb towards the house, a silent line of darkened figures, moving in the moonlight. Well, not wholly silent. I could hear the rustle of their footsteps and the heavy tread of two dark horses being led in single file behind, with bundles piled on their backs.

The floorboards in the next room creaked as Daniel Butler rose as well, and stealthily went out and down the stairs. A moment later from my window I could see his shadow going out to join the others, and to clap the shoulder of the man in front in greeting, and to guide the line of men and horses up around behind the house.

It didn't in the least surprise me that he was a smuggler, I had guessed already from the things he'd said about his less-than-honest trade, and from the character he'd painted of the brother who shared the command of his ship. Besides, this was Cornwall, and every house here had its smugglers.

I wondered what the men had carried up tonight, then I decided that I didn't need to know. It didn't matter.

It felt colder on my feet now standing there beside the window, so I turned away and headed back to bed.

And then I stopped.

Because the bed had started wavering. Across the blankets shadows played and shifted as the hanging curtains caught the breeze that blew in from behind me like a long, regretful sigh.

Another breath and it had faded like a swirl of smoke in wind, and I was once more in the corridor, just crossing from the bathroom and a few steps from my bedroom door, while all the house around me went on sleeping as though nothing had changed.

Chapter Twelve

'You're quiet this morning. You feeling all right?' Mark had already been up and out and hard at work for hours by the time I ventured outside. There'd been a sharp change in the weather, and all round the flowers were ducking in front of the wind, gusting damp and chilly for this time of year. Even the dogs hunched their backs to it, keeping their tails down and gathering closely around Mark and me as we walked to the greenhouse.

The truth was, I wasn't too sure *how* I felt. I was glad to be back. But if things had gone differently I might be taking this same walk with Daniel right now, and not Mark, and for some reason that left me feeling a little bit . . . well, a bit cheated, though I knew that didn't make sense.

Nor was it really fair to Mark, who was still looking at me with concern. I made an effort, and met his gaze brightly. 'I'm fine.'

He seemed prepared to take me at my word. His own attention was distracted by the dogs, who had gone wild because Felicity was coming out to meet us from the greenhouse.

Her good spirits, at least, were as buoyant as ever. Dancing her way through the onslaught of leaping dog bodies and wagging tails, she said, 'It took you both long enough. Wait till you see what we've done!' As we neared the doorway to the greenhouse she slipped in behind Mark, covering his eyes with both her hands. 'Don't look, not yet. You either, Eva. Close your eyes.'

'Felicity, what . . . ow!' Mark whacked his elbow on the door frame as he tried to step through blind.

'All right. Now.' Lifting up her hands with an enthusiastic flourish, she revealed the latest triumph she and Susan had achieved. They'd painted. Everything was green and ivory, beautifully elegant and restful. For the first time, it looked less like an old greenhouse than a tea room in the making.

Even Mark was forced to say a heartfelt, 'Wow.'

And that one word, because it came from him, was all the benediction that Felicity had hoped for. I could see it in her eyes, her brightened smile, and once again I marvelled that Mark couldn't see it for himself. She said, 'Of course there's still the floor to do, and all the rest, but doesn't it look wonderful?'

It really did. I told her so.

Susan was cleaning the paintbrushes in the new sink that the plumber had just installed, but when she saw us she turned off the water and came across. 'Well, brother? What do you think?'

Mark was still looking up. 'I think maybe you might have a tea room.'

'I told you.' But she seemed pleased, too, to have won Mark's approval. 'Now all we have to do is bring the tourists in, and Eva's got a start on that already. Did she tell you that she's found a duke who might have some connection to Trelowarth?'

'Really?' Mark turned. 'Who would that be?'

'Oh,' I said. 'The Duke of Ormonde.' I'd forgotten all about him, but for the benefit of Mark and Felicity I gave an account of his career, how he'd fought against the Jacobites initially and then switched sides and tried to bring the young King James across to take the throne when Queen Anne died. 'He was raising a rebellion right down here,' I said, 'in Cornwall, only Parliament got wind of it and voted to arrest him as a traitor, and he took off into exile.'

'A Jacobite rebellion? Here in Cornwall?' asked Felicity.

'I know,' said Susan. 'That's what I said. But it's quite romantic, don't you think?'

Mark asked, 'And how's this duke connected to Trelowarth?'

If I'd had Fergal's gift for lying I'd have answered that I'd read somewhere the Duke of Ormonde might have had a blood relation living here in 1715, but as it was I only glanced away and shrugged and said, 'I haven't really got it all worked out. I'll have to do a bit more research, yet.'

Susan said, 'You should ask Oliver. Remember him?'

I nodded. 'Yes, of course. I just bumped into him Wednesday, in fact, in Felicity's shop.'

'*Did* you?' asked Felicity. 'He didn't mention that to me.'

I felt the quick surge of new interest all round.

Susan asked me, 'And what did you think of him?'

'Well . . .'

'He's filled out a bit, hasn't he?' Susan grinned. 'Who knew he'd grow up to look like a film star?'

Mark said, 'I should imagine Eva's seen her share of film stars, Sue.'

'Well, I'll take him, if she doesn't want him. The point is,' she told me, 'if it's history you're after, he'd be a good person to go to, because he knows all sorts of obscure things. He researched a lot, when he set up his smugglers' museum. If he doesn't know the exact facts you're after, he might point you in the direction to find them.'

Mark looked doubtful. 'Would he be open on a Sunday?'

Susan said, 'If the museum's closed, he only lives upstairs. I'm betting if you knocked he'd come and open up.'

'Especially,' Felicity said, teasing, 'for the right sort of a customer.'

Oliver's museum was along the harbour road, and it *was* open. The force of the wind blew me in through the door and I had to lean all of my weight on the heavy wood to make it swing shut behind me and latch.

Inside, everything smelt of the salt of the sea and the old plaster walls and the wood dust that came from the floorboards. Brass ship's lanterns hung from the dark weathered beams overhead to create the illusion the room owed its brightness to them, not the more modern pot lights set into the ceiling. The ceiling itself seemed unusually low at first, but like most very old cottages here, this one's floor had been hollowed out so that it actually sat at a level below the street outside. Once I'd gone down the two steps from the door I could stand without bumping my head.

It was rather like stepping below decks, I thought, on a ship. With the posts and the beams and the lanterns and barrels and ropes worked so cleverly into the big room's design, I almost expected the floor to roll under my feet when I walked on it.

'Eva!' He'd been in the back, either reading or working because he was wearing his glasses, but he took them off, tucking them into his shirt pocket as he came forward to greet me.

I looked round the room. 'This is really nice, Oliver.'

'Thanks. I'm afraid I can't take all the credit, though. It was my mother's idea. She came from a smuggling family herself, and she had this collection of things she'd been gathering over the years, and she always said someone should build a museum to put them in, so . . .' With his hands spread, he gestured to what he had made. 'Mind you, she didn't stay to help me with it.'

I remembered his mother, a cheerfully no-nonsense woman. 'Oh? Where did she go?'

'Up to Bristol, to live with my aunt. Left me to fend for myself, so she has.'

'Well, you seem to be doing all right.'

'What, with this? The museum won't pay any bills for me.' Oliver smiled. 'It's a labour of love. No, I've got a collection of holiday cottages over St Non's way. I let them year round, and so far that's been enough to keep me in the black. I can't complain.'

'Holiday cottages? Really? You wouldn't have one sitting empty right now, would you?'

'I'm afraid not. They're all booked through September.'

'Oh.'

'Why, were you wanting one?'

'Thinking about it.' I nodded. 'I'm taking a bit of a break from my job and LA and . . . well, everything, after Katrina. You know. I was thinking I might rent a cottage round here, maybe stay for a while.'

He said, 'Choose the cottage you like, and I'll turf out the tenant.'

I smiled. 'You don't need to do that. But if one does come free in September—'

'It's yours.' He watched me looking round the room and asked, 'You want the tour?'

'Yes, please.'

He'd done a good job setting up all the exhibits so they flowed one from the other in a pattern that was logical, from the earliest days of the settlement here through the bold privateers of the Tudor age right to the heyday of 'free-trading' in the late 1700s, when practically everyone took part in it, sometimes including the revenue men who were meant to be keeping the smugglers in check.

There'd always been trade between Cornwall and Brittany, on the French coast, and neither wars nor taxes had been able to persuade the Cornish free-traders to give up what for them was a good livelihood, and more than that, a most diverting game.

'Like cat and mouse,' was Oliver's analogy. 'Everyone knew who the smugglers were, the real job was to catch them. And then, once you'd caught them, you had to make the charges stick, because the local juries here would only let them off again. That's why some of the revenue men in the end gave it up, helped themselves to a cut of the profits and turned a blind eye.'

I couldn't imagine the constable turning a blind eye to anything, though he had not seemed to me like a man to be easily fooled. He must surely have known what the Butlers were up to. But then again, those men I'd seen from my window had gone to great lengths to come up from the woods without anyone noticing.

'What did they smuggle in, usually?' I asked.

'Oh, brandy and tea and tobacco, French laces and silk. Anything that the government slapped a big duty on.' He hitched a barrel over and sat down while I examined a small gallery of drawings of Polgelly's famous smuggling ships.

I didn't find the one that I was looking for, and so I asked him, 'Did you ever hear of a ship called the *Sally*?'

He considered it a moment. 'No, it doesn't ring a bell. Was she a smuggler's ship?'

'I think so. She belonged to the Butlers who lived at Trelowarth.'

'The Butlers? I don't know them, either. What year would this be?'

'Early 1700s,' I said, trying hard not to sound too specific, because I could already tell from his face he was going to ask me,

'And where did you come across all of this?'

I shrugged. 'I read about them somewhere on the Internet, I can't remember where. I wasn't smart enough to bookmark it.'

'The Butlers. Did it give their first names?'

'Jack and Daniel.'

'Well, I should at least remember *that*.' He grinned. 'It

sounds enough like what I like to drink.' Which led him to his next idea. Glancing at the windows that were for the moment free of rain, he said, 'You've done the tour. Now let me buy you lunch.'

'That's what you do for all your tourists, is it?'

'Certainly.' His eyes, good-natured, challenged me to challenge him. 'What's it to be? Your choice – the Wellie or the tea room?'

I was torn at that, because I'd never been inside the Wellington. It hadn't been the sort of pub you took a child into, which had only made it all the more intriguing. But I settled on, 'The tea room, please. I'll do a bit of corporate spying while I'm here, for Susan.'

'Right,' said Oliver. 'I'll fetch my coat.'

We were the only customers for lunch, and it was clear the waitress had a crush on Oliver because she set my soup down with a lack of care that bordered on disdain. Oliver, not noticing, looked puzzled when he saw me trying not to laugh.

'What?'

'Nothing.'

'So, Felicity tells me Sue's put you to work.'

'Yes. That's what brought me down here today, actually. I was hoping I could find somebody famous in Trelowarth's past, a name that she could use to draw the tourists in.' I knew from how he looked at me he'd hit upon the obvious, as I had, so I told him, 'Yes, I know. I told her she should use Katrina's name, but Susan wasn't having it. I'll have to find her someone else.'

'A famous person in Trelowarth's past.' He wasn't sure. 'Well, there's the Duke of Ormonde, maybe.' We discussed that for a minute. He impressed me with his knowledge of the details of the Jacobite rebellion I had read about, which encouraged me to add, 'His name was Butler, right? James Butler.'

'Like your Butler brothers, you mean?' He considered this. 'It's a bit of a shot in the dark.'

'Oh, I don't know,' I told him carelessly. 'They might have been related.'

'You're determined to find Sue her famous person, aren't you?' Oliver was smiling, but he sympathised. 'I know, it would be brilliant if her plans worked out. I'd hate to see the Halletts lose Trelowarth.'

In surprise I set my spoon down. 'It's as bad as that?'

He gave a nod. 'It's bad.'

'I didn't realise.'

'Never fear,' he said, 'I'll do a little research of my own, and see what I can find. Even if the Duke of Ormonde didn't come this way, your Butler brothers might prove interesting enough themselves.'

'Thanks, I'd appreciate that.'

'Would you? Then you'll have to let me buy you lunch again.'

The waitress heard that part, and slammed my sandwich plate down with such force the table rattled.

This time even Oliver noticed. Watching our waitress depart he said, 'She's in a bit of a mood today, isn't she?' Then catching sight of my face, he asked, 'What?' again.

It took an effort to straighten my smile as I answered him, 'Nothing. It's nothing.' But I had a feeling that lunching with Oliver anywhere here in Polgelly might turn out to be an adventure.

Chapter Thirteen

Claire was pleased. We hadn't seen her for a few days, she'd been keeping to herself, and after supper I had walked out to the cottage for a visit, with the little mongrel Samson at my heels. The dog was lying in a warm contented coil now, underneath the narrow table that Claire used for mixing paints in her bright studio. I'd always liked to watch her work. I liked the mingled smells of oil paint drying slowly on the canvases, and brushes left to soak in jars of turpentine, and underneath all that the fainter scent of coffee sitting somewhere in a mug and growing cold because she had forgotten it as usual when she began to paint.

I liked her paintings, too. The landscapes had a quality of fantasy about them, as though she'd taken what was there in front of her and shaped it as it could have been. The Christmas cards she'd sent to us each year while both my parents were still living had been painted by her own hand, printed privately, so beautiful they'd sat out on our mantelpiece long after all the other decorations of the season had been cleared away. I wondered what had happened to them. After the death of my parents so many of those little links with the past had been lost.

Claire swept an edge of sunset colour underneath a cloud and said, 'I'm glad you got to spend some time with Oliver.'

'I nearly didn't recognise him.'

'Yes, he's changed a little, hasn't he?' Her sideways glance was twinkling. 'On the inside, though, he's still the same old Oliver he ever was. Where did you go for lunch?'

'The tea room by the harbour. And Felicity was right, the woman there can't make a scone to save her life. She'll be no competition for Susan.' Which was, I thought, as good a starting point as I was going to get for what I'd really come to talk about. I said, 'Aunt Claire?'

'Yes, darling?'

'If I ask you something, will you give an honest answer?'

The motion of her brush stopped on the canvas as she turned to me with eyes that seemed to know already what I was about to ask her. 'Always.'

'How much money would it take for Mark and Susan not to lose Trelowarth?'

She blinked, and set the paintbrush down. 'However did you hear of that?'

'I'm not allowed to say.'

Claire crossed to put the brush in turpentine, and slowly cleaned her hands. And then, because she'd made a promise to be honest, she explained how the investments had diminished and the taxes had increased. 'Mark's not in debt yet,' she assured me, 'but he will be this time next year if he can't turn things around.'

'I want to help,' I said.

'You are helping.'

'I mean really help. Financially. I know that Mark would never take my money, but it isn't mine,' I justified. 'Not really. It's Katrina's. And she wouldn't want to see Trelowarth struggling if her money could prevent it.' I paused long enough to glance at Claire and satisfy myself that she agreed with that before I carried on, 'I thought if I were to set up a Trust, Mark and Susan could draw on the funds when they needed them, keep the place going, and know that the Trust would be there for their children as well, and their grandchildren.'

I waited for Claire's arguments, and braced myself against them. There was no way I could properly explain in words why this was so important to me, why it seemed so right to me that something of my sister should remain here, something tangible.

Claire looked at me a long and silent moment. 'I think,' she said finally, 'that would be a lovely legacy. Katrina would be pleased. How can I help?'

We talked it over while we moved into the kitchen from the studio, and Claire made some suggestions as she put the kettle on to boil, and by the time she'd filled the Wedgwood teapot we had worked the whole thing out between us.

'I'll go see Mr Rowe at the bank in Polgelly tomorrow,' I said. 'He can help me get everything organised.'

Claire smiled. 'You'll have to fortify yourself then, for

the climb back up afterwards. Which biscuits would you like? I've coconut or chocolate.'

As she set the biscuit tin down on the table I shook my head. 'I'll have to walk up and down The Hill ten times a day, if I keep eating these.'

'Nonsense. You're too thin as it is.'

'There's no such thing in California as "too thin".'

Claire's dry and wordless glance said much about her view of California and its fashions, but she didn't say a word. She only opened up the biscuit tin and tilted it towards me till I took one. It was coconut. I shared it with the dog, who'd come to join us with expectant eyes and wagging tail. He settled by my chair as I asked, 'Have you seen the greenhouse yet?'

'I haven't, no.'

'They've painted. It looks wonderful.' I filled her in on everything Felicity and Susan had been doing, while we sat and drank our tea.

I liked this kitchen, liked the feel of it, the cosy warmth and comfort that owed more to Claire herself than to the decorating. She changed the feeling of the rooms that she was in. She made them welcoming.

And maybe that was why I felt my sister's presence here as well, this evening. It didn't take a great stretch of imagination to picture Katrina in the empty chair just at the table's end, with her chin propped on one hand the way she'd always sat when she was following the flow of conversation.

And when we took our tea into the sitting room I felt her come along and curl herself into the sofa at my side, so that I felt no need or inclination to get up, and when Claire told me I looked tired and brought a pillow and a blanket so that I could 'rest my eyes' I didn't argue, only lay my head back happily, still feeling that Katrina was right there with me.

Perhaps she was.

But when I woke, she'd gone.

I'd slept much longer than I'd meant to. It was morning, and the smell of toast still hovered in the kitchen. Claire had left a note: *Gone walking with the dog. Help yourself to what you like.*

But she had cleaned the kitchen and I didn't want to spoil its spotlessness, and having slept the whole night in my clothes I felt rumpled. My breakfast could wait, I decided, until I'd got back to Trelowarth and showered. I wrote my own note underneath Claire's, thanking her, and propped it back up on the table.

Then taking my coat, I slipped out the front door. It had rained in the night, and the leaves in the woods all held loose beads of water and when the wind chased through the branches and set them to shivering light little showers came scattering down on my shoulders and head, and my boots slipped a bit in the mud of the path, but I didn't much mind. And as I came out the far side of the woods there was sunlight at last breaking through the clouds over my head, and Trelowarth itself standing waiting to welcome me, and Susan coming out now to walk round to the greenhouse. I'd go out myself after breakfast and help her, I thought. And then I'd go down to the bank.

When I took my next step, though, the heavens suddenly opened with a fury, and a torrent of rain blown by wind struck me full in the face out of nowhere. I struggled to regain my footing, steadying myself against the onslaught of the sudden storm, and made a dash towards the house and shelter.

The wind was like a wild thing pursuing me. It shrieked as I blew through the back door and slammed it shut behind me, and the blast of rain that followed pounded on the wood like fists demanding entry.

I had water running in my eyes. I pushed my hair back from my forehead, stripped my jacket off and shook it out and turned to hang it on its hook with all the other coats.

Except there were no other coats. No row of hooks. No rack of boots.

The realisation hit me with the same force as the storm, and just as suddenly. I let my jacket drop. It made a puddle on the flagstone floor as, stepping from my muddy boots, I padded in on stockinged feet.

In the kitchen, the gnarled branches of the apple trees were scraping at the window and their dripping leaves cast ever-changing shadows in the dimness. All the dishes had been cleared away, the pots scoured clean and set to wait upon the fireless hearth that smelt of cold dead ashes. No one had been cooking here this morning.

Very quietly, I took my sodden coat and boots and stored them out of sight beneath some sacking in the little room that Fergal called the 'scullery', which looked to simply be a place for storing things and washing up, with wooden boxes, woven sacks and empty jugs shoved up against the walls, one small scrubbed table and a tall free-standing cupboard with an iron lock.

Then slipping from the scullery I tiptoed back across the

kitchen to the narrow back staircase that might let me get to the safety of 'my' room before someone saw me. I didn't have to worry about Daniel or Fergal, of course, but they weren't the only people living here, and they'd both said that Daniel's brother Jack might be returning any time. For all I knew, he might be home already.

I kept that thought in mind as I creaked lightly up the steep slope of the stairs to the first floor, and crept past the door of the room that Daniel had informed me was his brother's. It was closed, as were the other doors up here, but I was still relieved to reach the large front-corner room and shut myself inside it.

And relieved again to find the blue gown draped across the chair before the writing desk, where I had left it. This time it was easier to dress myself, though fastening the bodice with the pins still took some time and patience. But I could do nothing with my hair yet except comb my fingers through it and allow it to hang loose.

Prepared now, I sat on the bed's edge patiently, and waited.

Maybe I'd come back too early in the morning. It was difficult to judge the time with dark rain sluicing down the windows, driven hard against the glass by a rough wind that rose and wailed and died again into a weeping moan. It was a lonely sound.

The minutes passed. My shoulders stiffened, unaccustomed to the damp, and I got up and paced a little in an effort to get warm. I thought for certain that my pacing would wake Daniel in the next room, but the house stayed silent. Finally, after what seemed an interminable time, I raised the courage to cross over to the door between our rooms, and very gently eased it open. If he was in there asleep, I thought, I'd simply close the door again and wait.

But the blue-curtained bed was empty.

Moving cautiously past it, I knocked at the next connecting door, but that room, too, had no one in it. That discovery and the need for movement made me bolder, and in time I had repeated the manoeuvre with the other upstairs rooms, and then with those downstairs, and found that, for the moment, there was no one in the house but me.

I might have gone outside to see if they were there, but I remembered Daniel saying clearly that it was not safe for me to leave the house, and I agreed. I really didn't want to meet the constable alone.

The problem was, it had been a while now since I'd woken up at Claire's and come away without my breakfast, a decision I regretted now. It wasn't just the food – I could go hungry for a while with no real ill effects – but I had never coped too well with thirst. The more I tried ignoring it, the deeper it took hold, and if I didn't find some water soon I knew I'd get a headache.

I'd seen Fergal dipping water from a pail beside the kitchen hearth, but when I checked the pail I found it empty. I stood frowning for a moment till a blast of rain against the kitchen window gave my thoughts a jolt. Taking the pail with me, I went to open the back door and set the pail out in the rain. It took several minutes before I'd collected enough for a small drink of water, but that was enough. With my thirst partly satisfied, I put the pail back outside to get more, just in case I got thirsty again before Daniel or Fergal came back.

They'd be back soon, I thought. They had left the doors open, and surely they wouldn't have done that unless they'd been somewhere close by. In the meantime I felt sure they wouldn't begrudge me a handful of food.

And a handful of food was the most I could find in the scullery. One of the sacks held the barley that Fergal had used for his broth, but uncooked it was hard and inedible, and in the other sack there was just coarsely ground flour. I found two soft apples in one corner of an otherwise empty box under the worktable, but all the other food must have been in the tall cupboard, and that was locked.

I ate one apple, saving the other for later, and went in search of something that would help me pass the time.

It felt strange being in that house with no one else around. I wasn't used to it, and even with the wind and rain Trelowarth had a multitude of voices – stairs that creaked with no one on them, joists that settled with a sigh, and unseen mice that scrambled through the walls with tiny, furtive noises.

What had Daniel's wife done on the days he was at sea, I wondered? True, she would have likely had the house to keep and clean, and meals to make, if only for herself. And housework might have filled her waking hours with no time left for boredom. But for me this was a foreign country, really, coming from a place where I could flip a switch and instantly have music or the hourly news to chase away the loneliness.

I wondered whether Daniel's wife had ever gone upstairs, as I did now, to seek the comfort of the study where the fragrance of his pipe smoke lingered as though he were not far off. I scanned his books in search of something I might know. The books themselves were lovely things to look at, bound in half-calf leather so the scent of them alone enhanced the beauty of the room. Some had their titles stamped in gilded printing on the spine, and curious, I picked out a copy of Jonathan Swift's poems, so recently printed that I could still smell the sharp scent of fresh ink on the pages. As I read the satirical lines I was struck by the strange realisation that Jonathan Swift was alive right now somewhere and walking around, maybe forming ideas for *Gulliver's Travels*, a book that he hadn't yet written.

Now I'd noticed it, several of the books in this room were by writers who would have been very much alive in 1715: Alexander Pope, and William Congreve, and the poet Matthew Prior. It was thrilling just to hold those books in the same form in which the authors would have held them, in what likely were the first editions published, with their covers smooth and new and all the pages crisply cut.

I wondered how the writers would react were I to tell them that a woman living in this house three hundred years from now would know their names, and still be reading what they'd written.

Putting back the Swift poems I chose instead a folio of Shakespeare's plays, and flipped through till I found *The Merchant of Venice,* the first play I'd ever seen on the stage, when my parents had taken Katrina and me up to Stratford as children. Katrina had always said that one performance had started it all for her, switched something on deep inside her that told her that acting was what she was meant to do, what she'd been made for.

I settled myself in the chair by the window, and passed

the next hour or so quietly reading. It carried me back, as so many things did. I could almost imagine Katrina beside me, the two of us there in the dark of the theatre and lost in the magic the actors were weaving with just a few props and their voices. Of course it had helped that the young actor playing Bassanio had been so hugely good-looking that right from the opening scene, when he'd leant on a railing directly above us bemoaning his fate, he'd commanded our sympathy.

It had likely been his fault, as much as the play's, that Katrina had taken up acting. She'd met him in person once, years later, making a film, and had been unimpressed. 'A walking ego,' she had called him, when she'd come round to my place that evening as she sometimes did after a long day's shooting, to relax.

I'd made brown sugar sandwiches, my mother's bedtime specialty, and asked her, 'Really?'

'Really. And to think, for all these years he's been a fantasy of mine. I guess it's true, you should be careful what you wish for.'

I could hear her voice within my head again now, though I didn't need the warning. I already knew it to be true. I'd just come halfway round the world myself in hopes that at Trelowarth I could touch the past and hold what I had lost a little longer, and now here I was. I'd touched the past all right, but I had missed Katrina by three hundred years, and in this strange place I felt more alone than ever.

Evening came, and brought the realisation that I might be on my own for longer than I'd thought. I'd had to leave the study and the books with some reluctance and come back downstairs. The darkness here could not be held at bay by switching on a light, and though the house had no shortage of candles they had to be lit to be useful. Besides, since I'd now eaten the last apple, if I didn't want to starve I'd have to find a way to somehow cook the barley. I would have to light a fire.

The iron grate inside the kitchen fireplace had a dusting of cold ashes underneath, but it already held a stack of fresh wood waiting for a flame. Except I wasn't good with fires. Not even with a modern box of matches, which I didn't have to hand, although a quick search of the crannies near the kitchen hearth produced a metal tinderbox, the kind I'd only read about in books. I knew the theory of the tinder-box: I was supposed to take the flint and steel and strike some sparks onto a small pile of the tinder, in this case a mixture of wood shavings and bits of cloth. When the sparks caught on the tinder I was then supposed to blow on them and coax them to a flame that would in turn ignite the wood stacked in the fireplace. Foolproof.

Only this was me, and after working at it for what felt an hour I'd only managed to produce a few small sparks that flashed and smouldered and did no more than consume my precious scraps of tinder before burning out completely in a listless puff of smoke. My face was smudged, my temper frayed, my knees were stiff from kneeling at the hearth, but I'd been born too stubborn to let such a small thing beat me, so I focused all my concentration on the task and shut out everything around me that might serve as a distraction – every creak and groan the house made, and the rattle of the storm against the windows, and the wailing of the wind across the chimney-top above me.

And the door. I didn't hear it, either, so the sudden heavy tread of boots behind me on the floorboards made me jump. I turned, expecting Daniel. Maybe Fergal.

It was neither.

Chapter Fourteen

In the near-dark of this room the silent presence of the constable was something to be feared. My one advantage was that I had caught him off his guard as well – he clearly hadn't been expecting to find anyone at home.

I stood with care, and tried to calm my racing heartbeat with determination.

He recovered first. 'Mistress O'Cleary.' There was no attempt to make even a mocking bow this time, no need to show respect since there was no one watching. Those cold, uncompromising eyes grew narrow as he processed this discovery. 'Have they left you here alone for these past days?' His gaze moved briefly to the hearth and back. 'And with no fire. That was unkind of them. I confess when I did not see smoke from the chimneys I was myself convinced the house was empty.'

So that was why he'd come in unannounced like this –

because he'd thought he could. He'd thought there would be no one here to notice or to challenge him, and that he would be able to poke round at leisure, undisturbed.

Except I'd spoilt his plans.

Now, like some reptile who could change the pattern of his skin when needed, he appeared to be adapting to this new twist of events. I saw his features lose a little of their hardness in a calculated way, and when he spoke again his voice made a deliberate stab at being civil. 'Are you having difficulty?'

It was just as well that I was scared of him, because that fear prevented me from answering for long enough that I remembered I was not supposed to have a voice. I gave a wary nod.

'Stand aside then.' He did not appear to notice that my fingers shook a little as I passed the tinder-box into his outstretched hand. It took him time as well, but in the end he made a fire that grew steadily upon the hearth and cast a welcome light and spreading warmth into the dreary room.

When he straightened, it took all my effort not to take a backwards step away from him, because he seemed too close. 'Now, how then will you thank me for my aid, when you have not the use of words?' He saw my wariness increase, and seemed amused enough by it to push my panic button further, giving me a purposefully slow once-over, pausing on my loose hair. 'I can see you were preparing for your bed. Perhaps you need assistance there, as well?' He smiled at my reaction, and then went another route. 'But no, some wine, I think, will be enough. A bottle of the best that Butler has and you may count your debt repaid.'

I stood a moment at a loss, until I suddenly remembered there had been wine in the dining room when we had eaten lunch there – several bottles lying dusty in a corner near the sideboard. I had no idea whether they were Daniel Butler's best or not, but that's what he'd been drinking so the wine would not be bad.

I gave a small nod to excuse myself and hustled off in that direction, hoping that the bottles would still be there. And they were. I grabbed the top one, wiped the dust off with my hand and took it back to give to the constable, in hopes that would get rid of him.

He wasn't where I'd left him in the kitchen. Apprehensive, I stood still beside the hearth a moment, listening. He wouldn't have gone far, I knew. I'd only been a minute. But I also knew his aim in coming up here in the first place must have been to look around, and he was obviously taking full advantage of my absence.

Then I heard him. In the scullery.

My mouth went dry so suddenly I found it hard to swallow down the nervous lump that lodged itself above my heart. My jacket and my boots were in the scullery, and if he found them . . .

I could feel my fingers clenching round the bottle's neck so tightly that my fingernails were digging in my palm as I went through into the scullery to join him. To my great relief, I saw that he had not yet moved the sacking on the floor. His interest seemed to be directed at the pantry cupboard with its lock.

'Tell me,' he asked idly, 'does your brother always lock the food away when he does leave you on your own?' His glance toward me held no expectation of an answer, but his eyes were watchful on my face for my reaction. 'Or might there be more in here than food?'

I kept my own face neutral, trying hard not to react at all, not even when he walked towards the sacking. But he only kicked it to one side and reached for a short-handled axe that leant against the wall behind. I hadn't even known the tool was there, myself. The constable had sharper eyes.

'We must not let you starve,' he said, with mock concern. He brought the axe down with a force that broke the locked door cleanly and the cupboard swung wide open.

I hadn't been too sure, myself, what he might find inside. For all I knew there might be contraband behind the food, but after he had opened the few tins and shoved some sacks aside, he muttered something to himself and stood a moment, thinking. Then he turned his head and looked at me.

I really didn't like his eyes. They made my flesh crawl cold.

He'd thought of something, I could see it in the way his mouth began to curve. He asked me, 'Are you in the house alone?'

And how was I to answer that? He obviously knew that Daniel Butler and the rest were gone away somewhere, and if there had been anybody here with me I wouldn't have been trying on my own to light the fire. No matter how much my protective instincts warned me not to give a truthful answer, I knew full well that I wouldn't fool him if I lied. I gave a slow nod.

'Well then, I do think it would be wise were I to make a full inspection of this house and all its rooms, that I might satisfy myself as to your safety.'

There was nothing I could do to stop him anyway, but still he'd picked a clever way to word things so that neither I nor anyone could argue his intentions.

He carried the axe with him out of the scullery and when I followed he turned round and using the blade, pointed back at the kitchen. 'No mistress, wait there. I would do this alone.'

He was gone for a long time. Long enough for me to think about escaping to the stables or the woods, but with the storm outside it seemed a foolish thing to do, and anyway my fear was slowly melting into anger at his arrogant intrusion, and a part of me refused to give him any satisfaction, so I didn't run. Whatever happened, I'd at least be able to tell Daniel what the constable had done. And what he'd found.

With the wind at the window I couldn't hear what he was doing upstairs, though. I didn't know what he was touching, defiling. It was, I thought, rather like having a rat roaming unseen behind your walls, doing its damage.

I was happy to see, when he came back down, that his hard face had the look of frustration, as though he'd been cheated. Clearly he hadn't found what he'd been looking for.

Passing the scullery door he stopped briefly to throw down the axe he was holding. It fell with a clatter and thud on the flagstones. 'Well, Mistress O'Cleary.' His tone was a challenge. I saw his gaze fall on the bottle that I was still holding. 'Would that be my wine? Give it here, then.'

Heavily he sat beside me, took a small knife from his pocket and pried out the seal, and then took a long drink from the bottle itself. And another. Then wiping his mouth on his sleeve he said, 'It may be that I am approaching this wrongly. Perhaps I have only to ask, hm?' He angled his head and his eyes fixed themselves on my own. 'Have you had any visitors here to Trelowarth of late? Any men of high birth?'

Very carefully, I shook my head.

'You would do well to tell me the truth, mistress, for I remind you that this country's laws of high treason can give no protection to those who might shelter a traitor.' His voice held a velvet contempt as he added, 'Nor even for those who would take one to bed.' His glance flicked down my length and back as he drank deep from the bottle again, and when I failed to react to the insult he said, 'Do not flatter yourself that he holds you in any regard. Do you know why he gives you that gown? To give life to a ghost. Any whore could fulfil the same purpose.'

His smile had the power to cut just as cruelly as that small knife he'd used to open the wine, and that he now put back in his pocket. He stood. 'Think on that, while you seek to protect him from justice. I am not myself without mercy, you'll find, but I can do nothing to help you if you put the noose round your neck by your own choice.' Setting down the bottle on the table, he said, 'Take you good care of that fire I have made for you, Mistress O'Cleary. 'Twould grieve me to see you get burnt.'

I did not stand myself, nor look round as he left. The truth was that I'd started shaking too badly to stand. It was only the after-effect of the fear I had felt while he'd been here, my body's release of the tension I'd had to hold in, and no more. But in spite of the fire that now crackled so warm on the hearth it was some time before I stopped shaking, and even when I finally stood I still felt cold inside.

The wine that he'd left on the table might have helped warm me, but I didn't want to drink from any bottle he had held. It was as though he had a poison in him that was transferred by his touch and needed to be cleaned away. I took the bottle in my hand and carried it around to the back door where I upended it above the muddy ground.

And then I tilted my face to the rain until I felt clean, too.

The bucket I'd set out before was now half full. I brought it in and locked the door, then hauled the three-legged iron kettle to the hearth and emptied most of the water into it, saving some for drinking later. I'd lost my appetite, but knowing that my hunger would return and that I needed to keep eating to survive till someone came, I sifted barley from the sack into the water and I left it there to boil while I lit a candle and went up to see what damage the constable had done.

My anger returned in full force when I saw the effects of his search. Daniel's books lay strewn across the study floor, and in the bedrooms there were drawers pulled out and mattresses askew with no attempt made to return the rooms to order. He'd had the time to search and leave no sign of it, I thought, but it was obvious he'd wanted to let Daniel know he'd been here. Why, I didn't know. If *I* felt this much anger simply looking at the things that had been tainted by the presence of the constable, it stood to reason Daniel would be furious.

Unless that was the purpose of it all, provoking Daniel to retaliate, because, although I didn't know the laws of this time, surely there would be a nasty penalty for challenging the king's own loyal constable. Arrest, at least. And maybe more.

I fought my anger down, lit more candles to bring light into the rooms, and started tidying, returning books to their neat rows and righting chairs and trying hard to make things look the way they had before. I took the greatest care in the small room that had been Daniel's wife's, because to me the very thought the constable had been in here among her things seemed unforgivable, an act of violation.

And he had been here. He'd rifled through the clothing in the long box at the foot of the bed, leaving petticoat edges and sleeves hanging out. I restored them to order as best I could, smoothing the dresses in folds with as much care as if they'd belonged to Katrina. 'I'm sorry,' I told her, and closed the box gently.

And then I remembered. 'Oh, Christ,' I breathed, feeling the drop in the pit of my stomach. Because when I'd changed out of my own clothes into this gown, I had hidden my things at the bottom of one of the boxes that sat by the wall in my bedroom, and if he had taken the time to search this one, then . . .

'Dammit.' I yanked the door open between the two rooms and went through with a feeling of dread.

Both the boxes were closed. And the first one, the one where I'd hidden my clothes, appeared just as it had been before when I opened the lid. On the top were a few white shirts, fine to the touch, and below them two brocaded waistcoats, and then below *them* were my own things, still folded, with no indication that they'd been disturbed.

It appeared, from a glance round the room, that the constable's focus in here had been on the small writing desk, to the exclusion of everything else. He had sat at the chair, for it was in a different position than it had been earlier, and when he'd closed the lid part of a paper had caught in the hinge.

I crossed over and opened the lid to release it, to put it back into the tidily organised pile where it had been. It was a short statement of household accounts, written in a strong and heavy hand. Nothing of interest to the constable, apparently, or else he wouldn't have looked so frustrated when he'd finished with his search.

He'd been looking for something specific, I sensed, and I could feel a bit of satisfaction knowing that he hadn't found it.

I made very certain the doors were all bolted that night, having forced down a bit of the porridge I'd made and left the rest to cool beside the hearth. It was too much to hope that there'd be anything left of the fire in the morning, in spite of my amateurish efforts to bank it, so I took one of the tall glass chimneys from the sitting room and used it at my bedside as a shield for the one candle I left burning there, in hopes I might be able to use that to start a fire on the hearth if it were necessary.

I took off the bodice and skirt of the gown that had been Daniel's wife's, but I left on the simple chemise underneath in an effort to conjure up some of her courage – for it must have taken courage to have slept in this big house with all its shadows when the men were off at sea.

When Katrina had died I'd gone through all her closets as Bill had requested, and sorted a lot of her clothes to be given to charity, but I'd kept the comfort clothes, the ones that she'd most often worn, and in those moments when

I missed her most I still found putting on her favourite flowered shirt could bring her close to me.

As I drifted with eyes closed, the voice of the constable asked me again, 'Do you know why he gives you that gown? To give life to a ghost.'

I could have used that ghost for company right now, and so I huddled deeper in the blankets, hugging the chemise all the tighter around me and trying to work the same magic, alone in the dark.

Something clattered downstairs in the kitchen and brought me awake. I had slept through the sunrise, although not by much, for the shadows were still sharply angled across the floor, cast by the daylight that came through the east windows flanking the fireplace.

I sat up to listen.

And then I heard whistling, and booted feet climbing the stairs, and the whistle altered from a tune into a sharper blast, the way Mark whistled up the dogs when they were running wild, and from the hall a stranger's voice called, 'Are you yet in bed? You've let the fire go nearly out. And why the devil did you lock the doors?' He had grabbed the handle of my own door now, and swung it open as he talked. ''Tis hard to think that my own brother is now turning into an old . . .' Then he saw me sitting up in Daniel Butler's bed, so that his last word, '. . . woman,' trailed away unsure.

Jack Butler – because from the look of him and what he'd said he could be no one else – shifted in the doorway to a steadier position, his expression changing gradually from pure surprise to something that reminded me of how a man might look when he had seen a friend perform a feat that he had thought impossible. With a slight shake of his head he flashed a quick lopsided smile and said, 'Good morrow to you, mistress.'

I was not supposed to talk, I knew. According to the plan that Daniel Butler had decided on with Fergal, Jack was meant to think that I was Fergal's sister, too. I could still hear Fergal saying, 'Jack can never keep his mouth shut, and he'll never be convinced she came the way she says she did.' So I just nodded in reply.

'And is my brother in the house?'

I shook my head.

'Can you not speak?' He asked that jokingly, as though the situation still amused him.

When I shook my head again he looked surprised at first, since it was not the answer he'd expected, then the faintest light of envy touched his eyes. 'A woman with no voice.' He swore a cheerful oath and said, 'My brother always had the better fortune.'

He leant one shoulder on the door jamb, not as tall as his brother, nor to my eyes as good-looking, but with an easy charm that made it plain to me why all the mothers of Polgelly locked up their daughters whenever Jack came home. 'Well then, can you cook? For on my way here I did stumble on some mutton that was longing to come join me for my dinner, though I've no idea myself what I should do with it. Do you?'

My nod was somewhat less than certain, but it satisfied him. 'Good. Then let me give you back your privacy. Unless you do intend to wear that today? No? A shame, in my opinion.' And he left me with a friendly nod and one last smile.

Alone, I closed my eyes and raised both hands to hold my forehead for support as I exhaled a sigh. I may not have been relishing the thought of spending one more day alone here at Trelowarth, and having Jack Butler around would indeed make my life that much easier, but he wasn't quite the kind of company I'd wished for. He was going to be another complication.

Dressing quickly, I went downstairs where I found the joint of mutton waiting for me in the kitchen, on the table by the window that Jack Butler had apparently come in by. He had knocked a chair down in the process, and I set it upright while I tried to figure out how people in this time cooked mutton. I had no clue. In the end the only thing that I could think of was to roast it in the same way I'd seen Fergal roasting fowl, though forcing the spit through the mutton proved harder than I would have thought, and the spit and meat together were a heavy, awkward burden to try hanging in the hearth.

But at least Jack had got the fire going again, and set new wood on top of it, and in the cupboard that the constable had smashed open I found the tin of honey I'd seen Fergal use before, and if I copied Fergal's trick of basting roasting meat with honey, then I couldn't go far wrong.

And since Jack had also left a bunch of carrots on the table with the soil still clinging to them, I decided I could add them to the porridge I'd already made and thin it down to something that approximated Fergal's vegetable and barley broth, if I could find some water.

That problem solved itself a moment later when Jack Butler came in through the back door with a sloshing pair of buckets. 'We've no water in the house at all,' he said, as though I wouldn't know it. 'So I went and fetched us some.' He set the buckets down and took a seat himself, with an approving glance towards the mutton. ''Tis as well that you were here. That would have gone to waste had I attempted it.' And then he said, 'I did not mean to hurry you.'

He must have seen I didn't understand, because he made a gesture at his own head and explained, 'Your hair. You could have taken time to dress it, I would not have minded. You'll find me not so difficult,' he promised, 'as my brother.'

He was definitely chattier. Some people might have found it awkward spending time with somebody who didn't speak, but not Jack Butler. While I cooked he rocked his chair back on two legs and, shoulders to the wall, kept up a mostly single-sided conversation, asking questions that he answered for himself. 'So did he tell you all about me, then? Of course he did, or else you would have feared me as a stranger, though I doubt he would have thought I would be home before him.'

From the track his conversation took I gathered he'd concluded that his brother was still off aboard the *Sally*, which to me made perfect sense. It explained, too, why the constable had seemed so sure that no one would be in the house.

'And so you've been here all this time and on your own?' He would have answered that himself as well, I think, except he saw my face. He stopped. 'Have you then had a visitor?'

I nodded, once.

His chair came down, but slowly and controlled, and when he spoke again his voice had changed, no longer lightly teasing but more serious. 'A welcome one?'

I shook my head, and knew from how his eyes had altered that he didn't need to be told who, any more than he needed to have anything spelt out for him when I showed him the smashed cabinet lock in the scullery.

He was quick enough putting the pieces together.

'The constable came on his own? Did he search the whole house? Did he find anything?'

Here, instead of a nod, I was happily able to shake my head 'no'.

Jack Butler said, 'That must have spoilt his temper.' He seemed pleased by that, until another realisation crossed his mind and he looked down at me. 'Did he then do you harm?'

I shook my head, but he had seen my moment's hesitation.

'Are you certain?' He was looking at me clinically, not trusting what I'd told him, when I saw his face change once again, as though he'd just this minute noticed what gown I was wearing.

Though he obviously recognised it, he did nothing more than raise his gaze to mine a moment before going on without a comment, 'Good, for Daniel would have gutted him.'

I hadn't thought of that. I had forgotten that in this age men still felt an obligation to defend a woman's honour. Having lived so long where men were more likely to push their way past me than open a door for me, I hadn't even considered the fact that if I *had* been harmed, Daniel Butler might well have responded with violence. I gave silent thanks that the constable had only struck me with words, not his hands, even though I felt sure that he'd wanted to.

Thinking of it now, I wasn't certain what had stopped him, since it would have been another way to try provoking Daniel into action, if that had in fact been what he had intended. I remembered how the constable's dark gaze had raked my gown. It made me wonder if he'd seen a ghost himself when he had looked at me, and she had stayed his hand.

Whatever the reason, I was thankful for it, just as I was glad I'd taken time last night to tidy up the rooms before Jack had a chance to see them, for I knew there was no chance of keeping anything from Daniel if Jack knew it. Fergal might have been exaggerating when he'd said Jack Butler couldn't keep a secret – after all, a man who made his living smuggling had to keep a secret now and then – but I could understand what Fergal had been getting at. Jack Butler liked to talk.

About himself, mainly, but he was good-natured about it and, in spite of my earlier misgivings, after being alone in the house I found him welcome company. Besides, I felt better with someone around for protection, and I had a feeling Jack Butler was good in a fight. Not as good as his brother, I guessed, because Jack seemed like someone who didn't have much self-control, but he likely fought dirtier.

Still, he was not without manners. The mutton I'd roasted came out a bit charred, and my barley and carrot broth didn't have even a bit of the flavour that Fergal's had had, but Jack ate them without a complaint, and then ate them a second time, cold, for his supper.

It was not until afterwards, when twilight settled outside on the hills and Jack lit the candles on the table and the atmosphere inside the kitchen grew close, that he showed a small flash of his mischievous nature.

'So, mistress,' he asked, 'shall I help you to bed?'

I probably wouldn't have dignified that with an answer in any event, whether spoken or otherwise, but as it turned out I didn't have to give him a reply. The answer came out of the dimness behind us, surprising us both.

''Tis a kind offer, Jack.' Daniel Butler had settled himself in the doorway that led to the corridor, arms folded over his chest. 'But I think that would be my prerogative.'

Chapter Fifteen

Fergal was having none of it. Shouldering his way past Daniel Butler he said drily, 'You can both of you behave yourselves, or do you need reminding in the way of it? My sister has the wit to see herself to bed without the aid of either of you.'

I heard Jack say in surprise, 'Your sister?' and I was aware that Fergal answered him, but the bulk of my attention was still focused on the tall man in the doorway and the warmth within his eyes.

He looked as pleased to see me there as I was glad to have him back, and if we'd been alone I would have told him so, but I could only let my smile speak for me.

'. . . and that will be my only warning to you, so you pay it heed and mind your manners,' Fergal finished off, to Jack.

'Would I do otherwise?' Jack's voice was mild. He'd

turned to look at us. 'And I do fear you may be warning the wrong Butler in this instance.'

'Ay, I've said the same to him and all,' said Fergal. He had noticed the remains of what I'd cooked, an eyebrow lifting at the blackened meat. 'Where did you find this mutton?'

'I did meet with it upon the road on my way home,' said Jack, 'and in so sad a circumstance that pity moved my hand to see it liberated.'

Fergal's sideways glance was dry. 'And what else did you liberate?'

'Only the mutton. 'Twas all I could carry.'

Daniel, lounging comfortably within the doorway, asked, 'And who now has gone hungry by your hand?'

'None but a lazy merchant who was fool enough to leave his wagon unattended while he slept.'

'You'll try your luck one time too often,' was his brother's comment. 'You are fortunate you did not meet the constable upon the road. He would have had you taken for a thief.'

Jack shrugged. 'I am well liked by juries in these parts, they would have voted me my freedom. And in any case, the constable had other things to occupy his time.' His tone had sobered. 'He was here. He searched the house.'

I saw the narrowing of Daniel's eyes as Fergal, who'd been tearing off small chunks of mutton, tasting what I'd done with it, turned round with sudden fierceness. 'Christ's blood, Jack, and did you never think to stop him?'

'I had not the opportunity, he came and went before I did arrive. Your sister could not tell me what occurred, of course, but it appears she faced him on her own, and even had she had a voice she would have had no chance of stopping him herself. He must have been in a rare temper, from the treatment he did give that cupboard standing in the scullery.'

While Fergal went to check the cupboard, Daniel studied me with quiet calm, the kind of calm that sometimes silences the winds before the weather takes a turning for the worse, and it appeared to be a warning sign to Jack who quickly said, 'I asked her if the blackguard used her ill, and she assured me in her way that he did not.'

Daniel said nothing, but his eyes moved briefly past me as behind me Fergal stepped out of the scullery and said, 'He used the axe.'

The calm of Daniel's face grew deeper, settling over his whole frame, and Fergal said, 'Jack, come and help me take a look around the stables, will you? God alone knows what he might have done out there.'

'But—'

'Shift yer arse.' The terse instruction left no room for argument, and Jack made none.

Daniel moved from the doorway to let them go past, but he waited until they'd gone out to the yard and the back door had swung shut behind them and they had moved well out of hearing before he asked quietly, 'Are you all right?'

'He didn't lay a hand on me.'

'That was not what I asked.'

'I'm fine.' I half-turned away from those steady eyes that I suspected saw more than I wanted them to. 'It rattled me a bit, that's all. I mean, I'd just come back and all of you were gone, and it was raining, and I couldn't start a fire, and then I turned around and there he was . . .'

'You did not let him in?'

'He let himself in. I don't think he expected to find anybody here. He seemed to know you were away.' I paused, and glanced back. 'Were you off on your ship?'

'Yes.' He didn't elaborate. 'What did he do when he found you at home?'

What I told him was an edited account of what had happened, from the constable's starting the fire to his smashing the lock on the cabinet and going to search the upstairs. 'I'm fairly sure he didn't find what he was looking for,' I finished.

'No more would he. There was nothing here for him to find.' From his tone I could tell that he wasn't protesting his innocence, only saying he had better sense than to leave any evidence lying around. 'So he came back downstairs. And what then did he do?'

'Nothing, really. He drank some of the wine that I'd brought him,' I said very carefully, 'and then he left.'

'And only that.'

I nodded, and I saw a flickering of warmth behind his eyes. 'You must ask Jack to school you in the art of telling lies, for plainly you have not yet learnt the trick of it.'

I raised my chin. 'It's not a lie. He didn't touch me.'

'I am close enough acquainted with the constable to know that he has other means of doing harm.' He didn't press the point. Instead he said, as though he meant it, 'I am sorry that I was not here.'

'It's just as well you weren't. You might be up now on a charge of murder.'

'Yes, I might at that.' And with his smile the deadly calm that had been hanging round him broke and fell away. 'And do I have to call my brother out, or has he been behaving like a gentleman?'

'He's been behaving.' Mostly, I suspected, because of where he had discovered me, in Daniel's bed. Jack Butler might be reckless, but that didn't make him fool enough to trespass on what he would have believed was ground belonging to his brother.

'I would find that most unlikely,' Daniel said. 'And you forget I have the evidence of my own ears against it.'

I'd forgotten what he'd overheard as he came in – Jack's offer to escort me up to bed. And Daniel's answer. I surprised myself by blushing. I had lived so long in Hollywood I'd thought that there was nothing any more that could embarrass me. I covered it by saying it had only been a joke. 'He was no more serious than you were.'

'Was he not?' The smile held, and in that moment while he looked at me I swore that I could feel the air between us as though it had come alive. Perhaps it had.

But then he looked away again and everything was normal. 'You have done well with Jack. It does appear that he accepts you in your role, and does believe you cannot speak.'

'Yes, well, it wasn't all that difficult. Your brother talks so much himself I doubt I could have got a word in edgeways if I'd wanted to.'

I had never heard him laugh. I liked the sound of it. He asked, 'When was it he arrived?'

'This morning. Through that window, actually. I'd locked the doors.'

'And if you should be here and on your own again, I

trust you'll do the same, and keep them bolted fast till one of us returns. Nor should you hesitate to use the hole to hide from an intruder.'

'What hole?'

'The priest's hole.' With a glance at my uncomprehending face, he asked, 'Is it not used in your own time?'

I shook my head. 'We don't have any need to hide our priests.'

'No more do we. But such a hiding place does still have uses. Come.' He took a candle from the table and led me from the kitchen, through the hall and halfway up the staircase to the broad half-landing with its panelled walls. 'The tale is that the building of Trelowarth happened not long since King Henry had defied the Pope and set aside his queen to marry Anne Boleyn. The times then were as troubled as our own, and men who kept to the old faith were forced to say their prayers in secret, and to hide their priests whenever the King's agents came to call.' His fingers found the corners of a panel with a sureness born of practice and he gave a single push, and with a quiet click the spring gave way. A length of panel nearly my own height, hinged like a door, swung neatly outward.

In the space behind, a man could stand – or sit, if he grew tired – but he couldn't do much more than that. It would be dark and close, but safe.

'You pull it shut with this, when you are in,' said Daniel, showing me the metal ring attached to the inside, 'and none will find you.'

'Have you ever had to use it?'

'On occasion.'

It would be an uncomfortable place for a man of his height, and I said so, but he only shrugged.

'I had rather stoop here for an hour than be stretched at the end of a rope.'

It was not the first time he'd implied he earned his living in a way that wasn't legal, and I called him on it. 'Is the law so merciless with free-traders?'

He took the question in his stride. 'The law, in my experience, is more strict in its word than in its practice. And the constable does line his pockets well by his arrangements with the free-traders who choose to make their harbour in Polgelly, and does please himself to look the other way while we unload our cargoes. No,' he said, ''tis not my free-trading that so concerns the constable. He would see me hang for something far more heinous in his view.'

'For treason.'

Daniel swung the panel shut with a decided click, and turned. 'Is that what he did tell you?' He seemed curious, not angry, but I didn't have the courage to repeat the words the constable had said to me, however much they resonated in my mind.

I didn't need to. Daniel said, 'And did he tell you that you would be damned yourself for comforting a traitor to the Crown?' He smiled slightly without waiting for an answer, and a hardness touched his eyes although I knew it wasn't meant for me. 'I can but guess what words he used when he did phrase that speech. I am no traitor, Eva.' With a level gaze and even voice he faced me. 'I am loyal to the rightful King of England, as my father was before me, and will be so for as long as I do live.'

I knew that he was saying he was loyal to James Stuart,

still across the sea in exile, and I could have told him that there was no future in that loyalty because the Stuarts never would regain their crown, and all their dreams of restoration would be killed on battlefields and paid for with the blood of countless Jacobites. But if I told him anything, I'd interfere with what was meant to happen, maybe change what was to come, and that might have a far more devastating consequence.

He must have seen the conflict of emotions on my face, but he misunderstood their cause. 'I promise you,' he said, 'I will let no one do you harm.'

I couldn't hold his gaze. I looked away.

I hadn't realised he was close enough to touch me, but he did. He reached a hand to lightly take my chin and turn my face back round so that our eyes met, and he said again, more quietly, 'I promise.'

I couldn't speak.

Which probably was just as well, because at that same moment I heard Fergal coming back with Jack, and making noise enough to let us know it.

Daniel smiled, and let his hand drop. 'Damn the man,' he said, without an ounce of violence. 'Even now he is developing the instincts of a brother.'

He was right. For it was Fergal, in the end, who saw me safely up the stairs that night and checked in all the corners of my room before he left me, and stood waiting in the corridor until I'd put the key into the padlock he had given me, and turned it to secure the latch.

And next morning it was Fergal and not Daniel who instructed me on how to do my hair.

He brought a looking glass and pins into my bedroom,

sat me down beside the window, and with hands that were surprisingly adept and gentle, showed me how to wind the strands in curls and pin them into place.

I asked him, 'Is there anything you can't do, Fergal?'

'Likely not.' He'd moved to stand behind me and I saw him now reflected in the looking glass that I was holding, with his head bent, concentrating. 'Though I'll have to warn you this may not be in the latest fashion. I've not done this for some years, and even then I doubt I did it well. Ann used to say I made her look more like an ill-made bird's nest than a lady.'

'Ann?'

He'd caught himself, and in the mirror his eyes briefly flicked to mine, then down again. 'Ay.'

'Daniel's wife?'

'Ay.' Silence for a moment, then, 'When she grew too ill near the end to attend to her own hair I helped her, for she was determined that he would not see her as less than she wanted to be.'

I was holding the hairpins. I fingered one thoughtfully. 'Was she ill for long?'

'Ay, for some months. It started as a cough that would not leave her, and it wasted her away, and by the summer's end we'd lost her.'

I was silent in my turn, because essentially that was how I had lost Katrina too. I knew the pain of it.

'He'll have my head for telling you,' said Fergal.

'Fergal?'

'Ay?'

'Could you . . . could you do my hair a little differently than you did hers?'

His hands stopped, and again his eyes met mine within the mirror for an instant, and he nodded understanding. 'I was thinking that myself, I was. Come, put that glass down and I'll teach you how to do this back part, for we'll not be fooling Jack for long if I'm here in your chamber every morning doing this.'

'Where is Jack?'

'He's gone to fetch the horses back. Whenever we're away we loose the horses in the paddock at Penryth where there's a farmer who can see they're fed and watered.'

I hadn't even thought of the horses. They might have been starving in their stalls within the stable, and I wouldn't have known. But when I confessed as much Fergal just said, 'Well, you had other worries, I expect. And no harm done.'

I barely recognised myself when we had finished. All my hair had been piled up and fastened daintily, making a circlet on top of my head with a few curls escaping as though by pure chance. 'I'll never be able to do this myself.'

'Ay, you will,' Fergal told me. ''Tis nothing to facing down Constable Creed. Now then, put your pinner on your head,' he said, handing me a modest-looking cap of soft, white linen, 'and we're done with this fussing and on to the next of your lessons.'

'What next lesson?'

''Tis sure any sister of mine should know how to cook mutton without setting fire to it, and at the least, how to season a stirabout. Our ma,' he informed me, straight-faced, 'would be scandalised.'

Chapter Sixteen

The *Sally* didn't lie at anchor long. Next morning Jack was off again in his turn, and I stood with Daniel on the hill below the house and watched the sloop's white sails pass by the harbour of Polgelly far below us, heading east.

'Where is he taking her?' I asked, but Daniel only glanced at me and answered non-committally, 'I cannot say.'

'Because you still don't trust me.'

'Because,' he said, ''tis best that you do not concern yourself with certain things.' I felt him glance at me again although I kept my own face turned towards the sea and the departing ship. 'Are all the women of your time so curious?'

'The women of my time are many things,' I told him. 'Doctors, lawyers, heads of state. We can do anything a man can do.'

I couldn't tell if he believed me. 'Heads of state? Well, we have had a queen ourselves, till lately.'

'Not only queens. I mean elected heads of state, leaders of parliaments.'

'You jest.'

'You don't believe a woman's capable?'

He seemed to give the matter thought. ''Tis not that I dismiss a woman's capability,' he said, 'nor her intelligence. 'Tis only that I would be fair amazed to see society permit it. I would think that she would find herself opposed by members of my sex, and ridiculed by members of her own.'

I had to smile. 'Yes, well, that does still happen sometimes. But at least the opportunity is there. We can be anything we choose to be.'

I looked away again. The *Sally*'s sails had grown much smaller now, a little blot of white against the rolling blue of the Atlantic.

Daniel was still thinking. 'If in truth there is such freedom for the women of your time, then you must find it difficult to be here.'

I actually hadn't thought that much about it. I'd only been here for short periods, and I'd had more on my mind than my freedoms and rights. But if I were to stay here forever, I thought, he was right. It would not be an easy adjustment.

To know that my opinions would no longer count for anything in public, and that all the legal rights I'd come to take for granted were no longer mine; to be dependent for support on someone else because I could not earn my living.

Daniel watched my face a moment, then he turned his own gaze out to sea and said, 'My brother sails to Brittany.'

It was an open declaration of, not just his trust, but his respect.

I turned to look at him as he went on, 'There is a harbour there where he has friends who keep him well supplied with wine and silk and wigs for trade, and where there are young brides whose husbands are too often gone off to the fishing. 'Tis most likely more than one child in that town does bear a passing likeness to my brother.' He was smiling when his head came round. 'No doubt the women of your own time would be too wise to fall such victims to his wicked ways.'

'Oh, I don't know. There'd still be some who'd swoon.'

'But not yourself.' His tone was sure. 'My brother did remark upon the fact that you did seem unmoved by all his charms.'

'Was it a blow to his confidence?'

'Likely. Though he claimed that his purpose in telling me was to set my mind at ease, for his own mind has leapt to a certain conclusion since he did discover you in my bed.'

I wasn't used to the dark light of mischief that flared in his eyes, and not knowing him well enough to know the way to respond to his flirting, I treated it lightly.

'Well, at least it won't happen again. Fergal's given me padlocks.'

'Has he now? Thoughtful man.' He'd have said something else, but a sound from the road to the back of Trelowarth distracted us both – the hard clop of a horse's hooves, coming along at a purposeful trot.

Daniel motioned me to step towards him and I didn't argue, knowing that his size and strength, together with the sword he carried, would give me protection. It was not his sword he reached for, though. Instead he took the dagger from his belt and held it as he'd held it that first day I'd faced him in the study, with the blade all but concealed within his hand.

His other arm he offered to me as the rider came in view and I could see that it was not the constable, only an ordinary man on a high-stepping grey horse. I felt relief, but Daniel didn't drop his guard. 'Stay beside me.'

As we climbed the short slope of the hill towards the house, the rider turned the grey horse off the road into the side yard, and dismounted. From that distance I could only see that he was lean and wearing a white wig beneath his hat, and that his clothes looked to be fancier than those I'd seen here so far. This impression grew stronger the closer I got to him, and owed as much to the fabric his clothes had been cut from as to their design. His long jacket was dark-green brocade, with an elegant sheen to it, and his high boots were so gleamingly black that they looked as if they'd hardly been worn.

But his face, when he turned, was plain-featured and didn't quite match the effect.

He ignored me completely, and nodded a greeting to Daniel. 'Good morrow. I wonder if I might impose on your kindness. My horse has a shoe loose.' The accent was hard to place. Scottish, I guessed, though it held a faint trace of the Continent.

I could feel Daniel's shoulders relaxing. He said, ''Tis a dangerous road.'

'So I'm told.'

For a moment the men faced each other and waited, and then the newcomer offered his hand with a smile. 'The name is Wilson, Mr Butler, and I do bring with me the good wishes of our mutual acquaintance.'

'I am glad to have them, Mr Wilson.' Daniel sheathed the dagger in his belt so neatly that another person watching would have missed the motion altogether and not even known that he'd been holding it. He shook the stranger's hand and, looking up the empty road, he asked, 'You travel on your own?'

'I did arrive with my man yesterday. We took rooms at the inn at St Non's, and I charged him to stay there and wait while I came on alone to you here.' He had noticed me finally. His eyes held polite expectation as he looked at Daniel and waited.

'Forgive me,' said Daniel, as though it had been an oversight and not protective instinct that had kept him from bringing me forward. 'Mistress Eva O'Cleary, a guest of my house.'

Wilson bowed. 'Mistress O'Cleary, your servant.'

I wasn't sure how to respond, so I did what I'd seen women do in the movies – I made a deep curtsy, and hoped that was right.

To my relief, Wilson turned back to Daniel and asked, 'May I stable my horse?'

'In the back.'

There was nothing uneven at all in the horse's gait, confirming my impression that his mention of a loose shoe had been part of a script, as had Daniel's reply – like two spies trading passwords to make themselves known to each other.

I guessed, too, that their 'mutual friend' was most likely James Butler, the 2nd Duke of Ormonde, who according to the reading I'd done earlier would still be in England, waiting to learn what the House of Lords would do in answer to the charges brought against him of High Treason. He would be impeached, I knew. And soon. But no one here was yet aware of that.

'How fares our friend?' asked Daniel.

Wilson, if in fact that was his name, was walking several steps ahead of us, the horse's bridle in his hand. 'He is quite well, though incidents of late have tried his patience, as you likely can imagine. It has been suggested to him he might seek to cure his restlessness with travel.'

'If he has a mind to travel he has but to say the word and I will put my ship and crew at his disposal.'

''Tis most kind,' said Wilson with a nod of thanks, 'I will be sure to tell him so when next I see him.'

Trailing silently behind, still holding Daniel's arm, I tried to remember if any of the historical sources I'd read in my research had said how the Duke of Ormonde had escaped to France. I didn't think they had. Which left me wondering if he had made the crossing as a passenger aboard the *Sally*.

No doubt I was going to find out.

It was strange, knowing what I was seeing was history unfolding. How many historians would have paid money to walk in my shoes at this moment, I wondered? To be able to listen and watch while these men played their parts in a growing conspiracy, one that would lead in a few months to open rebellion?

From the glance Wilson gave me I guessed he was finding my presence a bit of a nuisance. His next words were proof. 'Surely Mistress O'Cleary will much prefer waiting out here while you show me which stall I may use for my horse?' And directly to me he said, smiling, 'You'll not want to ruin your slippers.'

He appeared to be expecting a response from me, but Daniel stepped in smoothly.

'She has not the use of speech.'

The man named Wilson raised his eyebrows. 'Does she not? And how then was she robbed of it?'

'It is my understanding she has been afflicted since her birth.'

'Remarkable.' He looked at me as though I were a scientific specimen, and I had the impression he'd just dropped me down a few points on the scale of intelligence. 'How sad,' he said, then turned away dismissively.

I knew Daniel would have to follow, so I lifted my hand from his arm and the look he angled down at me held quiet thanks. He said, 'Please go and let your brother know that we will have a guest for dinner.'

With a nod, I went. I looked back once, but they had gone into the stables with the horse already, and the yard was empty. When I brought my head back round I saw that Fergal had come out to stand within the open doorway, hands on hips. He frowned. 'I thought I heard a horse.'

I quickened my steps, knowing I'd have to be in the house with the door shut, and able to talk without worrying Wilson would hear, before I could tell Fergal what was going on.

'Has someone come?' he asked.

I gave another nod, but faintly, because something had begun to change in Fergal's face. He was looking at me strangely. With my next step I came close enough to see his eyes, to watch the question in them change to open disbelief. And then he raised his hand and crossed himself. 'Sweet Jesus.'

And before I could react, he started wavering and faded to a shadow and then vanished altogether like a breath of smoke dissolving in the air.

I stopped walking.

And suddenly I wasn't in the yard myself, but stepping out onto the open hillside from the Wild Wood, with sunlight breaking through the clouds above me and Trelowarth waiting patiently to welcome me, and Susan a small figure heading off towards the greenhouse.

I hovered in confusion for a moment before memories started swirling back – my evening spent with Claire, my sleeping over at her cottage, and my waking up to find she'd gone out before me. Coming back along the coast path through the woods, and then the sudden rain, and running for the house, and . . .

That had happened two full days ago for me, yet here I was back in the present day, and it was plain to see no time had passed. When I looked down I saw the deep impression of my footprints in the muddy ground that led to where I stood now on the soft grass of the hill, and everything was as it had been. As it should be.

Well, perhaps not everything.

I ran my hand down one hip to make absolutely certain, and my fingers smoothed across the silken fabric of the gown I was still wearing. And beneath its linen covering my hair was still pinned up in its elaborate style. Not things that could be easily explained, I knew, if anyone should see me.

It was that one thought that shifted me to motion, forced my feet to leave the spot where they had taken root, and lead me running uphill in a hurry to be safely out of sight.

At this hour of the morning Mark should already be out and working. I could only hope that he'd be keeping to his schedule. But in case he was still finishing his breakfast in the kitchen, I went in by the front door and made a beeline for the stairs.

I'd gone halfway up before I heard a door close overhead, and cheerful humming that I recognised as Claire's. There was no chance for me to make it to my room without her seeing me, and since her steps were coming down the corridor right now there likely wasn't even time for me to turn and go downstairs again. I'd never cross the hall in time.

I was panicking, pressing my back to the panelled wood wall, when the feel of that wood stirred my memory and I turned to push the panel on the landing in the way Daniel had shown me. Part of me didn't expect it to open, but it did, and just in time I slipped into the cramped and cobwebbed space and pulled the panel closed again behind me as Claire's footsteps neared the stairs.

I heard her light and even tread come down and cross the landing, passing close beside my hiding place, and without pause she carried on and down the final half-flight to the hall.

The dress looked different, here. I spread it on my bed and touched its folds with careful fingers, for the journey across time had left it faded, and the stitching of the seams showed through in places, weakened. Fragile.

Such a lovely thing, I thought. And now I'd brought it here, and there was likely no way I could ever take it back to where it properly belonged. My own clothes, left behind in Daniel's time, were easy to replace, but this . . .

'I'm sorry,' I said quietly, although I knew the people the apology was meant for couldn't hear me. I found a padded hanger in my wardrobe and I hung the chemise and skirt and bodice on it, then I covered all of them with Daniel's red silk dressing gown – his 'banyan', he had called it – because somehow it seemed right to me for them to be together. They were almost too bulky to keep in the wardrobe now, and anyone who opened up the wardrobe door would see them, but for the moment it would have to do.

The slippers and hairpins were easier. Wrapped in the soft linen cap they tucked tidily into the drawer where I'd already hidden my sleeping pills, wristwatch and phone. I'd left the watch and phone there even after I had figured out that stress was not my problem, since I didn't want to run the risk of taking either item back in time with me. Modern technology didn't belong in the past.

Nor do you, I reminded my face in the mirror.

But somehow the eyes that looked back at me didn't seem wholly convinced.

Chapter Seventeen

Mark and Claire were in the kitchen when I went downstairs. Claire glanced around as I came in and said, 'Got back all right, did you? Oliver telephoned. Something about an old book he found down in his archives that mentions a smuggler who lived at Trelowarth.'

'Really?' I felt a small charge of excitement. 'That was quick.'

'You're to meet him at one, if you're interested. He said he thought it was well worth a lunch.'

Mark said, 'That's the line he's using these days, is it?' With a grin he reached to take an orange from the basket on the worktop and began to peel it. 'Good one.'

'Give it up. He's helping me do research.'

'Oh, I'm sure he is.' He tried to school his features. 'And you're sticking to your story, are you, that you spent last night at Claire's?'

I looked to her for confirmation. 'Claire?'

But she was smiling. 'Just ignore him, Eva,' she advised, and crossed between the both of us to fill a glass with water at the sink. 'He knows full well you were with me, I rang him up to let him know.'

'And a good thing she did,' Mark said. 'I was beginning to think you'd gone the way of the Grey Lady. Though it's not really proof, is it, Claire only *saying* you were with her . . .'

I interrupted, disregarding that last bit to ask him, 'Who's the Grey Lady?'

'You know. The one who vanished at Trelowarth. Have you never heard about her?'

'No.' I had the sudden feeling I was standing in a draught. I moved and asked him, 'When was this?'

He turned to Claire. 'When was it? You're the one who knows the story.'

She considered. 'Oh, before my parents' time. I had the story told me when I first came to Trelowarth by an old man in the village who was nearly ninety then, at least, and he had been a young man when it happened. He'd seen it with his own eyes, so he said.'

'What did he see?' I had the strange sense that I knew what was coming.

'He saw a woman disappear.' She said it very plainly, as though such a thing were possible. 'Right here, behind the house. A woman he knew well. He said one minute they were talking, and the next she went all grey and then just faded into nothingness, and disappeared.'

The draught returned.

Mark saw me shiver and said, 'It's a story, Eva. People

don't just disappear.' He split the orange into sections, offering a piece to me.

I took it. Forced a smile. 'I'm only thinking it might be another tale to tell the tourists, that's all.'

'Why don't you ask Oliver?' he said, his eyes all innocence. 'He's good with local history.'

Claire told him, 'Actually, I'd think it would be more the sort of question that you'd want to ask Felicity.'

'Why Felicity?'

'Well, she's keen on ghosts and folklore. She'll be in the shop today, Eva, if you're going down to Polgelly. You ought to stop in for a chat.'

I had hit on a better idea. 'Why don't we all go? We could have fish and chips at the harbour.'

Claire shook her head. 'Susan and I have to go shop for tables and chairs,' she said, then went on in an offhand way, 'But Mark will come, I'm sure. He's always up for fish and chips.' I saw the glance Claire sent her stepson and I knew that she, like me, had noticed Felicity's feelings for Mark, even if he hadn't, and was trying to play matchmaker.

He fell for it. 'All right. I've got some work I need to finish first, though,' he said drily, 'on my blog.'

I smiled. 'Why don't I go ahead, then? I've got banking that I need to do, and I'll collect Felicity and Oliver, and you can meet us at the harbour. One o'clock?'

With that agreed, I headed out. I wasn't sure that I was really up to lunching in Polgelly, since I wasn't quite myself yet and a part of me just wanted to lie down and rest, to find my balance and restore it after all my travelling through time. But overriding my exhaustion was the lure of learning more about the Butler brothers from the book that Oliver had found.

And I did have a bit of business to attend to at the bank. If I surprised Mr Rowe with my request to put a Trust in place, in secret, for Trelowarth, he was too much the professional to let it show. Of course, he said, it could be done. It would take time, preparing all the paperwork and seeing to the finer points, but yes, it was quite possible. And with those wheels set spinning into motion, I moved on to my next stop.

Felicity had customers. I waited by the shelves that held the little dancing pisky figures, picking up the nearest one and weighing it within my hand until she had the time to come across and say hello.

'You want to watch those,' she advised me. 'Tricky things, those piskies.'

With their pointed hats and elf-like clothes and laughing eyes they looked completely harmless, but I knew the tales of piskies and their mischief. 'I'll be careful. What is this?' I asked, and pointed to a little sign among them with the words, 'Porthallow Green' carved on it.

'Don't you know that story? Well, you know Porthallow, surely? And according to the legend there was once a boy from there sent on an errand by his master, and it was dark before he'd finished and on his way home he heard a voice at the roadside say, "I'm for Porthallow Green." And the boy thought, well, it might be good to have a bit of company, even from a stranger, so he called out, "*I'm* for Porthallow Green," and quick as a wink, there he was, on Porthallow Green, with the piskies dancing round him. Have you really never heard this one?'

I told her that I hadn't.

'Well,' she said, 'one of the piskies called out, "I'm for Seaton Beach!" and the boy thought, *Well, why not?* So he said, "*I'm* for Seaton Beach," and there he was, with the piskies again. And they went on like that all night, all the way to the King of France's cellar, where they drank his wine and danced, and when the piskies brought the boy home in the morning to Porthallow Green, he still had his wine glass to prove it.' She smiled. 'Wouldn't happen today, of course. Think of the airfare I'd save if I could go and stand in a meadow and simply call, "I'm for Ibiza," and land on the beach.'

'But you'd have to rely on the piskies to bring you back home again,' I pointed out. 'They don't, always.'

'True enough.'

I asked casually, 'I don't suppose you've ever heard of anybody disappearing from Trelowarth?'

As it turned out, she had never heard the story of the Grey Lady. 'When was that, do you know?'

I did the maths. 'Claire said she heard it when she first came here to live, which would be nearly thirty years ago, and the man she heard it from was maybe ninety, so assume that he was twenty-five or thirty when it happened . . . ninety years ago?' I estimated. 'Give or take.'

'I'll have to ask around,' she said, 'but nothing would surprise me. You know Trelowarth's built right on a ley line?'

'A what?'

'Ley line. Sort of a geomagnetic conduit, if you like. A lot of ancient monuments and holy sites were built on top of ley lines. There's a line that runs clear under St Non's well and through the Beacon and Trelowarth to Cresselly Pool.' She laughed at my expression. 'I'm not making it up, honestly. Dowsers can find them, they're actually there. They've a powerful energy. All sorts of strange things can happen on ley lines.'

I certainly wasn't in any position to argue that, I thought. As I set my pisky back among his dancing brethren on the shelf, Felicity asked brightly, 'So, what are you doing down here in Polgelly?'

I turned and told her, 'Taking you to lunch.'

The tide was in, the wind was fair, and many of the fishing boats had gone to take advantage of the day, to ride the sea beneath a sun that warmed my shoulders even through the fabric of my shirt and felt like summer's kiss upon my upturned face.

I felt another happy moment of nostalgia, sitting on the whitewashed harbour wall enjoying fish and chips that had been wrapped in newspaper, the old way I remembered it. The rest was well-remembered, too: the biting tang of vinegar, the sharpness of the salt, the sound of seagulls wheeling greedily above me while the water lapped the wall below and, further off, the waves that crashed in rhythm at the entrance to the harbour and cast up a spray that carried on the breeze to cool my skin.

Felicity, beside me, smiled. 'You look as though you've eaten the canary.'

Mark said, 'That'll be next, at the rate she's going. Where are you putting it all, Eva?'

'I'm hungry.'

'You can chase that with a pound of fudge,' suggested

Oliver, who in this group had fallen very naturally back into his old childhood pattern, teasing me to focus my attention where he wanted it – on him.

Not that he had seemed at all put out that I'd brought Mark, nor that Felicity had joined us. Oliver, as I recalled, was nothing if not sociable, and with his easy-going ways he could adapt without complaint to any change of plan. But he was not about to let that steer him off his course, or change his purpose.

It was clear he had his eye on me. I noticed it today more than I had at our last lunch together, noticed how he looked at me and how his smiles lingered. And a month ago I might have even welcomed the attention. After all, he was a nice guy, and looked absolutely gorgeous in his plain white shirt and jeans, his blond hair golden in the midday sun and tousled by the harbour breeze. I knew most women would have thought him wonderful if they'd been in my place.

But when I looked at him today my only thought was that his face, though handsome, didn't have the same appeal as Daniel Butler's, and that Daniel's eyes in that same light would have been even greener than the sea beyond the shore.

I shrugged off Oliver's remark, and smiled. 'I doubt that I'll have room for fudge when I'm done with this.'

'If I take you for a walk, you will.'

Mark said, 'I thought you called her down to see a book.'

'I did. Only found it this morning. It came in a box with some others I bought at a sale last year, and it's been gathering dust at the back of my bookshelves.'

Felicity glanced over, curious. 'What sort of book?'

'A field guide of sorts to this area – natural history with small bits of colour thrown in – but it mentions some people that Eva's been after. She's trying to find Susan somebody famous who lived at Trelowarth,' he said, 'and these brothers, the Butlers, were smugglers. Infamous, not famous, but the local people loved them, so the book says. They were heroes here.'

Mark said, 'Like the Carter brothers up at Prussia Cove?'

'Exactly. But the Carters weren't in business till years afterward. They weren't even born when the Butlers were free-trading out of Polgelly.' He'd finished the last of his chips and he crumpled the wrapping of newspaper into a ball. 'I have to thank Eva for putting me on to them. I'd never heard of the Butlers, myself.'

Felicity was looking at him with the keen eyes of an old friend who will not be fooled. 'I'm surprised you found the book at all,' she said innocently, 'if it was at the back of your bookshelves.'

'Yeah, well, Eva asked me yesterday about the Butlers, and I had some time last night, so I just thought I'd look. You know.'

She smiled at him. 'Oh yes. I know.'

'Shut up.' Their banter had the easy back and forth that came with practice. 'Shouldn't you be getting back to work?'

'I've got five minutes still. And I was hoping to take one of you big strong men back to the shop with me. I've just had an artist ship over her paintings – they're huge, and I'll need help to hang them.'

Oliver was unenthusiastic. 'Mark's got bigger muscles. And while you're off doing that,' he said, 'I'll show the book to Eva.'

Which was clearly what Felicity had wanted to begin with.

I watched them go. 'She's fun.'

'She is that.' His gaze moved to me as he said, 'That was nicely manoeuvred.'

'What was?'

'Your inviting Fee out to have lunch with us. And with Mark. You've noticed she's head over heels for him.'

The fact that *he'd* noticed surprised me at first, till I realised he worked with Felicity and they were obviously close. 'Yes, well,' I told him, 'I didn't do *all* the manoeuvring, did I?'

He grinned. 'I've done my share of helping hang pictures. And Mark's muscles really are bigger. Besides, how do you know I wasn't manoeuvring for my own benefit?'

I ate my last chip and wadded the paper with careful hands. 'Oliver . . .'

'What?'

'I do like you.'

'But?'

'I just don't want you to think that I'm . . . that is, I'm really not looking for . . .'

'Hey.' I could hear the faint smile in his voice. 'It's a book, not an etching.' He rose to his feet from the harbour wall, held out his hand for the newspaper. 'Come on, let me chuck that in the bin for you, then you can come and look at what I've found.'

I wasn't fooled. He still had an agenda, but I knew there

wasn't a thing I could do to discourage him. Men who had Oliver's confidence weren't to be swayed by small things like the fact I had fallen for somebody else.

I formed that thought idly enough, but it struck me with a sudden force that stopped me in my tracks. I couldn't honestly have meant that, could I? Yet I sat here in the sunshine on the harbour wall and turned the thought a thousand ways, and every way I turned it, it was true.

Oliver, who had no way of knowing that I'd just been hit by something like a thunderbolt, asked whether I was ready and I numbly told him yes, I was, and went to see the book.

He'd left it set out for me on the small working desk beside the bookshelves in the storage room of the museum, in the back beside the little kitchenette that had a kettle and some cupboards and a sink and not much more.

The storage room itself was crowded thick with shelves and boxes and it smelt of dust that hadn't been disturbed in quite some time. Still, there was proper light to read by, and an antique wooden captain's chair that proved to be quite comfortable.

Collecting my still–rattled thoughts, I focused my attention on the book itself.

It was an older book, with cloth-and-cardboard covers frayed and dented at the edges and the binding at the spine so badly cracked and worn that whole sections of pages, stitched together, slid and shifted when I leafed my way along to find the place that Oliver had marked.

He came to stand behind me, leaning over, pointing to the lines that were of interest. 'There, you see? Below that bit about the Cripplehorn.'

But I'd already started reading in the paragraph before that:

At the western limit of the beach there is a rock the locals call the Cripplehorn, which at its highest point is measured more than ninety feet, and which extends beyond the cliffs to form a breakwater. Upon its eastern face two minor streams converge to form a fickle waterfall, at times a mere cascade, at times a cataract that rushes to the sand and draws a varied wealth of plant life from the rock . . .

After describing all this plant life in excruciating detail, and the several types of birds that liked to nest upon the Cripplehorn, the author made a detour from his scientific facts to state:

The base of the cascade conceals a narrow cavern safely set above the highest tide, which in former times reportedly was favoured by the Butler brothers of the nearby manor of Trelowarth for the storage of their smuggled cargoes. It is spoken still with no small pride that never once did any person of the village tell the secret of this hiding place, no matter what reward was offered by the local constable, so well-regarded were the Butlers for their generosity in sharing of the wealth they gained by working in defiance of the law. Their daring exploits were later recounted in a journal that was published by the younger of the brothers as A Life Before the Wind. *Proceeding westward, one encounters an uncommon wealth of avian diversity . . .*

That was all that had been written of the Butler brothers. After that the author veered off once again into his birds and plants and rock formations. I read through the paragraphs again to be sure I hadn't missed something of value, then I turned round in my chair to look at Oliver. 'This journal of Jack Butler's . . .'

He had known that I would ask that, I could see it in his smile. 'Yes. *A Life Before the Wind.* Poetic bastard, for a pirate. I've already looked it up, but I could only find two copies referenced, both of those in library collections in the States. There may be more, though. Give me time to do some hunting.'

He'd impressed me. 'And when was it actually published?'

'1739.' He didn't hesitate. 'Printed for some bookseller in London, in the Strand.'

I'd have to look it up myself. I felt a faint sense of surprise that, of the brothers, Jack had been the one to leave behind a journal. From the little I had seen of him, he hadn't struck me as the writing type.

But then again, I'd learnt in life that people could surprise me.

Mark, for instance, as we walked together up The Hill a short while afterwards, didn't tease me once about my afternoon with Oliver.

I sent a sideways glance in his direction. 'You all right?'

'I'm fine. Just thinking.'

There'd be no use asking what about, I knew. Mark rarely shared his thoughts. Instead I asked him, 'Did you know there was a cave below the Cripplehorn?'

He gave a nod. 'I used to play at pirates down there as a boy.'

'You never took me.'

'You weren't old enough. It's not an easy scramble down.

And when you did get big enough, I'd grown too old myself to play at pirates.'

'Did you take Katrina?'

'Once. She didn't really care for it. Too dark and damp. She liked the light.'

We walked a bit in silence with our thoughts. Which was as well because we'd reached the steep part of The Hill where speaking started taking up more air than I could spare. But still, I found enough to ask him, 'Will you take me now?'

Mark was more fit than I was, and his words came without effort. 'What, today?'

'God, no.' I took a gulp of air to fuel the burning muscles of my thighs. 'I just meant sometime.'

'Sure. There's not much there to see, though, and the climb back up is worse than this.'

'No climb,' I said, 'is worse than this.'

He grinned. 'Suit yourself. We'll go tomorrow, if you like.'

'Wednesday. Then Felicity can come along.'

Mark seemed to find that odd. 'Why would she want to?'

'You're an idiot.'

'I'm what?' He turned. 'Why am I an idiot?'

I linked my arm through his and told him fondly, 'You just are.'

And that was all the breath that I had left for talking till we'd finished with The Hill.

Chapter Eighteen

I dreamt of him that night; I dreamt of Daniel Butler lying in the bed beside me, only lying there asleep and nothing more. I heard his even breathing and I felt his warmth, the shifting of his weight against the mattress as he turned. His face in sleep was not so hardened as it looked by day. The lines were there, but smoother, and the slanting shadows of his lashes crossed his tanned skin peacefully.

It seemed to me we were not at Trelowarth any more. The room felt warmer, and the night air carried strange exotic scents I didn't recognise. But I paid no real attention to the room or to the bed, I was so focused on the man who shared it with me at that moment.

Then as I watched his face, his eyes came slowly open and he saw me too, and smiled . . .

The curtains at my window stirred in answer to the

cooler breezes blowing inland from the sea along the Cornish coast, and half-wakeful and half-dreaming still, I turned my own head hopefully. But nobody was there.

And in the darkness of the room it seemed the walls breathed out a sigh and I'd have sworn I heard a voice, not from the next room but from this one, and not talking now to Fergal but to me. I heard him.

'Eva.'

Not quite sure if I was sleeping or awake, I said, 'I'm here.'

No answer came except the wind, and in the silence following I found a sleep that was too deep for dreams.

Next morning I was up and dressed before the sun had touched the hills. Downstairs, the dogs rose from their resting places like a wagging entourage and, since both Mark and Susan were still sleeping and my mind was full of restless thoughts that wanted clearing out, I went with all the dogs still bouncing round my heels and took a walk.

I'd had some time now to adjust to the idea that I'd fallen half in love with Daniel Butler, but I still had no idea what to do about it. Any way I tackled it, the thought was still impossible. We lived in different centuries. For all I knew, we'd never meet again. And even if we did, who was to say that he would ever feel the same for me?

He couldn't, I decided, as I led the dogs up past the greenhouse by the path the tourists would be using when they came, an older path that wound along the high stone walls of all the older gardens where the birds were warbling joyously, unseen. He couldn't love me, I was nothing like the women of his time. I was a novelty, but that would soon wear off and in the end, when people chose someone to love, they chose their own kind. That was common wisdom, wasn't it?

So why, I wondered, had I chosen him?

I climbed the winding path in silence while the dogs ran round me, madly sniffing everywhere and tagging one another in the way that dogs will do. I nearly tripped on Samson twice, and still I didn't know the answer. They were strange to me and new, these feelings, yet I'd never been more certain in my life of how I felt, and that alone was something I found troublesome.

Why him? I asked a second time. Why couldn't it be Oliver who made me feel this way? Why did it have to be a man I couldn't have? It wasn't fair.

'It isn't fair,' I told the dogs, but they just wagged and grinned agreement as we reached the turning in the path where I could glimpse the ruined Beacon, rising as it always had above the blue Atlantic where the wind had carried off Katrina's ashes.

She hadn't stayed, I thought, so why should I? I wasn't bound here, and I'd done the thing I'd come to do, so why not simply leave? I knew it had to be this place that was affecting me, this place where strange grey ladies disappeared and ley lines ran below the ground, and if I went away then surely things would soon return to normal. I would leave and not be missed and Daniel Butler would forget me, and Trelowarth would go on the way it always had, without me.

Or at least that's what I thought, until I climbed the final few feet of the path and came out with the dogs beside the turning in the road between Polgelly and St Non's, and saw that Mark had cleared a broad and level place up here to make a car park that was wide enough for several cars, I noticed. Or a tour bus.

And standing there I realised that I couldn't leave. Not yet. I turned around again and looked back down the way that I had come, to where the glass roof of the greenhouse caught the early sunlight like a mirror, and I knew I couldn't leave till Susan had her tea room open and I'd signed the papers for the Trust to keep Trelowarth where it should be, with the Hallett family, for a good long time to come. There was nothing for it, really, but to set aside all thoughts of leaving, and resolve to stay.

And if there was another reason, one I was less willing to acknowledge, for my choosing not to go just yet, I pushed it far back in my mind and locked it there.

I set to work the next few days on doing what I'd promised Susan I would do. I sent the early press releases out, and made some phone calls to the local tour providers to convince them of Trelowarth's charms.

By Wednesday, when Felicity came up to help again, I could announce that *House & Garden* was considering a feature, and that one firm operating minibuses to St Non's was eager to include us in its schedule.

Susan, who'd been trying to decide which of the trees close by the greenhouse would be best used as the 'cloutie tree', stopped looking for a moment. 'Really?'

'Really. They do tourist runs from Plymouth, so they pick their people up at their hotels and stop at St Non's on their way down to Falmouth for lunch, but they wanted a different stop on the way back where their tourists could stretch a bit, walk around, and we're conveniently right on their route. So I said we could give them a garden tour and a traditional Cornish cream tea, and they went for it.'

Susan was delighted. 'Well done you.'

'I said they could start the beginning of August, is that still all right?'

She'd told me she'd need that much time to get all her work properly done on the tea room. She gave a firm nod. 'Yes. What do you think of this one?'

I looked upwards at the tree in question while Felicity stepped back and frowned and said, 'It ought to be a thorn.'

'Why?' I asked.

'Because most cloutie trees are thorn trees,' said Felicity.

Susan said, 'But this one's pretty.'

'No, it needs the proper energy.' Felicity held firm, and in the end we settled on the only hawthorn tree close by the greenhouse door.

'Well, I suppose,' said Susan, 'I could have Mark take down these other two beside it, so it has a little bit more presence.'

Felicity thought that would do very nicely. 'And you can put a little pond or something here beside it, for the water.'

'Water?'

'Susan,' said Felicity, 'you cannot have a cloutie tree unless it's next to water, that's tradition.'

'Ah.' Resigned, she took another look around, with hands on hips. 'Well, the pipes to the greenhouse run just over there, we could maybe tap into those somehow. I'll have to speak to Paul.'

I asked, 'Who's Paul?'

Felicity smiled knowingly. 'Her plumber. Do you know,' she said to Susan, 'I have never seen a project need more plumbing work than this one.'

Susan shrugged the teasing off. 'Is that a fact?'

'If you ask me, it's all the fault of that story Claire told us about how her grandparents met,' said Felicity. 'Good looking plumbers who strip off whenever it rains, and all that. It creates expectations.'

'Claire's grandfather didn't strip off in the rain,' Susan told her friend, amused. 'He took his shirt off, Fee, and he was only being chivalrous.'

'Yes, well, we've had a lot of rain,' Felicity remarked, 'and your Paul hasn't been chivalrous once, has he? That's all I'm saying. I'll tell you who's chivalrous,' she turned her gaze to me. 'Oliver. He's been all over these past few days, looking for leads on your smugglers.'

Susan smiled. 'Yes, well, that's men for you. You can hit them with a rock and it still doesn't put them off.'

I sent her a dry look. 'You can't possibly remember the rock throwing thing. You weren't old enough.'

'I didn't say I remembered.' She stooped to pull a straggling weed. 'Did you really knock him flat?'

'I did.'

Felicity said that was likely why he had his eye on me. 'Men always chase after the women who treat them the worst. You treat them nicely, they don't notice you.'

Her tone was light, and yet there was a wistfulness behind it that I heard and understood.

I said, as casually as I knew how, 'To change the subject, if I may, Mark said he'd take me on a field trip later, if the two of you would like to come.'

Felicity perked up. 'Oh, yes? To where?'

'The cave below the Cripplehorn. I've never seen it.'

Susan frowned. 'What cave below the Cripplehorn?'

'A smuggler's cave, apparently. You've never seen it?'

She had not. Felicity was fascinated. 'When would you be going?'

'Just after lunch,' I told them, 'if the rain holds off.'

The rain held off. And after lunch the four of us, with Mark in front, trekked off on our adventure.

The dogs had howled a protest at Mark's leaving them behind, but he'd been right. We couldn't bring them. While the path along the coastal cliffs was not too hard to manage, when we neared the Cripplehorn itself the path became a challenge, slippery rocks descending in uneven steps towards the beach, with a red-lettered 'Danger' sign warning the rocks were unstable and that those who passed this way did so at their own risk. As if to drive home the point, a large red-painted box the same size as a mailbox stood next to the sign, with the words 'Cliff Rope' lettered in white on its front, a reminder that several times yearly some tourist who took this path had to be rescued.

But Mark went down with the sure steps of a mountain goat, and I went after him, carefully putting my feet in the same places he had.

Around us the black rocks rose higher and sharper, more slippery because of the spray from the sea. And the sound of the sea itself grew even louder as wind-driven waves hit the beach.

The beach would not have met the Californian definition of a beach – there was no sand in sight, just hard round rocks and pebbles worn to smoothness by the water, shifting crunchingly wherever I set foot on them, all grey and black and lighter grey with clinging strands of dark-green seaweed trailed across the stones.

I'd never been down here. I stood a moment on the slipping pebbles and breathed in the sharp, wet, salty scents of sea and stone, and found I liked the feeling of the wind-flung mist against my face. There was no ship in sight today, but I could very easily imagine one – the *Sally*, maybe – sliding darkly past the Cripplehorn and coming in to anchor while her men cast off the smaller boat to bring her smuggled goods to shore. I raised a hand to shield my eyes and squinted at the vision while I tried to make my mind up who to give her as a captain, Jack or Daniel . . . who would be the taller figure moving in among the others on the deck, a silhouette against the sails . . .

'So,' said Felicity, as she came crunching up behind me, 'where's this cave?'

Mark pointed. 'There.'

In front of us the waterfall that tumbled down the Cripplehorn and hit the beach below in an uneven, narrow spray was flowing fast and full today, the streams that fed it swelled by all the recent rain. At times in summer it was no more than a trickle, but today it was impressive, as though it had somehow known there would be someone to show off for.

Susan, who'd taken her time down the cliff path, caught up to the rest of us now and moved past, looking hard at the waterfall, then at her brother. 'Why didn't you show me this ages ago?'

He gave her the same answer he'd given me, sort of – that she'd been too young when he'd played here, and when she'd been old enough he'd left off playing in caves. He seemed game to recapture the fun of it now, though. It was hard to keep up with him, dodging the worst of the wet of the waterfall, balancing carefully on the slick rocks. I looked down for a moment, unsure of my footing, and when I looked up Mark had vanished.

I stopped in my tracks in surprise. 'Mark?'

His voice seemed to come from the solid rock. 'Here.'

Then I moved to the left, and I saw it. The cleft in the rock was concealed by the fact that the opening faced the sea, sideways, so when it was viewed from the front all that showed was the unbroken rock of the cliff. And from the sea no one would notice it either, because of the cascading screen of the waterfall.

Mark waited till he was sure I had seen him before he moved forward and into the cave, and I followed. The sudden close of darkness was unsettling, but as my eyes adjusted to it I could see that it was not complete. Faint shafts of filtered light from somewhere overhead showed me the inward curving walls, the deeply worn and pitted floor that, while it lay above the tide's reach, was still flecked with shallow pools of moisture everywhere; the remnants of a row of barrels, little more than bits of wood and badly rusted metal now, that had been left to moulder in the shadows.

More unsettling than the darkness was the sudden change in sound, as though I'd cupped a hollow shell against my ear and shut out everything except the rushing echo of the sea and the more stealthy and insistent dripping of dark water into unseen pools within the cave.

And then Felicity came in and broke the silence with a voice that echoed, too. 'This is incredible.'

Behind me, Susan asked her brother, 'Did you bring a torch?'

'Don't need a torch,' he said. 'It spoils the effect.'

I knew what he meant. Any light, let alone the hard beam from a flashlight, would ruin the secretive feel of the cave. I could see the appeal this would have to a boy playing pirates.

Could see, too, why the Butlers would have chosen it to hold the goods they smuggled in from Brittany aboard the *Sally*. They'd have likely dropped her anchor round the headland at high tide, and under cover of the darkness rowed the contraband to shore. It would have taken several men to do the work, and I remembered how the book I'd read at Oliver's had said it was a point of pride that no one in Polgelly had betrayed this cave's existence to the constable.

When he had searched the house that day, the day he'd found me there alone, the thing that he'd been looking for had probably been hidden safe down here.

I wondered what it was.

Behind me, Susan moved towards the row of barrels. 'Look at these. Your Butler brothers left these, I expect.'

Mark didn't think it likely. 'They're not old enough. Besides, they weren't all empty when I played here. I'll lay odds that was Dad's private stash of whisky.'

'I'm surprised he let you play here,' Susan said.

'He didn't know. He would have had my hide if he'd found out.' Mark took an idle step away, and accidentally his foot kicked something out of place that scuttled with a rasp across the stone. He bent to pick it up.

I asked, 'What is it?'

'Just a bit of strapping from a barrel, I'd imagine.' He tossed it back into a corner. 'Not like the treasures we used to find.'

Felicity set down the spent candles. 'What sort of treasures would those be, then?'

'Lots of things. Musket balls, sometimes. Old coins. I've got some of them still, in a drawer somewhere.'

Susan, who had still not quite forgiven him for keeping the cave secret from her, said to him accusingly, 'I've never seen those, either.'

'Yes, well, pirates hide their treasure. They don't show it to their sisters, do they?'

'If they want to go on having meals cooked for them,' Susan said, 'they do.'

Mark's smile in that dim light was hard to see, but I could tell he knew, as I did, that when Susan set her mind to something she would not be swayed. 'I'll try to dig it up,' he promised, then he paused as a faint rumble filled the cavern.

Felicity, hearing it too, announced, 'Thunder.'

'So it is,' said Mark. 'We should start back, those rocks aren't so easy to climb in the rain.'

I hung back a bit and took one final look over my shoulder as though by force of will alone I could push through the barriers of time and see the cave as Daniel would have known it. But I only saw the darkness and the dripping stone and hollow walls that told me I had come too late. Three hundred years too late.

Outside, Mark's voice called, 'Eva?'

I turned again and stepped out of the silence through the cleft beneath the waterfall, and heard the singing of the sea.

Chapter Nineteen

Back at the house, Susan gave Mark no rest till he'd gone up to look in his room for the childhood treasures he'd claimed he still kept 'in a drawer somewhere'. In spite of his earlier vagueness, he must have known exactly where they were because it wasn't long before he came back down and set a slightly grimy biscuit tin between us at the kitchen table.

'There you are,' he said. 'My plunder.'

Susan gave it an experimental shake. 'What's in it?'

'Have a look and see.'

He put the kettle on to make the tea and watched with patience while we sorted through his 'treasures': small bits of polished glass and stone, a limpet shell, a tarnished metal button, the cork from a wine bottle, two shilling coins and a ha'penny, some woman's earring with worn plastic pearls, the promised musket balls, and underneath all that a length of rusted metal so misshapen that it wasn't recognisable as anything. Until Felicity reached out to pick it up and gently brushed the flakes away.

I stared, then, as the cold chased up my spine.

Susan asked her friend, 'What's that?'

'Some kind of knife.'

She looked to Mark, who shrugged and said, 'I think I found it in behind the barrels. Don't remember.'

It was in fact a dagger, small and neatly made to fit the hand that held it so precisely that whoever faced it in a fight would only see the blade. I knew, because I'd seen it twice myself already.

Susan touched it lightly. 'What's the handle made of?'

Felicity peered at it. 'Bone, I think.'

Not bone, I could have corrected her. Shell. Some sort of shell like abalone that could show its colours in the light. But it was mostly gone and what remained was crusted thick with dirt, and there would be no way I could explain how I had known. Instead I asked her, 'May I hold it?'

It felt strange in my grasp, cold and rough, not the smooth deadly thing it had seemed when I'd seen it in Daniel's hand just a few days ago. Just a few days . . . Had it been only that? It seemed an age, and I wondered again at how quickly he'd come to be someone I missed, when he wasn't there.

Susan said, 'It looks so old.'

And Felicity, watching me, had an idea. 'Eva, why don't you take that and show it to Oliver? He knows a lot about weapons and things. *He* could tell you how old it is. And what it's worth, even.'

Mark didn't think it would be worth much. 'Not in that state.'

But Felicity told him, 'You never know. The strangest things can fetch the highest prices, sometimes.'

My fingers closed protectively around the rusted knife. 'You wouldn't sell it?'

'*That?*' Mark looked as though the very thought were ludicrous. 'Of course not.'

Susan smoothly interjected, 'And you don't mind if Eva takes it down to Oliver?'

'If that's what she wants to do.' It was a bit of a challenge, but I wasn't paying attention, not really. My own thoughts were concentrated on the unaccustomed weight of Daniel's dagger in my hand, and I was trying to remember if I'd ever seen him when he wasn't wearing it.

Except for that one time when I'd surprised him late at night in bed, I didn't think I had. For all I knew he'd had it with him then, as well – it seemed to be his favoured weapon, and the one he reached for first when he was faced with any threat.

What threat had Daniel faced down in that cave, I wondered, that had made him draw his dagger? And why had he lost it?

Of the older stones still standing in the overgrown churchyard most had been so worn by weather and by time that it was difficult to read the date or name, and of the names I could read none was 'Butler'.

The Halletts were all here – Mark's father and grandfather and his great-grandfather and varied cousins and other relations, since this little church of St Petroc's had stood its whole life within view of Trelowarth and served all the families who'd lived there by turns.

It was really no more than a chapel of ancient stone set by the side of the road that ran up from Polgelly, wound past the back of Trelowarth and on to St Non's and beyond that to Fowey.

The tale went that back in the dark, misty times lost to memory a raiding ship from Ireland had wrecked upon the coast, and the sea and the black rocks had taken the lives of the people aboard her and spared only one man who, wanting to show thanks to God, had built with his own hands this little church upon the hill. It made a rousing legend, but there was no way of knowing what was true, or if he'd ever found his way back home to Ireland, or if in fact he ever had existed.

Time was good at erasing the tangible proof that a person had lived.

Behind me the gate to the churchyard creaked open and clanged like the chime of a clock. 'Morning,' said a man's voice and, turning to answer, I saw the church sexton approaching with his wooden-handled garden shears in hand. I remembered those shears, and remembered the sexton who, though he'd grown greyer, still walked with the stride of a working man. And he seemed to remember me, too, though his memory had likely been helped by the fact that my coming to stay at Trelowarth would have been a subject much talked about down in the pubs in Polgelly.

'Now Miss Ward, see, I thought it was you.' The broad smile, with its row of impossibly even teeth, took me right back again.

Feeling about five years old, I smiled back. 'Mr Teague.'

'You're a little bit bigger than my memory of you, I'll admit, but then it's been . . . what? Twelve years?'

'More like twenty.'

'Never.' He pretended shock. 'You'll have me feeling ancient, so you will.'

I didn't think it likely, and I said as much. 'You look the same.'

'You'll want to have a doctor test your eyes, my dear.' But he was pleased. And then he said, as though it needed saying, 'I was sorry when I heard about your sister. Never seems right when the young ones go. I'm told you brought her back with you?'

'Yes.'

'Good for you. The dead deserve to have a peaceful place to rest. She wouldn't find that in America,' he said with the certainty of someone who'd never set foot out of Cornwall himself, looking round at the shaded green churchyard with its leaning rows of grey stones. The vicars of St Petroc's came and went, but Mr Teague had been a fixture of this churchyard for as long as I'd been coming here – it had seemed to me that every time I'd chanced to pass this way he'd been here somewhere, with his crowbar or his mower or his old wood-handled shears, and he had always taken time to stop his work and chat a minute.

It occurred to me that Mr Teague might be the one to ask about the Butlers, so I did. He turned the surname over in his mind, and frowned a little.

'Butler. Seems to me as there might be a grave or two of that name.'

'I didn't see any.'

'Well, you wouldn't now, not if they're old as you say.

Let me just fetch the book from the vestry.' Setting his shears down beside the church's side porch, he took out his great jangly key ring and opened the old arched oak door with its black iron hinges. I could have gone in with him, but I preferred to wait out in the fresh morning air with the songs of the birds spilling out from the trees and the warmth of the sun on my back. In a minute or two he returned with a small book with plain cardboard covers, the kind of book that local history societies everywhere tended to publish.

Mr Teague turned the pages with work-calloused fingers, in search of the one that he wanted. 'In 1822,' he said, 'there was a survey done of where the graves were to that time, and the inscriptions that were readable were copied down. Ah, yes, Butler. There be two graves here, for Butlers. In the south-west corner. Come, I'll show you where they're to.'

The churchyard's south-west corner was the closest to the road, and Mr Teague had waged a battle here against the hawthorn hedge that had been planted at its edge along the bank. The hawthorn hedge was fighting back. It had begun to creep across the top of the flat stones set horizontal in the earth. The stones themselves, already partly hidden beneath moss and waving grass, were both so beaten and eroded by the weather I could scarcely make out any traces anywhere of letters, much less read what had been written there. But luckily, in 1822, the words had still been legible.

'Says here that one,' Mr Teague said, pointing, 'is Ann Butler, died 20th October 1711, at the age of 23. "Beloved wife", it says. And this must be her husband.'

He moved on. I held my breath for one long heartbeat without meaning to.

'Jack Butler,' Mr Teague read from the book. The stone had split across the centre, as though something had been dropped on it. 'No dates on this one, strangely. Just an epigraph: "My God will raise me up, I trust."'

I breathed again. Jack Butler would have died an older man, I knew, because he'd lived to see his journals published nearly a quarter of a century after the time when I'd met him. And the quote from the poem by Sir Walter Raleigh, an earlier seafaring rogue, seemed quite fitting for Jack.

I asked, 'So there are no other Butlers here?'

Mr Teague read down the list of inscriptions again. 'Not here, no. That's the lot. Were they relatives, then?'

'No, I'm doing some research for Susan's new venture.' I knew he'd have heard about *that*. 'You know, finding out who used to live at Trelowarth.'

'Well, here's the lad coming now that you ought to be asking about things like that.' Mr Teague gave a nod to the road where a cyclist was just coming round the sharp bend at the top of The Hill from Polgelly. I recognised Oliver straight away, even with his cycling helmet on.

'That is,' said Mr Teague, 'if you've not already been asking him.'

I caught a sly tone in his voice that made me wonder just what else was being talked around the village pubs, these days.

It hardly helped that Oliver, when he caught sight of us beside the hedge, slid to a stop beside the road and smiled a brilliant welcome. 'Morning, Eva. Mr Teague.'

The hard climb up The Hill had left him faintly winded,

and his T-shirt clung with perspiration to his chest and shoulders while the muscles of his legs beneath the biking shorts were perfectly defined.

'Oliver.' With one more knowing nod in my direction Mr Teague said, 'Well, I'll let you two young people talk. I've got my work to do.'

I said, 'Thanks for your help.'

'It weren't much.'

As he started to go, I remembered to ask, 'Mr Teague, could you tell me the date of Ann Butler's death one more time, please?'

His weathered fingers flipped the pages of the book again to find it – October 20, 1711 – and I thanked him for a second time and, as he headed back across the churchyard to the place he'd left his garden shears, I turned instead to Oliver. 'Do you have a pen?'

He found that amusing. 'Do I look like I have a pen?'

I glanced once again at his close-fitting T-shirt and biking shorts, and said, 'No problem,' repeating the date in my memory a few times to hold it there.

Oliver asked, 'Who's Ann Butler?'

'Daniel Butler's wife.'

'You've found out more about them, then, your Butler brothers.'

'Just a bit. That's Jack,' I said, and pointed to the broken stone. 'The younger brother.'

'So where's Daniel?'

'I don't know.' I wasn't sure exactly how I felt about not finding him. There might be peace, I thought, in knowing how he'd died, and when, and yet a part of me was happiest not knowing.

Oliver felt confident that he could track the information down, in time. 'I like a challenge.'

'So I see.' I nodded at the bike. 'You do this sort of thing for fun, then, do you?'

'Actually, today I'm off on business.'

'Business?' I know I looked as surprised as I sounded, but really, that outfit . . .

He grinned. 'One of my holiday cottages up St Non's way has a burst pipe. I'm meeting the plumber at ten.'

'Susan's plumber?'

'Don't know. Does she have one?'

I nodded. 'From Andrews & Son, in St Non's.'

'Then it might be. Working on the tea room for her, is he?' At my nod, he said, 'Felicity keeps telling me I ought to come by sometime and see how that's getting on.' And then, 'She also told me yesterday you'd found a knife, or something, that you wanted me to look at?'

'Oh. Daniel's . . . I mean, Mark's knife. Yes.' My slip seemed not to register with Oliver.

'Maybe I'll stop in on my way back, then. Have a look. You'll be in, will you?'

I had to admit that I probably would be.

'Then I'll see you later.' With a brilliant smile of promise he set off again, the bike wheels whirring as he picked up speed along the narrow road.

And watching him, I couldn't help but wonder if the tenant of his cottage was a woman. Because if she was, then her day was about to get better than she could have hoped, having Oliver and maybe Susan's good-looking young plumber at work on that burst pipe together.

I felt another tiny twinge of guilt that I could not return

the interest Oliver was showing in me. After all, I'd met him first, before I had met Daniel. But I couldn't help my feelings. *There's either a spark or there isn't*, my sister had once told me. There wasn't with Oliver. Whether I'd met Daniel Butler before him or after him, I knew it wouldn't have made any difference.

I looked down and said to Ann Butler's grave, '*You* understand, don't you?'

And I felt sure that she did.

Coming out of the churchyard, I stood for a moment, trying to decide whether I should take the more scenic path through the newly made car park and down to the house through the gardens from there, or walk back the way I had come, by the road. I chose the road because it had more shade, and started walking down again beneath the arching trees.

The day was going to be a warm one. Even the birds seemed to sense it and sang their songs lazily, saving their energy. Now and then something unseen, some small animal, rustled in the green and grassy banks along the roadside and fell silent. Everything seemed to be slumbering, and there were no dogs today bouncing out from the drive of Trelowarth to welcome me home.

The dogs were likely out wherever Mark was in the gardens. But the silence of the house did strike me odd.

And something else was wrong, as well. I couldn't put my finger on it, to begin with, and then all at once I realised I was walking on hard ground and not on gravel, as I should have been. I'd missed the sound of crunching steps, the shifting feeling underfoot. And even as that struck me, I heard someone coming whistling out the front door of the house.

It was the same tune that Jack Butler had been whistling on the morning when I'd heard him coming up the stairs, just after he'd climbed in the kitchen window. The same morning he had found me in his brother's bed. And if I had surprised him then, the jeans and T-shirt I was wearing now would raise his eyebrows even more.

I looked for somewhere I could hide myself, and quickly.

The trees by the roadside were too far away to make a run for them. I hugged the shadow of the house and moved towards the back.

Then, with relief, I heard another voice I recognised. And laughter. Daniel, I thought. Daniel out with Fergal, in the back. They'd get me safely in the house, before Jack saw me.

Moving faster now and with less care, I came around the corner.

Daniel, standing at the far edge of the yard, glanced up and saw me as I stepped from shadow into sunlight. But he didn't smile or nod or show in any way that he'd acknowledged my arrival. He was careful not to. And I saw at once the reason why.

The man who stood before him wasn't Fergal.

Chapter Twenty

It was not the best of places I could be. I couldn't duck back around to the side of the house because at any minute Jack could come round that way himself and find me there. And there was no place in the yard for me to hide. I could do little more than freeze there, like some creature who'd been flushed out in the open and had caught sight of the hunter.

Daniel shifted his position very casually, to draw the man in front of him a little further round. I recognised Mr Wilson from his clothes, the long coat of elegant dark-green brocade, the high-cut black boots, and the white wig beneath the wide brim of his hat.

And then Daniel looked straight at me over the other man's shoulder, the briefest of looks, and with a quick darting glance and a tilt of his head made it clear I should run for the stables.

I did. How I made it across that wide yard without losing my footing or making a noise I would never remember. I didn't risk looking behind me, not even when I'd reached the stables themselves and the relative safety of their shadowed stalls smelling thickly of hay. One or two of the horses looked over the boards at me, but it seemed they'd seen more interesting sights than myself in their time and they looked away, unimpressed. Scooting past all of them, I found a stall at the end that was empty and, slipping in, pressed myself close to the rough wooden wall as the after-effects of adrenaline set my legs trembling.

I had no idea how long I had been there before I heard Daniel come in, heard his boots on the floorboards and then his voice saying, ''Tis no trouble.' Then other boots behind his. Mr Wilson had come in as well, protesting, 'You need not be my groom, Butler. Stand back, man. I'll do that myself.'

I tried not to breathe. Not that they would have heard me, with all of the noise Mr Wilson was making with saddling his horse.

He said, 'He will be glad to know that he does have your loyalty.'

'When will you see him next?' asked Daniel.

'Two days hence. I'll tell him, also, that your ship is his, if he has need of her.'

'Ay. Tell him he has but to say the word.'

The big horse grunted as the cinch was pulled and buckled, and the jangling of the bridle told me Mr Wilson had the reins in hand.

The men were moving.

Daniel said, 'If you do chance to meet our constable

upon the road, you would do well to sing the praises of King George.'

'Faith,' Mr Wilson said, betraying his first flash of humour, 'if I meet your constable, I'll call him by his name and say his king sent me here to test the hospitality of those who claim to serve him. I may get myself a meal of it, if nothing else.'

I'd missed the sound of Daniel's laugh. 'You may, at that. I'll see you to the road.'

When they had gone, the quiet settled round the stables once again, with nothing more than the faint snort or shuffle of a horse to break it.

I heard the booted footsteps coming back, alone this time, and let my breath go with relief. My legs still shook and I was trying to convince them it was safe for them to move when all at once the man approaching broke into a careless whistle.

For the second time, I froze in place. It wasn't Daniel after all, but Jack.

He came into the stable unaware, and clucked a greeting to the horses, who replied with stamping hooves.

'Now, none of that,' he told them, firm. 'I've fed you once today already, and you've no call to complain.'

His steps were turning now towards my hiding-place. With nowhere left to go, I slid a little further down the wall and closed my eyes as though some sudden twist of childish logic would make me invisible if I could not see him.

'Why so nervous?'

Two thudding heartbeats passed before I realised he'd been speaking, not to me, but to the grey horse in the stall beside my own. I heard Jack's feet shift in the straw as he moved round till we were separated only by the thickness of the boards that made the wall.

He soothed the horse. ''Tis only myself, you great fool.' But he said it with affection, in the tone men use for animals when no one else is watching. Then he changed his voice again and said, 'My horse has turned fair skittish.'

I had not heard Daniel enter, but he answered from the doorway, 'Has he, now?'

His deep voice, calm and quiet, filled me with relief, but I stayed motionless against my wall and breathed in tiny, shallow breaths I hoped could not be heard.

Jack gave his horse's neck a pat and said, 'Perhaps he takes objection to the company he has been forced to keep of late. I cannot say I blame him.'

'Do you speak of Mr Wilson, or his horse?'

'Both. Though were I forced to choose the company of one above the other, I admit the horse did irritate me less.'

There was a creaking of the floor as Daniel crossed it. 'I would not have known,' he told his brother drily, 'from the civil way you did behave while Wilson was our guest.'

'I have no time to play at politics. I do but give a man as much civility as he deserves.'

'He carried his credentials from our kinsman.'

'Then our kinsman must be wanting in his judgement, if he puts his trust in Mr Wilson.' Jack turned and his shoulder shook the wall between us. 'Christ, can you not see it for yourself? Or has your dalliance with Fergal's sister blunted all your better sense?'

There was a pause, then Daniel said, more calmly still, 'Be careful, Jack.'

But Jack did not back down. 'She is not Ann, you

know that? Dress her how you will, she is not Ann.'

'I'm well aware of who she is.' It was the quiet, careful voice that I'd last heard when he'd been speaking in the kitchen after learning that I'd had to face the constable alone. The voice that seemed to warn those few who knew him that his mood was growing dangerous.

He would have known that I was somewhere in the stables, which was likely why he cut the conversation short by telling Jack, 'And it is none of your affair.'

I couldn't see the look that passed between the two men, but I felt the tension of it all the same.

'All right,' said Jack. 'I'll say no more of that. And it may be that you are in the right as well about your Mr Wilson, but you will forgive me if I test that point myself.'

He started saddling the horse, his silence stubborn until Daniel finally asked him in more normal tones, 'Where do you mean to ride?'

'To St Non's. Wilson left his travelling companion at the inn there. I'd be interested to know how he amused himself, and whom he might have met. I've no doubt the information could be had at little cost. Do you object?' He dropped that last phrase like a gauntlet.

'No.'

They said no more. The horse was saddled and led out, and Daniel stepped aside to let Jack do it, and silence settled once more over all the stalls.

He said my name, then. 'Eva.'

'Here.' I straightened stiffly from the wooden wall, and waited while he came to me.

His face showed no emotion when he saw where I'd been standing, but he would have known that I'd heard every word that Jack had said about me, and his own replies. And since I didn't want him thinking that I cared, I forced a smile and said, 'Should I come back another time?'

It smoothed the awkward moment over, and his smile, though slow in coming, warmed his eyes.

Fergal wasn't in a mood for smiling. Slamming down the plate and cup that he'd just carried downstairs to the kitchen where we sat, he wheeled on Daniel. ''Tis hardly something you can laugh about. Have you not thought what she might have faced had she appeared like that in front of Wilson or your brother, or the constable? You've seen the way it happens, when she comes and goes. You've seen it, Danny. So have I, and I'll admit it made me fear the devil's hand, and me a man of reason.'

Daniel told him in an even voice, 'You know it is not witchcraft.'

'Ay, I know it. And you know it. But another man might not. You've seen a witch trial, have you?'

Daniel didn't answer. Fergal looked away.

'Well, I have. And it is not a sight I'd wish to see again, nor yet the evil that the mindless mob does afterwards, the way they kill the wretched—'

'She is safe with us,' said Daniel, though his interruption seemed as much a warning to his friend to hold his tongue as it did an attempt to reassure me. From his face I knew he'd thought about the danger, too, before this, and if he had not entirely dismissed it he felt sure it could be managed.

'Is she, now?' asked Fergal, challenging. 'And how can you be sure?'

'Do you now doubt me?' Daniel's tone grew faintly

frustrated. 'Christ, any man who saw you so belligerent would think she *was* your sister.'

They'd been talking long enough as if I wasn't in the room, and I decided it was time for me to cut between them. 'If I may?'

I felt a little like a referee as both men turned their heads to look at me.

I said, 'There's not a thing that I can do about the way I come and go, or where it happens. If I could, I . . .' Daniel's eyes were too distracting. 'Well, I can't, that's all. But once I'm here, it seems to me the best thing I can do is to stay close to one of you, because you both know what it looks like when it happens. You would know if I was . . . leaving. And if someone else was with us you could maybe find a way to draw them off, or stop them noticing.'

I watched them both consider this, each in his way, and Fergal gave a nod.

'Ay, so we could. Though let us hope it never comes to that.' He fixed me with a gaze that seemed to recognise I hadn't really had a proper welcome, yet. 'So. Did you eat before you came, or will you want a second meal?'

'A second one?'

'Ay.' The empty plate that he'd slammed down before was still in front of him, and he gave it a nudge. 'See, the first one's been eaten, I've just brought that down from your room, where you've been lying ill these past two days.'

'Oh. I see.' Of course, I realised, he and Daniel would have had to think up some excuse to give to Jack and Mr Wilson. I felt a twist of guilt that I had put them to such trouble.

Daniel said, 'She ate it all again, I see.'

Fergal's mouth twitched. 'Ay, she has a fair appetite, so she does, even when she's feeling poorly.'

To me, Daniel said, 'And a good thing you came back before he burst all of the seams of his clothing.'

The mention of clothing drew my own attention to what I was wearing. Self-conscious, I crossed my arms over my T-shirt and faced him. 'I'm sorry, I seem to have . . . that is, the gown that you gave me is . . . well, it's . . .'

'I did notice,' Daniel said.

Fergal had turned away and was bent over a loaf of bread, cutting thick slices that I assumed were meant for me. He paid no attention as I looked at Daniel.

'I'm sorry,' I said.

'It was only a gown.'

No it wasn't, I thought, and his shrug didn't fool me. I wondered for a moment how he'd feel were I to tell him that I'd visited her grave – Ann's grave – and seen the grasses blowing round it in its quiet corner of the churchyard, by the stone that would be Jack's.

'You needn't look so troubled,' Daniel said. 'I do have other gowns.'

Fergal, without looking round, remarked, 'The flowered one would suit her.'

Daniel looked at me. 'It would at that.'

And so the flowered one it was. When I went upstairs after eating it was waiting on the bed, the full skirt trimmed with a broad edge of blue that matched the small sprigged flowers, like forget-me-nots, that danced across the bodice of the gown. The neckline of the bodice, low and rounded, had the same blue edge. Its simple lines were lovely.

I had trouble with my hair at first, but after two or

three attempts I got it right and set the little linen cap that Fergal called a 'pinner' tidily on top. If I could trust the little looking glass, I thought, I almost looked the part convincingly enough to leave my room.

The sound of my door opening made Daniel call along the landing from his private study. 'Eva?'

'Yes?'

'Is everything all right? Do you want help?'

I crossed the few steps to his open door and breathed the aromatic scent of pipe tobacco swirling from the room. 'No thanks, I'm fine. I . . .'

He was sitting in the chair where he had sat when we'd first talked in here, beside the little window with his shoulder to the wall. A book lay open in his hand but he'd stopped reading and was staring at me silently.

My voice trailed off. 'It is a lovely gown,' I said uncertainly. 'If you would rather that I didn't wear it, then—'

'It is not that.' He set his pipe down as his quiet gaze trailed up to judge the full effect: the gown, my hair. He said, 'You did your hair yourself?'

I raised a hand to check the placement of the pins. 'Did I get something wrong?'

'No.' Daniel stood and offered me the chair beside him. 'Will you join me?'

As I sat, he sat as well and closed his book, and would have tapped the ashes from his pipe except I said, 'It's all right, I don't mind you smoking.'

'Thank you.' Leaning back, he shifted round to face me properly. 'You move well in a gown. Do women wear them in your time at all? Or are you all in breeches, like men?'

'We still wear gowns sometimes. Not quite like these,' I

spread my hand across the lacings of the bodice, flat across my waist, 'but we do wear them sometimes.'

'I confess I am not sure which I like best.' He smiled. 'Where have you left your other clothing?'

'In the box that's in the bedroom. Underneath your shirts.'

'They will be safe there for the moment. But you really should let Fergal have them later, he knows corners of this house where even I would fail to find what he has hidden.'

Fergal seemed to have a lot of talents, and I said so.

'Ay,' said Daniel, 'there are few to equal him. It was his own idea to tell Jack and Wilson you had fallen ill, and he did play the role of nursemaid so devotedly at times that I was half-convinced myself.'

I shared his smile. 'You've been friends for a very long time, Fergal says.'

Daniel nodded. 'We have. Twenty years, more or less.'

'You must both have been young when you met.'

It was a rather clumsy way of asking him how old he was, but Daniel didn't seem to mind. Through the smoke of his pipe his eyes smiled at mine. 'I was fifteen, and Fergal a few years above that, when both of us came near to being pressed into the navy in Plymouth.'

My mother, with her love of history, had once painted me a vivid picture of the roving groups of rough men hired to forcibly recruit or 'press' unwary locals into hard military service, coercing when they could, using violence when they wanted. The strength of Britain's navy had owed much to countless lads who'd woken up from one too many drinks to find themselves aboard a ship and far from land.

'Myself, I was too green to do much but fight with my

fists,' Daniel told me, 'but Fergal is quick in his mind and his speech and he got us both out of the way of the press gang and onto a fishing boat, and these years later he still thinks me fully incapable of taking care of myself. That, I suspect, is why he does not leave.' His smile grew more reflective as he looked at me, and then he added, 'Fergal does not easily attach himself to people, and his loyalty, once won, is won for life.'

'Then you are fortunate to have it.'

'I was not speaking of myself.' His tone was patient, like a tutor's. 'If you find that Fergal seems more out of temper, you should know 'tis not from anger, but because he has been worried for your welfare and is far too proud to tell you so.'

I was touched by the thought, and I promised to keep it in mind. 'Have I really been gone two days?'

'You have.'

I hadn't figured out the workings of travelling in time yet, beyond the fact that I appeared to leave my own time and return to it seamlessly, so however long I spent here I went back to the same moment I had left, to find that nobody had missed me.

But the rules seemed rather different at this end of the equation.

Daniel must have seen me frowning, because narrowing his gaze against an upward waft of smoke he asked, 'What is it?'

I explained, as best I could. 'It makes no sense,' was my complaint. 'It's just not logical, it's—' Then I saw that he was laughing at me and I stopped. 'What?'

'You will forgive me, but you've come across three

centuries and what concerns you most is that the times will not be matched?'

'What's wrong with that?'

'Well, if a pig came up to me one day upon the road, full dressed and wearing boots, and asked the way to Plymouth, I can promise you it would not be the colour of his buttons that would interest me.'

I saw his point, but couldn't help but add in my defence, 'It's only that I'd like to understand what's going on.'

'I know.' His eyes acknowledged that. 'Like yours, my mind would seek to know the science. But there are things in life that lie beyond our understanding. Why they happen, we may never learn. And yet they happen.'

In his eyes the light of laughter was now fading into something more like quiet curiosity. 'What would it change,' he asked me, 'if you understood?'

'I don't know. Likely nothing.'

'You would still be here.'

I had no argument for that, and so I didn't offer any.

Daniel's pipe was dying and he knocked the ashes from it. 'When I meet a wind I cannot fight,' he said, 'I can do naught but set my sails to let it take me where it will.'

I knew that he was right. Some forces could not be controlled, and that was just as true for hearts, I thought, as for a ship at sea. I met his gaze and said, 'I'm not much of a sailor.'

'Give it time,' was his advice. 'Mayhap you'll learn.'

Chapter Twenty-One

There were a lot of other things I had to learn before that.

Fergal had decided that, to guard against the chance I might come back again one day and find myself alone as I had done before, I ought to know the workings of the house and its surroundings, from the little plot of vegetables that sheltered in a terraced garden up behind the stables to the well close by the yard where they drew water.

Leaning over the lip of the stone well, I looked at my rippled reflection below. 'Is it any good for drinking?'

'Ay, if you and I were horses, maybe. Me now, I would rather meet my thirst with ale and cider.'

I'd have happily poured him a big glass of cider to soften his mood at the moment. He'd been brusque and short-tempered, as Daniel had warned me he might be, and if I hadn't known it was his way of showing worry I'd have taken it to heart. As it was, I found it touching, even flattering, that this fierce man had taken on the role of my protector so completely.

Turning from the well, he said, 'This water will not harm you, but you're best to keep to ale for drinking, anyway. You do remember where the ale is kept?'

I answered back obediently, 'In the cask beside the cellar steps.'

'And if the ale runs dry, the cider is . . . ?'

'To be protected at all costs,' I quipped, to see if I could make him smile.

He did, a little. But he wasn't fully satisfied until I'd answered properly and told him where the kegs of cider that he prized so much were hidden. Having done that, I asked, 'Does Jack really not know where they are?'

'He does not. And I'll thank you to leave him in ignorance.'

'But if you're away and he's here when I run out of ale . . .'

Fergal drily assured me there'd be little chance that I'd run out of ale with Jack in the house. 'Even if you did, he would be off down to the Spaniard with his cup and bowl, he would not need my cider. But yourself,' he said, 'you cannot leave Trelowarth without Danny or myself, so if the cider keeps you safe another day, so be it.'

Turning from the well he led me off again to what I hoped would be our final stop, because my legs were having trouble keeping up to Fergal's pace. Against the north wall of the stable block stood a small shed with a rickety roof.

'And your firewood is in here,' said Fergal, and shoved the door open to show me the tightly wedged stacks of split wood. 'Though with luck you'll not have to come all this way out for it. I'll leave a fair supply stacked in the scullery.'

When we went back to the house I discovered he'd already been hard at work in the scullery, arranging the food in the cupboard so that I'd have no trouble finding the things that I'd need to make one of his stirabouts. 'If we have cheese, which we usually do, it will be at the back in that tin there. And this,' he said, raising the lid of a small keg nearby and lifting a leathery long something out of it, 'this is salt beef. Bane of a sailor's existence, that is, but we always keep some for the *Sally*. I'll leave this lot here, then you'll need never fear you'll have nothing to eat.'

I took the length of salt-cured meat from him, feeling its strange texture, hardened like wood. 'And you *eat* this?'

'Well, not like that, no. Break your teeth if you tried. No, you boil it and soak it to draw out the salt, and then cook it with other things into a broth. Here, I'll make it for dinner and show you.'

He started off by showing me the way to use a tinderbox to light the fire, explaining as he went, and, while I doubted I could match his skill, at least it let me see the steps more closely than I'd seen them when the constable had done the task. And with the fire lit Fergal kept a close eye on me while he was cooking, to see I was paying attention. I was. Fergal's hands were the hands of a hard-working man, and his knuckles were scarred from a lifetime of fighting, but he cooked as deftly as any trained chef I had seen. A true man of abilities.

'Fergal?'

Turning around with his knife in his hand he asked, 'Ay?'

'Thank you.'

'For what?'

'Taking care of me. I've never had a big brother before.'

'Have you not?'

'No. I had an older sister, but she died this past winter.'

He looked at my face for a moment. 'God rest her soul.' He crossed himself respectfully and turned back to his work.

I asked him, 'You don't honestly have seven sisters, do you?'

'When did I say that I did?'

'You told the constable.'

'Well then, it's certain I told him the truth, for I'd never tell lies to the constable.'

I couldn't help smiling. 'Me neither.'

'See then,' he said with a nod of approval, 'and did I not say that you were an O'Cleary?'

The moment of companionship sat easily between us while the kettle on the hearth steamed with the scents of salted beef and boiling cabbages and carrots, and it struck me just how comfortable I had begun to feel here, even with the things I had to learn, the things I didn't know.

'And so the people at Trelowarth,' Fergal asked me, 'are they not your family, then?'

I took a minute to explain my whole connection to the Halletts, my relationships with Mark and Claire and Susan.

Fergal listened intently, as though he were storing the facts in his memory. 'And what do they think when you vanish from their time? Where is it you tell them you've gone?'

'They never know, so I don't have to tell them anything.

Things work a little differently at that end,' I explained. 'When I go back, it's like I've never been away, I step back into the same moment that I left.'

I watched him think this over. Daniel had been right about the quickness of his mind, he didn't miss much. 'But the last time you went back you were in different clothes.'

'I was.'

'And no one noticed?'

'I'd been walking on my own, there wasn't anyone to see me.' But the thought of clothes reminded me that, 'Daniel said I ought to give my other clothes to you, so you could hide them.'

'Did he, now? Well, bring them here then, and I'll see what I can do.'

And that was why, when Daniel came to join us in the kitchen several minutes later, he found Fergal deep in fascinated study of my jeans.

'You see now, Danny,' Fergal told him, barely glancing round, 'this is a work of genius, this is.' And he ran the zipper up and down to prove it. 'Look at that. I've never seen its like in all my years. And see this seam, with every stitch so even. Sure my own granny could never sew a seam like that, and she was known through all the county for her needlework, she was.' He smoothed the fabric with his roughened hand in wonder and appreciation. 'A pair of breeches as fine as this would last a man a good while. 'Tis a shame,' he said to me, 'that you are not a larger woman, else I could take these in trade for the trouble you've caused me.'

Daniel pointed out with flawless logic that if I had been a larger woman I would not have fit into the borrowed gowns. 'Then she would have no clothes and you would have a pair of breeches you could not wear for fear the constable might see them.'

Fergal shrugged. 'So let him see them. I could tell him they were made for me by seamstresses in Ireland, where all the finest fashions have their start.' But he'd already started folding up the jeans. My shirt had been a plain white T-shirt, which was slightly less exciting, though I saw him take note of the tag. ''Twas made in India. So are the trade routes open still, in your time?' Without waiting for an answer, he went on, 'Myself, I've never been to India. Jamaica, now, I've sailed there twice, but never yet to India.'

I was thinking, as he said that, of the black beach in Kerala on the southern coast of India, where I had gone to visit with Katrina on her holiday from filming in Mumbai. I felt the touch of Daniel's gaze and raised my own to meet it, but I only glimpsed the speculation in his eyes before he looked away respectfully and changed the subject.

With his head tipped slightly back, he sniffed. 'What the devil are you cooking, Fergal?'

'Beef broth.'

'And what are you using in place of the beef?'

Fergal sent him a suffering glance. ''Tis salt beef, so that Eva will know what to do with it.'

'Eating it,' said Daniel, 'would not be my first suggestion.'

'Are you wanting something purposeful to do?' asked Fergal drily. 'Because I was just saying now to Eva that we need a bit of firewood for the scullery, and if you have the time to speak your mind about my cooking, you could surely spare a bit of time for walking to the woodpile.'

Daniel smiled, and looked at me. 'Will you come?'

'To the woodpile?'

'It is a chore that can be made more bearable by company.'

I yielded to the smooth persuasion of his smile, and went out with him into the strong sunlight of the stable yard.

'Did Fergal show you where the well was?' Daniel asked me as we passed it.

'And the garden, and where to find things in the house. He even showed me where the cider was.'

'Did he indeed?'

I nodded. 'He wanted to be sure I wouldn't die of thirst if I ran out of ale.'

'And what if you ran out of cider, too? What then?'

'You wouldn't be away that long.'

'If all was well, we wouldn't, no. But many things can happen while a ship's at sea,' he said. After a moment's thought he carried on, 'There is one other place you would find ale if you had need of it, though 'tis not in the house and the only way down to it wants a sure foot and some courage.'

I gave a nod. 'The cave below the Cripplehorn, you mean. Yes, I—'

'What do you know of that?' he asked me, in a tone too casual.

I didn't see the need to lie. 'I read about it in a book, and then my friend who lives here . . . well, he used to play down there when he was little, so he took me down to show me what it looked like.'

'And what does it look like?'

I couldn't really tell if he believed me, but I said, 'It's mostly empty, only a few old barrels left, although I don't think they were yours.' I couldn't tell him that his dagger had been there, as well. I only told him, 'If it helps, the book did say that no one ever gave away your hiding place.'

We'd nearly reached the woodpile, but he stopped and turned to face me, and his eyes held open disbelief. 'The book says that?' He clearly found the thought improbable. 'It mentions me?'

I gave a cautious nod.

'By name?'

I tried remembering exactly. 'It didn't say your name. It said "the Butler brothers of Trelowarth".' I found his gaze too steady to meet comfortably.

'And why, pray, would it mention us at all?'

I shouldn't tell him anything, I knew. And yet I couldn't bear to have him look at me like he was looking now, as though he thought I'd made the whole thing up.

I took a breath. 'Because you were such well-known smugglers. Well, that is, you *used* to be well-known. The book was old.' I didn't tell him Jack would one day write a book himself. I thought that might be pushing things. 'It was really only a field guide, about birds and rocks and trees, with little bits of local history. All it said was you were smugglers, and the people here respected you, and that you used the cave below the Cripplehorn.'

Daniel stood a moment looking down at me, his eyes unreadable, and then he let it pass and looked deliberately to one side as though gathering his thoughts. When his eyes came back to mine, they weren't so hard.

'How did you come across this book, then?' There was something gentler in his voice, as well, that made me more aware of just how close to one another we were standing, there beneath the trees that edged the stable yard, in quiet shade.

I raised my chin and told the truth. 'I wanted to find out about you.'

'Did you? Well,' he teased, 'you should not trust the things you read in books. If there is something you would know, you've but to ask.'

The problem was, when he smiled down at me like that I found it difficult to phrase a simple question, or to speak at all. And anything I might have asked seemed unimportant, suddenly.

To my relief he looked away again. With slightly narrowed eyes he judged the movement of the clouds above our heads. 'We do have time, I think, to walk awhile.'

'But shouldn't we . . . the firewood, I mean . . . and Fergal's dinner—'

'Will be every bit as inedible an hour from now. Salt beef,' he promised, 'cannot be destroyed. A single piece of it would outlast any civilisation.'

And so I let him lead me past the woodpile, up the slope of field that lay beyond the stables and the ordered garden plots where Fergal grew his vegetables.

The wind blew wilder here, and whipped my skirts about my legs and made it hard to hear when Daniel spoke ahead of me. He had to turn his head to ask the question over. 'Do you ride?'

I told him that I did. Not all that well, but I could ride.

'Then I shall introduce you to my favourite mare, and

mayhap someday you may ride her,' he said. 'Come, the field's not far.'

I wasn't sure at first which field he meant. The hillside had been altered through the centuries so that I had to work to get my bearings here, and what I'd always known as garden plots with walls and hedges was now open land with long grass chased in ripples by the wind, and the dark of the woods lying off to my left. We climbed to the top of the hill where the road was. *That* still had the same shape, although it was more of a track than a proper road, rutted and grassy and curving in ways that had never made sense to me until this moment, when I saw the great tree that stood in its way.

The tree was an ancient one, oak from its shape and the way it stood spreading its limbs in defiance of any assault the winds wanted to make. The road, too, had run straight towards it until, clearly meeting its match in the tree, it had veered to the side and gone round it instead, curving off round the hill and away to St Non's while the tree held its ground as it had done for years, maybe hundreds of years. It looked stubbornly capable of standing there a few hundred years more, but I knew that it hadn't. This tree wasn't part of the grounds of Trelowarth that I knew. I'd never heard tell of it.

'Really?' said Daniel when I said as much to him. 'Was it cut down?'

'I don't know.' I would have to ask Oliver. He might have come across something about it, I thought, in his reading.

'There's no one round here would dare cut the Trelowarth Oak,' Daniel informed me. 'The old ways die hard in these parts, and a lone tree is still seen as sacred. An oak even more so. Ask Fergal sometime about oak trees,' he said with a smile. 'For all that he does not believe in witches, he does yet keep the old beliefs.'

The Irish and the Cornish and the Welsh were Celtic peoples, bound by their shared myths and superstitions, and I didn't doubt that Fergal's 'old beliefs' were not so different from Claire's grandmother's. I found myself curious, all of a sudden, to know just what Fergal *did* think about oak trees.

The leaves of a low branch brushed softly against my blown hair as I stepped from the field to the roadway with Daniel. The church lay behind us, sedately unchanged though its churchyard was smaller and lonelier looking, exposed on all sides with no sheltering woods and no stone wall built round it. I stole a quick backwards glance over my shoulder, but from where we were I could not see Ann Butler's grave.

Daniel saw me look behind. 'You've naught to fear,' he said. 'The road is lightly travelled at this time of day, and I am with you.' To reassure me further he slowed his steps so they matched my own and leisurely he walked close by my shoulder.

Round the bend again, we came to a long field on level land that had been fenced and gated. Through the grass there ran a darker line that marked the cut banks of a narrow stream that crossed the paddock, passed beneath the fence and underneath a wooden bridge set in the road before it carried on its way to feed the waterfall that tumbled down the Cripplehorn.

Daniel told me, 'This is where we turn the horses out to pasture when we are away from home.'

I'd guessed as much. The field was shaded well by trees, and with the running water and the green, abundant grass it made a perfect place for horses.

'They must hate to see the stables after this,' was my remark.

'Ay, I have little doubt they curse me when I come to fetch them in.'

There was just one horse in the paddock now, a bay mare who stood against the treeline at the far end of the field and eyed us both expectantly. And she did seem to be cursing Daniel when he whistled sharply to her now. Her head came up, but she stayed obstinately in her place of comfort by the trees.

He grinned, and whistled once again.

The mare stayed put, but I could hear the distant clopping of a horse's hooves responding to the call, then more hooves following and growing quickly nearer, coming briskly down the road. I turned, and Daniel moved a step towards me, and although I didn't see his hand move this time to his belt I knew he would have taken out his dagger and be waiting, just in case there might be danger.

There was no time for the two of us to move where we could not be seen. The horses were already at the turning of the road . . . and then they came around and crossed the little bridge in single file and we saw Jack on horseback, leading them.

Or so it seemed at first. Until I noticed that his hands were strangely still upon the horse's neck, and moments after that I saw the rope that bound them, and the warning in his face as he caught sight of us.

Behind him, with an air of satisfaction, rode the

constable. And with him came a shorter man whom I had never seen before, and half a dozen others who began to look uncomfortable as they caught sight of Daniel standing quiet by the roadside.

Daniel took a step that brought him close in front of me, so close that I could see the dagger's blade glint in his fingers where he held it very casually below his coat's turned cuff.

And then he stepped into the road and with his other hand reached out to catch the bridle of his brother's horse and bring it to a halt. 'Well, Jack,' he said, in the same tone he might have used if he had caught his brother coming home too drunk. 'And what is this?'

Chapter Twenty-Two

The answer came, not from Jack Butler, but the constable, who'd reined his horse up deftly just behind. ''Tis an arrest. And there will be another yet, if you do not let loose that horse.'

Daniel ignored the threat. 'What is the charge?'

'This merchant here,' – the constable inclined his head towards the shorter, rounder man behind him – 'was cruelly robbed upon the road but several days ago, and lost a purse of silver and a joint of mutton to your brother.'

The mutton. I recalled Jack's cheerful boast about the theft, and I could feel my heart sink suddenly inside me as I glanced at the indignant, unforgiving merchant's face. He was a thick-jowled man of middle age, his waistcoat stretched across a stomach that had seen its share of hearty meals, but though he looked a fool he did not look to be a liar, and his accusations would bear weight.

Jack looked less cheerful now, avoiding Daniel's eyes, his own eyes lowered to the rope that bound his wrists together. His character was normally so reckless that I wondered why he hadn't bolted anyway, and chanced his horse's speed against the constable's pursuit.

The constable was moving forward now, aware he had his foes against the wall and wanting only to enjoy it. With his boot a mere hand's-breadth from Daniel's shoulder, he looked down in mocking sympathy. 'And will you come to see your brother hang?'

I didn't breathe the whole time Daniel stood there with his gaze locked to the constable's. The calm had settled over him so evenly it seemed the very wind had lost its nerve and ceased to blow, and for that moment even I feared it would end in violence.

But he moved at last, a slight shift of his stance and nothing more, and for some reason that small movement was enough and I could breathe again.

He said, 'Where is your warrant?'

And just like that, the tables turned. I saw it in the briefest hesitation of the constable, and in the faces of the men behind him.

Daniel said, 'You surely have a warrant?'

'We are riding now,' the constable assured him, 'to obtain one from the justice of the peace. If you will kindly stand aside.'

But Daniel had already turned towards the merchant. 'Tell me, sir, where did this most distressing robbery take place, and when?'

The merchant, keen to share his story, named the date, and said, ''Twas early in the morning, so it was. The sun was barely up, and I had travelled all the night in this man's company.' He stabbed a finger through the air in Jack's direction. 'Offered me protection, so he did, and said he'd ride with me a ways because he knew these parts and knew the dangers of the roads, and so I let him ride beside my wagon. And at sunrise I complained of being weary and he told me it was safe for me to sleep, that we had passed the place of greatest danger and I would no longer need his aid.'

Daniel considered this, and gave a nod. 'And so you slept?'

'I did, sir. And when I awoke, I found he had repaid my trust by making off with one fine joint of mutton and my purse, sir.'

'A bold theft, indeed,' agreed Daniel. 'And bolder to do it by daylight, when he could more easily have overcome you at night, without fear of a witness. How did he subdue you, then?'

The merchant frowned. 'What?'

'Well, surely when you woke and saw him stealing your belongings, you did all you could to stop him. Did he strike you? He does look a man who might resort to violence.'

Jack, as though he thought his brother had gone mad, glanced back at Daniel with a dark expression, but it went unnoticed as the merchant's hard expression altered.

'No, he did not . . . that is, I was not awake . . .'

'Ah.' Daniel gave another nod. 'But how then did you see him take the mutton and your purse?'

The constable, a step ahead of where this line of questioning was leading, said impatiently, 'One does not need to see the thief in action to be sure that he has stolen.'

'Does one not?' asked Daniel, calm. 'I do apologise. 'Tis only that it seems to me this good man here might have been set upon by any rogue while he was sleeping, for in these parts there are many, I am sure you will agree, who would do mischief.'

The constable held his gaze. 'One or two, ay.'

'And as this merchant seems an honest man, I only seek to try his memory so that he may satisfy himself that he does not accuse the innocent.'

'The innocent?' The word all but exploded from the constable, as though he had been pushed beyond his limit.

Daniel looked at Jack. 'You will admit you rode beside this merchant's wagon through the night, and that you offered him protection?'

Jack's eyes settled on his brother's, wary. 'Ay, I did.'

'And when you parted ways, was he asleep?'

'He was.' Jack caught on slowly, adding, 'I was certain we had come past all the points where we might be accosted, and as I was keen myself to get back home I thought it safe enough to leave him there to carry on his way without me.'

Daniel turned back to the merchant. 'If you are convinced, sir, that this man did rob you, though you saw it not and could not swear an oath to it, by all means take your case before the Justice of the Peace.'

But he had sowed the seed of doubt. I felt a fleeting twist of sympathy for the merchant as I watched him wrestle with his own misgivings, trying to decide what he should do.

Then Daniel in one motion sheathed his dagger in his belt and drew a small bag from the lining of his coat as he went on to say, 'Whatever you decide, sir, I am sorry for the loss that you have suffered, and I would not have you leave here thinking all Polgelly men are thieves.' Holding out the soft bag, which looked weighted down with coins, he said, 'This likely will not match what has been taken from you, but perhaps it may restore your faith in those who live here.'

I watched the merchant take the purse from Daniel's hand and open it, and from his quick reaction I could tell that it contained more money than he had been robbed of. Quite a bit more, it appeared, because he closed it with a hurried gesture, squirrelling it tidily away into his own coat while the constable objected, 'Careful, Butler. You do seek to interfere too much.'

'I only seek to show good Christian charity to one who is in need of it.'

'By paying him with profits from your own illegal trade.'

The merchant interjected, 'Come now, come now, sirs, I would not be the cause of any argument between you.' Giving the front of his waistcoat a pat, he gave Jack a once-over. 'I do now confess I am not altogether convinced in my mind that this man was the culprit.'

The men who'd assembled behind, and who appeared to have been drawn into the whole affair to serve and aid the constable as his reluctant deputies, reacted now with unconcealed relief, from which I gathered none among them had been keen on taking Jack to see the Justice of the Peace.

I knew little of laws in this time, but I had vague recollections of reading at school about children who, in Queen Victoria's day, had been sentenced to hang for the theft of a loaf of bread, and that had been more than a hundred years later than this.

Jack, too, breathed his relief, though his cockiness showed in the half-bow he aimed at the merchant. 'I am in your debt, sir.'

'Not at all,' said the merchant. 'The fault was all mine.'

Daniel didn't allow that. 'An honest mistake, to be sure. Will you dine with us?'

'Dine with you?'

'Ay, as a show of our gratitude. My house does lie but a short distance in that direction.' He pointed, and the merchant after brief consideration gave a nod.

'I will, sir. Many thanks.'

The constable snorted. 'You fool. These men would play you like a fiddle, and that purse you have so lately won will be back in their hands by nightfall, mark me well.'

Which was as good as saying that the Butlers were both thieves and scoundrels, there in front of everyone, and Jack's temper flared. 'Then come and guard it for him, if you have a mind to.'

It was not an invitation, really, so much as a dare. I had the sense Jack Butler often said things without thinking first, his reckless nature making him as reckless with his words.

I watched the constable react, and saw him hold back his own anger in response and slyly turn things to his own advantage. 'Very well, then. I will dine with you as well. 'Tis very kind of you to offer.'

Daniel kept his own face neutral. To the other men, he said, 'I do regret we have not room enough for all of you to join us, but if you ride on now to Trelowarth House and say to Fergal that I've sent you he will find you ale to drink at least, and water for your horses.'

The men – there were five of them now I could count them – broke ranks for a moment to ride forward, splitting to both sides of the road as they came round the standing horses of the merchant and the constable and Jack. One man, an older man, stopped briefly beside Daniel.

'Thank you, Danny.' He inclined his head, and Daniel answered with a nod.

'Peter.'

''Twas not our doing,' the man said by way of apology, as he moved on and regrouped with the others who, safely past now, heeled their horses to quicken their pace as they carried on round the bend into the trees.

The silence they left in their wake had a dangerous edge.

Only the merchant seemed unaware of it, as his gaze shifted over to me. 'Mrs Butler,' he said with a gracious bow. 'I pray you will forgive me, as your husband has.'

The constable cut in, 'That is not Mrs Butler.' From his tone it seemed that the suggestion had offended him, and not for the first time I found myself wondering what his connection had been to Ann Butler.

Daniel let the comment pass, and made the introductions while Jack looked at me as though he had just noticed I was there.

'You're out of bed,' said Jack, with some surprise. Which

wasn't the best choice of words, but as the merchant's eyebrows lifted, Daniel saved my reputation with the simple statement, 'She has been ill these past days.'

I felt the keen appraisal of the constable. 'She does look well recovered.'

Jack did not agree. Whether from chivalry or from wanting to make up for his earlier comments to Daniel about me, he swung himself with hands still bound together from the saddle, landing lightly on his feet. 'Let Eva ride my horse. It is a fair walk back, and she will tire.'

He held his wrists expectantly to Daniel, who reached once more for his dagger and with one swipe sliced the ropes.

The tension that had been between the brothers when I'd overheard them in the stables was still there, and Jack avoided Daniel's eyes and called to me instead. 'Come Eva, let me help you to the saddle.'

But when I drew near the horse the hands that took my waist and lifted me were Daniel's, sure and strong. He sat me sideways, which was terribly uncomfortable and hard on my one hip, but I held on as best I could and tried to look the part while Daniel took the horse's bridle in his hand again and started walking.

To the merchant he said, 'Where would you be bound, sir?'

'For Lostwithiel.' He explained he would be there by now except the theft had made him break his journey at St Non's to sell some of his wares to have the means to live by. While the merchant told his story I saw Daniel slide a sideways glance accusingly at Jack, who kept his own gaze fixed with studied nonchalance upon the road ahead.

'Fortunately,' said the merchant, finishing his tale, 'the landlord of the Cross & Oak is, like yourself, a man of understanding and compassion. He let me have my room for no more than my promise I would pay him, and now thanks to you I can make good upon that promise.'

He patted the bulge of the purse in his waistcoat again while the constable sent him an unimpressed look.

'You'd do well to take care where you travel,' the constable warned. 'These are dangerous times here in Cornwall.'

'Dangerous times all over, sir,' was the merchant's reply. With a nod of agreement he said, 'Everywhere the countryside is verging on unrest, and every town is plagued with troubles. I've heard little these past months that does not touch upon the young Pretender's plans for an invasion.'

The constable asked him, in a calculated tone, 'And what do you perceive to be the people's mood when they do speak of it?'

The merchant shrugged. ''Tis none of my affair, sir, for I'm neither Whig nor Tory and I take no part of politics.'

'There are some here who take too great a part in it,' the constable remarked, his eyes on Daniel.

Daniel didn't bother looking round. He said, 'There are some I can think of who would rather have a king who was not only born in England but can speak the English tongue.'

The constable's eyes narrowed. 'Such talk comes close to treason.'

'Does it?'

'Ay, and with your kinsman up before the Lords for just such an offence, I should be watching what I said if I were you.'

The merchant looked from one man to the other, settling on Daniel with surprise. 'Your kinsman? Do you mean to say you are related to His Grace the Duke of Ormonde?'

Daniel nodded. 'Distantly.'

That impressed the merchant. 'A great man, the Duke of Ormonde. Very truly a great man, and I know several who did serve in his campaigns upon the Continent who feel the same. He brought us peace.'

Again a sound of rough amusement from the constable. 'A peace that served his own needs more than ours. More than Queen Anne's. He should be vilified, not honoured.'

'With respect,' the merchant said, 'those accusations—'

'—come from men of higher station than yourself and I,' the constable reminded him. 'From men who better stand to know the truth.'

Beside me, Daniel turned his head. 'And has the truth become the property of those who can afford it?'

The dark eyes of the constable held Daniel's with a challenge. 'Do you think yourself an equal to the House of Lords?'

'The House together? No, of course not. Man by man? That would depend,' said Daniel evenly, 'upon the lord.'

The constable smiled, but it wasn't a smile of amusement. 'Perhaps you'll have the chance to test yourself against them sooner than you think.'

The merchant took that as a joke and laughed. 'I see that we shall have a lively dinner conversation, sirs. 'Tis sure I do look forward to it.'

Still wearing that reptilian smile, the constable said, 'Let us hope O'Cleary's skills will stretch to feeding all of us.'

I caught the edge of Daniel's own smile as he looked away again. 'I shouldn't worry,' he replied. 'When I left Fergal he was cooking food that would fair satisfy a sailor.'

Chapter Twenty-Three

I would have paid a lot to see the constable eat salt beef, but I didn't have the chance to. When we reached Trelowarth Daniel passed me solemnly to Fergal who in his turn made a show of fuss about my health and took me upstairs to my room, supposedly to rest.

He closed the door behind us quietly. 'Never mind, I've had the story from the men who came before, but in your own words tell me what you saw and what was said.'

I told him, speaking low so we would not be overheard, and Fergal nodded once or twice and cursed Jack Butler's rashness in that half-forgiving way reserved for family members who bring trouble in their wake. 'You lock the door and stay in here until myself or Danny comes to fetch you.' Giving my shoulder a pat of reassurance, he went out and waited briefly in the corridor until he'd heard me lock the door behind him.

Left alone I looked around the room and weighed my options. So far it had been a crazy day. I'd risen earlier than usual this morning in my own time, and a part of me was tempted by the bed and by the knowledge that I likely had at least an hour to spend in here alone before the merchant and the constable had finished with their dinner and were gone.

But then, I wasn't confident I *could* sleep while the constable was in the house. I felt too much on edge.

The problem was there wasn't much else I could do here while I waited. There was nothing to tidy and no books to read. I was stumped till I noticed the tinderbox set on the mantelpiece. Not that I needed a fire, it was warm in the room, but the starting of fires was a skill I still needed to work on, and practising would at least keep me distracted from what might be happening downstairs.

This tinderbox, like the one in the kitchen, was made of plain metal and held a worn flint and a ring of hard steel on a soft pile of bits of charred cloth. Kneeling on the hearth, I tried to focus and remember what Fergal had showed me that morning, the steps that he had taken.

I still found it much harder than it should have been, and clearly I was doing something wrong, because this time I couldn't even raise a proper spark. It proved a frustrating endeavour, but it *did* help pass the time. Before I knew it, I heard footsteps in the corridor and Fergal called my name outside the door.

I set the flint and steel aside and, standing stiffly, went to let him in.

'Our visitors are gone, so you can come downstairs again when you've a mind to. Just be careful how you go, for there's a wee bit of a storm wind blowing down there at the moment.'

I could tell what he was getting at the second that I stepped onto the landing. Jack's voice, raised in anger, carried clearly up the stairs.

'Have I not told you that I'm grateful? Should I bow to you and kiss your boots as well?'

'We keep a code, Jack.' Daniel now, his own tone dangerously level. 'We have always kept a code. We do not take what is not ours.'

''Tis noble of us, surely, but—'

'You robbed a man.' He fired the accusation like an arrow, straight across his brother's argument. 'We are not thieves.'

A silence followed.

Fergal, who had no doubt heard the brothers arguing like this before, kept walking down the stairs, but I stopped halfway down, unsure, not really wanting to intrude.

Jack's voice dropped slightly, but they'd moved into the kitchen now and I could still hear every word. 'King George might not agree with that.'

'The Prince of Hanover is not my rightful king,' was Daniel's stubborn answer, 'and for that I owe him nothing, for a free trade is a fair trade. What we sell we have already bought and paid for in good faith, we have not stolen it from strangers who can ill afford the loss.' I heard him exhale with impatience. 'Have you never stopped to wonder why, in spite of Creed's advances and his bribery, not one among the people of Polgelly has betrayed us? 'Tis because they do respect us, Jack. They know that we are honest men.'

'Well, *you* are,' Jack acknowledged. 'I myself have never

owned that reputation. Nor, in truth, have I considered it worth owning. Being honest cannot furnish me with all I want.'

'And will that make you happy, having everything you want?'

The answer came back with defiance. 'I will let you know.'

A hand came gently round my elbow. Fergal had come back up the few stairs to where I stood. 'Come on now, they are only talking.'

'I think they want privacy.'

He seemed amused at that. 'And can you hear them where you're standing now?' There was no need for me to answer, and he gave a knowing nod. 'If they were caring about privacy, I promise you they'd talk where they would not be heard. Besides, I think the worst is over.'

He was right. We came into the kitchen to find both the brothers in a kind of stand-off, like two soldiers on opposing sides who'd used up all their ammunition but weren't ready to step off the battlefield.

They noticed Fergal's entrance more than mine.

Daniel asked him, 'Fergal, will you tell Jack there are things in this life greater than himself?'

To which Jack countered, 'Fergal, will you kindly tell my brother that I suffer from a weaker moral nature than his own, and so he should not hold me to his standard?'

Fergal looked from Daniel to Jack and said drily, 'I had rather tell the pair of you to mind that there's a lady present. And,' he said to Jack, 'if you think Danny's yelling at you for the theft alone, then you're a greater fool than I'd have known you for. He feared you would be hanged, you flaming idiot, and him not able to do aught but stand aside and watch. He'll never tell you that himself, but there's the reason.' Glancing round at Daniel he said, 'And you know it, too, so you can stop pretending you're so hard.'

The fight drained out of Jack, first, and he looked across at Daniel as though looking for some proof of Fergal's statement. 'Were you truly worried?'

Daniel asked him, 'Were you not?'

Jack shrugged, attempting to look brave. 'A jury would have set me free.'

'Creed did not mean to use a jury,' Daniel said, and then he raised his own broad shoulders in a shrug and added lightly, 'And finding another first mate for the *Sally* would not be a simple task.'

'First mate?' Jack grinned a challenge. 'You meant to say "captain", I'm sure.'

But the tension was broken, the unspoken bond of affection restored.

Fergal passed through into the dining room and returned with a bottle of claret and cups and, having settled both Butler brothers at the kitchen table with the bottle there between them, he got down to work cleaning up after the dinner, with me as his helper.

I scraped and washed the dishes while he wiped them and returned them to their places, making sure that I was watching so I'd know the spots myself.

And all the while I listened to Jack's story of his capture in St Non's.

Jack had gone to the inn, as he'd said, to enquire after Wilson. He'd met with a friend there who'd stood him a drink. 'We did pass the time merrily,' Jack said. ''Twas then that the merchant himself must have seen me and gone out in search of a constable, and Creed being there in the town he replied. He didn't dare set a foot in the inn, though. He has better sense. Nor indeed did he take me when I stepped out into the street, for again there would be witnesses, and doubtless men among them who'd have come to my defence.'

'Where did he take you, then?' asked Daniel.

'In the wood, before the mill. It is a lonely stretch of road, that, and he fell upon me in a proper ambush with a cudgel, like the coward that he is.'

'A cudgel?'

'Ay.' Jack gave the bruised back of his head a rueful rub, in memory. 'You do not think I'd let myself be bound without a fight, if I were conscious, surely? No matter who it was doing the binding, nor how many men he had gathered around him.'

Fergal, who'd already talked to the men who had been with the constable when they'd stopped in at the house, gave a nod and said, 'Ay, well, they would have been there from their duty to the law and not their loyalty to Creed, I'll warrant. Likely they were just as pleased as Jack was to see you there by the roadside, Danny.'

Daniel's thoughts had travelled back a few steps. Tipping the bottle of claret he emptied the dregs into his cup and turned to his brother again. 'So, your time in St Non's . . . was it worth all the trouble?'

Jack met his gaze squarely. 'Did I find out aught about our Mr Wilson, you mean? Ay, I did.' With a pause for a quick drink himself, he went on, 'His true name is Maclean. And the servant he travelled with did call him

"Colonel Maclean" once or twice, says my friend.'

Daniel smiled and relaxed.

'Do you not find it telling that he did not use his given name with us?'

'All who are close to this venture do guard their true names out of caution,' was Daniel's reply to his brother. 'But Colonel Maclean is a good name to have, Jack, for that is the name of the duke's private secretary.'

'So he is on our side, as he claims.'

'Ay. Indisputably.'

'I hope that you are right,' said Jack. He still looked unconvinced, but having just patched up one quarrel with his brother he did not appear to be in any rush to start another. He set down his empty cup. 'This wine has given me a thirst for something stronger,' he confessed. 'I think I will go down to try the Spaniard's rum.'

Fergal, beside me, turned round in disbelief. 'You know that Creed will be more keen than ever for your blood, now.'

'He will not try a second time today.' Jack's tone was certain. 'And the lads will gladly see me safely home again this evening.'

Daniel didn't raise an argument. But when his brother left the house, I saw his face and read the worry on it.

Silence fell again upon the kitchen, and to break it I asked, 'Who is the Spaniard?'

Fergal's eyes made that familiar crinkle at their corners. ''Tis not a who, but a what,' he corrected. 'The Spaniard's Rest, down by the harbour.'

A pub, I thought, giving a nod of my own. 'Where by the harbour?' I asked.

Fergal told me, and I said, 'In my day we call it the Wellie. The Wellington.'

'What sort of name is that, then?'

How could I explain to them without revealing details of the wars that were to come – the Duke of Wellington, Napoleon, and Waterloo? I only said, 'He was a famous soldier, Arthur Wellesley, Duke of Wellington. A hundred years from now. A lot of names were changed to honour him.'

But Fergal still preferred 'The Spaniard's Rest', and said so. With a sideways look at Daniel, he said, 'And where are you off to, then?'

Daniel had stood to his full height and was stretching his shoulders a little bit wearily, his one hand moving in that automatic gesture to his belt to see his dagger was in place. 'To keep an eye on Jack.'

'He would not thank you for it, Danny.'

'Perhaps not.'

'Then sit down, you great idiot. Creed wants your own blood more than he craves Jack's, and you know it.'

Daniel's silence acknowledged the fact as he reached for his hat.

'Danny . . .' Fergal tried again.

'He is my brother,' Daniel said, as though that answered everything.

And Fergal, seeing that there was no winning, sighed. 'Well, take your sword, at least.'

Daniel shook his head. 'There'd be no room to draw it, in the Spaniard.' But I noticed that he tucked a pistol in his belt as well before he left us, and I couldn't help but wonder just what sort of crowd went drinking at the Spaniard's

Rest. A rougher clientele, I reasoned, than I would have found in the Polgelly pubs of my own time.

'They'll both wind up dead by the roadside,' was Fergal's black prediction, as he gave the fire on the hearth a savage stir with the poker, 'and Creed will come and say it is an accident, he will, and I'll be left to kill the bastard with my own two hands.'

I braved his blackened mood to ask a question. 'Fergal?'

'Ay?'

'Why does the constable want Daniel's blood?'

Fergal set the poker back in place and I could sense his hesitation, so I tried to help him.

'It can't be just the free-trading,' I said, 'because I'm sure he makes a profit from that, doesn't he?'

His mouth twitched in the way it always did when I'd amused him. 'Ay, he does.'

'So I'm assuming that it's personal.' I cleared my throat and asked him, 'Does it have to do with Ann?'

He slowly turned his head. 'Why would you think of that?' But I could see from his expression that I'd hit the mark. 'What did Creed tell you?'

'Nothing. No, it's just . . . oh, I don't know. The way he sometimes looks at me. He doesn't like to see me wear her clothes.'

'Well now, the only one who has a say in that is Danny,' Fergal said. 'And he's not bothered by it.'

I wasn't sure I'd have agreed with that, entirely, but instead of arguing the point I asked, 'Was he in love with her? Constable Creed, I mean.'

'Love?' Fergal's mouth twisted slightly, a grimace instead

of a smile. 'Not the word I'd have used for it, no. Not what Ann would have called it herself, neither. No,' he said, looking away, 'he was Ann's brother.'

That one I hadn't seen coming. 'Her brother?'

'They shared the same father, though Creed's mother died before he was grown halfway to manhood. He took little notice, they say, of his father's new wife, or of Ann. Not at first. But as Ann grew, he started to take an unnatural interest.' He spat in the flames. ''Twas a kind of obsession. An evil one. Smothered her with it, he did. Couldn't bear it if she looked at anyone else.'

'And she looked at Daniel.'

'She did, ay. And Danny looked back.'

I thought about this. 'So I'm guessing the constable wasn't too pleased when they married.'

'He was not. But see, Ann had a mind of her own, and she did what she wanted. She feared Creed herself at times, but she would never have shown it.' He glanced at me, and this time there was nothing hard behind his smile. 'You share that with her, anyway – the both of you too proud to let your fear show when you feel it.'

'I'm not proud at all.' I met his gaze with honesty. 'When the constable's anywhere near me, I'm scared to death.'

Fergal's face softened. 'Well now, you needn't be. He'll have to come through myself first to get to you, and after me there's still Danny left standing, and he's not so easy to get by.'

'So long as he's not lying dead by the roadside,' I pointed out, remembering his earlier prediction.

Fergal shrugged aside the words. ''Twas only myself talking, that was. You pay it no heed, now.'

I did try to take his advice.

Hours later, alone in my bed, I tried focusing on the soft sounds of the sleeping house – the scuttle of mice through the walls and the creak of the beams in the ceiling above me, and Fergal's snores rattling down the long corridor. I tried telling myself that if Fergal was so unconcerned about things that he was able to sleep, well then, I should be able to sleep, too. But I couldn't shake off my worries.

The images rose in a taunting progression, dissolving to worse ones of Daniel approaching the dark shadowed trees of The Hill with his unhurried stride, to be met by an ambush as Jack had been, beaten and bound while the constable looked on with cruel satisfaction . . .

I turned over sharply to stop my imaginings, tugging the blankets with me as I rolled on to my side. The weather had changed, growing cooler and damp, but I'd left the windows halfway open anyway, so I'd be able to hear any noise from the road. There was no wind tonight, and instead of the rush of the leaves and the rattle of window-glass, I could hear nothing right now but the hoot of an owl from the woods, and the slumbering roll of the waves on the shingle below the black cliffs. Now and then something made a faint sound, some small animal, maybe, that rustled the grass with its passing, and after that silence again and that horrible stillness that seemed to be waiting.

And when, after what felt like hours, I finally heard the shuffle of approaching footsteps, my rush of relief was short-lived. The steps sounded wrongly uneven, and in those first moments the horrible images rose once again and I half-thought that Daniel *had* met with the constable's men, and was staggering wounded now up the long hill from Polgelly.

I bolted from the bed, taking the top blanket with me to wrap round my shoulders for warmth like a shawl, but by the time I reached the window he'd gone past already.

From the floor below I heard the door swing open and slam shut as though it had been kicked. And then a dreadful clattering as though he'd fallen over.

I was halfway to my own door when I heard a burst of laughter, and Jack's cheerful voice so slurred with drink I couldn't catch the words. I couldn't catch Daniel's reply, either, but the deep quiet tone of his speech reassured me and made me relax. He was only bringing Jack home. He was safe.

And the reason his footsteps had sounded unsteady outside became obvious as the men started to climb the stairs – Jack must have been so drunk that he could barely stand, and from the swearing going on I gathered it was taking a bit of work for Daniel to keep his brother upright.

'Left foot . . . *left* foot. There you go,' said Daniel.

Jack hushed him with an exaggerated 'Shh,' and, 'do you want to wake the house?' And then he fell into another fit of laughter.

Something slammed against my door with an almighty thump and scuffle and the laughter stopped abruptly.

Daniel swore.

I pulled my door half-open and looked out into the corridor to find Jack lying senseless like a barrier in front of me and Daniel reaching down to take Jack's shoulders in a firm grip as he hauled his brother upright.

The smells of a night at the pub hadn't changed much

in three hundred years. Rank tobacco and hard liquor mingled in all the stale scents that assailed me, and Jack was so completely gone that I decided I'd be safe to speak. Keeping my voice low, I asked Daniel, 'Is he all right?'

Briefly startled, he glanced round. 'What? Oh, he's fine. You can go back to bed,' he assured me. 'I'll have him out of your way in a minute.'

I pulled my door all the way open and folded my arms in the warmth of my blanket-shawl, looking at Jack, who had slumped to the side again and would have fallen if not for his brother's strong arm. 'Are you sure he's all right? He looks sort of . . . well, sort of . . .' The word 'dead' came to mind, but I stopped short of actually saying it.

'Ay,' Daniel told me, 'I know how he looks, but there's no need to worry. I've seen him look worse.'

'If you say so.' I would have gone back in my room, but Jack's eyes had come open, and from his suspended position he stared at me, trying to focus his thoughts.

'Eva?'

Damn, I thought. He'd heard me speaking. Heard my voice.

Jack pushed clear of his brother's hands, making an effort to stand on his own, his expression incredulous. 'Eva,' he said, 'you can—'

That was the most he got out before losing his balance again. He swayed once and pitched forward to land like a fallen log, stretched on the carpet before me, unconscious.

I stood in my doorway, not sure what to say, feeling awful I'd opened my mouth in the first place, and knowing that I should have stayed in my room and just let them go by. I watched Daniel, waiting, expecting a lecture.

And after a moment he thoughtfully raised one hand, rubbing the back of his neck. Then giving a nod to his brother's prone figure, he said, 'There now, didn't I tell you I'd seen him look worse?'

Which was so far from what I had thought he would say that it caught me off guard, and I laughed without thinking.

Which caused us more trouble.

Chapter Twenty-Four

'What the bleeding Jesus are you doing?' Fergal's exasperated words shot down the passageway like shrapnel as he came towards us, shrugging on his shirt and looking none too pleased to have his sleep disturbed. 'As if a man in his condition is a sight a woman needs to see,' he chastised Daniel, firing him a dark look as he nodded at Jack's crumpled form. 'What were you thinking, Danny, dragging Eva from her bed at this hour?'

I thought of stepping in to say that I'd already been awake, but Fergal didn't look in any mood to hear it and Daniel didn't need me to defend him. He stood calm against the onslaught, bending down again to lift his brother up and sling him senseless half across one shoulder.

Fergal studied Jack, frowning, and asked, 'Was he into the rum?'

'Ay.'

'And fighting, I see.'

I looked at Jack, too. In the dark I had missed seeing how the one side of his face was all bruised.

'Well,' said Daniel, 'I would think that was for reputation more than anything. 'Twas a wound to his pride, being taken by Creed's men in daylight – he purposely looked for a fight at the Spaniard to show that he was not so weak.'

'Ay, for he's looking the picture of strength, so he is, at the moment.'

'He won the fight,' said Daniel.

'Was he standing when he did it?'

Daniel smiled at that. 'He was. He was using his feet well enough till we came up the stairs just now. Then he fell.'

Fergal assured us he'd heard it. 'The same as I heard you two laughing. And what would have happened if Jack had heard Eva?'

'He already had,' Daniel said. ''Twas an accident.'

Fergal shot a glance between us, swore beneath his breath, and raised his shoulders as though bracing for a load before the movement altered slightly to a shrug. Resigned, he told us, 'Well, there's nothing to be done for it. With luck the drink will keep it from his memory.' Stepping closer he expertly shifted Jack's weight from Daniel's back to his and said, 'I'll see him to his room myself,' and waved off Daniel's protests with, 'You've done enough already.'

There was no arguing with Fergal, when he'd set his mind to something.

Daniel let him go, and turned to me instead.

I said, 'I'm really sorry.'

'You did nothing wrong. And Fergal is not truly angry, he is only—'

'Worried. Yes, I know.'

I'd started shivering a little and my voice had changed because of it, and Daniel looked beyond me to the darkness of my bedroom.

With a slight frown he remarked, 'You have no fire.'

'I didn't think I'd need one when I went to bed, it only got cold afterwards, and Fergal was asleep by then, and I'm afraid I'm not too good yet with the tinderbox,' I said. 'I know the theory, but it never seems to work for me.'

'It only takes a bit of practice. Shall I show you?'

I was torn. On the one hand I was cold, and that was obvious. Not only would a fire be very welcome, but it probably would seem a little odd if, after standing here and shivering and telling him I couldn't start a fire myself, I told him not to bother. But the problem was that if I told him yes, then he would come into my room and I would have to try to act as though I weren't the least affected by it, and if I was already this nervous and aware just standing near him in the doorway, who knew what kind of a fool I might make of myself if I had to stand next to him here in my bedroom. At night. In the dark. But there really was no other answer to give, so I told him, 'Yes, please.'

Daniel must have been into the rum himself, down at the Spaniard. I caught the faint scent of it on his breath as he stepped into the room, but the drink didn't seem to have had an effect on him. Free of Jack's weight he moved surely and easily, taking the tinderbox down from the mantel and crouching beside the cold hearth of my fireplace. I followed, and did likewise.

Through the window on the eastern wall the moonlight cast a slanting square of pale light onto Daniel's hands, so I could see what he was doing.

Choosing a piece of charred cloth from the box he set it on the hearth and said, 'You hold the steel like this.' He slid his fingers through the oval ring until it reached his knuckles, then made a fist to secure it. 'And the flint in your other hand, and strike the two together, thusly.' Steel met stone, a sharply ringing sound, and raised a single spark that scudded sideways on the hearth and quickly died.

He held his hand out, straightening his fingers in the steel ring so that I could take it from him. 'Try it now.'

I hesitated. 'Couldn't you . . . ?'

''Tis better learnt by doing,' he insisted, with his hand still stretched toward me, waiting.

Silently I took the steel, amazed at how that brief and sliding contact of our fingers made my insides leap. The steel itself was cold but where he'd held it I could feel faint warmth, and shifting my own grip I tried to hold on to that small sense of shared contact while he handed me the flint.

I tried to strike the two together in the way he had, but my attempt was clumsy. Adjusting the angle at which I was striking, I tried again.

'Patience,' he said. 'It is never done quickly.'

'I'm learning that.' The edge of my frustration made my words come out more sharply than I'd meant them to, and Daniel's own tone grew indulgent, in the way an expert tries to make an amateur feel better.

'You'll soon have the way of it,' he told me. As my efforts went on he asked, 'What do you use in your own time, then?'

'Matches.'

'Matches?' I'd somehow astonished him.

'What's wrong with matches?'

'Nothing, if you seek to fire a cannon, but I would not think them practical for household use.'

I paused for a moment to send him a puzzled frown. 'Sorry? I mean, what do you call a match?'

He described what a match was, in detail, and smiling I nodded with new understanding.

'We'd call that a fuse,' I said. 'No, modern matches are like . . .' I tried to remember what he called the match-like lengths of tightly twisted paper that they used here to transfer a flame from one source to another. Spills, that's what they were. 'Well, they're like little spills,' I told him, 'only with their ends dipped in chemicals that self-ignite when you strike them on something rough.'

'Indeed.' I'd forgotten that he had a very scientific mind that would find certain things intriguing. 'Spills that light themselves,' he mused. 'What are the chemicals you use to make this happen?'

'I don't know. I . . . ow!' I'd hit the flint too wildly and the steel had bashed my thumb instead. I took a breath against the sudden pain and said, 'You see? I'm hopeless.'

He fell silent for a moment while he watched me in the darkness. Then his hands reached out to close around mine calmingly. His quiet voice assured me, ''Tis not such a complicated thing.'

I couldn't have replied if I had wanted to. The breath I'd drawn had somehow lodged within my chest and I could only sit there being glad that in the dark he wouldn't see the foolish way that I'd reacted to his touch.

He carried on, 'It wants some effort, yes, and patience, but then . . .' Tightening his hold he moved my hands for me, his fingers curving slightly round my knuckles and the steel. '. . . but then, what in this life that is of any worth does not?'

I couldn't answer that one, either. *Get a grip*, I urged myself, but Daniel's touch was sending all my senses into overdrive. He'd shifted closer in the dark until our shoulders almost brushed, until his words came close against my ear when he said, 'If you give them time, the flint and steel will make a spark. They cannot help but do so.'

I knew just how they were feeling. Flint and steel were not the only things in this room striking sparks off one another, though I doubted Daniel noticed the effect that he was having on me. He was only being nice, I told myself. For all that he might flirt with me from time to time by daylight, that was all it ever was with him – flirtation – and he was too much the gentleman to try the same game on with me here in the darkness of my bedroom, at this hour, with us alone.

If he was sitting close to me it was because he had to sit that close to hold my hands the way he needed to, and that touch was itself a light and helpful one, designed to show me what to do and nothing more.

I was being a terrible student, I knew. My head bent lower still, my focus narrowing more fiercely on the task as I tried shutting out the knowledge of his nearness. But it wasn't any use. Each time he breathed, the faintly mingled scents of rum and pipe tobacco warmly brushed my hair, and it occurred to me that if I turned my own head just a little bit towards him, we'd be close enough to . . . close enough to . . .

'There,' he said.

From our joined hands a shower of small sparks cascaded to the hearth, and two of them fell squarely on the piece of charred cloth kindling where they glowed like tiny eyes against the dark.

Releasing my hands, Daniel bent forward, shielding the cloth with his cupped hands while he breathed on the growing sparks. They glowed more surely now, their reddish light cast upwards to illuminate the hard edge of his jawline. And then suddenly the light turned golden, dancing up between his fingers as though he'd created it by magic. When he took his hands away there was a proper curling flame along the charred cloth.

'You see? 'Tis as I said. A simple thing,' he told me.

Taking up a bit of splintered wood he held it to the cloth until it caught the fire as well, before he carefully positioned it beneath a larger length of log.

I found my voice. 'And what's the trick to doing that?'

'There is no trick. 'Tis only patience, once again.'

I watched him while he crouched there by my hearth and brought the fire to life with expert and unhurried movements, shifting this bit here and that bit there and sitting back to wait for the result, his focus idle on the flames.

I found I couldn't take my eyes from him. We were no longer touching but I still could feel his hands on mine, and still my heart was beating much more loudly than it should have been.

Each bit of wood that caught the spreading fire on the hearth threw more light out to chase the shadows from our corner of the room, but I saw nothing more than Daniel's now familiar features, nothing more than that, and I could only sit and stare like some infatuated schoolgirl.

A simple thing, he'd said, and so it was. A random meeting and a touch – that's all it took to make a spark that could, with care and time, become a flame . . .

'Here, try it for yourself,' said Daniel, shifting to make space for me and holding out a sturdy length of stick. 'Or do you fear to burn your fingers?'

My imagination could have read a double meaning in those words of his, but pushing those romantic fancies firmly to one side I met the challenge in his face and took the stick from Daniel's hand and concentrated on the hearth until the fire leapt to the largest log and raised a dancing blue along its length.

Approving, Daniel turned his head to me and I could see those flames reflected in his smiling eyes.

I should have looked away. I should have smiled back and looked away, but the emotion I'd been feeling surfaced suddenly, betraying me before I could conceal it, and whatever he had been about to tell me fell forgotten in the silence as the smile in his eyes took on a faintly puzzled aspect, and then finally shuttered over into something that I couldn't read.

The large log cracked and settled on the smaller ones beneath it, and I pulled my gaze away and strove for something normal. 'So,' I said, with no idea what came after that.

After a moment Daniel filled the pause himself. 'You have your fire,' he said, and standing to his full height stretched his shoulders.

I stood too, before he had a chance to offer me a helping

hand. I didn't trust my own reactions to his touch just now. Lowering my head I mumbled, 'Thank you', and I would have stepped away except my foot caught in the trailing blanket I'd wrapped round me and I half-tripped as I tried to pass him.

Daniel moved to steady me – a gentlemanly gesture, just one hand around my arm, but all that did was knock me more off balance.

'Sorry,' I said, putting out both hands from instinct.

He'd reached out as well. My fingers landed on his chest as his clamped firmly round my elbows and I closed my eyes without exactly knowing why. Maybe because I was trying to keep my composure, to behave like a twenty-first century woman instead of some swooning Victorian heroine, to not let him see just how incredibly, hopelessly, helplessly hard I was falling in love with him.

'Eva.'

Opening my eyes, I met his own and found them not quite as unreadable as they had been before.

In fact, they weren't unreadable at all.

We looked at one another for so long I started wondering if time, instead of flinging me from place to place, had stopped completely. The air grew charged between us with a thousand things unsaid, and with a growing sense of wonderment I thought, *He feels it, too. My God, he feels the same way I do.*

And he did. I sensed it in the subtle change in how he held me, in the way his fingers shifted on my arms, and all at once I felt uncertain in a way I'd never felt before. I wanted him to kiss me and I feared it at the same time without really knowing why. I felt a mix of joy and dread and everything between, as though someone had thrown a switch and scrambled all my circuits.

When his hands slid to my shoulders I believe I held my breath; and then he took hold of the edges of the blanket that had slipped and with a careful touch rewrapped me in the woollen folds, his features set in studied concentration as he crossed the blanket's ends and tucked them under.

There was an instant just before he let me go when I felt sure he meant to say something, but in the end he only gave a nod. 'Good night,' he said, his measured tone the same as it had ever been.

The doorway that connected his room to my own stood partway open and I watched him cross towards it. Halfway through with his hand on the latch he turned back to say over his shoulder, 'And Eva?'

It astonished me I had a voice at all. 'Yes?'

'Lock your door.'

With which advice he pulled it shut behind him, leaving me hugging the blanket around me and feeling a warmth that had nothing to do with the fire.

Chapter Twenty-Five

'You're in a rare fine mood this morning.' Fergal somehow made that seem an accusation. I had found him at the far end of the yard beside the stables, chopping firewood, and although he hadn't asked to have my company I'd plonked myself down happily upon a nearby log to watch. He swung the axe so hard it cleaved the length of wood in one blow and stuck deep into the broad scarred stump beneath, so that he had to wrest it out again. As he straightened he glanced sideways at me, openly suspicious. 'What's the cause of it, I wonder?'

'I'm just happy.'

And I was. Almost ridiculously happy, in a way that couldn't be stamped out by anything. Not Fergal's grumbling, nor the gnawing in my stomach that reminded me I hadn't eaten breakfast, nor the fact the sun lay hidden by a bank of cheerless cloud. The world was beautiful this morning, because Daniel Butler liked me.

I'd replayed the moment several times since waking, to be sure, and every time I had replayed it I'd been more convinced it hadn't been imagined. He had liked me. And he'd wanted me. And that – to use a phrase he'd used himself – was a beginning.

So this morning seemed a miracle, no matter what the weather or the moods of those around me, or the fact that Daniel wasn't even here.

He'd gone out just after daybreak. I knew because I'd been awake myself, my own mind racing, and I'd heard him walking back and forth across the creaking floorboards in the next room, heard him twice approach the locked connecting door, then stop, and turn away again. And in the end he had gone out and down the stairs and in a little while I'd heard the sound of hoofbeats passing from the stables to the road, and they had faded up the hill and left the wind alone behind.

That same wind brushed my face now as I looked at Fergal. Jack had been asleep and snoring loudly when I'd passed his door upstairs on my way out, and at this distance from the house there wasn't much chance of my being overheard, but still I kept my voice as quiet as I could when I asked, 'Do you know where Daniel's gone this morning?'

'No.' The axe swung down again as Fergal shot another glance my way that held more interest than the first. 'There's no one tells me anything these days, it seems.'

The axe stuck in the stump again and this time when he yanked it free he turned the blade and ran his thumb across a small nick in the metal, frowning.

'Is it broken?' I asked.

'Sadly, no. 'Tis indestructible, this relic. It belonged to Danny's uncle, and is doubly as cantankerous.'

I smiled at the thought of Fergal being bested by a thing as stubborn as himself, and then I thought of something else, and asked him, 'What was Daniel's uncle's name? Was he a Butler, too?'

'A Pritchard. Why?'

'I only wondered. There aren't many Butler graves up in the churchyard, that's all, only Ann's and—' Just in time I caught myself and stopped before I gave away a bit of knowledge Fergal shouldn't have. Not that I knew how Jack had died, or when, except that it would happen twenty years or more from now, but still . . .

Fergal, true to form, missed nothing. 'Have you walked over my grave as well?'

'Fergal.'

Setting more wood on the stump, he shrugged. 'You needn't fear. I've no great wish to know my future. No man should.' Then a thought seemed to strike him. He glanced at me sideways. 'Nor should anyone, I'm thinking, know what lies in store for someone else, for that would be a burden, would it not?' His eyes met mine with understanding. 'Take this whole rebellion, now, that Danny's got himself involved in. If you were to know that it would fail and could not tell us so, I'm guessing that would cause you to be troubled in your mind.'

He knew already, I could see that. He knew as surely as I did that nothing would come of the venture.

'And,' he said, 'if that were how you felt, I'd have to tell you not to waste your worries. Anyone with any wits at all knows well enough the Duke of Ormonde cannot carry through his plans.' He turned his head away and calmly spat upon the ground, a gesture that I took to be a sign of his opinion of the duke. 'And Danny knows it, too, believe me.'

'Then why does he . . . ?'

'Why does he take part in it?' He shrugged. ''Tis how he's made, and how he reasons things. To Danny, knowing that the battle will not end the way he wishes does not make it any less worthwhile to fight.' He swung the axe with forceful certainty. 'I'm only saying. What you know or do not know, you needn't let it be a burden. Things will happen as they will.' With a sweep of the axe blade he cleared the cut wood from the stump and looked round for a new length of log to be split. There was none.

'You could always cut down that one,' I suggested with a nod towards the slender, deeply leaning tree behind him. 'It looks like it's ready to fall over all on its own.'

'What, the rowan?' He glanced back himself to confirm it. 'I'll never touch that one.'

'Why not?'

''Tis the whispering tree, is the rowan. The witches' tree. Show it your axe without asking permission and you'll have bad luck all your days.'

I thought of the great ancient oak tree that stood in the way of the road in this time, and had vanished somehow by my own. Daniel had told me I ought to ask Fergal sometime about oak trees, and lone trees, and Celtic beliefs, and since Fergal seemed talkative I asked him now.

'Well, the oak is more sacred again than the rowan,' said Fergal. 'Legend says that its roots are well bound in the otherworld, and that the tree itself serves as a doorway between the two realms of the shadows and light. Never fall asleep under a lone oak, they say, else you'll wake . . .' He broke off.

'Where?' I prompted him.

'Somewhere you never were meant to be.'

As though on cue the wind chased lightly through the trees that edged this corner of the stable yard, and suddenly I heard the sound of heavy rolling wheels approaching, and a horse's clopping steps, and a man drove around from the side of the house in a cart being drawn by a sturdily built chestnut mare. The cart rolled to a stop just in front of us as Fergal set down his axe and stepped forwards to shake the man's hand. 'Morrow, Peter.'

'O'Cleary.' The man gave a nod, and then angled it round to include me, too.

Fergal said, 'You'll have met my sister yesterday, I'm thinking.'

Then I realised why the man's face seemed familiar. He'd been one of the men on the road with the constable. I remembered him best because he'd been the one who had spoken to Daniel before riding off with the others, the one who'd said, ''Twas not our doing.'

He looked as though the episode still shamed him as he gave another nod to me and said, 'Mistress O'Cleary.' Then taking a sack from the seat of the cart he told Fergal, 'I'm just off to market. I thought you could find a good use for this.'

'Did you, now?' Fergal took the sack and looked inside. 'You know me too well, Peter. Wasn't I saying this morning I fancied a conger pie?' Thanking the man, he said, 'But you've no need to be giving me anything.'

'Well.' The man looked to the side. ''Twas a bad business yesterday. And you had to make your dinner stretch to extra mouths and all, because of it. I minded that you had a taste for conger.' With another nod, he wished us both good day and turned the cart around and headed off.

The sack was wet and smelt of fish, and peering in I saw the coiled body of a large, dead eel.

Fergal said, 'It may be ugly, but it makes a grand pie, conger does.'

I might have made a comment, but just then the back door opened and Jack Butler took a few unsteady steps into the daylight. He stopped as though he'd hit a wall, and then came on towards us, walking gingerly, his head held in both hands.

'Christ,' he said, with his eyes shut as though even the sound of his own footsteps caused him pain. 'Where the devil is Daniel to?'

Fergal held back his answer until he had sauntered a few paces forwards himself to stand close beside Jack, and he spoke at full volume. 'Left this morning, didn't he, though where he's gone I couldn't say.'

'Jesus.' Gripping his temples more tightly, Jack let his eyes open a fraction and squinted at Fergal. 'You bloody old—'

'None of that now,' Fergal warned. 'Not in front of my sister.'

Jack turned his head a fraction, wincing at the movement, till he saw me, too. 'Eva. Good morrow.'

As I nodded in reply I saw a flicker of remembrance cross his face. He said, 'Do you know, I had the most unlikely dream of you last night . . .'

I'd been dreading this, but Fergal had apparently been waiting for it. 'Did you, now? And will I have to mind you to recall your manners?'

'No, it was nothing improper.' Jack made the mistake of forgetting his hangover and the small shake of his head made him wince again. 'She was speaking.'

The Irishman shot him down there on the spot with one dry look. 'Oh, ay? In what language?'

'In English, of course. She was speaking to Daniel.'

'How hard were you hit on the head, then?' asked Fergal. 'Or was it the rum?'

'It seemed real.'

'Ay, I'm sure that it did.' Fergal's tone was indulgent. 'And I'm all the time seeing little wee men when I've drunk too much whisky, myself.' He handed the wet sack to Jack and the younger man blanched at the smell.

'What,' he asked in a weak voice, 'is that?'

''Tis your dinner,' was Fergal's reply. 'Or it will be, when Eva and I are done gutting it. Take it on into the house for me, will you?'

Jack turned whiter, if that could be possible, and the bruising on his face stood out sickly. 'Take it yourself, you great bastard. I'm going back up to my bed.' He threw down the bag at his tormentor's feet and with one final glare of reproach turned and headed back into the house.

Fergal grinned as I looked at him.

'What?' he asked. 'Would you deny me entertainment?' Hoisting the heavy wet sack full of eel he followed after Jack and asked me, 'Bring the axe, if you can manage it.'

Which sounded to my ears more like a challenge than a mere request, and with a smile I went back to the stump to fetch the axe. For a short-handled tool it was heavier than I'd expected. It took me a moment to manage a comfortable grip on the handle, and by the time I turned and started back across the yard both Jack and Fergal were already in the house.

And then I heard the rider, coming down the hill.

I couldn't see the road from where I stood, but I could tell there was no cart this time, only a single rider, turning now to come around the house at such a leisured pace I knew it must be Daniel, and I stopped there in the stable yard and quelled the nervous flutter in my stomach as I turned my head expectantly to welcome him.

The dark bay horse stepped round the corner with a certain arrogance, well-suited to the black-garbed man who rode him. I was unsure which of us was more surprised to see the other, but my fingers tightened round the handle of the axe instinctively, an action that did not escape his notice.

With a smile that bordered on a sneer he brought the horse between the house and me, and reined it to a halt. 'Mistress O'Cleary,' said the constable. 'Good morrow.'

I nodded and lowered my eyes, a false show of respect, before lifting my chin again so I could meet his gaze squarely and show him I wasn't afraid. My acting skills weren't in a league with Katrina's, I knew, but I must have pulled it off with some success because his eyebrows lifted slightly in response.

His dark gaze slid down to the axe in my hand and returned to my face, and he murmured, 'Well, well. A show of spirit, is it? Very inadvisable.' He briefly glanced towards the house, then leaning forward in his saddle told me confidentially, 'In fact, I should be careful altogether were I in your place, lest it occur to me to use a different bait to draw your lover out. A more . . . attractive bait, perhaps, than I have used before?'

He slowly looked me up and down. I felt that look as though he'd put his hands upon my body, and I had to steel myself to stand there while he did it, and not move.

The back door banged, and Fergal's voice called, 'Eva!'

Still I couldn't move. My legs seemed weighted to the ground.

'Eva!' Fergal's voice was firmer. 'Come to me.'

I found a little of my courage then, and with a death-grip on the handle of the axe I forced myself to move out of the shadow of the tall bay horse and step around so I could cross the stable yard to Fergal. I walked carefully, and did not run, aware that Creed was watching.

More than watching – he was following, his horse's steps deliberate.

Fergal asked him, 'Have you business here?'

The constable shrugged the question aside. 'Your sister,' he told Fergal, 'wants to have a care when carrying that axe. I might mistake it for a weapon.'

'Would you, now?' The words held open insolence.

As I reached Fergal's side he held out one hand for the axe and I gave it to him gratefully. He turned it in his fist to take a firmer grip and said to Creed, ''Tis best, then, that I carry it myself, so you'll have no mistake.'

The threat was boldly made, even for Fergal, and I held my breath beside him as the two men glared at one another. And then Fergal glanced at me and told me, 'Eva, get inside.'

Surely, I thought, he wasn't about to take on the constable? Openly fighting a man of the law wasn't something a man could just do without paying a price, and though Fergal was fierce I would never have thought him so reckless.

I hesitated, showing my uncertainty, and with impatience in his eyes he turned his head again and said more forcefully, 'You're looking pale. You need to go on in the house. Now.'

He was looking pale himself. Or rather, grey.

And then I understood.

I felt the change beginning, saw the landscape start to waver and reform, and in a kind of frozen limbo I watched Creed's head start to turn, as well, towards me.

And then suddenly the rhythm of hard hoofbeats sounded further up the hill, and Fergal said, 'Here's Danny coming now,' and Creed, distracted, turned the other way to look towards the road.

I did run, then.

I ran the few steps to the back door of the house and swung myself inside the darkened corridor in panic, as the walls around me melted into fading, shifting shadows and dissolved as though they'd scattered on a breath of wind.

Time blinked. And I was walking down the shaded road outside Trelowarth House, still in the lovely flowered dress whose thin and fraying hem now brushed the gravel of the drive where I stopped, my legs now trembling much too violently to carry me.

The small dog Samson bounded with his usual exuberance around the corner of the house, tail wagging, but a few feet off he paused, and laid his ears back slightly.

'It's all right,' I reassured him as I crouched and held my fingers out towards him. They were shaking, and I couldn't make them stop, just as I couldn't stop the coldness that had started creeping through my body, settling in my bones. I drew a breath and once again, but this time for myself and not the dog, I whispered, 'It's all right.'

Chapter Twenty-Six

The room beside my own was bright with midday sunshine, but I still felt cold. I'd started to think I might never feel warm again. Each time I started relaxing, the thought of how close I had come to disaster this morning would set off a new round of shivers.

A burst of hard wind from the sea set the windowpanes rattling as I moved further in, stirring dust from the floorboards with each careful step. No one knew I was in here. The door to the passage was closed; I'd come through the connecting door from my own bedroom, with Ann Butler's flowered gown bunched in my arms.

This was the second of her gowns that I had taken from the time where it belonged, and it seemed right somehow to bring it here to hide, inside this room that had been hers.

Against the far wall, in the space below the attic stairs, a sloping built-in cupboard held the out-of-season clothes that no one needed till the winter. Shoving the mass of woven sleeves and woolly things aside, I tugged a hanger free and slipped the flowered gown onto it carefully, then slid the hanger back in place behind the other clothing where the faded blue gown and the banyan hung already, quietly concealed.

My fingers lightly brushed the silk of Daniel's banyan, and I closed my eyes. I felt his presence here more strongly than I had before, so strongly that it almost seemed that if I were to close my eyes and wish with all my heart, then maybe . . . maybe . . .

'So you're back.' Claire's voice, approving. Coming through the open doorway from my bedroom she asked, 'Did you have a nice walk?'

I closed the cupboard door as nonchalantly as I could and turned, my eardrums buzzing from the sudden surge of guilty blood pressure. I gave a nod and told Claire, 'Yes, I went up to the church.' It seemed an age ago, to me. I cleared my throat and added, 'Mr Teague was there. He hasn't changed.'

Claire smiled. 'He never will, you know. I've no doubt when he finally passes over he'll keep walking through that churchyard every day in spirit, keeping things in order. Was he pleased to see you? I expect he was. He likes a bit of company, does Mr Teague.' Her keen glance swept the little room. 'God, look at all this dust. I must have words with Mark and Susan's cleaner when she comes. I'm sure that cupboard wants a clearing out as well.'

I forced a shrug. 'You're better off to leave that till the winter, aren't you? When you take the coats out and put all the summer things away.'

'Well, I suppose.' She turned her gaze on me instead. 'I don't know that I've ever seen you with your hair up, Eva. What a lovely way to do it.'

I was taken by surprise. I had forgotten. In my hurry to get safely back inside the house before somebody saw me, and to change into my proper clothes, I'd overlooked my hair. Reaching up to make certain, I fingered a hairpin and said, 'It's a little bit fussy . . .'

'No, leave it up. You'll want to look your best for lunch.' She smiled. 'You have a visitor.'

•

Following Claire through the door to the kitchen I heard a knife's blade striking on the cutting board and thought at first, *Oh, Fergal's cooking something*, and for that brief moment following, while my mind adjusted to the modern room instead, I felt a bit off balance. Out of step.

Mark was sitting at the table writing idly in a notebook while Susan, standing near the sink, chopped vegetables for one of her trademark huge salads. Her attention, though, appeared to be on Oliver, who lounged against the worktop not too far from her, still in his biking shorts and fitted shirt that showed the muscles of his arms and chest in perfect definition. The wind had dried his hair so that only the bits near his temples were still slightly damp from the effort of cycling the hilly road back from St Non's.

He grinned as I came in. 'I'm back.'

'Like a bad penny,' Claire said with affection, giving him a once-over. 'Does your mother know you're dressed like that?'

'My mother bought the outfit,' he returned, his wit as quick as ever, but Susan didn't let him get away with it.

She smiled her teasing smile and asked, 'No, really. Are you on the pull, or something? Trying to look all manly and athletic?'

Mark, from his seat at the table, drily commented that wearing Lycra shorts was not the best way to look manly.

'That, dear brother,' Susan told him, 'is a matter of opinion.'

Their brief exchange of banter had been all the time I'd needed to shake off my momentary sense of being in the wrong place, at the wrong time. In Oliver's defence I said, 'He's cycled over to St Non's and back this morning.'

Mark glanced up at his friend and asked, 'Crisis with one of the cottages, was it?'

'Burst pipe,' said Oliver. 'Oh, and it *was* Susan's plumber,' he told me.

She looked at him, reddening slightly. '*My* plumber?'

'Paul, from Andrews & Son. Had the pipe fixed in no time,' said Oliver. 'So I thought I'd just drop round on my way back—'

'Conveniently at lunchtime.' Claire met the full charm of his boyish smile with motherly indulgence. She asked Susan, 'I suppose we can feed him?'

Susan thought it possible.

Oliver tried to look indignant. 'I *am* answering a summons, as it happens.'

Claire glanced at me. 'Oh, yes?'

'I'm here to see Mark's knife.'

Mark raised his head. 'My what?'

'Felicity said you had some old knife . . .'

'Oh.' The fog cleared. 'That one. Hang on, I'll get it.'

He rose and left us for a moment while Claire counted

out the cutlery for five of us and started setting places at the table. 'Oliver, what will you drink?'

'Water, please.'

I heard Fergal's voice speaking again in my mind. *Me now, I would rather meet my thirst with ale and cider, same as everyone.* It faded again, but when Claire set my own glass in front of me I was half-tempted to ask her for cider.

I didn't, of course. But it seemed so much harder this time to fit back in the slot I belonged in. Especially here in the kitchen, where I spent so much of my time in the past, I found things didn't feel right. I missed seeing Fergal's black scowl and quick smile, and Jack rocking his chair on two legs with his back to the wall and his eyes full of mischief, and Daniel . . . I really missed Daniel.

'Your hair looks amazing like that,' Susan said to me, mixing her salad. 'You ought to put it up more often.'

'Thanks.'

Oliver confessed he hadn't noticed. 'You didn't have it up this morning, did you, at the church?'

'No. I . . .' Lifting one hand, I self-consciously pushed in a hairpin more firmly. 'I felt like a change.'

Susan teased us both, 'Are you two having early morning trysts now in the church-hay?'

'Right,' said Oliver. 'With Mr Teague about? Not likely. No, your PR wizard here was scouting out the final resting places of Trelowarth's famous smuggling Butler brothers.'

Mark, returning with his treasure box in hand, said, 'Them again?'

Susan said, 'Well, it's colour that we're after, Mark, and

smugglers do provide it. That's what brings the tourists in.'

Mark shrugged and set the box down and we all leant in to take a look at his assorted treasures.

Oliver was taken with the musket balls, although he made a small correction. 'If you found these in the cave, I'd think it much more likely that they came from a pistol than a musket. I can't imagine someone having room to fire a musket in that space, they'd use a pistol at close range.'

I looked at the seven small metal balls lying so deadly and still on his palm.

'Can't you tell from the size of them what sort of gun they were fired from?' I asked.

'Well, not really. Both muskets and pistols were smooth-bored, they didn't leave marks to identify, and because of how they worked, the balls and shot were smaller than the barrel of the gun, you had to leave a bit of room to wrap a bit of paper round them before loading. Standard navy issue muskets used a larger ball, but blunderbusses and some other muskets could use smaller shot, like these.' He stirred the balls round with his finger. 'But at a guess, I'd still say these came from a pistol, just because of where you found them.'

I was thinking of the pistol I'd seen Daniel tuck inside his belt last night when he'd gone to keep an eye on Jack, down at the Spaniard. Just last night . . .

My eyes closed briefly on the memory as I tried to focus on what Oliver was telling us.

'I've got a matchlock pistol down at the museum that takes shot about this size.'

'A matchlock pistol?' Susan asked. 'What, do you use a match to fire it?'

'Not a match as we would think of it. A match in those days was a sort of . . . well, a sort of . . .'

'Fuse,' I said.

'Exactly.' Oliver's glance praised my research. 'A slow-burning fuse, that's right. You have been swotting up, haven't you?'

Mark took the dagger with care from the box. 'Right then, Einstein, how old would this be?'

'Wow,' said Oliver, rolling the metal balls back where they'd come from and taking the dagger with reverence. 'That's really beautiful.'

Only a man who loved history, I thought, could find beauty in something so ruined by time. He turned it so the sunlight from the window caught the small bit of the handle that remained. 'That's shell, I think.'

Score one for Oliver. I waited, frankly curious to see how close he'd come in his assessment to the truth.

He said, 'Now *this* could be a smuggler's knife.'

'Why's that?' Mark asked.

'Well, someone who spent time at sea. They all had knives this size. A multi-purpose gadget, really, good for cutting rope or cutting food or eating with. You wouldn't be without one on a ship. But this,' he turned it to the light again, 'is really lovely workmanship. You see here, if I hold it just like this,' he said, and palmed the handle, 'you would barely see the blade. Whoever made this knew what he was doing.' Looking at it closely he considered Mark's first question. 'How old is it? Hard to say with this corrosion, but I'd hazard Restoration era maybe, from its shape. The 1660s, 1670s, somewhere in there.'

He'd impressed Mark. 'That's pretty precise.'

'Yes, well. I have a thing for knives, actually. Care to sell this one?' He knew what Mark's answer would be, I could tell from the smile in his eyes.

'Not much point,' Mark said, taking the knife back and tucking it safe in the box with the rest of his treasures. 'There wouldn't be much value to it, not in that condition.'

If Oliver knew what the dagger's true value was, he didn't bother to share it. Instead he gave up with a shrug that made Claire give a cluck of her tongue and come over to study a tear in his sleeve.

'You've a bad scratch under there,' she told him. 'Let me get a plaster.'

'No, I'm fine,' he reassured her. 'It was just that blasted tree. You know, the one beside the greenhouse.'

'Susan's hawthorn tree.' I pulled my mind deliberately away from Daniel's dagger and my speculations, all unpleasant, as to how it might have ended up there in the cave below the Cripplehorn. 'She's just had all the shrubs around it cleared away.'

'Well, thanks for that,' he said to Susan, who replied, 'It's Cornish culture, idiot. We're making it a cloutie tree, just like the one at St Non's well. It's great for tourists – let them tie a little strip of fabric on a branch and make a wish, like people did back in the old days. For luck.'

'Ah.' Oliver rubbed his sore shoulder. 'You're off to a grand start, then.'

As he helped himself to salad, something made me think to ask him, 'Oliver?'

'Yes?'

'Have you ever heard tell of a tree called the Trelowarth Oak? A big old oak tree that once grew at that really sharp bend in the road?'

'The Trelowarth Oak? Sure.' With a wicked grin he said, 'I actually *do* have an etching of that one, if you ever want to come look at it. Up in my sitting room.'

I let that pass. 'What happened to the tree itself?'

He speared his salad. 'Methodists.'

'I'm sorry?'

'Well, the local people thought the tree was magical, or something, and the Methodist minister wasn't having any of it, so he had the tree chopped down.'

'When was this?'

'1800s sometime. I can look it up for you.'

Across the table Susan shook her head and said, 'What silliness. They cut the whole tree down?'

'They did. And burnt the stump and dug that out as well.'

But not the roots, I nearly said. They couldn't have destroyed the roots.

The roots that, in the Celtic legends, bound two worlds together, so the tree became a doorway . . .

The sound of far-off laughter caught my ear – a man's laugh – and I raised my head to look, and in that shadowed instant I could see the room begin dissolving into something else, and saw a shape like Fergal's cross to where the open hearth had been . . . but then I blinked and everything was back the way it had been.

'You all right?' Beside me Oliver was frowning faintly with concern. 'Got a headache, or something?'

'Or something.' I picked up my own fork and gave a tight smile. 'But I'm sure it will pass.'

Another shadow swept across the window as the figure of a man went by, his footsteps falling hard along the path to the back door. A man dressed all in black.

Chapter Twenty-Seven

A cold hand clenched my chest and made it difficult to breathe until I reassured myself that I was firmly in the present, with my friends still sitting round me, and the constable had not in fact crossed into my own time. The man who'd passed by was a stranger to me, taller than the constable and broader through the shoulders.

Oliver had seen him, too, and as the first knock sounded at the back door he pushed back his chair and rose. 'I'll get it.'

From the brief exchange of voices in the corridor I gathered both men knew each other, but when Oliver came through into the kitchen he looked straight at Susan first, then stepped aside. The man who followed him was ruggedly attractive in a way that made it difficult to judge his age. The only thing I could have said with certainty was that he wasn't young – his well-cut auburn hair had turned to silver at his temples and his jawline had begun to lose the chiselled definition that it would have had when he was in his thirties.

He seemed to hesitate a moment, like the rest of them. Until Claire broke the tension with a smile of welcome. 'Nigel. Good to see you.'

'Claire. Mark.' He greeted them both, gave a brief nod at me, and looked over my head. 'Susan.'

Susan didn't answer him, and when I saw her face and saw the way that she was looking at him, and the way that Mark and Claire and Oliver were watching *her*, I finally figured out who this must be: the man she'd been with up in Bristol. Her ex-boyfriend.

Nigel's gaze stayed fixed on Susan till she found her voice.

'Hello, Nigel. What brings you to Cornwall?'

'I'm celebrating, actually.' His smile was lopsided, disarming, and I watched as she responded to it with the instant understanding of someone who'd shared a longtime intimacy with this man and knew his moods and his expressions.

With a slowly spreading smile herself she guessed, 'You got the promotion.'

'I did.'

'Well, that's wonderful. Really it is. You deserve it.'

He said, 'It means moving to London, of course. Thought I'd take a run up at the weekend and start looking round for a flat. I was hoping,' he added, 'that I might persuade you to come.'

She had to steel herself. I saw her do it, saw the silent effort that it cost her to resist him as she said, 'Look, we've been through all this. And anyway, you don't need me to help you choose a flat.'

'Don't I?'

'Nigel,' Susan began, but he wouldn't be put off.

'It comes to this,' he said. 'I love you. And I'm miserable without you.'

'Nigel,' Susan tried again.

'Please, hear me out. I know you think we haven't got a future, but I think you're wrong. I want to prove it to you, if you'll let me.'

Then in front of us, as though we had all disappeared and he and Susan were the only people in the room, he took a little velvet-covered ring box from his pocket.

'Nigel.' Susan's voice had lost its force and faded to a level that was just above a whisper. She looked shaken by emotion as he crossed the room towards her.

'Susan Hallett.' Like the hero in a fairy tale, he got down on one knee and pried the lid up on the ring box as he asked her, 'Will you marry me?'

'It's her decision.' Mark reached a gloved hand among the thorned branches and with his shears snipped off an unwanted shoot that had sprung from the roots of a red-petalled rose. 'No one else's.'

Two hours had passed now since Nigel had turned up and made his proposal, and Susan and he had gone off for a drive to discuss things. Like Mark, I was filling the afternoon hours with work while we waited for them to come back, though I realised my efforts to photograph some of the lovely old roses now coming into bloom here in the Quiet Garden might all be for nothing if it turned out Susan answered 'yes' and moved away to London.

'She couldn't run her tea room, then,' I said, 'and she's put so much work into it.'

Mark shrugged and let the shoot fall with the other ones discarded at his feet. 'It wouldn't be the first time a project here has been abandoned. Dad did everything in stops and starts. That's why we have a glasshouse,' he reminded me, 'and why it's sitting empty.'

I'd forgotten about Uncle George's unsuccessful foray into rose breeding. 'Well, at least he tried,' I said in his defence. 'And now you have the greenhouse.'

'So we do. And that, as well,' he added, with a nod down at the sunburst coloured rose beside the one that he was tending. 'My dad's one and only hybrid.'

'Really?' Lifting my camera, I snapped off a photograph. 'What is its name? And if you tell me something Latin, Mark,' I warned as he prepared to speak, 'I swear I'll have to hit you.'

'It doesn't have a Latin name. Or any name, officially.'

'Why not?'

'Dad never gave it one. It was still being field-tested when he died.' He looked at me a moment and decided, 'I suppose that we could name it, if you like. It only takes a bit of paperwork.'

'What would you call it?'

'You choose.'

I touched a leaf with gentle fingers. 'You can name them after people, can't you, roses?'

He could see it coming. 'Eva.'

'Can't you?'

'Yes.'

I raised the camera for a second time to take another picture of the fragile-looking rose that held the colours of the setting sun. 'Let's name it for Katrina, then.'

I heard his silent argument and answered it.

'It's not the same,' I said, 'as using her name for publicity. You know it's not. She loved this place, she loved these gardens, and it's just a way of seeing she's remembered.'

Mark's eyes told me just how likely he considered it she'd ever be forgotten, but he thought it over. 'Right, then,' he said finally. 'The Katrina Ward it is.'

The garden walls were built to block the wind and yet a dancing breeze brushed past my cheek as though Katrina were announcing her approval.

I'd been feeling her around me very strongly all this afternoon, as though she felt I needed my big sister. And I did. Above all, I needed to borrow a bit of her courage.

I still felt off-balance because of my run-in with Constable Creed in the stable yard only this morning. I knew I might not be so lucky the next time we met. Even if I managed not to disappear in front of him, he might make good his threat and come at me to get to Daniel. Odds were, if I left Trelowarth I'd remove that risk.

And yet, I'd risk another kind of pain by leaving.

If I'd wanted proof of that, I'd had it when I'd looked at Daniel last night, and he'd looked at me, and suddenly my choices had seemed more confused than ever.

Susan was facing that sort of a choice now, I thought. I'd seen the conflict in her face and heard it in her voice, and knew her heart was being pulled in two directions. And it occurred to me that there was someone else here who had faced that same choice long before myself or

Susan, so I went off now in search of her advice.

I knew where I'd find Claire. I heard the lovely mellow tones of the piano long before I stepped inside the house, and knew that she was in the big front room. I went in quietly. I'd always loved to watch Claire play. The music took her so completely, shaped her mood and flowed from her so easily it seemed to be her own invention, her own voice. I recognised the peaceful, almost wistful notes of Chopin, and they seemed to be so perfectly in tune with my own feelings at the moment that I didn't interrupt. Instead I focused my attention on the bookshelves, searching out with idle fingertips the worn spines of the old books that my mother had once given Uncle George.

I paused at a thick book whose title intrigued me, and was lifting it down when Claire finished her prelude, the final note drifting to silence.

I told her, 'Don't stop, that was lovely.'

'I wasn't sure I would remember it all,' she confessed with a faint smile. 'I haven't played that one in years. Not since I was your age, in fact.'

'And when was that?' I teased her. 'Yesterday?'

Her smile grew warm at my flattery. 'Seems like it, sometimes.' She looked to the window. 'Is Susan not back yet?'

'Not yet, no.'

'Oh, well. One can't rush a decision like that.'

I decided that made a good opening for what I'd wanted to ask her. 'Aunt Claire?'

'Yes, darling?'

'When you met Uncle George . . . I mean, it must

have been a change for *you*, to move here. And not only geographically. You were changing your whole way of life, taking on Mark and Susan and everything. How did you . . . that is, when someone is making that big a decision, how . . . ?'

'How do you know it's the right one to make?' She was watching me kindly. 'Are you asking on Susan's behalf, or your own?'

Before I could answer, a door somewhere opened and closed and the sure tread of footsteps approached from the back of the hall, and we turned to the doorway as Oliver entered the front room.

On cue, from the small knowing smile on Claire's face. She greeted him with, 'Didn't we get rid of you once today?'

He'd changed his clothes at least, although the jeans and T-shirt he now wore weren't that much less revealing than the biking shorts. 'I've just had a delivery that I thought might interest Eva,' he explained, and held a small wrapped packet up to show us. 'Mark said I should come right in.' He looked around the room. 'Is Susan not back yet?'

Claire answered as I had done, 'Not yet, no.'

Oliver lifted an eyebrow. 'You don't think she'll actually marry him, do you? I mean, he's a nice enough bloke, Nigel, but he's not right for her. I could have told her that, first time I met him. They're chalk and cheese, aren't they?' He sauntered across for a look at the book I was holding. 'What's that?'

I angled the cover to show him.

He read out the title: '*The Wife's Guide for Keeping a Garden and House*?'

'Newly revised in . . .' I flipped to the title page, briefly consulting the date, '1692.'

'That would explain why it's falling to pieces, then.'

'Only the binding. The pages are fine.'

He looked at the page I'd been reading. '"For Making a Stirabout"? What's that?'

'A stew, sort of.'

'Ah. And it doesn't concern you at all that the next item down is "A Cure Against Vomiting"?'

I cast a dry look up over my shoulder. 'It's meant to be a full instruction book for housewives. Home remedies, recipes, how to do laundry and clean things.' All useful, I thought, for a young woman setting up house at the end of the seventeenth century. Or for a woman who found herself thrust back in time to the start of the eighteenth.

Oliver said, 'If you're wanting to read something, try this instead.' And he gave me the packet.

As I took it from his hands I felt the quick touch of excitement and I knew what it must be before I'd even got the wrapper off and seen the book inside, bound in smooth leather with faded gilt letters that spelt out the title: *A Life Before the Wind*. Jack Butler's diary. 'Oh, Oliver! Wherever did you find it?'

'I have sources.'

And he must have had to pay them well. The book was an original edition, from the look of it. 'You'd really let me borrow this?'

'I wouldn't, no,' he told me, and then smiled at my reaction. 'You're to keep it. It's a gift.'

I shook my head. 'I'll buy it from you.'

'Sorry, no. A gift's a gift,' he said. 'You're stuck with it.'

I would have argued further if I hadn't been distracted by the sound of tyres on gravel from the drive outside. All three of us fell silent while we listened, waiting.

One car door banged shut. And then the tyres rolled off again.

When Susan came to join us, she was on her own.

'I've told him no.' She stood within the doorway, looking tired. 'Our lives are just too different, it would never work.' Her weariness seemed more pronounced as she glanced round the room. 'Mark's in the gardens, I expect? I'll go and hunt him down and let him know, so he'll stop worrying.'

Oliver stepped forwards, not the charmer any more but the dependable old friend who could be leant on in a crisis. 'You don't need to hunt him down, I know exactly where he is. Come on, I'll take you to him.'

When they'd gone, I looked at Claire and noticed her expression, and I said, 'You're not surprised.'

'No. Nigel wasn't the right man for her.'

'Because the gap between them was too great?'

She shook her head. 'Because it wasn't meant to be.' Her eyes were wise. 'Every relationship has its own obstacles, darling. And as you said, your Uncle George and I had our share of them. As would you, if you were to meet someone here.' From her smile I assumed she meant Oliver. 'There would be practical choices you'd have to make. Where you'd live, that sort of thing. Where you'd work. And there'd be differences in lifestyle that might take some getting used to. It's one thing to spend a summer at Trelowarth, or let a cottage for awhile, and quite another to live all year in Polgelly,' she said knowingly. 'The social structure here is . . . well, you'd find it rather different from America, I'm sure. It's never easy, changing how you live.'

I gave a nod of understanding, looking down.

'But,' Claire continued, 'all of that amounts to nothing, if you love him.'

As I raised my head, she met me with a smile.

'Believe me, Eva dear, if *I* was able to adapt, there's hope for anyone.'

Chapter Twenty-Eight

I heard the voices speaking low to one another from the wall behind my bed.

'You'll need my help, I'm thinking.'

'I've enough men aboard the *Sally*.' Daniel's voice.

I drifted in that drowsy plane between sleep and full consciousness, not wanting to wake up and lose the moment.

Daniel said, 'I cannot take you.'

'So then take Jack.'

'And waste the whole night arguing which one of us will take the helm? I thank you, no. Nor can I send Jack in my place,' he went on, as though cutting off an argument, 'because the message clearly states it must be me.'

A pause, then, 'For one woman,' Fergal said, 'she can create uncommon difficulties.'

'I rather think you put it in her nature when you made her an O'Cleary.'

They were talking about *me*, I realised. And their voices were very distinct, not as muffled as they'd been before with the distance of time in between us.

Rising to awareness like a diver pushing upwards from the depths, I brushed aside the clinging fog of sleep and forced my heavy eyelids open.

It was morning, fully light, and I was lying on the linens of the big four-poster tester bed, and though the doorway to the corridor was closed, the one connecting Daniel's room to mine was open. Fergal stood square in it with his back to me.

I blinked for a moment, adjusting, and tried to remember.

I'd fallen asleep in my own bed last night. I'd been reading. I'd started Jack's memoir, but after ten pages or so of his exploits I'd started to drift, and then . . .

'I pledged her my protection,' Daniel said, and from his voice I judged that he was standing just the other side of Fergal, in his room. 'I'll not feel easy in my mind unless I know that you are here to guard her if she should return.'

Which would have been my cue to say something, had not another male voice spoken up before I had the chance to. From the next room, Jack's voice asked, 'Return from where?'

I hadn't heard his footsteps in the corridor, or heard the door of Daniel's room swing open, but from Fergal's quick reaction I could only guess that Jack had somehow caught them by surprise.

'I was about to say,' said Daniel quietly, 'should she return to health.'

In my doorway Fergal shifted so he blocked the view

more solidly, his shoulder all but welded to the door frame.

Jack used a phrase I'd never heard, but it must have been rude because his brother told him, 'Mind your tongue. We have a woman in the house.'

'Do we, now?' The floorboards creaked as Jack stepped forwards, and I looked round frantically to find a blanket, anything to cover my modern pyjamas, as he went on, 'These past days you have sent me twice on errands to do nothing of importance, and in all that time I've neither glimpsed nor heard your sister, Fergal. And yet both of you keep telling me she's here, and only ill.'

'And what would either of us have to gain by saying so, were it not true?' asked Daniel.

Jack came closer still. 'You see, I cannot tell you, and that troubles me. It troubles me as much as does the memory of her voice.'

The only blanket I could see lay folded out of reach across the clothes-press, so instead I scrambled underneath the sheets and pulled them to my chin. The sound, though slight, caught Fergal's ear. He turned to look towards the bed as Jack asked, 'How is she this morning, then?'

My gaze stayed locked with Fergal's as I marvelled once again at his ability to show no outward sign of his reactions when he wanted to conceal what he was thinking. His expression hadn't changed, though he did wait a moment before telling Jack, 'She is asleep.'

I took the hint and closed my eyes.

'She is a quiet sleeper,' Jack remarked.

'See for yourself, then, if you'll not believe us.' Fergal must have stepped aside because the floorboards creaked much closer to the bed, and in the pause that followed I tried hard to concentrate on breathing lightly, evenly.

After what seemed an eternity Jack broke the silence and whispered contritely, 'I'm sorry, I—'

'Call me a liar again,' Fergal said, 'and you'll wish that you hadn't. Now out with you. Both of you. Give her some peace.'

I felt someone's fingertips trace lightly over my cheek, maybe brushing a stray bit of hair aside, and I knew whose touch it was even before Fergal said, 'Danny, both of you. Out.'

Daniel said, close above me, 'I think she looks better this morning.'

'She does, ay,' said Fergal. 'I'd not be surprised to see her up and about by the afternoon. But now she needs her rest, so *out*.'

He left no room for argument, not with that tone.

The light touch left my face and I heard both the brothers retreat through the next room and, trading muffled arguments, start down the stairs. Fergal crossed to shut the connecting door firmly behind them.

I opened my eyes as he turned round to face me, his own dark eyes crinkling with laughter. 'I have to confess,' he said, low, 'I'm beginning to think that you may be a witch after all, for you do have the devil's own luck with your timing.'

Returning his smile, I felt suddenly, heart-expandingly happy in a way I hadn't felt for years, the way I'd felt when I'd awakened on those childhood summer mornings at Trelowarth with Katrina in the bed beside me and a day of new adventures spreading bright before us.

This felt so exactly like that, in fact, that for an instant I had to sit still while I took it all in, the warm familiar blend of sounds and smells and half-remembered sights that strummed a chord within me deep as instinct, wrapped me comfortingly in the certain knowledge I was *home*.

Fergal was saying, 'And more luck for you that I haven't yet eaten your breakfast, it's still on the tray.'

He had brought me a thick slice of bread spread with cheese, and a cup of cool ale. Fetching the tray from the desk in the corner, he set it on the bed and stood, arms folded, while I sat upright to eat.

'You did that very neatly,' was his comment. 'How the devil did you manage it?'

Daniel and Jack were downstairs, now. I heard the occasional tramp of a boot or the swing of a door underneath us, and knew it would be safe to talk if I kept my voice quiet, like Fergal's. 'I'm sorry?'

'Turning up like that, in the bed.'

'I don't know,' I said honestly. 'I just woke up, that's all.'

'This is your room in your own time, then?' Seeing my nod, he gave one of his own, as though he'd suddenly made sense of why Daniel had given me this room to sleep in.

Curious, I asked, 'How long have I been gone this time?'

'Eight bleeding days.'

'And Daniel has to go somewhere?'

'He does. And he can tell you all about that for himself, I'm thinking, once you're up and dressed.' At which he stopped, as we both noticed something obvious.

Tugging at my T-shirt sleeve, I said, 'I'm sorry, I—'

'You'll need the wardrobe of a queen, if this keeps up,' he told me drily. Leaving me a moment on my own he went next door to Daniel's room and came back in through the connecting door weighed down by the most beautiful gown I'd yet seen, of a quiet green colour that shifted when catching the light like the leaves of the trees shaded deep in the woods.

I touched the fabric as he laid it on the bed beside me. And I couldn't. I just couldn't.

'Fergal, I can't wear this.'

'Why not?'

'I've lost two gowns so far. Ann's gowns. It's just not right. And if I lose another—'

Fergal cut me off. 'This was not Ann's.'

I stopped. My hand fell still against the fabric as I looked at him.

'Last week,' he said, 'Danny took the *Sally* down to Plymouth on some business. He came back with this.' He flipped one sleeve so it lay straight across the bodice. 'There are slippers to go with it.'

'For me?'

'Well, fair to say it wasn't meant for me.' Straight-faced, he said, 'The colour is my favourite, but the cut would never do me justice.' Digging briefly in a pocket he produced a handful of hairpins. 'You'll need these as well, will you not?'

'Thanks.'

I would have said more but a sudden rise of voices underneath us made him lift a warning finger to his lips, until the hard slam of the front door and the crunch of footsteps outside on the path made him relax. Crossing to the window, Fergal watched whoever had just left stride off towards the road.

'That's Jack away to lick his wounds,' he said with satisfaction. 'You can come down when you're ready, then, for Danny will I'm sure have things to say to you.'

And taking up my finished tray he left me on my own to dress.

The gown was of a different design than the others. More modern, I supposed. Just as the fashions I was used to changed each year, so too the fashions of this time must have evolved as well according to the current style. The sleeves were still close-fitted to the elbow and turned back above the wrists to show the ruffles underneath, but the bodice had a different shape and cut and fastened at the side instead of at the front, which made it difficult to manage on my own.

I'd nearly reached the point of giving up when Daniel's voice behind me asked, 'Do you need help?'

I hadn't heard him coming up the stairs. I hadn't even heard the door between our two rooms open, but the thing that marked a smuggler, I supposed, was his ability to move round without drawing much attention to himself.

He'd changed his own clothes slightly from the last time I had seen him. The leg-hugging breeches tucked into his boots weren't the brown ones he usually wore but a dark navy blue, and the full white shirt left open at his throat was new as well, and of a finer-looking linen than the ones that I remembered. But his smile was just the same.

I was foolishly pleased to see him, but after the moment we'd shared in this room after lighting the fire I also felt a new degree of nervousness.

I looked away, still fumbling with the fastening. 'It's a little bit difficult.'

Taking that as a yes, he left the doorway and came to help. His fingers gently moved my own aside and did the task with expert ease.

'It suits you well, this gown,' he said. 'I did not know for certain it would fit.'

I stood quite still beneath his touch and thanked him. 'It was very thoughtful of you.'

'And expensive. This one garment cost me a full case of brandy,' he said, 'and a dance with the seamstress's daughter.'

The lightness of his tone relaxed me slightly. 'I hope she was pretty.'

'She danced like an ox, but I reasoned a gown that was bought for the price of a dance could not help but have happiness in it.' He'd finished. 'There,' he said, and turned me round to face inspection.

I kept my gaze hard on his shirt lacings. 'You shouldn't have gone to so much trouble, you know. Once I go back to my own time it's as good as lost, just like your wife's clothes. I can't seem to find a way to bring them back.'

He gave a shrug. 'And that is why I bought you this one.'

'So I wouldn't lose any more of hers?' I said it wryly, but he didn't take it as a joke.

'I bought the gown,' he told me very carefully, 'so that you could be done with borrowed things.' His hand still rested on my waist. 'I thought it time that you had something you could know was yours alone.'

My chin came up at that, and as my gaze met his I knew

he wasn't talking any more about the gown itself. The constable had told me once that Daniel only let me wear Ann's clothes to bring her ghost to life, and even though I'd known Creed's words were poison there'd been part of me since then that couldn't help but wonder just who Daniel really saw when he was looking at me.

Looking at the darkness of his eyes now I saw nothing but my own reflection there, and felt those doubts begin to fade.

His eyes asked a brief question, asked it and searched mine to read the reply before his one hand slid slowly under my hair to the back of my neck and he lowered his head.

The kiss began simply enough.

Just a brush of his lips on my cheek, reassuring and warm. But then one of us – I think it might have been me – moved a fraction, a turn of the head and our mouths met in earnest, but he remained a gentleman, not rushing things, not taking it for granted that I had any experience.

Until I kissed him back.

The rules changed, then.

Another minute more and he was holding me with both arms, which was just as well because I would have had a lot of trouble standing upright on my own. God knows I lost all track of time and Daniel must have done as well, because Fergal had to cough twice and swear once before either of us paid him any attention.

And even then all Daniel did was draw back with his forehead still resting on mine as he angled his head to the doorway.

'Yes?'

Fergal folded his arms. 'Were you coming downstairs, then? Or would you rather wait till Jack gets back so we can all sit down and talk this through together?'

Half-amazed I had a voice, I asked them both, 'Talk what through?'

Fergal said, 'He has to take the *Sally* out tonight, by order of His Grace the Duke of Ormonde.'

Daniel exhaled, patient. 'By request, not by his order. I am asked to do a favour for my kinsman, and no more than that.'

'Without a proper crew . . .'

'I will have men enough.'

'And not a one of them who's fit to raise a sword to guard your back should things go wrong.'

'You are more needed here,' said Daniel.

This, I thought, was where I had come in – the two men arguing.

As Daniel straightened from me I drew one long breath to calm my pulse because it was still racing from the kiss. I tried to think. And looking up at him I said, 'You won't let Fergal come with you because you want him to stay here at Trelowarth and look after me.'

Daniel half-smiled, not dropping his hands from my waist. 'I will only be gone a short while. And I'll be in no danger.'

'Then take me along.'

He had not seen that coming. 'What?'

'Take me along,' I repeated. 'Then Fergal can come, too. You can tell your crew I'm there to do the cooking, or whatever, and I'll keep out of the way, and with both you and Fergal there I'm sure that nothing will—'

He interrupted. 'No. It is impossible. On any other voyage I'd consider it, but not on this.'

'Why not?' I stood my ground. 'You said yourself there'd be no danger.'

Trapped by his own words, he looked at Fergal who was standing in the doorway fairly daring him to answer.

He was caught, and the three of us knew it. If he admitted the dangers involved in this 'favour' he'd been asked to do, then Fergal wouldn't rest until he'd found a way to go along. And if Daniel stuck to his story that there was no danger at all, then he'd have no good reason to leave me and Fergal behind.

And frankly, the idea of being left behind with Fergal in the foul mood that I knew he'd be in if he didn't get to go with Daniel wasn't that appealing to me.

Fergal, from his doorway, said, 'It seems a fair idea, Danny, taking her along. And you can tell the crew I'm there to guard her virtue.'

Daniel exhaled harder this time, giving in. 'The crew will hardly need an explanation why you're with us, I'll not need to tell them tales.'

'And who says you'd be telling tales?' He sent a pointed glance towards the pair of us, Daniel's hands still resting on my waist, and with a final dry look turned away.

Chapter Twenty-Nine

The evening brought a soft wind and a softer light that settled on the woods, where all the lilting voices of the birds and hidden creatures had been soothed to drowsy silence. Fergal, for all the heaviness of his boots, made little sound himself as he walked on ahead of me, moving in his dark clothes like a shadow through the trees. I tried to copy his stealth, but the hem of my long green gown brushed with a rustling sound over grasses and twigs and small shrubs, at one point flushing out a rabbit who leapt suddenly across my path, a startled streak of brown.

Fergal wheeled round at the small burst of noise, and then seeing what it was, relaxed and motioned me to follow on more quietly.

I did my best.

This was the first time I had been along this path – the same path I had glimpsed so long ago while walking through the Wild Wood. The path that had appeared and disappeared again and which I now knew led towards the sea. The scents of salt and spray grew ever stronger as we neared the south edge of the woods, where the dimness of the tangled branches overhead gave way to sudden light.

The path angled downwards here, sharp to the right, winding down the black rocks at the edge of the cliff – a wider and less treacherous descent than the one to the shore at the foot of the Cripplehorn, but I still had to be cautious and watch where I put my feet. The flimsy slippers made my steps less confident, and the swing of the heavy gown tested my balance so that I was grateful for Fergal's strong steadying hand as he helped me along.

I was vaguely aware of tall masts and the shape of a ship, but it wasn't till we'd nearly reached the bottom of the path and I could raise my head and take a proper look that I first really saw the *Sally* riding at anchor, not far out from shore.

I'd only ever seen her that one time before, when Jack set off for Brittany, and then I had been watching from the hillside at Trelowarth and I hadn't seen her clearly, just her graceful lines retreating as she'd headed out to sea.

Now, from closer up, I saw that she was not a very large ship, maybe fifty feet or so from bow to stern, with four square gunports set along her curved side high above the water level, and two soaring masts thick-laced with rigging and collapsed sails that flapped hopefully at every breath of wind.

Moored in the lee of the sheltering headland, her hull painted black like the high cliffs behind her, she shone like a lady, her trim gleaming white.

'Ay, she's beautiful,' Fergal agreed when I said so myself. 'Built at Deptford, she was, and there's few that can equal her speed.'

I'd sailed a bit with friends in California so I knew my starboard from my port, but I didn't know much about ships of this age. Didn't know what the names of the sails were, or how to tell one class of ship from another, and yet from simply standing here and looking at the *Sally* I could tell exactly why both Jack and Daniel were so keen to have her solely for themselves. She was too lovely to be shared.

Fergal gave a wave and though I hadn't seen a man on deck before, I saw one now, who waved in answer. And another man appeared. And then another.

I stood on the pebbled shore watching them lower a boat that one man rowed across to us. Fergal lifted me over the wet of the waves at the shoreline and settled me on the hard seat without giving any explanation to the other man of who I was or what I might be doing there. The fact that I was there with Fergal seemed to be enough to mark me out of bounds.

Still, when the dinghy scraped hulls with the *Sally* and I was helped up to the ship's main deck, Fergal came after me, facing the men down and setting things out in plain terms. 'This is Eva, my sister. She's coming along. She's no voice of her own, but if any of you gives her trouble I'll hear of it, see?' He didn't threaten them with what he'd do if they *did* give me trouble, but I gathered that they knew him well enough to fill those blanks in for themselves.

The youngest of the men looked like a teenager, the oldest seemed to be approaching sixty, and they all had that rough look of men who ended their hard days at sea by drinking late into the night at quayside taverns. But to my relief, not one of them looked hard enough to get the best of Fergal in a fight.

That helped me feel less nervous as they scattered to their duties.

Fergal squinted skyward as though judging the position of the sun. 'There'll be two men to come yet,' he told me, 'and Danny. We might as well wait for them in comfort.'

I didn't really want to leave the deck. I'd never been on an old ship, and I liked how the canvas and rigging above me was creaking and fluttering, and how the deck itself shifted in time with the rise of the waves, and how the wind and the sinking sun felt on my uplifted face. But arguing with Fergal was a lost cause at the best of times, and all the more impossible out here because I couldn't use my voice, so I gave in and let him lead me down below.

There was a single deck down here, with a grated trapdoor that I guessed would lead further down into the hold. What cargo might lie down there I could only imagine, but here on this deck I could count eight brass cannon, their wheeled mounts fastened to the inner hull with ropes to curb the recoil when they fired, their muzzles resting at the gun ports to each side. Towards the rear of this main space the sleeping quarters for the crew announced its purpose with its hammocks hanging off to either side, slung from the beams overhead so they ran in the same line, from bow to stern. Behind them was a separate space enclosing Fergal's galley and a table where the men could eat, and at the back of that there was a heavy door.

'The captain's cabin,' Fergal said. 'You'll sleep in here.' He didn't add the word 'alone' but then he didn't need to – I already knew he'd be keeping a watch on my door to see I wasn't bothered by the crew. Or by their captain.

I hid my smile and felt a twinge of sympathy for Daniel, especially after I'd entered his cabin and seen the comforts he'd be forced to do without.

There were windows here, for one thing – a broad row of them that ran across the squared wall of the stern, and two of them stood open on their casements to the fresh salt air. A definite relief from the close staleness of the cabin where the crew slept. Candle-holders had been fitted to the walls with brackets, and a small carved desk of heavy wood stood off to one side underneath a shelf of charts and papers. Near the farther wall there swung a hammock that looked comfortable and wide and had been fitted with a pillow for the sleeper's head.

I'd never slept the whole night in a hammock. With my luck, I thought, I'd tip out on the floor and break my neck. I was crossing to inspect it when I heard the splash and pull of oars outside the open window as the boat went out again.

'That'll be somebody coming,' said Fergal. 'Wait here.'

He left me and went up, and in a while I heard the boat come back, the creak and bump of wood on wood as it drew up against the *Sally*, and the thump of booted feet that landed on the deck above me in a cheerful rise of voices, Daniel's own among them. I couldn't hear what he was saying, the heavy wood deck and the walls of the cabin effectively muffled his words, but his laugh carried easily in through the window.

And then he was coming downstairs.

Fergal came with him into the cabin. He didn't look pleased. 'William's cousin be damned. William's ill, sure enough, but that lad you've brought with you is never his cousin.'

Daniel gave a smiling nod to me and answered Fergal, 'No, I did not think he was.'

'Then why the devil did you let him come on board?'

'Because he told the story well enough, when he did meet myself and Michael on the shore. He had the password right and all. It seemed a shame not to reward such effort. And,' he said, more serious, 'because we have an hour or so to wait yet for the tide, and if I'd left the lad on shore he would have run straight off to tell the one that sent him.'

'Creed.'

'I should imagine so, yes.'

'Creed,' said Fergal, 'cannot stop you sailing.'

'He can make a nuisance of himself, or send another vessel in our wake to watch and follow us. For now, he thinks he has his spy on board in safety. Let us keep him thinking so.' With all that settled, Daniel turned to me. 'How do you like my *Sally*?'

I replied the ship was lovely. 'But I have my doubts about the hammock.'

'Do you?' He considered it. 'It holds my own weight well enough, and I have seen a bed like that sleep more than one man on a crowded voyage, so you need not worry.'

Fergal said, 'She needn't, ay, considering that neither your own weight nor that of any other man will be in there tonight with her.'

His tone was dry, but Daniel matched it with the glance

he gave his friend. 'It may be I should toss you back on shore as well, together with Creed's spy.'

'You go and try it.' Fergal, unconcerned, half-shrugged to stretch his shoulders. 'What's the plan, then?'

Above me I could hear the steps and voices of the men. Hard footsteps tramped towards the stern, in my direction, and although I knew the angle of the ship's hull meant that nobody could see me from above, I still drew back a pace from caution. The footsteps stopped directly overhead.

'There he is,' Daniel's voice drifted down.

Other steps shuffled forwards to join him at the rail, and a younger man's voice complained, 'I can see no one.'

'Our passenger,' said Daniel, 'is a man much wanted in these parts. He does well to be careful and keep to the shadows until you can collect him.'

'Me?'

'Ay. Rowing would be William's job if he were here to do it, and you did say you had come to do his work.'

A doubtful pause. 'But I see no one there.'

'Nor will you, till you land the boat and call the password. Now away with you, and fetch him back so that we can be off. The tide has turned.'

I heard the scraping of the boat against the *Sally*'s side again, and as the rhythm of its splashing oars moved off, I heard another sound – a laboured clanking, unfamiliar. It wasn't until the *Sally* began to turn slightly as though she were drifting, that I realised what I'd heard had been the anchor being raised. From above came the creaking of ropes and the sound of the great sails unfurling to gather the wind.

The *Sally* gave a forward surge of joy. As her stern came round, my windows gave a clear view of Creed's spy, who'd nearly reached the beach. Even if the luckless lad had strength enough to turn his craft and row on back to catch us, he would have surely known there was no point to it. He'd never be allowed on board again now that his game had been discovered. Instead, as I watched, he drove the boat on to the shingle and leapt out, knee-deep in water and wading ashore with the wide, flailing motions of somebody in a great hurry.

The last glimpse I had of him as we slipped out of the shadows of the headland, he was scrabbling up the rocky path towards the clifftop. Not an easy climb for someone wet and tired from rowing. Still, he could count himself fortunate, I thought, that he'd been sent off in the boat and not simply dumped over the *Sally's* side.

Fergal said much the same thing minutes later when, taking his role as my chaperone seriously, he came down below decks with Daniel. The two of them joined me at the windows in the stern.

Fergal told Daniel, 'You've only made him angry now. You should have cooled his temper with a swim.'

'And if he could not swim?'

A shrug. 'We would have one less fool to waste our time with.'

Daniel smiled. 'You are a hard man, Fergal, and I do fear what would happen to me should I ever fall from your good graces.'

'Then take care that you do not,' was the advice returned, although I caught the fleeting play of light in Fergal's eye that spoilt the sternness of his warning. He was leaning to the window, looking back at the retreating shore. 'He'll be running straight to Creed.'

This time the shrug was Daniel's. 'Let him go. There will be nothing Creed can do. There is no vessel in Polgelly harbour that can catch the *Sally* when she runs before the wind.'

I believed him. I could feel the pull and power of the ship's sails as we altered course a second time and set Polgelly squarely at our back.

Beside me Daniel straightened from the window, the top of his head nearly brushing the beams of the cabin. 'Are you troubled by sea travel?'

'Pardon?' I asked.

'Do you feel any sickness?'

'Oh. No, I'm all right.'

'Good. You will find the comforts greater here,' he told me, 'in the cabin, but I should think that you would find the journey more diverting from the quarterdeck.'

It was an invitation, and I willingly accepted it.

Above, the air smelt cleaner and the sunlight from the west had taken on that warmly golden glow that marked the final hours of the evening. We were headed south, and opposite the sinking sun the purple of the coming night had started creeping up into the wide bowl of the sky above, where soon I knew the evening star would make its first appearance.

Watching the men work the sails and the ropes with experienced ease, I gave myself up to the sinuous rising and roll of the ship's deck beneath my feet, leaning at times to the will of the wind at an angle that tested my balance.

But I didn't mind. I was looking at Daniel for most of

the time, because seeing him here on the Sally was proving a small revelation. It occurred to me that, though I'd seen him smile and even laugh before, I'd never seen him totally content until this moment. He looked the same person, but . . . different. He looked so at home here, the voyager, eyes to the distant horizon, relaxed at the helm.

The same thing that made me so nervous, this whole thought of venturing into the unknown, seemed to cause him no bother. In fact, it appeared to be one of the forces that drove him. Like Tennyson's Ulysses, with his plans to bravely sail beyond the sunset, Daniel had the look of someone who would not be bound by lines on maps or dragons that were drawn there, but would set his own course to discover what lay at the end of it.

I watched him till the cooling night breeze chased me down below decks once again, where Fergal set me to helping him parcel out hard bread and ale to the men with a stew made of fish that he'd somehow prepared in a cauldron secured on a firebox of bricks in the galley.

The food was simply made and roughly eaten, but I gladly ate my share and then retired to my private cabin where, with Fergal stationed like a sentry in his galley just outside my door, I braved the swinging hammock. It embraced me like a lover's arms, and sent me off to sleep with dreams of ships and sails and distant shores that lay beyond my view.

Chapter Thirty

They were loading the last of the boats. The sloped deck of the *Sally* gently rose and fell beneath me as I held the rail for balance. Even with the hanging mist I still could see the shore, the little cove curved round its sheltered bit of sea, green hills that echoed those we had just left and small square houses stacked in cosy clusters up the slopes, with only the slight difference in the architecture telling me that we had crossed the narrow stretch of sea dividing Cornwall from the Continent, and had arrived in Brittany.

The crew were hard at work still bringing up the *Sally*'s cargo. I tried purposely to keep my gaze averted so they wouldn't think me nosy, but I had already seen the bales of wool.

A true free trade, I thought. They swapped the raw materials that were, by British law, so hard to come by on the Continent, for finished goods that were considered luxuries to those back home in England, just as Daniel had explained to me.

He'd gone ashore himself on the first boat, and I'd assumed I would be coming on this final one with Fergal when the crew had finished loading it, but even as I smoothed my hands across my gown to tidy my appearance Fergal strode across the deck and set me straight.

With a curt nod he said, 'I'll be away myself, now. Time you got below.'

'What?'

'You'll be safer in the cabin,' he elaborated. 'Come.'

He took me there himself, and quickly looked around to see that everything was as it should be while I grappled with the fact that they were leaving me behind, that I would not be going with them when they went ashore. I hadn't been expecting that.

I wasn't good at hiding how I felt. My own face must have held a mix of irritation and dismay, but if it did then Fergal chose not to react to it. He simply faced me, hands on hips, and asked me, 'Can you fire a pistol?'

'Pardon?'

Crossing to the desk he pulled the top drawer open just enough to show the pistol lying there. 'You'll find it primed and loaded. Do you know the way to fire it?'

'Likely not.'

'Then let me show you. Pay attention now,' he told me, as he took the pistol from the drawer and led me through the steps.

'Fergal . . .'

'Not that you'll be needing it.' His glance was reassuring. 'There will be only three men left aboard with you, and none of them will give you any trouble. I could trust them with my mother. Still,' he added, with a shrug, ''tis always best to think the worst of everyone, for that way you'll be seldom disappointed.'

'Fergal.'

'Ay?'

I knew the answer, but I had to ask him anyway. 'Can't I come with you?'

He half-turned and fixed me with that dead blank stare that meant I'd caught him off his guard, and then he made a great show of considering the question. 'Well, you *could*, were you a fishwife or a whore, but since you're neither you'll do best to keep here safely in the cabin,' he advised me in a dry tone that asked whether I had any sense at all. 'What sort of men would you be thinking that we are, to take a woman in to shore?'

'Well . . .'

'You watch from this window and see how many women from the village leave the safety of their homes to welcome *us*,' he said. 'More likely when they see the *Sally* drop her anchor they all scurry out of sight to guard their precious virtues.'

'Well,' I said, 'that's probably because they think it's Jack.'

Again I got the blank look, then his eyes began to crinkle at their corners and he grinned. 'Ay, like as not they do.' He handed me the pistol. 'Bolt that door, now.'

When he'd gone, I set the pistol back in place within the drawer. It felt too dangerous to hold. Above my head I heard the heavy tramp of feet as those last crewmen bound for shore climbed down into the waiting boat, and when the splash of oars passed by I took a step back from the windows so that I was partly shielded by the curtains at their edge. I didn't want to be caught watching like a child left behind; but that was how I felt.

Still, there wasn't any point in sitting stewing in self-pity when there wasn't anything that I could do about it, other than find some way to amuse myself while everyone was gone.

The captain's cabin wasn't fitted out for entertainment. I could only see that single shelf of charts and papers on the wall beside the desk, with several books wedged in among them, and the books at first glance didn't hold too much appeal. One was mathematical, another was in Latin . . . the third appeared to be either *by* Alexander Pope or about him, since his name was printed on the spine, which meant it might not be too terrible. But when I tried to take it from the shelf it was so tight against the others that it brought the book beside it out as well and sent it tumbling to the floor.

The unknown book fell both face down and fully open and I scooped it up as quickly as I could, so that the pages wouldn't bend. I'd planned to simply close it and return it to the shelf, but when I turned it over in my hands I saw the scratchy lines of handwriting in black and blotted ink, and realised what I held was not a printed book.

It didn't seem to be a journal or a log book, either. There were no divisions for the dates and times, just paragraphs of writing.

Then a sudden thought occurred to me. I closed the book and opened it again at the beginning, to the words that I'd suspected I might find there, written in that same uneducated hand: 'Jack Butler, His Book'.

Jack was midway through his memoirs, from the look of it. The memoirs that he'd find a way to publish later on in life, and which in turn would find their way to me three hundred years from now.

I hadn't had a chance to read much more than the first several pages of my copy of *A Life Before the Wind*, the book that Oliver had no doubt paid a shocking sum of money for. He might have saved himself the bother, I thought smiling. I could read the whole thing now for free. After all, it wasn't really an invasion of Jack's privacy if all this was already published openly in my own time. And from my first quick glance at the initial page, it seemed that he had published it exactly as he'd written it – the words had not been changed.

With that decided, I put Alexander Pope back on the shelf instead and settled down with Jack's book in the gently swinging hammock.

It felt curious and strange to read the same exact words I had read two nights ago, the same account of Jack's and Daniel's upbringing, but this time as a manuscript. And this time I was able to go further on. The focus stayed on Jack, of course – he'd clearly set himself up as the hero of the narrative – but now and then he widened out his viewpoint to include things like,

It was at this time that my brother Daniel, going up to London, chanced upon two men who were then being pressed into the Queen's service, and taking it upon himself to intervene he did effect their rescue and did find himself indicted for a Trespass for his troubles. Having languished several weeks in Newgate he was finally brought to trial, whereupon it was discovered there were none who would appear against him, and he was happily acquitted to rejoin us . . .

I could remember Fergal making mention of that episode when I had overheard him arguing with Daniel in the next room on the first day I had come to their Trelowarth – the Trelowarth of the past. He had been reminding Daniel that the Duke of Ormonde's battles weren't their own. 'When did the flaming Duke of Ormonde ever think to do you favours?' I recalled him saying. 'Never, that's when. Did he think to put his hand in when they had you up to Newgate? Did he come to pay you visits?'

Evidently not, although from what I'd read so far it didn't seem the Butler brothers needed anybody's intervention. They appeared to lead charmed lives. Just reading Jack's accounts of his own captures and escapes, and the few tales he told of how both he and Daniel had outwitted Queen Anne's agents while at sea, I was ready to believe the only luck they had was good luck.

With one notable exception.

And at summer's end my brother's wife succumbed to her long illness and was laid to rest with God.

He said no more about Ann's death, nor its effect upon the family, though I thought the constable came into things a little bit more often after that, a darker presence in the background of the narrative.

And the narrative, in spite of Jack's poor grammar and the challenge of his handwriting, made for some fascinating reading.

So much so, that when I turned a page expecting to find more of the description of a riot that had happened just this spring at celebrations for King George's birthday, and instead found that the sentence I'd been reading simply ended there, with blankness after, I was disappointed.

Flipping ahead to make sure there was nothing more, I closed the book regretfully. Oh, well, I thought. At least I had the finished version waiting for me in the present day. I'd have to be content with that.

I was starting to swing myself out of the hammock when the *Sally* lifted suddenly and rocked as though a wave had struck her broadside. As the hammock swung me back again I gripped it with my free hand, though in truth there was no danger I'd fall out. It was, as everyone had promised me, completely safe.

But that safety felt relative, now.

The *Sally* rolled a second time as something blotted out the daylight from the windows at the stern, behind me. Still clinging tightly to the hammock I turned round to see another ship's hull sliding ominously past, so close that I could see the gilded scrolls of woodwork on her gun ports.

The sight brought me out of the hammock in one swift decided move, planting my feet on the unsteady floor while I tried not to panic.

I couldn't see anything out the stern windows except the dark rise of the black-painted ship and one narrow slice of the grey sea and mist-shrouded shoreline that seemed too far off now to be any help, and I felt a new sense of frustration with Daniel and Fergal for leaving me here.

I'd be safer here, would I?

It didn't appear so. The unknown ship had started a slow turn that brought her bow around to face the offshore winds. I watched her black stern swinging out away from ours until the two ships rested almost parallel to one another with the hard slap of the waves against the *Sally*'s hull the only sound of protest.

I'd expected some reaction from the three men left on board with me, but so far I'd heard nothing, not so much as one stray footfall on the upper deck. Maybe, I thought, my three would-be protectors had slipped into hiding – something they wouldn't have done unless there was a reason *to* hide.

I knew that I was speculating; knew I had no way to tell if this new ship was friend or foe, but the mere sight of that black hull sliding past with all its gunports standing open, and this strange, unsettled silence that now hovered over everything inclined me to believe the worst.

Hiding wasn't exactly an option for me – I didn't know the *Sally* well enough to know where I'd be safe. At least here in the captain's cabin I had that strong bolted door between me and whatever came. And more, I had the pistol.

It had slipped my mind initially, but now I crossed to take it from its drawer again with hands that weren't quite steady.

I had barely closed the drawer again when I heard the quiet splash of oars approaching, almost furtive . . . heard the creak as they were lifted, and the scrape and bump of something on the *Sally*'s starboard side.

Gripping the pistol I closed my eyes briefly, preparing myself for the obvious since there was no way to stop it.

The *Sally* was going to be boarded.

Chapter Thirty-One

Not knowing, not seeing, just hearing the sounds of the men coming over the sides was the worst part by far. I'd seen too many pirate movies and my mind was freely fitting images to what I heard above me, matching every shuffling step to some crazed killer carrying a cutlass in his hand.

So when I heard the first thump of a man's boots coming down the stairs, I had the pistol waiting, cocked the way Fergal had shown me. As the boots approached I raised the pistol higher, and when the handle of the cabin door first gave a rattle I prepared to fire.

But then the intruder did something I hadn't expected.

He knocked.

And Daniel's voice said, 'Eva? Let me in.'

The rush of relief was so great that it set loose a wave of adrenaline that made my fingers fumble on the bolt until I concentrated.

Daniel looked surprised to see the gun. 'Are you all right?' He swung the door shut firmly at his back. 'Has something happened?'

I kept my voice low, so the crew wouldn't hear. 'There's a ship.'

'Yes, I know.' Relaxing, he reached out to take the pistol from my hand. He let the hammer down with care. 'There is no need for you to worry. Did you think that I would leave you so defenceless?'

I was on the brink of saying that I hadn't thought he'd leave me in the first place, but I caught the words in time before I spoke them. It was not his fault, I knew, that social customs were the way they were; that men and women here were bound by different rules. And if I was feeling left out, I had no one but myself to blame. I'd asked to come along.

I said, 'I just thought I should be prepared for anything.' And then, because he didn't look entirely convinced, I changed the subject while he put the pistol in its drawer. 'Did you get all your business done on shore?'

'We did. And bought ourselves a boat into the bargain, to replace the one that Creed's boy rowed away in, else we'd find it a damp walk between our mooring and the beach when we got home.'

The tramping of men up and down between decks let me know that whatever they had traded for the wool was now being unloaded and stored in the *Sally*'s deep hold. Soon the great creaking winch would start hauling the anchor up. So much, I thought, for my grand sea adventure. In no time at all we'd be finished and back at Trelowarth.

Holding in my disappointment, I crossed to the windows and focused my gaze on the black ship that had given me those few unsettling moments. 'Is that ship a free-trader, too?'

Daniel leant on the edge of his desk. 'No. She is, by her colours, a French naval frigate.' He seemed unconcerned.

'She's a much bigger ship than the *Sally*.'

His practised eye measured the looming black hull. 'Ay, she'll be close on 400 tons, and has 32 guns to our 8, and she'll be carrying at least ten men for every one of ours.'

I said, 'That's hardly reassuring.'

'On the contrary, for that description fits in every way that of the ship I have been sent to meet.'

So this wasn't an ordinary smuggling run, then. 'You're supposed to be meeting another ship here?'

'My instructions were to that effect.' Daniel tipped his head slightly as though trying to get a clear view of the French ship's rigging. 'Though I must confess they did not name the ship in question.'

The scenery of my own view through the windows at the stern began to slip a little sideways as the *Sally* caught the wind and started slowly nosing out along the grey line of the shore. We glided once again into the French ship's shadow.

Daniel must have sensed my nervousness. He said, 'This is no place for us to make an introduction, with so many watching eyes. It will be better if we seek a quieter stretch of coastline where we can heave to and see what they intend.'

Looking at that line of gilded gun ports I fought back my own misgivings. 'Yes, of course.'

He wasn't fooled. 'Are you now wishing you had stayed back at Trelowarth?'

'No.' That came out too quickly. I said it again, 'No, I'm glad I came.'

He didn't comment on that, and his silence made me turn self-consciously to find he was still leaning on his desk, arms folded, watching me with thoughtful eyes. I asked him, 'What?'

He seemed to think a moment longer, then he said, 'You will not wound me, Eva, if you speak the truth. I would have honesty between us.'

'I am being honest.'

He didn't argue that. He only straightened from the desk and crossed to stand beside me, looking out the windows while the steadily retreating shadow of the black French frigate brightened into grey waves that broke hard upon the rocky shore to spray their mist and hide the rise of greening cliffs behind. 'It has a wild beauty all its own, the Breton coast,' he said, 'but I would doubt it could compare with India.'

My turn for silence. I thought he had missed that small slip I had made back when Fergal had noticed the tag in my T-shirt that said 'Made in India', and I'd been thinking of the time I'd spent there with Katrina, and he'd watched my face . . .

'You have been there,' said Daniel. He spoke the words surely, a statement of fact.

'Yes, I have.'

'And where else have you travelled?'

I scrolled through the list in my memory. 'A lot of places.'

'Is it that you think my mind so limited and narrow that I will not comprehend the truth? Is that why you conceal it?'

'No, I—'

Daniel turned his head. His eyes met mine. 'There is no map for this, no ordered rules of conduct, so we must invent them as we stumble through, and I would argue that the first rule must be honesty.'

I wasn't all that sure what he was wanting me to answer. My expression must have shown that, for he gave a tight-lipped sigh and looked away again.

'You are glad that you came,' he said. 'You, who have seen and done things I can scarcely imagine; you, who have freedoms in your time the women of mine cannot contemplate. Doubtless you thought that this voyage would be an adventure, and yet you have spent this day shut in a cabin alone and in fear for your life, and you say you are glad that you came. You'll forgive me,' he said, 'if I do not believe you.'

I understood him then. 'All right.' I took a breath. 'I didn't like being left behind when you all went ashore. I didn't expect it.'

His gaze swung back to mine. 'And I apologise. I should not have assumed that you would know you could not join us.' I could see him thinking further. 'You do understand the reasons?'

'Yes.'

'It would not have been safe.'

'I know. I really do, it's just . . .' I paused, and tried to put it into words. 'You talk of travelling. Well, even in my own time there are countries where a woman has to live with limitations. She can't get an education, or go out of doors unless her husband lets her, but that's not the way I live. And when you're used to certain freedoms, it's just very hard to lose them.'

I wasn't thinking, when I threw that last bit in, that Daniel would have first-hand knowledge from his time in Newgate prison of how losing freedom felt, until he told me slowly, 'I assure you, Eva, I do have a high regard for liberty.'

'I know you do.'

'And whatever custom may decree in public, in my family every woman has been free to speak her mind.'

'Behind closed doors.'

He smiled and said, 'I've found that there are many things more safely done behind closed doors than in the public view, by men as well as women.' Then, more serious, 'Do you think I am free to say exactly what I please, and when? In truth you'd be mistaken. If I stated my opinion of the current state of politics, I'd soon be clapped in irons for treason.'

He was right, I knew. 'But even if you can't state your opinions, you can act on them.'

'Not openly. No, you and I are both confined to showing but one part of us in public, and another to our friends. As for the whole of us . . . well, that must be reserved for those few people we are fortunate enough to love and trust.'

He glanced at me then and appeared to mistake my continuing silence for sulking, because he said, 'Would it be any comfort if I told you you'd missed nothing of importance on our trip to shore this morning? That even

Fergal could not rouse himself to anything but boredom? Would that help?'

'Not much.' But still I smiled. 'Did Fergal tell you that I asked to come along?'

He clearly hadn't, from the lift of Daniel's eyebrow. 'And what did he say to that?'

I told him, and he gave a short laugh, his eyes warming. 'Well, 'tis certain you've won his affection, for had any other woman asked him, Fergal would have thought it a fine joke to tell the crew.'

I said, 'I thought he might have told you, that was all.'

The laughter faded from his eyes but left the warmth. 'I've no need of Fergal to tell me when you are unhappy. Not even he can match my knowledge of your moods, I think, or know the way to read them in your face.'

The ship rolled and I put a hand against the window for support. It was no more than that, I thought – the movement of the ship, and not the words that Daniel had just said, or how he'd said them, or the fact that he was standing half a step from me.

Looking up at him I said, 'I'm not unhappy.'

'Are you not?'

'It's not unhappiness. It's . . .' Trying to find some way to describe the confusion of emotions I was feeling, I looked past his shoulder seeking inspiration. 'Daniel?'

'Yes?'

I touched his arm and for a moment he misunderstood and stepped in closer, so my cheek was pressed against the roughness of his jacket when I gripped his arm more firmly, turning him so he could see what I was seeing.

In the *Sally*'s wake a tall black ship was following,

her bowsprit spearing through the waves with predatory purpose.

He briefly tightened his embrace, his mouth brushing over my hair in a quick kiss of apology or promise before he released me altogether. 'Keep back from the windows,' he told me. 'And no matter what may happen . . .'

'I'll stay here,' I said.

He gave a nod. 'If there is any danger, I will come for you. I promise. Oh, and Eva? Lock—'

'—the door. I know.'

The quick flash of his smile was my reward for that as he stepped out and shut the door behind him.

Whatever signal passed between the French ship and our own it must have proved this was indeed the ship that Daniel thought it was, the one he had been sent to meet. He brought us hard around into the wind so that we all but stopped, and the next sound I heard was the orderly scramble of men going over the side of the *Sally* and into the boat.

I knew Daniel was with them. I caught the timbre of his voice above the now-familiar slap and splash of oars as they rowed off.

And so I settled in to wait, and let myself slide down the wall till I was sitting curled against it with my legs tucked up and my head resting comfortably on my knees. I sat like that a long time, drifting idly with my thoughts, rocked by the *Sally*'s gentle motion on the water, and at last that combination brought my heavy eyelids down and I was lulled to sleep.

My dreams were deep and pleasant, filled with Daniel's smiling eyes, his touch, his voice . . .

'You cannot stay here,' he said quietly.

'I want to,' I replied. 'I want to stay.'

I felt him lift me, then, and reaching up I linked my arms around his neck and snuggled to his chest before the hardness of it warned me that I was no longer dreaming.

Blinking stupidly, I looked around, or tried to. It was night, the only light within the darkened cabin coming from a single candle set upon the desk, the curtains drawn across the curving sweep of windows. Daniel shifted me a little higher on his chest. I must have been a burden with the weight of my green gown, but he made no complaints. He only said, 'You cannot sleep here on the floor.'

I wasn't totally awake yet. 'Didn't mean to. I was waiting.'

'So I see.'

'You took a long time.'

'Ay, we had a fair lot to discuss, and then the cargo to bring over.'

They'd already transferred cargo from the French ship to the *Sally*? I'd heard nothing. 'Did I sleep through that?'

'Apparently.' He set me on my feet but kept a light hold on my arms as though he thought I might topple over. 'Fergal was guarding your door for the most of it, I only came with the final load.'

Fergal. Guarding my door. With my reason returning, I looked at the door, which I knew I had locked. 'How did you get in?'

He raised one hand and briefly let a brass key dangle from his fingers. 'The captain's advantage. I've brought you some supper.'

Now that I thought of it, I hadn't eaten anything since breakfast and my stomach did feel hollow.

On the desk beside the candle lay a hunk of cheese half-wrapped in muslin, two pears and a few round buns that looked a little squashed as though he'd brought them in his pockets, which he very likely had done.

'Thank you.' Picking up a bun, I took a bite. 'It's very good. What is it?'

'French loaf.' He had crossed behind me to the bookshelf, and now slid a panel just below it to the side and rummaged in the recess.

The food had a restorative effect on my senses. It struck me how quiet the ship seemed. 'Where is everybody?'

'There is one man standing above on his watch. All the rest are yet aboard the French ship by her captain's invitation, having supper with her crew.'

I raised my eyebrows. 'Even Fergal?'

'Fergal,' Daniel told me, 'has few weaknesses, I will admit, but he is very partial to French cookery, and when he did discover that this French ship in particular has lately paid a visit to the Islands of Canaries and is carrying a goodly load of strong Canary sack, that decided the matter.' He'd found what he was looking for. He straightened from the recess with a flash of silver showing in his hand, and slid the panel shut.

'And what is "sack"?' I asked.

He answered by carefully lifting a green bottle out of his deep jacket pocket. 'This,' he said, and set the bottle down upon the desk, 'is sack.'

'And Fergal likes it, does he?'

'More than cider.' Daniel set the two small silver cups

he'd taken from the cupboard in the wall down, too, and easing out the bottle's cork began to fill them. 'Will you have some?'

'Please.' It tasted like sherry, but stronger.

A burst of raucous laughter drifted over from the French ship, and the distant lilt of music, and I said, 'It sounds as if you're missing all the fun.'

He raised his own cup, unconcerned. 'For my part, I would rather have your company.'

Despite the plainness of the food, that supper was the best I'd ever eaten. No fine restaurant, no expensive gourmet offering, could match the simple wonderment of sitting there with Daniel in candlelight, the ship's boards creaking to the gentle rocking of the dark sea all around us that made all the world seem, for this one evening, very far away.

We talked about our families. I didn't tell him I already knew some details of his own from reading Jack's book, and anyway it didn't matter. Daniel settled in and told the tales to me himself, and then he asked about my family so I talked about Katrina and our summers at Trelowarth and the reason I'd come back.

'And you came all that way,' he asked, 'because your sister wished to rest where she had once been happy?'

'Yes.'

'Was she not happy elsewhere?'

'Yes, of course she was. Just not in the same way. Trelowarth was – it *is* – a very special place.'

'Trelowarth,' he countered, 'is rooms gathered under a roof, nothing more.' He refilled his cup and my own. 'I would argue 'tis never the place, but the people one shares it with who are the cause of our happiest memories. That is why we find that having lived them once, we never can recapture them.'

I'd never really thought of that. But now I wondered if he wasn't right, and if that might not be the reason why, though Claire and Mark and Susan had done all they could to make me welcome, nothing at Trelowarth in the present felt exactly as I'd hoped it would. The place was the same, but the times had moved forward. My sister, my parents, were no longer there. And the girl I had been then . . . well, she too was gone.

I said, 'The Moving Finger.'

Daniel looked a question at me, and I gave myself a shake and told him, 'Sorry, it's a reference from a poem, a very lovely one.' I quoted the whole stanza for his benefit:

'The Moving Finger writes; and, having writ
Moves on: nor all thy Piety nor Wit
Shall lure it back to cancel half a line,
Nor all thy Tears wash out a Word of it.'

He said, 'You're right, it is a lovely poem. I do confess I'm not familiar with it.'

'No,' I said, 'you wouldn't be. It isn't written, yet. That is, the original version in Persian, that's been around for—' I tried to remember when Omar Khayyam had lived – 'well, for a few hundred years. But it won't be translated to English until the next century.'

'Rather a long time to wait.' He glanced at me as though I'd just done something that intrigued him. 'I'm surprised you thought to share it. You are usually more guarded with your knowledge of the future.'

He was right, I thought. Again I blamed the sack, and told him so.

'I see.' There was a trace of mischief in his half-smile as he took the bottle in his hand. 'Then let us fill our cups again,' he said, 'and you can tell me about India.'

Chapter Thirty-Two

Even with the fortified Canary wine relaxing me and spreading warmth through all my weary muscles, I found it near impossible to will myself to sleep.

So I lay there in my hammock watching Daniel sleep, instead.

He'd had more wine than I'd had, and the day's events had been much harder on him, and he'd drifted off while he was sitting in his chair with legs outstretched beneath the desk, head falling forwards till his chin was nearly resting on his chest.

It didn't look the least bit comfortable, especially since now and then he'd jerk his head up with a sudden start and let it slowly droop again, and on the third time that he did this I felt certain that I heard a crack of protest from his neck.

I lay a moment more in silence and debated what to do.

And in the end I swung myself out of the hammock and went quietly over to wake him.

I'd forgotten, from the time that I'd encountered him at night in the front bedroom of Trelowarth, just how quickly he could wake. My hand had barely touched his shoulder when his eyes came halfway open.

'Eva?'

'You're not comfortable.'

He closed his eyes again. 'I am.'

'You're not. That chair's too small,' I said. 'Let me sleep there. You take the hammock.'

'No need.' His voice had the cavalier slur of a man who'd had too much to drink and was past really caring; who'd happily sleep in a ditch if he had to.

But I cared. With a bit more persuading I managed to get him to stand. He was less steady on his feet than I'd expected, and I had to steer him to the hammock with his arm around my waist, and when he obligingly lowered his long body into it he didn't let go, but kept his arm there so that I was pulled partway into the hammock, too.

I tried to straighten. 'Daniel.'

He'd already started falling back to sleep.

If he'd been sleeping deeply it would have been easy to dislodge his hold and step away, but as it was his arm lay heavily and firmly round me, keeping me in place. And to be honest, once I'd thought about it, I was not all that inclined to step away.

He'd said a hammock held the weight of two men when it needed to. I took him at his word, and since I was already halfway in I cast propriety aside and slipped in properly, turning a bit so my head nestled onto his shoulder. I let the rhythm of his heartbeat, strong and sure beneath my cheek, chase off my worries.

He had been right earlier, when he'd suggested that I'd been expecting adventure; that I'd seen a certain romance in the notion of a smuggling run to Brittany. But the romance of the voyage could no longer mask the actual reality of what was going on, not with the cargo we now carried from the French ship we'd been sent to meet in secret by the Duke of Ormonde's orders.

I might be prepared to believe that what Daniel had taken in trade for the wool at our first port of call had been only the usual brandy and lace, but whatever the French ship had given us now had to do with the coming rebellion. And although I knew the rebellion would fail, I had not learnt yet what that would mean to the man lying next to me, or to his brother and Fergal, or even the men on this ship, and their families. In the history books they likely wouldn't even rate a mention, just as Shakespeare's Henry V, having read aloud the list of noblemen who'd died at Agincourt, had then dismissed the countless others lying lifeless in the mud as 'none else of name'.

But these men were not nameless to me. Not to me, I thought, laying my hand on the chest of the man at my side in a move that was faintly protective. Daniel half-woke again, drew me more closely against him and lowered his head so his wine-scented breath warmed my temple, and went back to sleep. And in time, as the ship creaked and rocked with the wind and the waves, I slept, too.

When I woke to a knock at the door there was light in the cabin – a grey light that spilt round the edge of the curtains.

I shifted, not wholly remembering, and felt the weight and warmth beside me.

Daniel hadn't moved much in the night. He still held me against him, my head cradled into the curve of his shoulder, his hand lying heavily over my hip. It couldn't be comfortable for him, I thought. If nothing else, he'd likely lost all circulation in his arm. Carefully I eased out of the hammock without swinging it too much, and crossed to answer the door.

Fergal's face was impassive. His dark gaze briefly rested on my rumpled gown and loosened hair before it flicked beyond me to where Daniel lay asleep, and then returned without expression. 'Waken him, would you?' the Irishman told me. 'He's needed on deck.'

He turned away, not waiting for an answer and not making any comment on the way that he had found us, but I sensed his disapproval.

I tried talking to him later, as we washed the dinner plates together in the galley alcove, on our own. I did it quietly. I told him, 'What you saw . . . it wasn't like that. Nothing happened.'

Fergal didn't answer. Didn't even glance around.

I tried again. 'I said—'

'You're not meant to be speaking.' His hard sideways glance cut me off. 'And the other is none of my business.'

I knew where the coldness was coming from; knew he was not angry but concerned, and I could only guess that his concern was not for me, but for his friend. He'd have seen how losing Ann affected Daniel, and no friend would ever wish to see that twice. No matter how well Fergal liked me, I felt certain that he viewed what was developing between myself and Daniel as a road to sure disaster.

And I wasn't so convinced that he was wrong.

My troubled thoughts stayed with me as the *Sally* slowly settled back into the shelter of her private mooring place below the dark woods of Trelowarth, with the black cliffs at her back.

We had slipped in on the rising tide and darkness was beginning its descent upon the pebbled shoreline, cloaking our activities from idly prying eyes. And by the time the men had off-loaded the cargo with efficient speed and silence, there was barely light left in the cabin for me to make out Fergal's features when he came below to fetch me.

'Danny's waiting at the cave,' he said.

We were the last to leave. The other members of the *Sally*'s crew had scattered to their own devices with a stealth that marked them true-born smugglers.

Fergal handed me down into the Breton rowboat that we'd brought back to replace the one we'd lost to Creed's accomplice. I could see the smashed remains of that one sitting on the beach as Fergal rowed us quietly across towards the Cripplehorn.

The constable, it seemed, had not been pleased to find his spy left on the shore. And despite Jack's claims no local jury would convict the Butler brothers, I knew better than to underestimate the constable. What Creed could do within the law and what he'd dare to do outside it were, I knew, two very different things.

The boat scraped bottom on the shingle. Fergal held it steady while I scrambled out to stand beside the waterfall, which, having passed midsummer, had thinned down to a trickle that shifted and danced down the long drop from overhead, splattering onto the already wave-wet rocks close by my feet. It was a good thing I already knew about the hidden entrance, otherwise the sudden figure stepping from what looked like solid rock might have unnerved me into jumping even higher than I did.

Daniel touched my arm. 'We'll have to put the boat up. Will you wait inside a moment?'

With a nod I sidled past him through the long cleft in the stone.

The rush of silence struck me with the same swift force that I remembered from the day I'd come down here with Mark. The sea sounded suddenly very far off, and the lyrical dripping of water from somewhere came echoing back from the walls of wet stone.

This was not the unused and abandoned space I'd seen that day, though. The scents of the sea and the salt-dampened rocks were overlaid here with more human ones – pipe smoke and new wooden barrels and candles that had only just been extinguished, the smell of their smoke still a sharpness that lingered unseen. The one candle they had left burning sat stuck in its own melted wax on a small tin plate set on the top of a barrel – one barrel among many others that stood stacked in staggering rows down the long curving wall to my right. I couldn't tell from looking at the barrels what was in them, but I would have bet the bank it wasn't anything to drink.

More likely, I decided, they held guns or arms of some sort that were meant for the rebellion. From the articles I'd read I knew the Duke of Ormonde's plans had been to raise a loyal army in the west of England that would fight beneath his banner in support of young James Stuart when he came across the sea to claim the throne so many in these times believed was his by right of birth.

James Stuart would come, I knew. He would land in the north, up in Scotland, and men throughout Britain would rise in his name, and would pay with their lives, and their cause would be lost in the end. All for nothing, I thought. All the risks that these men were now taking to bring back these guns or whatever they were, and to hide them down here, it was all wasted effort.

I felt a sudden heavy sadness in my chest, and yet I knew that, even if I did warn Daniel of what was to come, he would do nothing differently. He stood with his king, no matter what the odds or consequences, because that was where his heart and honour told him he must stand. Fergal had explained this at the woodpile when he'd said, 'To Danny, knowing that the battle will not end the way he wishes does not make it any less worthwhile to fight.'

I heard a quiet step behind me on the stone and Daniel's head came round the corner of the entrance. 'Done,' he said. 'Would you mind fetching me that candle, Eva?'

Being closer to it, I nodded, and crossed to lift it from the barrel, being careful where I put my feet upon the floor with all its slippery rocks and damply filled depressions. As I lifted up the candle on its small tin plate the flame dipped briefly sideways, dancing light across a gleaming length of metal near the barrel's bottom edge – the blade of Daniel's dagger, lying on the floor. He must have dropped it there by accident, I thought. I nearly bent to pick it up . . . but then I stopped myself, remembering Mark's treasure box, and Daniel's dagger buried at the bottom of it.

Here was where he'd lost it. And where Mark, in time, would find it. It was not my place to interfere.

Daniel must have seen me hesitate. 'Is everything all right?'

My fingers folded to a tight fist at my side, to stop me reaching for the dagger as I wanted to. 'I'm fine,' I said, and turning I walked back to him, the candle held in front of me. It hardly shook at all.

He took it from my hand and thanked me for it, then to my surprise he blew it out. 'I would not wish to see our work destroyed by fire,' he said, by way of explanation.

'Won't we need the light for walking home?'

Which was, I later thought, a really stupid thing to ask a smuggler who would hardly want to call attention to his presence in the woods at night. But Daniel only smiled, a smile I couldn't see but clearly felt against my lips as he bent close to lightly brush his mouth across my own – the barest kiss, because there wasn't really time for more than that, with Fergal waiting just outside.

'Sometimes,' said Daniel, ''tis better to be in the dark.'

Chapter Thirty-Three

We slept late the next day. Jack was up and about before any of the rest of us. I heard him moving round the house and whistling round the kitchen on his way out to the stables. In the room beside me Daniel woke and stirred. I heard his feet thump to the floor, and then the quiet movements while he dressed and went downstairs.

I thought of drifting back to sleep, but in the end I rose and dressed as well. It took a little while, and by the time I got down to the kitchen Jack was back indoors and arguing with Daniel, though this wasn't like the argument I'd heard them have before. More like a stubborn disagreement.

'Ay,' said Jack, 'I know what you were thinking, but I'm saying you were better to have let the lad come with you and then tossed him over halfway through the crossing, for that might have been an accident and no one could have called it any different.'

Daniel's level look spoke for itself, but he elaborated anyway. 'I do not murder beardless lads. Good morrow, Eva.'

With a nod I took the bucket from its hook beside the hearth and slipped between them.

Jack said, 'Beardless lads who have been shamed in front of Creed may prove more dangerous than you might yet expect.'

I would have liked to have hung about longer to hear what Jack thought Creed's unsuccessful spy might try to do to seek revenge, but being on thin ice already with Jack I knew it would be best if I kept to the things that a sister of Fergal's would logically do. And right now, that meant fetching a bucket of water to start cooking breakfast.

The well had a simple design with a winch and a rope and a hook for the bucket, but hauling the bucket up full was more work than I'd thought it would be. I was leaning my weight on the winch in an effort to speed up the process when Jack banged his way out the back door and started across the yard.

Catching sight of me, he changed direction and came over, saying curtly, 'Stand aside.' I couldn't help but think the force he threw against the winch was more from a release of temper than from any real desire to help me. The bucket all but flew up from the darkness of the well, and when he yanked the bucket from its hook it sloshed a wave of water out to protest such rough treatment.

'There.' He thrust the bucket in my hands and turned away, strode off four steps and wheeled again to add, 'If you *do* have a voice, you might use it to persuade my brother that there is a time when men must act to aid themselves, and not for honour.'

If I could have answered back, I would have told him there'd be no point in my telling Daniel anything. He was the way he was, and there was no force that could change him.

As I'm sure Jack knew already. With a final glare he turned and carried on towards the stables while I slowly lugged the water back across the yard.

Fergal, newly awake and still yawning, met me at the kitchen door and took the bucket from my hands, following my backwards glance with his quick knowing eyes. 'Don't you worry at all about Jack, he's all bluster. He's only been penned up alone in the house these past days, and he's wanting a breath of air.'

I didn't worry about Jack, as it happened. I knew he would live to a good age. It was the other two men that I worried about.

'Breakfast,' said Fergal. 'And then I'll be leaving you here to take care of the dinner.'

'Why? Where are you going?'

'Lostwithiel.'

'Why?'

'Not your business. Now, breakfast.'

'Does it have to do with the guns you brought back?'

Fergal turned then and gave me a look. 'I do hope that I never go forwards in time, for I'd not long survive in an age filled with women so curious.' Setting the bucket down hard on the hearth he said, more firmly, 'Breakfast.'

But I knew that I was right. And when he rode off in his turn an hour later, I wished hard that he would meet with no adventures on the road.

Daniel was busy upstairs with his books.

The pleasant scent of pipe tobacco met me on the landing when I went up with a mind to make my bed. Instead I went the other way along the corridor and found him in his study, deeply absorbed in a book that looked, even for this time, quite old. Glancing up from his seat by the window, he took the pipe from his mouth for a moment and asked, 'Did you want me?'

A loaded question, I decided, if I'd ever heard one. Resisting the impulse to answer it, I simply told him, 'I'll be starting dinner soon. It's fish – that's all that Fergal's left. How do you like it cooked?'

'However you desire to cook it,' was his answer, with a smile. 'Did he gut them first for you, at least, before leaving?'

'He did, yes.'

'A good man.' Setting his pipe on the table beside him, he rounded his shoulders to stretch them.

I looked at the book he held. 'What are you reading?'

For an answer he turned it round, holding it open at the title page so I could read the words myself. *The Sceptical Chymist*. The 'chymist' had me stumped a moment, then, 'A book of chemistry?'

'You know the science?'

'Only what I learnt in school.'

'Which was, no doubt, beyond what even the greatest of our current men of science could yet fathom.' Giving a nod to the book he said, 'This man, Robert Boyle, had a very great intellect, although he dwelt too much I think on alchemy. But when I was naught but a babe he conducted experiments dealing with fire and combustion, chemical combustion. I had hoped to find them detailed here, but this book was published before that time. Still, it makes for fascinating reading.'

'What's got you interested in chemical combustion?'

'You. Your self-igniting spills.' He flipped a page and settled back. 'It does occur to me that phosphorous might have some useful qualities, but as for the other chemical or chemicals that one might need—'

I cut him off in something close to panic. 'You can't do that.' But he could, I knew. It was the way his brain worked, turning everything he could not understand into a puzzle to be solved. A sort of game. Except, 'You can't be messing round with self-igniting matches, Daniel. They're not meant to be invented till the 1800s.'

He turned another page. 'Then if I do invent them I shall swear to keep the secret in my family until then.'

'Don't joke. You can't do this.'

'Why?' Holding his place in the book with his thumb, he closed it and faced me with an air of intellectual debate. 'What harm can there be in increasing my knowledge?'

'A great deal, if that knowledge isn't something anyone should have in this time,' was my argument. 'Anything you do that you weren't meant to do could change the future, change the way that things turn out.'

'How do you know this?'

'Well, it's common knowledge. Common sense.' The first rule of time travel, really, I thought – so ingrained in society's psyche through novels and films that it took on the weight of a fact.

'But what proof do you have?' Daniel asked. 'Has a man ever done this?'

I said, 'I don't know, but—'

'Have learned men studied the matter?'

'They have theories . . .'

'But how are they tested?' he challenged me. 'Theories are fine things, but I do confess that my own common sense tells me there is an order to life that cannot be so easily changed by the will of one man.' He spread his hands to indicate the study. 'All of this, this life that I have lived, it has already passed and faded from the memories of the people of your own time. It is rather like that poem you did speak of, with the moving finger writing words that cannot be erased. My page is written,' he said, 'and not even I can change a line of it.'

I wasn't sure which one of us was right. I said, 'But *I'm* not meant to be here. *I* might change things.'

Daniel looked at me a moment, then he set his book aside and stood and closed the space between us with his slow deliberate steps. 'How do you know,' he asked, 'that here is not exactly where you're meant to be?'

I didn't have an answer for him, partly because my mind, as always, had lost all its power to form coherent thoughts with him so near. And partly because I wanted so badly for him to be right, even though we both knew that the thing was impossible. I shook my head and repeated those words: 'It's impossible.'

'Why is it?' His eyes gave no quarter. 'Where is your proof?'

I had no hope of winning the argument, not with him standing there looking at me like that, but I still tried. 'Where is yours?'

Daniel took my hand and held it to his heart so I could feel its beating. 'Here,' he told me quietly. His other hand came up to hold my face and tilt it up while his began a slow descent. 'And here,' he murmured, with his mouth against my own.

It was a thorough and persuasive kiss that made my senses spin until I couldn't think of any reason not to be convinced.

When he drew back, the look he slanted down at me was so intense it stopped my breath. Intense, yet somehow questioning. He held my face still warm within his hand and asked me in a slightly roughened voice, 'Would you desire more proof than that?'

I knew what he was asking, then. Knew, too, that I'd be complicating things beyond repair if I said yes. Because if I already found it difficult to leave him as things were, that would be nothing to the wrenching loss I'd feel when I was forced to leave him after this.

Looking up, I gave a nod and watched the question in his eyes give way to warmth. And then he lifted me, the trailing gown and all, and he was kissing me again and we were moving from the study down the corridor towards the corner bedchamber.

The door swung open with a crash and Daniel kicked it closed again behind us, and I heard the scraping of the key turned in the lock, and we were on the bed together and to tell the truth, I wasn't much inclined to notice anything besides that for a while.

* * *

Time hung suspended. And for once, I had no question of my place in it. I was exactly where I was supposed to be, where I belonged, with Daniel Butler lying in the bed beside me. I could hear his even breathing, feel his warmth, the shifting of his weight against the mattress as he turned. His face in sleep was not so hardened as I'd seen it look. The lines were there, but smoother, and the slanting shadows of his lashes crossed his tanned skin peacefully.

Then as I watched his face, his eyes came slowly open and he saw me too, and smiled.

I closed my own eyes tight to hold the moment. Until I remembered how I had come into the past from the present this last time, and quickly I opened my eyes again.

He was still there.

Misreading my relief, he asked me, 'Are you back to doubting whether I am real?'

His tone was dry, and so I kept my answer light. 'After what just happened, yes, I might be.'

'I shall choose to view that as a compliment.' The smile deepened briefly. 'Or did you intend the opposite?'

My gaze still held by his, I gave my head the slightest shake against the softness of the pillow and replied, 'It was a compliment.'

I watched the green eyes darken in that now familiar way, as Daniel bridged the space between us with a kiss that somehow managed the impossible and left me with an even stronger sense of longing than I'd had before.

He drew back, his expression turning serious, and let his head fall to the pillow close beside my own, his one hand sliding from my face into my hair where he absently wound a long strand round his finger as though he were making a curl. 'I have known many women, Eva, but for all that, I have only loved but twice. I cannot say that I am well accomplished in the way of it, nor that I was the very best of husbands. I do hold the things I love too closely, sometimes, and I can be contrary for nothing but the sake of it, and I know well that I am not the easiest of men to make a life with.'

I held my breath and lay there watching him, and waiting.

He was studying my hair, now loosely spiralled in his fingers. 'I have only loved but twice,' he said again. 'The first I took for granted, and now she is in her grave and gone. I would not wish . . .' His hand closed briefly, tightening. 'I would not wish to make the same mistake with you.'

I'd held my breath too long and had forgotten how to let it out, and when I did my head felt light. 'Did you just say you loved me?'

'Ay.' His eyes were back on mine again. 'And I would have you marry me.' He must have thought that sounded too imperious, because he caught the words and phrased them differently. 'I'm asking,' he said, gently, 'will you marry me?'

I felt my eyes fill hotly with the unexpected depth of my emotions, and I tried to blink the wetness back, to hold to that last ragged edge of reason. 'I love you, too,' I said. 'But . . .'

Daniel waited through the moment's silence, finally prompting, 'But?'

'I'm hardly ever here. I come and go, I can't control it. You can't want to have a life like that.'

His face relaxed. ''Tis you I want.' He trailed his fingers

warmly down my cheek and brushed away the single tear that had escaped my lashes. 'I care not on what terms.'

He didn't try to catch the next tear, or the one that followed after that. His gaze stayed steady on my own.

'Say yes,' he said so quietly it might have been a whisper. He moved his hand against my face so that his thumb could brush across my trembling lips as lightly as a kiss. 'Say yes.'

As if there were another answer I could ever give him. 'Yes.'

I'd never seen him smile like that. I knew that for my whole life I'd remember it, as I'd remember everything about this moment – the angle of the sunlight spilling through the bedroom window and the even warmer light in Daniel's eyes.

And how his touch felt, gentle on my face.

'Whatever time we have,' he said, 'it will be time enough.'

Chapter Thirty-Four

Fergal stood behind me in the shadows of the church.

We hadn't needed any witnesses. Apparently the laws had not been written yet that made them a requirement. In fact, according to Daniel, we could simply have exchanged vows on our own, there in the bedroom at Trelowarth with no priest around to hear us, and then sealed the deal by making love – which had, I admitted, seemed rather appealing to me at the time.

But he'd laughed then and gathered me close and said we had in essence already done all of that. 'The promise is the same no matter where we choose to say it, yet it seems to me more meaningful to say it in a church.'

'We'll have to wait, then.'

'Why?'

'Well, because we'll need a licence, or they'll have to

read the banns, or . . .' I had paused, because I'd noticed he was looking at me strangely.

'All we'll need,' he'd said, quite certain, 'is a payment that will satisfy the vicar.'

He'd been right, of course.

Finding the vicar himself had been more of a challenge, but eventually he had been traced to the house of some friends in the neighbouring parish, and Fergal, returning from Lostwithiel, had headed back out to go fetch him. And that was how I came to be here, with an hour to go till sunrise, standing in the aisle of St Petroc's church by candlelight with Fergal at my shoulder and the vicar off discussing terms with Daniel in the vestry.

I felt a surge of nervousness again and smoothed the skirts of my green gown till Fergal told me, 'Quit your fussing. You look fine.'

Obedient, I stilled my hands and then, not knowing what else I should do with them, I clasped them both behind me. I whispered, 'They've been in there a long time.'

'You're meant to be my sister, and a Catholic. I'd imagine that's what's keeping them.'

'Oh.'

'You've no call to worry. For the price that Danny's offering, the vicar will be sure to keep his disapproval to himself.'

I looked away again. 'Like you.'

'What's that?'

I shook my head and murmured, 'Nothing.'

Fergal took a step around to stand where I could see him. 'Do you think I disapprove?'

'I think you care about your friend,' I told him with a

shrug, 'and you don't want to see him hurt again.'

'I want,' he answered carefully, 'to see him with a woman who will love him in the way that he deserves, and know the value of the man whose heart she carries.' In his voice I heard that same fierce challenge I remembered from the first time we had met, when we'd squared off across the corner bedroom with me in my borrowed gown and him as mad as blazes. 'Has he found that?'

Looking up, I met his eyes and saw that underneath the challenge lay what looked to be affection, and not sure that I could speak around the lump of pure emotion in my throat, I gave a nod.

'Well, then,' he said. 'Why the devil would you think I'd disapprove?'

'I'm sorry.'

'So you should be. Leaping into judgement.' There was humour in the dark glance angled down at me. 'If I truly disapproved, you'd not be here.'

'Where would I be, then? At the bottom of the well?'

'Most likely, ay.'

'Big scary man,' I called him, low.

He didn't hide the smile, this time. But he did step back again where he had been before, behind my shoulder, where he could more clearly see the vestry door.

The flickering candles had burnt at least half an inch lower before Daniel came through that door with the vicar beside him – a middle-aged man with stooped shoulders who looked as though he wasn't fully awake. But he seemed game enough for the task at hand.

'Have you a ring?' he asked Daniel, before we began.

Daniel looked an apology at me and started to say

something but with a shake of my head I reached over and slipped off the Claddagh ring, holding it out, and his fingers brushed warm on my palm as he took it and handed it on to the vicar.

It was, I thought, a fitting thing to use Katrina's ring for this. A way to feel her standing at my side, where I had always thought she would be when I married.

With a cough the vicar set the ring with care upon the pages of his open prayer book, ready for his blessing. 'Since I am told she cannot speak, I'd ask Mistress O'Cleary to—'

'Her name is Ward,' said Daniel, and the vicar stopped.

'I beg your pardon?'

Daniel said, 'Her name is Eva Ellen Ward, and in this place of God she has a voice. For surely this is not a place where anyone should speak aught but the truth.' He held the vicar's gaze directly. 'Nor where anyone should fear betrayal.'

The vicar paused. Then nodded slowly. 'No, indeed.' He turned to me. 'Now, Eva Ellen Ward, is it your wish that you be married to this man?'

I looked at Daniel, grateful for his giving me the chance to say the words out loud. 'It is.'

'Then let us now begin.'

The ring felt strange on my left hand instead of on my right. My thumb kept seeking out its smoothness there and twisting it around to feel the clasped hands and the heart, till Daniel caught my hand in his and held it while we walked.

We were taking the longer way back through the fields,

having let Fergal go on ahead of us. The rising sun had just begun to push its way above the hills that lay to the east of Polgelly, and over the wet grass our shadows stretched long.

He'd been right. The words we had just said to each other had seemed much more meaningful, spoken aloud in the church, than they would have done if we'd exchanged our vows privately yesterday. Something of the solemnity of the traditional service still clung to me, keeping me silent till Daniel's hand lightly squeezed mine.

'You are lost in your thoughts. May I know them?'

'I doubt they'd make sense to you.' Turning, I showed him a smile. 'I'm still sorting things through.'

'And what is it,' he asked, 'that needs sorting?'

'You know. How we're going to manage this.'

His turn to smile. 'The same as any other married man and woman might. How else?'

'But we,' I said, reminding him, 'are not like any other married couple, are we? We can't really make plans for our future, not like normal people can.'

'Why not?'

I answered with a dry look. 'We're lucky enough if we make plans for supper. I might disappear before then.'

'Life is always uncertain,' he said with a shrug. 'We cannot let the fear of what might happen stop us living as we choose.' His fingers twined more tightly round my own.

And then to lighten things, I said, 'At least I didn't disappear in church.'

'No, you did not.' He swung my hand a little as we walked on further, then his steps began to slow. 'You did not disappear in church,' he echoed. Stopping, he looked down at me. 'Nor when we were on the *Sally*.'

I knew his thoughts were travelling the same path mine already had, and coming to the same conclusion.

'I know,' I assured him, 'I've noticed the same thing. Whatever's been happening seems to be tied to Trelowarth itself.' And I told him about the Grey Lady who'd vanished years before me.

He was thinking. 'So then if you left, it would most likely stop.'

'It's possible, yes, but I don't know for certain. It's only a theory.'

'And theories are meant to be tested, are they not?' Not waiting for an answer he went on, 'Perhaps we ought to go away for a short while, to Bristol, or to Plymouth. You did say you always return to the moment you left your own time, yes? Then there is no danger. If we have guessed wrongly you'll merely go back as you would have done had we stayed here. But if we are *not* wrong . . .' There was no need to finish the sentence.

'We could hardly be sure,' was my argument, 'after just one trip away. There'd be no guarantee.'

'No. But we could repeat the experiment, surely. I gladly would go where I needed to go, if it kept you beside me.'

I looked away briefly, in thought. We were standing where, three hundred years from now, the Quiet Garden would be coming into bloom with Mark's beloved roses, safely walled to shield them from the sea-blown weather, but just at the moment there was nothing here but sloping field with wildflowers speckled through the bowing grass that tumbled down towards the roof and chimneys of the house below.

I asked, 'You'd leave Trelowarth?'

'I can serve the Duke of Ormonde and the king aboard the *Sally* just as well as I could serve them from on land, mayhap a good deal better. And rebellions all must have an end.' With a faint smile he brushed back the hair from my eyes where the wind kept on blowing it. 'Ill or fair, I mean to be alive to see the end of this one. And there has been talk that if this new attempt to set King James upon his throne should founder, he will send the Duke of Ormonde to the Spanish court for aid, and I should think the duke will need assistance there.'

'In Spain.'

'Have you been there as well?' His eyes crinkled with humour.

'Well, actually, yes.'

'Did you like it?'

I lifted my chin. 'Very much.'

'Then,' he said, 'we will take it in small steps. Beginning with Bristol.'

Sealing the bargain, he drew me in close for a quick kiss that lengthened to something more, making me hold to his waist for support, and my hand touched the top of the knife handle slung at his belt.

Drawing back in surprise, I looked down at the dagger, and Daniel's gaze followed mine. 'What is the matter?' he asked.

It was not the same knife. This one had a bone handle, a cruder design. I said only, 'You have a new knife.'

'Yes. I've mislaid my favourite, but 'tis not a matter for concern. Most likely it is somewhere on the *Sally*.'

I should tell him, I thought. I should tell him I knew

where it was. But I couldn't, because if I did, then it wouldn't be there in the cave for the boy Mark to find it, as he was supposed to. And if I changed that, then what else . . . ?

'Eva?' Daniel was holding me, watching my face. Waiting.

I shook it off. 'Sorry.'

And then for the first time I realised the *way* he was watching me; noticed the look in his eyes as the landscape around us began to change, wavering.

I tried to cling more tightly to him, knowing that I couldn't, and my voice this time was no more than an anguished whisper. 'Sorry.'

Daniel's arms came more closely around me. I saw his mouth moving, and knew he was telling me something. I thought he was saying he'd wait for me, but he had already started to fade and I only caught one faint word: 'Wait.'

Then the wind rose and swirled and collapsed on itself in a rush of unbearable stillness.

My eyes were shut tightly.

I kept them that way, not only because I knew if I opened them I'd only see the green walls of my empty bedroom at Trelowarth, and the empty bed that I was lying on alone, but because I felt them filling with the stinging heat of tears.

I thought I'd learnt the pain of loss, but this was nothing like I'd ever felt before. I'd never in my life felt so alone.

I turned my face into the pillow just in time to catch the first sob rising from this newly hollow place inside me, and the tears came with it, swelling in behind my eyes and spilling over with a force I couldn't stop or fight.

And through it all, the thing that seemed to me the most unfair was that the birds outside my window went on singing as though it were just like any other morning.

Chapter Thirty-Five

That whole week was horrible. My emotions stayed close to the surface, and I had to concentrate hard to not vent them at every small irritant. Susan had noticed I wasn't myself, but I heard her explaining to Mark it was likely a mixture of grief and fatigue.

She was right.

Her solution was, too. She kept giving me things I could do round the tea room, unchallenging tasks that would keep my mind busy without really needing much effort. I wiped down the newly bought tables and set them at just the right angle and clipped on the tablecloths, placing a bud vase for one single rose at the centre. I sent all the glasses and cups through the new built-in dishwasher, stacking them clean in their place on the shelves.

Wednesday morning I sat with Felicity, folding the menus.

She was, if it were possible, more quiet and absorbed in thought than me, and since this seemed so foreign to her nature I was finally stirred to push my own self-pity to the side enough to ask, 'Are you all right?'

'What?' Glancing up, she said, 'Oh, yes, I'm fine.' She focused on the menu's fold. 'I'm really fine.'

She wasn't, though. Her hands shook very slightly and I recognised the barest hint of puffiness around her eyes. She had been crying.

When the door swung open at our backs Felicity looked swiftly up, face wary and yet hopeful, then her eyes dulled. 'Hello, Paul,' she told the plumber.

'What's the problem?' he asked cheerfully, his muscled shoulders and broad chest set off to good advantage in a black T-shirt this morning. In his fitted jeans and workboots, with his handsome face, he looked like the embodiment of most young women's fantasies, and yet it seemed Felicity could barely spare a glance for him as she explained the difficulties Susan had been having with the sinks.

She clearly was preoccupied with something – or with someone – and I had a good idea what. And whom.

I found Mark working in the field. The weather had been dry this week and he'd been busy T-budding the root stock that he'd planted this past spring.

Budding was a learnt skill and not everyone could do it as efficiently as Mark could. Moving doggedly along the rows of plants, he bent at each to make a shallow T-shaped cut above the root, and into that he tucked a single bud stripped from the stem of the variety of rose he wanted this one to become. Protected by a rubber patch, the tiny grafted bud would hopefully begin to take by autumn, and lie dormant through the winter months until Mark came next February with his shears to prune the whole plant back to just above the bud.

From that new stump, the bud would grow and flourish, and become a rose as lovely as the ones that were now blooming in the next field over. Some things only needed time to find their proper footing. Time and patience. Others, sometimes, needed a swift kick.

Mark glanced up as I came across the field towards him, and he gave a nod, but didn't break the rhythm of his work.

'What did you do,' I asked him bluntly, 'to Felicity?'

He'd been treading lightly round me all week long, uncertain of my mood, and when he looked up now I read the caution in his gaze. 'What did she say I did?'

I told him, 'Nothing.'

'Ah.'

'You made her cry.'

He looked away and took a deeper interest in the plant that he was budding, though his tone remained a shade defensive. 'All I did was tell her that I didn't have the time to see an art show with her Saturday, in Falmouth. She had pieces she was showing there, and—'

'What the hell,' I asked him, plain, 'is wrong with you?'

'I'm sorry?' Mark had raised his head again, surprised.

'You heard. You've got this lovely, lovely girl who's totally obsessed with you, and you're too blind to see it.'

He looked down again and said, so low I nearly didn't hear it, 'I'm not blind.'

'What?'

'I'm not blind.' Emphatic, with an edge of rare impatience. 'I can see she likes me, and for what it's worth, I like her, too.'

'Then why . . . ?'

'Is this your business?'

'No.' I met his glare head-on. 'But someone needs to sort it out.'

'It's sorted.'

'I can see that. You're all angry, and she's crying, and—'

'It wouldn't work.' He threw the words down with a hard finality that left no space for argument, but my emotions were already raw and I was in a mood to argue.

'Why is that?'

'Because Felicity's an artist.'

'And?'

'She needs her freedom,' he explained. 'Like Claire.' Then, seeing I was looking unenlightened, he went on, 'When I was young, Claire used to go away for days, for weeks, sometimes, to do her work. She'd up and take her canvases and off she'd go. She still does, every now and then.' He raked the hair back from his face, a gesture of control. 'I used to hate it, waking up to find she'd gone. Some men can live like that. My father could. I can't.'

'Felicity's not Claire,' I said.

'Felicity's a butterfly.' Unmoved, he pointed out, 'She's barely been down here a couple of years, who knows when she'll be off again.'

I had known Mark long enough to know his body language, and from how he held himself I knew his inner conflict was a real one, but the memory of Felicity's sad eyes spurred me to say, 'Your famous theory, yes. The butterflies. There's just one little problem with it.'

'Is there, really?' Mark was probably as close as I had ever seen him to the loss of his own temper, but he held it in. 'And what would that be?'

'It's all crap, that's what.'

'And you would know.'

My own pain tumbled over, then. 'I know that life's too short to live by stupid theories,' I shot back. 'I know that if you have the luck to find someone who loves you, then you love them back, you don't care on what terms.' I used the phrase of Daniel's though it hurt my heart to say it, and because I drew some strength from just remembering those words I carried on, 'Whatever time you have with somebody who loves you, Mark, it should be . . .' Something caught hard in my throat, and made me pause to fight it.

Still defiant, Mark asked, 'Should be what?'

I got the words out somehow, just above a whisper. 'Time enough.'

And then I turned, because I didn't want to argue any more. Before I'd gone ten steps he called out, 'Eva?'

I glanced back. I'd never seen Mark looking so torn up inside.

'Love isn't everything,' he said.

I shook my head. 'It is, you know. It's all that matters, and I hate to see you throwing it away.'

I left him standing there, to think on that.

I'd been purposely avoiding picking up Jack's memoirs since I'd come back, even though the book still sat with patience on my bedside table, bookmarked to the place where I'd left off.

I'd read beyond that now, of course, that day I'd spent aboard the *Sally*, so there really was no harm in reading what I knew already. But I wasn't too keen, any more, to learn what happened next.

It was only now, with what I'd said to Mark still nudging gently at my conscience, that I drew the curtains closed against the light of afternoon and curled up fully clothed upon my bed and reached my hand out for the memoirs.

I could always stop, I told myself. I didn't have to go beyond what I'd already experienced. It would be enough to feel this closeness for a while, not just to Daniel but to Fergal, too, and Jack, whose voice came through the printed pages as though he himself were telling me the stories.

While I read I could imagine that the walls around me were those other walls, the bed a larger bed with posts and curtains, and the room beside me not an empty one but home to an inhabitant who paced the floorboards restlessly on booted feet.

When I approached the place where the pages I'd been reading on the *Sally* had gone blank I read more carefully, prepared to put the book down. There it was – the bit that I'd read last, continued over to the facing page, and then . . .

I stopped, confused.

Because there was no more beyond that. Nothing written by Jack's hand, at any rate, although the person who had edited the memoirs had inserted this parenthesised apology:

Jack Butler's own account ends here. What follows is the Reverend Mr Simon's learned lecture on the usefulness of this account in teaching moral lessons to those young men who are tempted to pursue the ways of decadence, for let them be reminded that Jack Butler, having turned his back on both his earthly king and on that other King who rules all men, did thus commit himself to suffer an untimely end; and such an end as does befit a traitor to the Crown, for it was on the very first great anniversary of the accession to the throne of that good King George the First, whom he did so despise and seek to overthrow, that he did chance to fall afoul of the lawmen of Polgelly, and while fleeing from their constable was killed by one sure pistol shot and sent thus in disgrace before his Maker.

'No.'

I didn't know I'd spoken till I heard my own voice echo in the silent room, but even as the echo died I knew it didn't matter.

Daniel had been right. The words were written there already, printed long before my birth, and there was no amount of wishing that could change them.

'Hard luck,' was Oliver's opinion of the way Jack Butler met his end. Head tilted, he tried to remember his history. 'If it happened on the anniversary of King George's accession to the throne, then that would mean he died in . . .'

'August. August 1st, to be exact,' I said. 'I looked it up.'

'Ah.' Leaning on the corner of the desk in Uncle George's study, Oliver angled a penetrating look down at me while

I worked. It was Saturday, and he'd come up to help with cleaning windows at the greenhouse in advance of next week's opening, but somehow he had found his way in here instead. I didn't mind. His company was welcome in my current mood.

He said, 'You've really taken this to heart, haven't you? Maybe I shouldn't have found you that book.'

I couldn't reveal why the knowledge of Jack's death depressed me as much as it did. All I said was, 'It just seems unfair, his being killed like that.'

'Come have lunch,' he suggested.

'I can't. I've got this press release to finish.' Searching through the papers at the side of my computer I let out a tight sigh of frustration. 'If I ever find my proper notes. You don't remember, offhand, what the name of that big prize was that Trelowarth won back in the 1960s, do you?'

'Sorry, no. Mark would know it, but he won't be back till late tonight.'

I glanced up. 'Back from where?'

'From Falmouth. He and Fee are at the art show.'

'Mark went with her?' I stared at him. 'You're sure?'

'Do you know,' he said, 'that's the first time I've seen you smile all day.'

'Is it? Sorry. I've just been a little out of sorts, that's all.'

'Susan might know what the name of the prize was,' he said. 'I'll go ask her. I ought to be out at the greenhouse now, anyway.' Straightening, he told me, 'Sue will be happy, at least, with the way your Jack Butler died. Adds a bit of drama to her story of the smugglers, for the tourists. Just as well, because I still can't find anything to tie the Duke of

Ormonde and his Jacobite rebellion to this area. Mind you,' he said, 'it wasn't much of a rebellion to begin with. Never really got off the ground. The Duke of Ormonde buggered off to France before it happened. He knew Parliament had voted to impeach him and he didn't wait around to be arrested.'

I couldn't really blame him, and I said as much. And then I asked, more slowly, 'Did he go to Spain, afterwards?'

'He did, yeah. Why?'

'I just wondered.' I wondered, too, whether he'd brought any kinsmen along on the voyage, to help raise support for the Jacobite cause.

Oliver remarked that when people like the Duke of Ormonde fell, they landed firmly on their feet. 'And they always choose warm places for their exiles. Spanish women, Spanish wine, I'm sure it wasn't any hardship. It was those he left behind him here in Cornwall did the suffering.'

I didn't really want to ask him, but I had to. 'Why? What happened to them?'

'Well, they were arrested, weren't they? King George learnt what they were up to, and he had them rounded up before they had a chance to rise. They had to watch King James land up in Scotland, watch him lose his battle, couldn't do a thing to help him. Some were executed, afterwards, and some transported to the colonies, and—' He broke off, looking at me. 'You all right?'

'I'm fine.' I schooled my face and looked away. 'You said King George found out what they were planning. How?'

'The Duke of Ormonde sent his private secretary down here as a messenger – a Scottish colonel, can't recall his name. McSomething, anyway.'

'Maclean.'

I could have told him that the man had used the alias of Wilson; could have told him what he'd looked like, that he'd worn a dark-green coat and powdered wig and high black boots, and that his horse had been a grey. I could have told him that Jack Butler hadn't liked him much; that Jack had nearly lost his life in going to St Non's to make enquiries as to Wilson's true identity, and that he'd learnt that Wilson's name was actually Maclean. I'd been there when Jack had told us that, when Daniel had assured him that Maclean was 'indisputably' a man to trust. The Duke of Ormonde's secretary.

Oliver nodded. 'That's right,' he said. 'Colonel Maclean. He came down to Cornwall and met all the people preparing to fight on the side of the Jacobites, and then . . . hang on.' His mobile was ringing. He took it out to check the number while I looked away, and just for an instant I saw in my mind's eye a man in a dark-green coat standing in the stable yard with Daniel, the both of them laughing and shaking hands.

Oliver put his phone back in his pocket.

'And then?' I made the prompt quietly.

'Then he betrayed them,' was Oliver's answer. 'He knew all the names of the people he'd met, and he gave every one of them right to King George.'

It wasn't the knowledge itself that was hardest to bear, it was knowing that I could do nothing about it, that even with all that I knew I was powerless. Useless.

I'd felt this before, while Katrina had battled her

illness. I hadn't been able to stop that from happening, either. I hadn't been able to save her. I would have paid any price then to be able to *do* something, anything, not just stand helplessly by. And I would have paid any price now. But the truth was that, once again, I could do nothing.

I couldn't warn Daniel. I couldn't save Jack. I was trapped here in my own time and I couldn't simply leap back into theirs by force of will alone, however much I wanted to. I had to wait. And worry.

I was grateful when the day of Susan's opening arrived, because it kept me moving constantly, with no real time for thinking about anything except the task at hand. Things went splendidly well – the first coachload of tourists arrived spot on time and the weather held fair and Trelowarth looked beautiful, and the photographer sent down by *House & Garden* got the whole thing very brilliantly recorded for her magazine. The interviews with Mark and Susan went off like a dream, and when the visitors all crowded into the Cloutie Tree to sample their Cornish cream teas before leaving, their chatter was glowingly positive.

By the day's end even Mark was admitting that Susan had proved him wrong.

'Say it again,' Susan challenged him, mischievous.

Crossing the carpeted floor of the big front room, Mark sank with visible weariness into the big armchair by the piano and leant his head back. 'You were right,' he repeated, with slow perfect diction. 'And I was . . .'

'Yes?'

'Less right.'

I looked up from my magazine. 'That's all you're going to get,' I said to Susan. 'And be happy with it, because it's more than *I* got.'

Mark partly opened his eyes. 'When were you right?'

I sent him a calmly superior look. 'Falmouth.'

'Oh.' His eyes closed again. 'Well, yes, all right. I was wrong about that, I'll admit it.'

Amazed, Susan said to me, 'Sorry, am I delirious, or did I just hear my brother say that he'd been wrong?' Her gaze swung, curious, to Mark. 'What have I missed?'

He said, 'None of your business.'

I knew that he'd gone out a few times since then with Felicity, and though they weren't yet what I'd call a couple they were at least making a start on it. Susan, who knew and approved of their changing relationship, wasn't aware that I'd argued with Mark. We had kept that a private affair, between us, and we'd settled it in the same way that we'd made peace when I had been little – the day after going to Falmouth, Mark had set up the badminton net on the side lawn and brought me a racquet, and though I was rusty at playing he'd graciously let me win two of the games. That, I knew, was the way he said 'sorry'.

We traded glances now as Susan sighed and said, 'Fine, be like that. You can't dampen my mood, I'm too happy.'

I told her, 'You ought to be. Today was perfect.'

'Can't rest on my laurels,' she said. 'We've still got the coach tour from Cardiff tomorrow.' She turned again to look at Mark. 'By the way, you don't know what's become of Dad's display stand, do you? The one we unearthed when we cleared out the greenhouse? I thought we might salvage the sign from it, if nothing else.'

'Sorry,' Mark said. 'I'm painting it.'

'Painting it? What on earth for?'

'Well, I'll need it for Southport,' he said.

Susan stared at him as though she didn't know him. 'What?'

'The Southport Flower Show. You want to read my blog more often. I announced last week that we'd be going.'

'But you never go to shows. Not any more.'

'A man can change.' A glance at me. 'Besides, like Eva said, we need to raise our profile.'

For a moment Susan looked at him in silence, then she said, 'Right. Now I *know* I'm delirious. Eva?'

'I'll get us drinks, shall I?' Setting my magazine down as I stood, I asked, 'Is there wine in the fridge, still?'

Mark thought that there was. 'Need some help?'

'Susan's delirious, and you're knackered. I'll manage.'

I wasn't sure where Claire had got to, but the house was quiet when I crossed the hall. The kitchen door stood slightly open. Pushing it, I felt it thud on something that not only stopped its inward swing but bounced it back towards me. Damn, I thought. One of the dogs must have decided to stretch out behind the door to take a nap, and now I'd clouted him, poor thing.

I heard a scuffle and a thump and then the door was yanked back open from the inside, all the way this time, and I could see the thing that had been blocking it was not a dog at all. It was the body of a man stretched out face down across the flagstone floor, his black hair wetly matted where a dark red trickle had begun to stain his collar. It was Fergal.

Shocked, I raised my gaze to find a pistol levelled steady at my chest.

I couldn't focus on the man who held it, because I'd already looked beyond him to the hard eyes of another man who stood close by the fireplace.

'Mistress O'Cleary,' the constable said, 'do come in.'

Chapter Thirty-Six

I couldn't move, at first.

Not that I wanted to, really. The last thing I wanted to do was step over the threshold into that unwelcoming room. But the man with the pistol had lowered it and now reached forwards to take a rough grip on my arm with his other hand, hauling me in.

'Shut the door,' said the constable. For all his calmness, he sounded displeased. 'Mr Hewitt?'

Someone else moved in the shadows behind him. 'Yes?'

God, I thought, how many of them were there? Trying to shake myself out of my nightmare paralysis, I took a wild look round the room and counted two more faces, making five of them in total. Small wonder Fergal hadn't stood a chance.

He lay now almost at my feet, and with relief I saw his ribs move slightly.

'Did you not,' the constable was saying, 'tell me you had searched the house?'

'I did,' the man named Hewitt protested. 'I swear I saw no one. She must have been hiding.'

The constable acknowledged this. ''Tis why they call it "searching". Would you be so kind as to go try again? With Mr Leach's help.'

The man who'd been holding my arm turned his head, gave a nod, and let go of me, slipping from the kitchen in the wake of the disgruntled Hewitt. Left there standing by the door, I tried to show the bravest face I could, my shoulders straightening a little as the constable regarded me with shuttered eyes that took no notice of the injured man who lay between us.

Almost casually, he asked me, 'Were you hiding?'

I remembered not to talk in time, and shook my head. My hands had started trembling and I curled them into fists so they would not betray my weakness.

But he seemed to see it, anyway. His mouth curved into something that could not be called a smile. 'In bed, then.' Spoken with a certainty supported by the way his gaze raked over my appearance, and I realised for the first time that the summer frock I'd worn all day, a loosely fitting peasant-styled frock of plain cream cotton, would to him and all the other men look like a chemise. Dressed as I was with my hair loose, I could understand why he had assumed I'd been in bed.

His sneer was more apparent when he asked, 'Were you alone?'

For an answer I lifted my chin a half-inch to imply such a question was not worth my answering.

One of the men near the window-wall said, 'Mr Creed,' and the constable's stare sliced the dark air between them.

'Yes, Mr Pascoe? You've something to say?'

An older man moved to the edge of the firelight, his features familiar. 'I'll ask you to mind how you speak, sir. The girl's done naught to warrant such insult.'

I recognised him then. I'd seen that same mix of defiance and shame on his face when he'd ridden as one of the constable's deputies on the day Jack was arrested at St Non's, and the same unvoiced apology in his quick glance the next day when he'd stopped off in the stable yard to bring the conger eel for Fergal. Fergal hadn't called him Mr Pascoe, though. He'd called him Peter. That implied the two of them were friends, of sorts, and meant I might have one man in this group who would defend me.

The constable had brushed aside the protest. 'It can be no insult, surely, to request the facts.' He followed my quick downward glance towards Fergal. 'You fear for your brother? A touching display, but I'll warrant he'll live long enough for his hanging.'

I wasn't so sure. He appeared to be breathing more shallowly now, and defying the constable's presence I knelt on the flagstones and stroked Fergal's hair lightly, trying to find where the injury was.

When the man Peter took a step forwards, the constable stopped him. 'No, leave her,' he warned. 'Keep your watch.'

My fingers touched the broad gash at the base of Fergal's skull and I put pressure on it, hoping that would help to slow the bleeding. They had hit him from behind, a ruthless blow with something sharp enough to leave a cut and with the weight to bring him down – a jug, it looked like, from the jagged shards of earthenware that seemed to have been kicked into the corner by the door behind me.

One shard the size of my hand pricked my knee as I shifted position to check Fergal's pulse at his throat. It was there, faint but steady.

The constable's men, Leach and Hewitt, had finished their search of the upper floors. Coming back into the kitchen, Leach said, 'No one.'

'Then we wait.' The constable relaxed in his position by the fireplace. 'I have waited long enough for this already, I can wait a little longer.'

It was the note of satisfaction in his voice that made me look in his direction, and he said, 'Ah, but perhaps you have not heard, Mistress O'Cleary, that the House of Lords has passed a law suspending those protections that did lately shield your lover. And as keeper of that law here in Polgelly I now have the right to enter any premises I choose, arrest whomever I suspect of plotting treason to the king, and see them sent to London where, I promise you, they will find no reprieve.'

My fingers slid protectively to Fergal's shoulder as Leach crossed towards us to take up his earlier position, standing guard.

As I shifted a little bit further away from him, my knee came down full onto the piece of the broken jug. I could feel it cut right through the fabric that covered my leg, but I bit my lip hard and said nothing, not wanting to draw any more attention to myself.

The men had fallen back to an uneasy silence, waiting. Listening.

It might have been a quarter of an hour before I heard the measured tramp of footsteps coming.

Leach had brought his pistol up and cocked it with an evil click to hold it aimed directly at the door to the back corridor, so that whoever stepped inside would have no hope of—

'Mr Creed?' The voice that called from outside in the yard was more a boy's voice than a man's, and wavered from exertion. 'Mr Creed?'

The fifth man, who stood nearest to the door, looked to the constable, who nodded, and the boy was swiftly ushered in.

He was stocky and round-faced and in the firelight I saw nothing in his face that was familiar, but his voice struck a decided chord within my memory when he said, 'I know where Mr Butler's to.'

This was, I thought, the same boy who had come aboard the Sally as a spy, and been put off again by Daniel. The same "beardless lad" Jack had argued might cause us all trouble some day. Jack had clearly been right, and just as he'd predicted, the boy was now trying to prove himself worthy to Constable Creed.

'I did just like you said,' said the boy, still half-breathless, 'and kept myself close to the Spaniard, and two of the men come out talking and one of 'em said to the other that it would be best when the day was well over, for one year of King George was naught to celebrate . . .' Pausing, he added, 'I noted his name for you, seeing that's treason and all.'

Creed's eyes narrowed. 'Go on.'

'Well, the other replied that the king would have no more

years after this, and their own work this night would help in sending him where he belonged, and they both laughed, and then the first asked was it midnight at the cave still, and the other told him ay, but both the Butler brothers would be at the cave before that. Both of them together, I did hear it plainly said,' he finished proudly.

Creed was frowning. 'And where is this cave they spoke of, then?'

The man named Peter dropped his gaze, and gave a faint shake of his head towards the man beside him, while the young man, Hewitt, shifted till he stood behind the constable, and gave a careless shrug. The bully Leach appeared to miss all this, and clearly didn't know about the cave below the Cripplehorn himself, but even as my hopes began to rise the boy spoke up, 'Why, I was thinking that you knew it for yourself, sir, or I would have shown you sooner. I can take you there.'

'Then do it.' Creed looked blackly at the men around him, as though he were trying to assess just how much use they'd be, but in the end he only said, 'If there be any man who is uncertain of his duty to the law, then let him tell me now, for I stand always ready to remind him.' Only silence met his challenge. 'No? Then let us waste no more time. Mr Leach, you will remain here with O'Cleary.'

'And the girl?' Leach asked.

'She comes with us.'

This proved too much for Peter. 'Mr Creed!'

When Creed looked round as though astonished any man would speak in such a tone to him, the older man said bluntly, 'Sir, I'll not allow it.'

At my knee I felt a movement, very faint. I braved a

quick look down and saw that Fergal's hand had moved a fraction, and his fingers had begun to curl. I didn't know just how aware he was of what was going on, or how much he could hear, but to be safe I slipped my hand in his and lightly squeezed to warn him not to move again.

Creed's eyes were dangerous. 'You'll not allow it?'

'No, sir. First off, she's not dressed. It isn't decent.'

This apparently had bothered Hewitt, too, for he put in, 'There is a chest of women's clothes upstairs, I'll just go up and—'

'No.' Creed's voice cut sharply through the offer. 'Those clothes do not belong to her.' To Peter, he said, 'Offer her your coat then, Mr Pascoe, if it troubles you, and let that be an end to it.'

But Peter, growing bolder, said, 'And any rate, the way down to the cave would be too rough for her, too rough for any woman in the daylight, let alone the dark.'

He hadn't realised what he'd just admitted, I felt sure, until the constable's hard features altered subtly and his voice smoothed to the tone I found most frightening.

'So, you know it, then? The way down to the Butler's cave.'

The older man's jaw set, but he didn't answer either way. And in that silence I felt sure the constable would win; that I'd be taken with them down to wait in ambush in the cave below the Cripplehorn, and Fergal would be left here helpless on his own with Leach. And Leach's pistol.

In a panic I tried thinking. Then I felt the ragged sharpness of the broken wedge of earthenware still lodged beneath my knee, and very slowly and with care I inched it forwards till it rested underneath the hand I'd linked with

Fergal's. No one noticed. Still more carefully, I guided it up into Fergal's palm and closed his fingers round it, pushing at his arm until his hand was tucked beneath the outflung edge of his dark coat, against his side.

Leach wouldn't see it there. But now when Fergal woke, I thought, at least he'd have a weapon. If he did wake.

He'd gone still again.

Creed said, in that same elegantly soulless voice I'd learnt to fear, 'I do confess that I have never understood the loyalty these Butler men command, and yet I truly cannot help but be impressed by it.' He looked from Peter back to Hewitt and then to the silent man who stood between the window and the door. 'It is a pity there'll be no one from Polgelly on the jury to defend them when they're brought to trial, for Londoners will surely be less sympathetic to the Butlers' charms.' He turned to Leach. 'I know you'll be occupied watching O'Cleary, but were I to leave you his sister as well could you manage it?'

Leach looked me up and down, leering. 'Oh, ay, I could manage her fine, Mr Creed.'

Peter moved again sharply in protest, and Creed's gaze swung round.

'You object to that also, Mr Pascoe? Perhaps you'd prefer, then, to stay behind with them.'

'I would, ay.' The older man's face was distrustful, but Creed only told him, 'So be it,' and took a step backwards to clear the way.

Peter, still clearly disturbed by my state of undress, began shrugging his coat from his shoulders as he crossed the floor, and the constable reached to take hold of the back of the coat's heavy collar, as though to assist him.

And then his hold tightened, and swiftly his free arm swung forwards and drove hard at Peter's chest.

It happened so fast that at first I was not really sure what I'd seen. With a cough and a look of astonishment Peter collapsed to his knees, arms pinned back by the constable's grip on the coat.

'You may stay, as you wish,' Creed said lightly, and as he drew his arm back I could see the knife blade brightly red, a deadly thing. Peter coughed again, and Creed yanked back once with his other arm to wrench the coat completely clear, then watched without expression as the older man fell face-first to the floor and lay unmoving.

'Now, then.' In the small, shocked silence Creed, uncaring, wiped the bloodied knife blade on the coat's dark sleeve. 'Does anybody else prefer to stay behind?'

The men, including Leach, stayed silent.

'No?' The constable glanced round for confirmation. 'Then let us go.' He waved the knife from Leach to me and told him, 'Get her up.'

'You said—'

'I lied.' Creed's eyebrows rose as if to show surprise that anyone would have thought otherwise. 'If Butler has his men around him, he may need persuading to submit to his arrest. Besides,' he added, 'if I left her here with you she might distract you from your duties, Mr Leach.'

Leach didn't answer him out loud, but he was grumbling something underneath his breath as he reached down to roughly grab my arm and haul me to my feet.

Creed gave his knife a final close inspection. Satisfied, he tossed the coat across to me, and turned away before I caught it.

'Cover yourself,' he said.

The boy who still stood just inside the door was staring dumbly at the body on the floor. If he had ever seen a murder done at all, I thought, he'd never been this close to one, because the stunned uncertainty was written plainly on his face.

The constable stopped walking just in front of him, and waited. 'Well?'

The boy, misunderstanding, seemed to think that Creed was asking his advice, and answered, 'Shouldn't we . . . that is, sir, should we not attempt to move . . . ?'

Creed frowned. 'Move what?' He turned his head, his own gaze following the boy's. 'Oh, that. No, leave him there. It was unfortunate that in our efforts to arrest O'Cleary he attacked and killed poor Mr Pascoe, but we can at least console ourselves in knowing that a charge of murder added to his treason will ensure the judge assigns him an unpleasant end.' He looked back at the boy, impatient. 'Now, this cave.'

'The . . . yes, sir. Yes.' The boy recovered. 'I can take you there.'

'Then do so. Mr Hewitt?'

'Sir?'

Creed shot one final glance behind him, cold and purposeful. 'Bring Butler's whore.'

Chapter Thirty-Seven

I saw fire on the hillside.

At first my mind just lumped that observation in with all the other things about the night that seemed surreal – the violent drama I'd stepped into, Fergal lying senseless on the floor, the man named Peter being killed before my eyes, and now the fact that I was being hurried by the hands of strangers over the dark field that lay between Trelowarth and the woods . . . why *shouldn't* there be fire on the hill as well, I wondered?

But even through the fog of shock that masked my sharper senses I could see it was no random fire, nor any strange imagining.

The Beacon had been lit.

I'd never seen it lit in my own lifetime. I had seen my parents' snapshots of the Beacon being lighted for the Silver Jubilee of Queen Elizabeth, before my birth, and Claire had sent me pictures of it burning on the eve of the Millennium, when all of Britain's ancient beacons had been set ablaze, but what the photographs had captured was a fraction of the full effect.

The sight was truly awe-inspiring, flames of brilliant gold that speared the star-flecked sky and shifted shape in random sprays of sparks. At any other time I might have marvelled at it, but my mind had narrowed in its focus and refused to be distracted long by anything that fell outside the needs of self-protection.

I had little memory afterwards of passing with my captors through the wood or scrambling down the jagged slickness of the rocks onto the beach – it blended into one long, nightmarish descent where I was scraped by branches, cut by rocks, and finally hit the shingle with a bruised knee and the taste of my own blood upon my tongue. It wasn't serious. I'd bitten through my lip to keep from crying out when I had whacked my knee, but still the pain of it was real, and my lip swelled so much that when we'd found the entrance to the cave and stumbled in and Creed had set the shuttered lantern that he'd carried from Trelowarth House in place on top of one wide barrel, opening its sides to let the light spill out, the man named Hewitt looked at me with pity and discomfort.

I felt pity for him, too, because I knew he couldn't come to my defence the way he might have liked to. Both of us had seen what the result of that would be. I drew the stiff edges of Peter's jacket tighter round my throat against the penetrating dampness of the cave and turned away from Hewitt's gaze.

The constable was watching us. Without a word he took

a long look round the shadowed cave and said, 'This is a most agreeable arrangement. Have the Butlers used it long?' He aimed the question straight at Hewitt, but it was the boy who answered.

'Why, they've always used it, sir. 'Tis common knowledge in the village. I was shown it by my father, years ago.'

'Is that a fact?' Creed took his pistol from his belt, examining its workings with an attitude of unconcern, but I could see his underlying tenseness. He looked not unlike a predator prepared to spring, and I was sure the people of Polgelly would be made to feel the depth of his displeasure with them. Taking out the knife he had just used to kill a man he turned its point to make some small adjustment to the flintlock mechanism of his gun.

And that's when I remembered.

It was over there, I thought, just *there*, between the barrels to my left, that Daniel's own dropped dagger had been lying on the floor the last time I'd seen it.

If I picked it up I knew I would be changing what was meant to happen, but then I'd already changed things once tonight by being here. A man lay dead because of me, because he'd tried to help me, and however that one act had changed the future it was done, and there was nothing I could do to change it back. All I could do was try to stay alive myself, and if I had a weapon I'd be bettering my odds.

The challenge was to find a way to get from where I stood to where I thought the dagger lay. I was deciding how to do it when my thoughts were interrupted by a noise approaching steadily outside the cave: the heavy crunch of footsteps over shingle.

Creed held one hand up to warn the men to silence, and aimed his pistol at the entrance as a second sound rose up now with the shifting steps – the sound of someone whistling a careless tune I recognised.

My heart dropped. Jack.

And then in almost sickening slow motion all the things I'd seen and heard tonight slid into place like pieces of a puzzle, and I knew then why the Beacon had been lit. I could hear again the boy's voice telling Creed what he had overheard the one man tell the other as they left the Spaniard's Rest: that he'd be happy when the day was over, for a year of King George on the throne was not a thing that should be celebrated.

God, I thought, that must be it. In my time the Polgelly folk had marked a royal jubilee by lighting up the Beacon, so it made sense the people here would do the same. Uncaring fate had brought me back on the first anniversary of King George's rule, the same day when, according to the note in Jack's unfinished memoirs, Jack 'did chance to fall afoul of the lawmen of Polgelly, and while fleeing from their constable was killed by one sure pistol shot.'

I knew what was about to happen. Knew because the constable was with me, and the men who walked around us *were* the 'lawmen of Polgelly', and the night was not yet over.

Jack would die, because I'd read it on a printed page and printed pages weren't meant to be changed. Like in the lines I'd quoted on the ship to Daniel from the *Rubaiyat*, The Moving Finger had already written what must be.

But then I thought of Daniel telling Fergal, 'He's my

brother,' and God help me, I just couldn't stand there silently and watch another man be killed.

As Jack was stepping through the opening into the cave, I made a sudden lunge against the constable and shouted, 'Jack, get out! Warn Daniel! Run!'

The pistol's deafening report in that confined space drowned my words and I could not be sure he heard them, and a second after that I couldn't see him for the powder smoke that seared my throat and stung my eyes and drifted like a white cloud through the cave, but as it cleared I saw the place where Jack had stood was empty.

The constable's shot had gone wide. Several feet away the boy took an unsteady step and stared at me with wonder and bewilderment, and then he touched a hand to the new spreading stain upon his chest and stumbled once again, and fell.

Creed's eyes, much closer, had held wonder too at first, but by the time I met them they were freezing over into something terrifying. With the gun still in his hand he swept his arm out savagely and struck me full across my face. I felt the pain against my cheekbone and the trickling warmth of blood start down the bruised skin of my temple, but although I staggered back I didn't shame myself by falling down.

When Hewitt made a move as though to protest, Creed stopped him with the cold reminder, 'This is none of your affair. Nor yours,' he told the other man, behind. 'Now go, the pair of you, and bring Jack Butler back.'

The two men hesitated, and he wheeled on them. 'I told you, go!'

And without any further argument the men edged off. I

heard their footsteps scraping on the shingle, walking first, then moving off more quickly, breaking to a run.

Creed didn't move, but still I felt the space between us shrinking.

'So,' he said. 'You have a voice.'

I tried to think. I hadn't said that many words, and with the pistol's firing it was likely that he hadn't heard me clearly, so there was a fair chance that he wouldn't know I wasn't Irish, wasn't who he thought I was. And even though he knew that I could speak, my safest course now might just be to keep my mouth shut and not risk him finding out that I did not belong here.

'A clever play on Butler's part,' he said, 'and on your brother's, for it made me ill-inclined to ask you questions, as they no doubt hoped it would.'

The knowledge that he still thought I was Fergal's sister would have eased my mind more if he hadn't been reloading the pistol while he talked, brushing the used powder out of the firing pan and re-priming it deftly.

'But now that I have heard you speak,' he said as he took practice aim towards the entrance of the cave and idly sighted down the barrel, 'I've a mind to find out for myself how well you sing.'

I watched the pistol swing around to point at me.

He said, 'You can sing, can you not, Mistress O'Cleary? You will find it is a useful art, for keeping your own head out of the hangman's noose. Come now, tell me what does Butler mean to shift from here tonight, and where will it be bound?'

Shaking my head once I took a step backwards, reminding myself he was trying to frighten me. Doing a fabulous job of it, certainly, but he had no real intention of killing me yet. He still needed me for the same reason he'd told his men earlier – Daniel would never submit to arrest without force or coercion, and I was the constable's leverage, his bargaining chip.

He wouldn't kill me yet, I told myself again, and clinging to that little fragment of uncertain courage I stepped back again and hoped he'd think I was retreating from the pistol. I knew well enough I didn't have a hope of moving out of range – I'd seen the damage his last shot had done the boy, who had been standing further off from Creed than I was standing now – but the dagger, Daniel's dagger, was still lying on the damp stone floor somewhere between the barrels just behind me.

My thoughts had not yet focused through my fear enough to let me form a plan of what to do with it, but having any weapon seemed a better thing than having none at all, so I kept inching backwards with a single-minded purpose while Creed said, 'You do know, do you not, what does befall a woman like yourself in Newgate? And for what? The law is very clear for those who comfort traitors. In the end you will be forced to testify to what you know, and he will hang regardless, and your suffering will be for naught. Speak now, to me, and I may yet persuade the courts to show you mercy.'

The voice that answered wasn't mine. It said, 'A kind offer, but I rather doubt she'll accept it.'

I turned my head, astonished, to see Jack not twenty feet from us, inside the entrance to the cave. Keeping his own pistol levelled on Creed and his gaze firmly fixed on the constable's face he remarked, 'You have given her small cause to think you'd be merciful.'

The constable shrugged. 'Men can change.'

If Jack felt fear he was hiding it well. He looked calm and completely relaxed as he took a step forwards and ordered me, 'Eva, go now.'

I heard Creed's gun, still pointed at me, give an ominous click.

'Butler, I should have thought saving yourself would outweigh any chivalrous impulses.'

Jack gave a half smile and said, 'Men can change, so I've been told.' Still coming forwards, he said again, 'Eva, go now, he'll not shoot you.'

The constable lowered his eyebrows at that. 'Will I not? And what makes you so certain?'

'Because it is not your design. You'd not even shoot me, if I gave you the chance.'

'You seem very certain.' Creed's voice had an edge. 'Why not put your own pistol aside, and we'll see?'

Jack answered without stopping his advance, 'All right.'

And as I watched in horror he replaced his pistol in his belt and held his hands out slightly from his sides, to plainly show he was unarmed.

Creed's pistol swung away from me to aim at Jack, and as it moved I took advantage of the fact to back away between the barrels, where I'd seen the dagger on the day we'd brought the cargo back from Brittany.

I'd nearly given up when I saw one faint edge of something metal gleaming in the lantern's light, and cautiously, my eyes still on the men, I stooped to pick it up. My hands weren't large enough to hold the dagger's blade concealed as Daniel did, but still I tried to keep it pointed straight so it was hidden by my wrist as much as possible.

Neither Jack nor Creed appeared to notice.

Jack had covered half the space between them now with his sure, certain steps, and all the while his gaze stayed steady on the constable. 'You want us dead, myself and Danny, but you will not shoot me now, for should I die by your own hand, the people of Polgelly will demand to know the cause of it, and even your authority has limits in this place.' He tipped his head to one side, questioning. 'Or do you think those two men you presumably sent after me, the ones I did see running for the woods, will yet return to lend you aid?'

Creed said, 'The people of Polgelly have no choice. The laws have changed.'

'Yes, I have heard. We may be taken without benefit of warrant, may we not, and sent to London for our trials? More reason not to kill me now,' said Jack, his hands still at his sides as he came closer, 'when you could leave that pleasure to the executioner, while you stand by the gallows and enjoy the entertainment.' Without turning his head he repeated, 'Go, Eva.'

'She stays,' said the constable. 'For if you claim to know the law, then you will also know that trials do have need of evidence, and she can yet supply that.'

Jack said, 'Eva cannot testify.'

'You think I am a fool?' Creed was dismissive. 'She can speak.'

'She can. But not against my brother. Or against myself, in fact, if that would so reveal my brother's crimes.'

Jack knew. I saw it in the faint curve of his mouth before

he dropped the bombshell with the satisfaction of a small boy who liked watching things explode. 'For if *you* know the law,' he said, 'then you will know no judge will have a woman as a witness at the trial of her husband.'

Creed stood thunderstruck. 'Her husband!'

'Ay, that was my own reaction, I'll confess, when Danny told me, but the vicar did assure me it was true, and for my part I now can see it was a good match wisely made.' The glance Jack sent my way held reassurance, but beneath it was full knowledge of the danger we were in. 'So you see,' he finished off, 'she'll be no use to you.'

The constable's cold eyes had taken on a colder purpose. 'Oh, I disagree,' he said. 'I can imagine quite a few ways that I might use *Mrs* Butler, and I'll keep your brother well informed of all of them while he does rot in Newgate.'

He turned his head to leer at me, and that brief shift of focus was the chance Jack had been waiting for. Arm's length now from the constable, he closed the distance in a final surge of motion, one hand reaching for possession of the pistol.

It was over in an instant.

With the gun's report still ringing in my disbelieving ears I watched Jack stagger back and fall, and felt a sudden stinging in my eyes that wasn't from the burning whiteness of the smoke.

'No,' I whispered, blinking back the pricking blur of tears.

I'd saved him, hadn't I? I'd made a choice and changed things so this wouldn't have to happen, so he wouldn't have to die.

But he *was* dead. There was no question of it.

'No!'

I must have spoken that more strongly, for the constable glanced up and with a twisting of his mouth turned back and spat once with contempt on Jack's unmoving body. 'Now,' he said, preparing to reload his pistol as he'd done before, 'we've but to wait for your brave husband, have we not? I must admit I did have some misgivings as to whether he would truly hold your life so dear that he'd agree to let me take him prisoner. A mistress, after all, is but a mistress. But a *wife* . . .' His tone was confident and mocking at the same time, and it struck some switch inside me that I hadn't known I had.

I didn't afterwards remember when I moved, or how, but in the next breath I was somehow there in front of Creed and Daniel's dagger was no longer in my hand.

He dropped the pistol with a clatter to the weeping stone and raised one hand to grasp the dagger's handle in his turn. It looked so strangely out of place there, stuck hilt-deep into the centre of his chest.

His face was angry as he yanked the short blade out and tossed it clattering aside, and looking at the rush of bright red blood that followed seemed to make him even angrier, because he raised his head and started cursing me . . .

The words froze on his lips.

I saw the change in his expression, saw the darkness of his glare give way to fear, and heard the horror in the word he whispered: 'Witch!'

He was already fading as his legs gave way beneath him and he dropped hard to his knees, this man who had so often fed upon the fear of others rattling out his final breath with terror in his eyes. And then he fell and his grey shadow tumbled down and thinned to nothingness.

Jack's body faded, too, and all the dimness of the cave around me shuddered once and melted into the back passage of Trelowarth House, and I was standing ready to walk through the kitchen door.

Except I couldn't move.

The night had sent me back too traumatised. I couldn't seem to manage the transition, I could only stand there trembling with the tear stains on my bruised and swelling cheek, wrapped in the rough coat of a dead man that weighed heavily upon my shaking shoulders.

I'm not sure I ever would have found the will or strength to move if I had not heard footsteps clipping with a cheerful and familiar beat across the kitchen floor, though even when the heavy door swung inwards and Claire stood there in amazement at the sight of me, I couldn't think of anything to do but fling myself into her arms and cling there weeping like a child who'd just awakened from a nightmare.

Chapter Thirty-Eight

Shock does strange things to the mind.

My senses telescoped to focus on a few small random details while the rest of what was going on I only grasped in fragments. Which was why I knew that Claire had seven buttons on her shirt but didn't know how we'd come halfway up the steep back stairs.

I heard somebody entering the kitchen and Mark's voice below us called me, 'Eva?'

Claire answered for me, still guiding me upwards, 'She's here with me, darling. I gave her a nasty hard whack in the face with the kitchen door, probably blackened her eye.'

A tiny voice deep in my mind argued, *That's not what happened*, but they had moved on to the subject of doctors and whether I needed one.

Claire said she wouldn't be sure till she'd had a good look at it. 'I'll let you know.'

And the next thing I knew I was soaking alone in the tub in the bathroom upstairs. On the edge of the tub sat a small dish of guest soaps, impractical things shaped like roses, six roses, quite violently pink.

Very slowly, my shaking subsided.

I wasn't in the bathroom any more, but in my bedroom.

'There, now.' Claire was beside me again. I could feel the slight dip of the mattress as she took a seat on the edge of my bed, leaning over to tuck the sheets round me. The cool of her hand smoothed my damply hot forehead while my eyes stayed fixed on the place where a small flake of paint had been chipped from the wall near my headboard.

Claire's tone was gently undemanding. 'Do you want to talk about it?'

No.

I couldn't form the word yet, but my head moved slightly on the pillow and she understood.

'All right.' I felt her hand against my forehead for a second time, and then she left.

At least, I thought she did.

But in the middle of the night I briefly woke from fretful dreams, and rolling over in the tangle of my blankets I was sure I caught a glimpse of someone sitting in the shadows of the corner by the fireplace, watching over me.

The house was quiet when I woke.

No laughter floating up the stairs, no whispers from the room next door, no movement but the swaying of the curtains at my windows as they sought to catch the currents of the spindrift-scented summer breeze before the wind's inconstant nature dropped them limply back to lie in wait against the window ledge.

The room felt warm. Too warm to be the morning. And the shadows were not in their proper places.

Without thinking I turned slightly on the pillow and the sudden painful pressure on my swollen cheek called back the night's dark memories in a swift, depressing rush.

I'd killed a man. I'd stabbed a man and killed him, and although he'd murdered others in his turn and would have doubtless murdered me, the fact remained that I'd done something I had always thought I'd be incapable of doing, and that wasn't such an easy thing to wrap my thoughts around.

And if my thoughts were horrible for me, I knew it would be even worse for Daniel, coming to the cave to find his brother dead. That the constable lay dead as well would be at least a minor consolation, but it wouldn't be a balance for the loss of Jack, in Daniel's view. Or mine.

I closed my eyes to shut the memories out. It didn't work. Against the blackness of my mind I saw the play of images, and I remembered everything. The only part that seemed less clear was how I'd come to be up here, in my pyjamas, in my bed . . . then I remembered that as well, and looked around for Claire.

I'd need to talk to her, I knew. I'd need to give some explanation for the state she'd found me in last night, though for the life of me I really didn't know what I could say, where I'd begin.

But knowing Claire, I wouldn't have a choice. She might be patient and prepared to wait, not rushing me, but in the end she'd want to have the answers to her questions.

Getting up and getting dressed took time. My limbs were stiff and everywhere I saw the scrapes and bruises that the night had left. The sight of my face in the mirror wasn't nearly as bad as I'd feared it would be. My eye had been left unaffected; the worst of the swelling had kept to the curve of my cheekbone and most of the bruising was up by my temple, the cut that had bled barely visible where it ran into my hairline.

In fact, if I left my hair down and allowed it to swing forward slightly it covered up most of the damage.

The damage that showed, I corrected myself.

There was worse on the inside that, while it was simpler to hide, would be harder to heal. But I hid it the best that I could, and went downstairs, composing a speech in my mind as I went, forming lines and discarding them, finding a few that I liked and rehearsing them mentally so they'd sound normal.

I needn't have bothered. Nobody was there.

As I moved through the rooms I tried keeping my thoughts in the present day, focusing on what was actually there, but I found the lines blurring and shifting at random; and when I came into the kitchen my steps dragged a little. I didn't want to be in here, didn't want to think of everything I'd seen in here last night, or to remember Fergal lying on the floor just there, between the Aga and the door, the fight knocked cruelly out of him.

I thought of Fergal's dark impassive eyes and his dry wit and felt a twist of pain not knowing what had happened to him. With the sharp edge of that broken piece of pot held in his hand he would have had at least a chance against the constable's man, Leach, who'd been left to guard him. But that was only if Leach hadn't used his pistol, and assuming Fergal ever had gained consciousness again.

I couldn't bear to think of Fergal dead.

And yet I knew they all were, now. The world had turned and they were dead and in the ground, and there was nothing I could do about it. Daniel had been right the day he'd said to me, 'This life that I have lived, it has already passed and faded from the memories of the people of your own time . . .'

He'd been right, too, when he'd theorised that altering the past might prove impossible. By calling a warning to Jack as he'd entered the cave I had saved him from being shot then by the constable, but time had found another way to do what must be done, and even with my interference Jack had died the way that he'd been meant to. Even Daniel's dagger that I'd used to kill the constable had, in the end, been thrown back to the cave floor and had scuttled to the shadows to lie waiting till Mark came to find it. History hadn't changed.

At least, I didn't think it had. I only knew the present seemed to be exactly as I'd left it. It just felt a little emptier.

As if on cue, a shadow passed the window and I heard the back door open and Felicity came in, balancing a plastic washing-up tub stacked with cups and saucers while she chatted on the mobile phone held wedged against her shoulder.

'No, no,' she was saying, '*all* over the floor. Well, we've switched it off, yes, but the thing is we've got a big tour group arriving a half hour from now, and . . . oh, would you? Thanks, that would be wonderful, Paul. You're a prince.'

Carefully sliding the tub onto the worktop so the china didn't clink too much, she rang off and greeted me, 'Hi. I didn't wake you with the last load, did I?'

Not sure what she meant at first, I glanced towards the sink and for the first time noticed it was nearly brimful, too, with soaking dishes, and a second empty washing-up tub sat off to the side.

'No,' I said. 'What's going on?'

'The dishwasher's leaking. We were putting these through so they'd be good and clean for our afternoon crowd, only something went wrong in the rinse cycle and we wound up with a flood in the kitchen and lovely baked soap on the dishes.' She held up a teacup to show me and tapped the hard crystals of soap. 'Just like rock. I've been scrubbing it off.'

I grasped at the chance to do something to keep my thoughts occupied. 'Want some help?'

'Claire said to let you rest.' She looked more closely at my face. 'She really got you with that door, didn't she? How does it feel?'

I didn't correct her assumption of how I'd been injured, I only assured her it wasn't as bad as it looked. 'I'm fine, honestly.'

Working together in under ten minutes we had both tubs restacked with clean cups and saucers.

'Come on,' I said, lifting the nearest tub carefully. 'I'll help you carry these back.'

It was going to rain. The air felt unmistakeably heavy and carried the scent of a summer storm underneath clouds that were gathering grey. As I followed Felicity up to the greenhouse I noticed that the thorn tree now wore flutterings of cloth strips left by some of our new tourists, and it made a proper cloutie tree beside the charming tea room.

As we came inside the smell of scones fresh from the oven overpowered all my other senses for a moment, and my stomach rumbled as I set my plastic tub of dishes down behind the serving counter. Susan straightened from behind the broken dishwasher and dumped a sodden rag into the bucket at her feet. She looked remarkably controlled, I thought, considering the crisis.

'Thanks,' she said, and sent a smile to both of us. 'The floor's dry now, at least. Did you get hold of Paul?'

Felicity nodded. 'I did. He'll be here in a minute, he said.'

'Right, then.' Looking around, Susan noticed my face. 'God, Eva. That must hurt. Claire said it looked pretty awful.'

'I'm fine,' I repeated. But she'd reminded me I wasn't in the clear yet, and I glanced around in my turn. 'Where is Claire?'

'She's gone up to keep an eye out for the coach, let us know what the numbers are.'

'Let's get these tables set, then,' said Felicity.

We weren't quite finished when I heard the steps crunching down the curved path from the gardens above, but it wasn't the tour group just yet. Only Paul, looking as though he'd rolled straight out of bed to answer Felicity's emergency call, with his blue denim shirt hanging unbuttoned over the close-fitting T-shirt beneath.

Susan brightened. She was crouched behind the counter with him, showing him the problem, when another set of footsteps sounded briskly on the gravel and Claire came inside. 'They're here,' she said. 'Just coming down. The guide said forty-one.'

Susan stood, as did the plumber, who gave Claire a friendly nod and a 'Good morning'. He was chattier with Claire than with the rest of us. He asked, 'Where's this group from, then?'

Claire wasn't sure, but Susan told him, 'Wales. They're going on to St Non's after us.'

He said, 'Bad day for it,' and stretched his shoulders. 'Looks like rain.'

'We only have to give them tea,' said Susan cheerfully. 'They didn't want a garden tour.' Setting out plates she asked Claire, 'Forty-one, you said?'

Claire seemed oddly distracted. 'What? Oh, yes, that's right.' She'd caught sight of me now. 'Eva, darling, you ought to be resting.' A motherly kind of reproach, but she said it with patience, the same sort of patience she'd shown when I'd strayed out of bounds as a child, and I felt the same need I'd so often felt then to just curl up at her side and tell her everything, because she'd understand.

But would she, this time? How could anybody, even Claire, believe my story, much less understand it? She would put it down to stress, or grief, or even mental illness, and she'd worry . . .

'Here they come,' said Felicity, as the first tourists came into view on the path, and the next fifteen minutes were blissfully busy, keeping me from thinking about anything but filling and delivering the teapots – my assigned task – while the others served the scones with jam and clotted cream and Paul the plumber tried to keep his focus on the dishwasher, which couldn't have been easy since the tour group seemed to mostly be young women, not a few of whom were pretty and the bulk of whom appeared to have *their* focus fixed on Paul.

Susan and Felicity were both too deeply occupied to take much notice, but I knew Claire heard the comments and the giggling and I saw her smile a few times, then I saw her smile more knowingly in Paul's direction as it grew apparent he had eyes for one young woman in particular, a lively girl with laughing eyes who seemed to draw our plumber's gaze each time he straightened from his work, and when she went outside with friends to have them take her picture by the cloutie tree, his frequent glances followed her with interest.

Passing Claire as I returned from filling yet another teapot, I nodded at the little group of tourists by the cloutie tree and shared a conspiratorial smile. 'Susan has some competition.'

'So it seems.' She raised a hand to brush the hair back lightly from my swollen cheekbone. 'That looks rather better than I feared it would. I'm glad.'

I drew a breath. 'You didn't hit me with the door.'

'I know I didn't. But I had to tell them something, darling, didn't I?'

A laughing shriek from outside interrupted us. The rain had come at last, in a great sudden lashing downpour that was pelting on the glass roof of the tea room like a drum roll and cascading down the windows as the small group of young women by the tree, caught unawares, made an impressive dash towards the door and tumbled through it, out of breath and dripping on the floor. Two of them had been wearing hooded anoraks and so escaped the worst of it, but the dark-haired girl Paul had been watching was soaked to the skin in her light cotton blouse.

And then Paul stood and shrugged his denim shirt off and stepped forwards, drawing all the female eyes now with his T-shirt closely sculpted to his muscled chest and shoulders and his lean flat stomach. 'Here.' He gallantly offered his shirt to the wide-eyed young woman, who took it and gave him a suddenly self-aware smile in return.

At the far edge of my vision I could see Felicity nudge Susan, and they stared together for a moment before Susan shook her head and made some comment to Felicity. No doubt she was remarking on how weird it was that history was repeating; that our plumber had done just what Claire's own grandfather had done, such a coincidence.

And then a kettle whistled to the boil and she turned back again to give it her attention, and the moment passed.

But not for me.

For me the moment stretched as though it were a string and I'd just figured out the pattern of the beads to thread upon it. Because I was watching Claire.

I saw the misting of her eyes, the strange emotion of her smile, the way she watched Paul watch the Welsh girl slide his shirt around her shoulders, and it all made sudden sense.

But still, it seemed so unbelievable that I could only clear my throat and say to Claire, 'That's just the way it happened with your grandparents.'

She turned her head and turned her smile on me, and then I knew beyond all doubt.

'My dear.' Her voice was quiet, meant for me alone, a confidence she must have felt quite sure I'd understand. 'They *are* my grandparents.'

Chapter Thirty-Nine

The rain had stopped. From time to time the wind chased through the taller trees that edged the wood around Claire's small back garden, shaking leaves and letting loose a scattered showering of water droplets, sparkling as they fell like little diamonds in the spears of sunlight breaking through the branches and the ever-shifting clouds.

Claire came out with two mugs of tea and handed one to me and edged her chair around so that, like mine, it faced the little sundial with its butterfly's bronze wings forever poised for flight.

We sat there for a moment saying nothing while a bird sang somewhere, steadily, within the cooler shadows of the wood.

Then I said, 'So you knew who he was.'

'Paul? Oh, yes. From the moment I saw him. And my grandmother, too. Of course I wasn't *sure* I'd get to see the moment when they met, I wasn't certain of the date, but I did hope . . .' She glanced at me. 'I'm sorry, darling, that I haven't been more help to you this summer, but I thought it best to let you find your own way through, without my interference.'

'But you did know what was happening.'

'Of course,' she said. 'It happened much the same for me, although you travel from this time into the past, while this time *is* the past, to me.' Her gaze had settled calmly on the sundial, and she spoke as though we were discussing something very commonplace. 'The first time that I travelled back to this time, I was young, like you. Alone, like you. My parents had divorced, you see, and both of them had taken up with new people and suddenly there I was, with stepbrothers and stepsisters and our family home sold, and no place that was really my own any more, and I began to feel a great nostalgia for the days when I'd come down here as a child, when both my grandparents were still alive and living at St Non's. When life was simpler.' Stretching out her legs, she took a sip of tea before continuing, 'I was struggling along on my own as an artist by then, no real ties or commitments to bind me to anywhere, so I came down into this part of Cornwall on holiday and spent a lovely fortnight rediscovering the place, and that of course,' she finished off, 'meant coming to Trelowarth, for a cream tea at the Cloutie Tree.'

She'd always loved to hear the story of the day her grandparents had met, and over the course of her own visits to them they'd formed a tradition of making a pilgrimage out to Trelowarth to share a cream tea.

'It wasn't the same,' she said, 'with them not there,

but nonetheless it was a brilliant summer day and all the roses were in bloom and I stayed afterwards and wandered through the gardens as we'd always done. My grandmother had loved the Quiet Garden best of all, so I went up and had a little moment there, communing with her spirit. But when I was done and ready to come out again, I couldn't find the path.'

She had been more perplexed than panicked. It felt strange to lose her bearings in a place she'd known so well. Eventually, she'd found the path – not where she'd thought it ought to be, but she did find it, and began to make her way back down towards the Cloutie Tree, a bit disoriented, only to discover that the tearoom wasn't there.

'There wasn't even a greenhouse. I thought I was losing my mind,' she confessed, 'as I'm sure you'll appreciate.'

I managed a small smile. 'Yes. What did you do?'

'Well, I *did* panic then. I turned tail like a coward and ran to the house and I banged at the door until somebody answered. That was when I met your Uncle George.' Recalling that meeting, she said, 'I was lucky he didn't call in the authorities right there and then, and have them drag me off to Broadmoor. I know I must have sounded like a madwoman. But George . . . well, he was always kind to strays.' He'd brought Claire in and listened to her tale and made her tea.

'I'm not sure where the children were,' she said. 'Mark must have been at school, and Susan was most likely upstairs napping.'

He'd been widowed for a year by then, though at the time she hadn't known that. She'd been too caught up in her own strange predicament to notice much of anything.

I knew just how she'd felt.

'Then someone telephoned – the telephone was in the hall, I think, and George went off to answer it, and then . . .' She paused, as though unable to describe exactly what had happened next, before it seemed to strike her that with me, the process didn't need describing, so she simply said, 'And there I was again, back where I'd started, in the Quiet Garden.'

Everything was back where it was meant to be. The tearoom was in its place again, and she had gone inside to settle her bewildered nerves with one more pot of tea. After an hour in the Cloutie Tree amid the normal ebb and flow of patrons and inconsequential chatter, she'd convinced herself that what had happened must have been a daydream, an imagining.

But still, she'd packed her car up hastily that afternoon and cancelled her hotel and driven north across the moors to switch the subject of her paintings to the wilder-looking coastline on the other side of Cornwall, up near Boscastle.

Three months had passed before she'd found the nerve to venture back.

'I couldn't stop thinking about it,' she told me. 'I couldn't stop thinking of *him*. I'd begun to have dreams . . .'

It was autumn, by this time. The tourists had mostly departed, the streets of Polgelly were quiet, and up at Trelowarth the roses were reaching the end of their season, the gardens being readied for the winter.

She'd gone right up and knocked at the door of the house. 'I'd decided, you see, that the only way to get the whole episode out of my head would be to prove to myself that it couldn't have happened.' And as she'd expected, the door of Trelowarth was opened by somebody else – a man not unlike George in appearance, but with reddish hair and a leaner build. 'He was quite pleasant. I asked after George and he told me the only George Hallett he knew was his grandfather, and he'd been dead a long time.'

I felt my eyes widen. 'His grandfather? Then he was—'

'Mark's eldest,' Claire supplied. 'Stephen. A charming man. Very artistic he was, with these gardens, though all of Mark's children were artists in their own way. Something they got from their mother.'

'Felicity.'

'Yes.'

I was pleased by that.

Unseen, the wind stirred the trees at the edge of the garden and shook loose a new spray of lingering raindrops that fell near our feet and chased over the face of the sundial. The butterfly, frozen in bronze, stayed unmoving, still counting its moments.

Claire settled deeper in her chair and took another sip of tea. 'After talking to Stephen, I didn't know what to believe. What I'd seen. I only knew that there was something . . . something pulling me . . . no, pulling is perhaps too strong a word. Something inviting me to stay here. I went down into Polgelly to the pub to have some lunch. To think. And there, two tables over, was a man, a very old man, and he watched me for a little while, and then he just came over with his pint and sat right down and introduced himself.'

He'd thoroughly disarmed her with his easygoing attitude and they'd begun to talk, about her painting and her grandparents and all that she remembered of St Non's.

'And then our talk turned to Trelowarth and the

gardens and he told me that his wife had been a Hallett, and through her he had inherited a cottage on the grounds and if I wanted I could have it for the winter, do my work there. So—'

She spread her hands, and at the gesture I looked round.

'*This* cottage?'

'Yes.'

'So this was home for you in your own time, as well.'

Claire gave a nod. 'It still is, come to that. I still go back and forth, my dear. Not quite as often, any more. The process seems to slow with age, but even so it's really not a thing one can control.'

Of course, I thought; and with a dawning sense of understanding I recalled what Mark had told me on the day we'd argued in the field: 'When I was young,' he'd said, 'Claire used to go away for days, for weeks, sometimes, to do her work . . . She still does, every now and then . . .'

I said, 'It can't be easy, though, with Uncle George gone.'

'It was never easy.'

When all this had begun back in her own time, for the first few weeks after she'd moved her things into the cottage nothing untoward had happened. And then one day while walking in the gardens she'd heard voices, and passing the half-open door in the high wall she'd found Mark and George pruning roses.

George had smiled at her. 'Hello,' he'd said. 'You came back.'

She'd been lost after that.

But it hadn't been easy.

'It was,' she said, 'a very different life than I was used to.

You think women have achieved things now, you want to wait and see what's yet to come. And then of course there were the children and their feelings to consider, and the more I fell in love with George the more it all became so very complicated.'

In the woods the bird had stopped its song. Some little creature rustled briefly in the undergrowth and then was gone, and all I heard then was the whisper of the wind among the leaves and further off the plaintive crying of a gull above the shore.

'I went away,' she told me quietly. 'I found it all too much, you see, and once I had returned to my own time I left my cottage and I went away to London.'

She had stayed away for nearly a full year.

'What brought you back?' I asked.

Her answer was a simple one. 'I loved him.'

We sat quietly together in the garden for a moment while I turned this over in my mind, and then she shook the memories off and looked at me.

'Do you feel that you can talk about it yet, my dear? I rather think your story might be more exciting than my own.'

'Oh? Why is that?'

'Because.' She reached across and lightly touched my hand. My left hand. 'Your ring is on a different finger now, and knowing you that is no accident,' she said. 'You've taken a rare interest in the smugglers of Polgelly. And the coat you wore when you came back last night was stained with blood.' Her hand moved up to smooth the hair back from my swollen cheekbone. 'Then there's this. He didn't do that, did he?'

'Who?'

'The man you've married.'

I had always marvelled how Claire could just accept things, never doubting, taking everything in her stride, and now I finally knew the reason for it. Nothing would surprise her, I thought, after what she'd lived, herself.

I shook my head and told her, 'No. He would never hit me.'

And I settled back, and told her all of it, beginning where we'd started once before here in this garden, with the voices in the next room and the path that wasn't there.

It took some time to tell it properly. Enough time that we'd gone through one more pot of tea and half a plate of sandwiches before with difficulty, haltingly, I reached the point where I had stabbed the constable.

'And good for you,' was Claire's pronouncement. 'What a bastard.'

'Yes, well let's just hope he wasn't meant to father somebody important later on.'

Claire didn't think it very likely. 'Anyway, your actions can't change history, as you said.'

'That's Daniel's theory,' I corrected her. 'He thinks that what has happened is already cast in stone, and can't be changed. That's why I couldn't stop Jack being shot and killed, no matter what I did.' That knowledge didn't make it easier to say the words. 'It was his time to die.'

Claire's quiet glance was comforting. 'He seems a very clever man, your Daniel.'

'Yes.' Which brought to mind another theory Daniel and I shared. 'Claire?'

'Yes, darling?'

'When you went away that time, and stayed away so long,' I asked, 'what happened? I mean, did you travel back in time at all?'

She shook her head. 'No. When I wasn't at Trelowarth, nothing happened.'

'And when you *were* here,' I pressed further, 'did you ever travel back in time when you were in Polgelly, or St Non's?'

'No. Only here.'

I felt a twist of hope. 'So then it *is* tied to Trelowarth.'

Claire agreed that it did seem to be. 'Perhaps it has something to do with Felicity's ley lines.'

I frowned. 'But why us, though? Why are only the two of us affected? Why not Susan, or Felicity, or—'

'Darling, it's a mystery, and it likely will remain one. I don't know what brought your Uncle George and I together, and I doubt I ever will. He called to me, somehow,' she said. 'That's all I truly know. He called to me, or else I called to him.' The sun was setting now, the shadows growing longer on the sundial as she looked at it serenely. 'We were both a little lost, I think, and so we found each other. How does anyone find anyone?'

I didn't have the answer. I was thinking about Daniel, lonely after losing Ann, and of myself without Katrina, looking desperately for somewhere to belong. Which one of us, I wondered, had first called out to the other across time?

I watched the sundial too, and drew a breath that caught a little in the place above my heart. 'But it's so hard,' I said. 'I mean, what if I never do go back again? What if the whole thing just stops, or . . .' My next breath caught more painfully.

I thought of Fergal, telling me he wouldn't ever want to

know his future. 'Nor should anyone,' he'd told me, 'know what lies in store for someone else, for that would be a burden, would it not?' If he were here, I thought, I could have told him it was just as great a burden, sometimes, *not* to know.

I said as much to Claire. 'It's just so hard,' I said, 'not knowing what will happen.'

She looked at me, and in the fading light her eyes were filled with understanding and with sympathy. And knowledge.

And she asked me, 'Shall I tell you?'

Chapter Forty

Mr Rowe slid the last of the papers across his desk to me and sat back as discreetly as he could within the confines of his office to wait while I read through them.

'Perfect,' I said finally. 'Thank you.'

'Not at all.' He watched me initial the pages and sign them. 'And here,' he said, pointing to one line I'd missed. 'You are sure about this? It's a very large Trust.'

'Quite sure, Mr Rowe. It was never my money,' I tried to explain. 'It belonged to my sister, and this is what she would have wanted.'

'But this new arrangement leaves nothing,' he said, 'for your personal use.'

'I have other accounts.' Which of course was a lie, but I said it convincingly, and with a smile, and he seemed reassured.

'Ah.' He gave a nod.

I signed the final page. 'There's nothing else I need to do?'

'No, nothing. From now on we'll see to everything. Mr Hallett and his sister and their heirs can rest assured that the Trelowarth Trust will be well managed; they won't have to do a thing but let us know what monies they require, and when.'

'And you'll explain this all to them? They're just off to London today, but they'll be back on Tuesday.'

'Then I shall contact them on Wednesday.'

'I have a letter here, for both of them.' I drew it from my handbag. Passed it over. 'If you wouldn't mind, when you do see them, could you give them this as well?'

'Of course.' He stood when I stood. Shook my hand when I thanked him. 'It's been a great pleasure,' he said.

'And for me.'

I left the bank and stepped back out into the midday sunshine and the narrow crowded street. The mood of the tourists down here in Polgelly had subtly shifted, as though they had only just realised that summer was nearing its end and so, too, were their holidays. Gone were the leisurely couples and families, replaced by a purposeful horde who were actively looking for fun and impatient to find it, thronging the pavements and pushing through shops in their search for it.

People perched all down the harbour wall as always, with their newspaper-wrapped fish and chips and their rattling striped paper bags from the fudge shop, but even those people seemed restless now, keeping one eye on the time while they ate, no doubt very aware there were still many things left to do in the limited hours of the day that remained.

I knew just how they felt.

I was running a bit late myself when I wended my way

through the crowd by the harbour and ducked through the door of the Wellington.

I'd never seen the inside of the pub, and the brightness disarmed me a moment. From the outside the Wellington looked every year of its age, whitewashed walls leaning slightly on ancient foundations, a little bit rough and disreputable, much as it might have looked back in the day when it went by the name of the Spaniard's Rest, when Jack had come to drink rum here and Daniel had made sure his pistol was tucked in his belt before venturing in. Knowing some of that history, I'd somehow expected the inside of the pub to look a little dark and dangerous, a den fit for smugglers and thieves.

Seeing the white stuccoed walls and the honey-warm wood of the tables and booths and the light dancing in through the multi-paned windows surprised me, so much so that Oliver, already comfortably settled in one of the booths with a view of the harbour, glanced up with a grin as I joined him.

'Not quite what you'd pictured?' he guessed.

'Not a bit.'

'I know, it disappointed me, too, when my Uncle Alf brought me in here for my first legal pint,' he admitted. 'After the way all us kids had been warned off the Wellie so long, I'd expected there'd be knife marks on the tables and a band of cut-throats in the public bar, but no such luck.' Draining the dregs of the pint he'd been drinking, he levered himself from his seat and asked, 'What can I get you?'

Normally I would have had something non-alcoholic at lunch, but this wasn't a normal day. 'Half of whatever you're having, please.'

Oliver didn't question my choice, crossing over to the

bar to place our order with the barman while I bent to read the menu, but when he came back and took his seat again he held my half-pint ransom. 'All right,' he asked me, curious. 'What's wrong?'

'I'm sorry?'

'First you ring me up and ask me out to lunch,' he said, 'which in itself is rather odd, you must admit. And now you're drinking in the middle of the day. Not,' he qualified, with roguish charm, 'that I'm complaining about either, mind, but it does seem a little out of character.'

I pointed at my half-pint. 'Can I have that?'

'When you tell me why you need it.' Leaning slightly back he looked me over, taking stock. 'You're either working up the nerve to proposition me,' he guessed, 'or else you're getting set to break my heart.'

'Oliver . . .'

'In case you're undecided, I say go with option number one, it's so much more enjoyable for everyone involved.'

I told the table, 'I won't need to rent a cottage from you, after all.'

A pause. 'You're staying at Trelowarth, then?'

I shook my head.

'I see.' He took a drink himself. 'So, option number two, then.'

I said, 'Oliver.'

'What changed your mind?'

I shrugged and deflected the question because there was no way to answer it honestly. 'I thought I'd do a bit of travelling.'

'Alone, I take it?'

Glancing up, I saw he wasn't expecting an answer. The

smile in his eyes, though resigned, held a trace of regret.

He said, 'Well, I *did* try.'

'You did.'

Leaning confidentially towards me he pretended to look pained. 'Was it the biking shorts? Were they too much?'

It felt good to laugh. I told him, 'No, I rather liked the biking shorts. It was just that . . . well, I couldn't . . .'

'Say no more.' He slid my glass across the table to me. 'I mean, you're not the first woman to feel a passion in my presence that's so strong she runs away from it.'

'Is that a fact?'

'It happens all the time.'

He raised his menu, feigning nonchalance, while I regarded him with fondness. How like Oliver, I thought, to try to make this whole thing easy for me, when with any other man it might have been so awkward.

On impulse I told him, 'You really are wonderful.'

He answered without looking up. 'An unfortunate side effect.'

I had to smile. 'Side effect? Of what?'

'Brain damage, actually. Somebody nailed me right here with a rock, once.' He showed me the place on the side of his head and his eyes, meeting mine briefly over the top of the menu, lost their teasing light. Just for a moment. 'I've never got over it.'

And then he dropped his gaze back to the menu and said, 'Now, let's see what you're buying me.'

'How did he take it?' asked Susan.

I carefully helped her manoeuvre the last of the show roses into the van. 'He was fine. He did get a bit drunk, though.'

'He's rather adorable when he gets drunk.' With a smile she admitted, 'I'm not sure that *I* could resist him, in that state.' Securing the roses, she took a look round. 'Is that all of them?'

'I think so, yes.'

'I do wish that you'd change your mind and come.'

'I can't.'

'But you've never been to Southport, and the flower show's quite fun. Besides, I'll need someone to play with. Fee won't have much time for me, will she?' She emphasised that with a meaningful glance past my shoulder to where Mark stood close to Felicity, talking, beside the front door. But in spite of her complaining, Susan didn't look at all put out. In fact, she looked well satisfied by how things were developing. 'Do come,' she said.

I explained that I would if I could. 'But I can't change my travel arrangements.'

'Too bad. Maybe next year, then.'

'Maybe.'

She dusted her hands on her jeans. 'Look, you've been such a help. I can't thank you enough.'

She was talking, I knew, about more than our loading the van, but I'd played such a small role in launching the tea room that I couldn't take any credit. I said, 'It was nothing.'

'Of course it was something. I mean, our new website, and all that publicity, bringing the tour groups on board. Not to mention the trouble you went to, to find me those smugglers to spice up the brochures. And now Mark,' she said, with a nod at the van, 'doing this. It's your influence, Eva. We couldn't have done it without you.'

I wanted to say, 'Yes, you could,' but her eyes were so earnest I kept my thoughts private and hugged her instead. 'You take care of yourself.'

'And you. Don't you forget us,' she told me. 'Come back any time.'

My hug briefly tightened, and then I released her and said, 'Have a good time in Southport.'

Felicity, when it was her turn to wish me well, gave me a gift.

'I remember you liked him,' she said, as she passed me the little bronze sculpture. My pisky, the one I had held and admired in her shop on that day when she'd told me the story of Porthallow Green and the piskies who'd taken the young boy adventuring, whisking him dancing from place to place as the mood took them. The pisky looked up from the palm of my hand with his wide knowing smile.

Felicity said, 'It's insurance, to see that you'll find your way back to us. Just tell him, "I'm for Trelowarth".'

'I'll do that.' I closed my fingers round the little figure. 'Thank you.'

Mark stood and waited beside the front door as though knowing I'd want our goodbye to come last.

When it did, it was all at once harder and easier than I had thought it would be.

'Summer's end,' he said. 'Just like old times.'

'So it is.'

But it wasn't like old times, not really, and both of us knew it. Those lazy, long-ago summers when the four of us children had run at our will through the gardens and roamed the Wild Wood and played laughingly all through the streets of Polgelly, those summers were gone and would not come again.

Still, the gardens remained, and the roses returned, and there'd be other summers to come and new memories to make.

Mark said, 'You used to stuff your pockets full of fudge before you left.'

I smiled. 'I might still do that. What time does the fudge shop close?'

'Don't know. Just mind, if you go down the hill you have to come back up,' he told me, 'and I won't be here to carry you.'

'You've carried me enough this summer. All of you.'

'Yeah well, you needed it, I reckon.' His keen eyes were understanding. 'Better now?'

I nodded. Wanting to be honest with him, I said, 'Mark, I don't know when I'll make it back again, or even if . . . that is, it might be quite a while.' I let my gaze drop to the ground between us, feeling at a loss, and Mark stepped forwards, wrapping me within his solid arms.

'It took you twenty years the last time,' he reminded me. 'However long it takes this time, it won't make any difference.'

'It's not you,' I tried to tell him. 'I love all of you, I do. I love Trelowarth. But . . .' I couldn't find the words.

He found them for me. 'It's not home.'

Grateful, I rested my cheek against his for a moment and shook my head.

He took a step away and stood there looking down at me, the same old Mark, the same slow smile, the comfort of his hands still so familiar on my shoulders. 'That's all right,' he said. 'I didn't really think it would be. After all, Katrina's ashes wouldn't settle at Trelowarth, either.'

I'd forgotten that. I felt my smile wobble but it must have had my heart in it because he flicked a finger lightly down my cheek the way he'd done when I was small and he was feeling brotherly. 'I'm sorry that I won't be here to drive you to the station.'

'Claire can see me off.'

He gave a nod, and leant to kiss my forehead. 'You take care.'

'You, too.'

It was past time for them to leave. I stayed there standing in the drive while they went off. I waved, then tucked both hands deep in my jacket's pockets as the van blurred very briefly in my vision.

From the region of my feet I heard a mournful little whine, and looking down I saw the small dog Samson sitting with his gaze fixed up the road where Mark had gone. He whined again, and trembled slightly, and I bent to give his head a pat of reassurance.

'It's OK,' I told the dog, 'you'll see him soon.'

I felt the small bronze pisky weighing heavy in my hand, and in a softer voice I said again, more certainly, 'You'll see him soon.'

The pisky's smile held mischief mingled with its knowing wisdom as I looked at it a moment, and I marvelled again at Felicity's craftsmanship, giving this small bit of metal such life. I remembered her saying, 'In Cornwall, one truly feels magic could actually happen.' And thinking again of the legend of Porthallow Green, I held tight to my pisky and gave it a try.

Eyes closed, I said, 'I'm for Daniel Butler.'

But the wind that brushed my upturned face was all the answer I received.

Beside me, Samson whined again, and I opened my eyes. The other dogs had taken off already with the happiness of schoolchildren released from supervision, and I could see them bounding in a joyous pack along the path towards the Lower Garden.

Beyond that lay the green rise of the fields above the darker smudge of woods that tumbled down to where the black cliffs met the sea, with the wind raising ridges of white on the water as far out from land as my vision would stretch.

Above those waves the white birds wheeled and spiralled in the air and I was suddenly reminded of what Mark had said about Katrina's ashes, and I thought back to the day when we'd released them on this hill, when they had gathered in the wind and danced away.

In search of somewhere else, so Mark had thought. Except I knew now in my heart that wasn't right. Not some*where*.

Someone.

And I thought I knew, at last, where she had gone.

CHAPTER FORTY-ONE

He didn't call back till the following morning.

I worked the times backwards: if it was nine here, that would mean in LA it was one in the morning.

'Eva?'

I heard the sounds of a party around him – the clink of a glass and an outburst of laughter and over it all the pervasive loud beating of dance music.

'Bill, hi.' I sat at the edge of my bed. 'Thanks for getting back.'

'I would have called you earlier, but I was on the set, and then it got too late, I figured you'd be sleeping,' he explained. A pause. 'How are you?'

'Fine. I'm fine. And you?'

The party sounds receded slightly as though he had stepped away a pace or two in search of a more private corner. 'I'm managing. You know.' Another pause. 'You're still in Europe?'

'For the moment, yes. In Cornwall, at Trelowarth. Did Katrina ever talk about Trelowarth?'

'Yes.' He knew where I was headed. 'That's the place, then?'

I nodded, forgetting that he couldn't see me. 'I scattered her up in her favourite spot, up on the hill at the Beacon.'

'Good choice.'

'No, it wasn't.' I gripped the phone tighter and lowered my head, and in a stumbling rush I told him what had happened, how the ashes had refused to settle, swirling on the wind and chasing out across the sea. 'You wanted her to be where she belonged,' I said, 'but Bill, it wasn't here.'

'Hey.' From the hoarseness of that single word I guessed what it was costing him to try to reassure me. 'Sure it was. I mean, where else—?'

'With you.' I heard my voice break, just a little, and I steadied it to tell him, 'She belonged with you.'

For several heartbeats afterwards the muted party noises were the only sounds that carried down the line. Perhaps, like me, he was imagining Katrina's ashes blowing westward over the Atlantic. Heading home.

'I just . . . I wanted to apologise,' I said. 'I got it wrong. You were the great love of her life, Bill. Where *you* were, that's where Katrina would have wanted most to be. That's where she should be.'

His lighter clicked, and I could hear his deep pull on the cigarette, and then the long exhale. 'She still is, Eva. She's here with me, every day. You didn't get it wrong.' Another pause, and I could sense that he was searching for the words that would convince me of that, grant me absolution. After half a minute more he said, 'Trelowarth's just a place, you know?'

Trelowarth, said Daniel's voice, warm in my memory, *is rooms gathered under a roof, nothing more.*

My eyes stung. 'Yes, I know.'

We left it there.

I'd been afraid the day would stretch unbearably. This was still new and strange to me, this knowing what was yet to come, and thanks to Claire I knew that what was coming would not happen until dark. I'd thought the waiting might be my undoing, but the fact was there were still things left to finish, and the knowledge that I wouldn't have another chance to finish them made every hour fly faster.

It took me till that afternoon to get the files in order that I'd wanted to leave Susan, so she could take care of any future PR work herself. And when I'd switched off the computer there was still the packing left to do.

The afternoon had given way to evening almost before I had noticed, and by the time Claire came round after supper I was only just then finishing the final task of pinning up my hair.

She sat and watched me. 'I must say, you do that very neatly, Eva. Who taught you how?'

'Fergal, actually.'

'The Irishman?' She placed him with a nod. I'd told her all about the people living at Trelowarth in the past, and Claire had an efficient memory. 'It sounds as though he helped you quite a bit this summer.'

'Yes,' I said. 'He did.'

'I'm glad. It makes a world of difference, having someone to confide in.'

There was something faintly wistful in her voice that made me feel a twinge of guilt at leaving her, until I realised that I wasn't really leaving her alone.

I thought about that evening in her garden when she'd told me what the future held in store for me, and how she'd come to know it. She'd begun a little curiously in my view, by asking whether I remembered when she'd told the story of the Grey Lady who'd vanished at Trelowarth.

'Yes, of course,' I'd said.

'Do you remember when I said it happened?'

'Yes, before your parents' time, you said.' And I'd looked up at her in sudden realisation.

Claire had met my eyes. 'My parents, dear, aren't born yet. Not in this time.'

'And the Grey Lady . . . ?'

'Is you.'

She had explained it all again to me, how in the future she would meet an old man in the village who would tell her of the woman who had disappeared before his eyes when he was young. And he would know exactly who I was. He'd know my name.

She'd told me his name, too, and I had tried to take it in, but even so I'd had to stop her midway through her tale to make sure I'd heard her correctly.

'And *he* was the old man you met in the pub,' I'd said, just to be certain, 'the old man you rented this cottage from.'

'Yes.'

'But you said that the cottage had come to him

through his wife's family. And she'd been a Hallett.'

'That's right.' Claire had waited patiently, her gaze expectant on my face, until I'd sorted through the possibilities and reached the only answer.

'Susan.' I had been surprised at first, but then it seemed so right that I'd repeated it with pleasure. 'His wife was Susan.'

Claire had nodded. 'It was, he said, a very happy marriage. He had lost her just the year before I met him, and he clearly still adored her.'

I had thought a moment, making sense of everything. 'So you believe him, then. That I'm the Grey Lady?'

'Oh, yes. He might have been a very old man when we first met,' she'd admitted, 'but there wasn't any problem with his memory. Everything he ever told me would happen did happen, my darling. And he was quite sure about this. As I said, he was there.'

'*Will* be there,' I'd corrected her, vaguely. 'I haven't gone anywhere, yet.'

I'd looked towards the sundial with its butterfly forever frozen on the brink of flight. Below them waved the ring of bright geraniums I'd helped Claire plant – the only mark I'd left upon Trelowarth in this time, and even that was passing. Soon the blooms would fade and nod and die and no one would remember them. 'Aunt Claire,' I'd said, asking the question she hadn't yet answered, the one that most mattered to me.

'Yes?'

'Did she ever come back, this Grey Lady who vanished?'

Claire had turned to me fully that time, and our eyes had met. 'No,' she had told me, 'she never came back.'

And I'd felt a small catch of emotion then, tight round my heart, feeling almost like hope.

I could feel it again, growing stronger as I covered my hair with the white linen pinner and turned around now to face Claire so she'd have the full effect. 'There.'

'Very nice.' Claire looked me up and down, admiring the lines of the dress. 'He chose that for you, did he? Clever man. The colour's lovely.'

The green had a soothing effect on my nerves as I lifted the skirts to adjust them and took a look round to make sure I'd done everything. Both of my suitcases sat neatly packed on the furthermost bed. 'I suppose,' I said slowly, 'I'm ready.'

We each took a suitcase, and carried them down the short way to the first landing, setting them down while I sprang the stiff panel that hid the old priest's hole. 'You're sure this will be OK?'

'Darling, it's been here for centuries now without anyone knowing. It's quite the safest place to leave things,' she said. 'Better than a cupboard.'

To prove it she tucked one case neatly away in the narrow dark space, taking care not to pull at the delicate fabric of Ann's faded gowns that we'd hung in here earlier, next to the coat that had been the man Peter's, and Daniel's silk banyan that I'd first brought back. I slid the second case into its place and positioned Felicity's pisky on top of it, leaving him there with his all-knowing smile to watch over things as I stepped back a pace, letting the panel swing closed again.

Someday, I thought, when Trelowarth House fell to the elements, some archaeologist might stumble over those twenty-first century cases of clothes sharing space with an old bloodstained coat and the banyan and two eighteenth-century gowns, and might wonder about them, and try to form theories explaining the puzzle of how they had come to be there in one place . . . but I'd lay odds that none of the theories would ever come close to the truth.

And the walls held their silence, no whispers this evening as I followed Claire down the staircase and through the bright kitchen and out the back door with the dogs coming, too, keeping close to our heels in a tail-wagging pack, ever curious, seeking excitement.

They seemed to find it in the scents that rode the cooling night breeze blowing shoreward from the sea, and with their noses bouncing happily from air to ground and back again they snuffed their way around the yard, some venturing with interest to the stable building doorstep, no doubt hoping that their master had returned.

I stayed with Claire, and went no further than the honeysuckle vine that climbed the wall beside the kitchen window. There was light here slanting out across the softness of the grass and casting shadows through the vine's leaves in a finely tangled net that made a pattern on my green silk gown.

I asked Claire, 'Are you sure we're not too late?'

'Darling,' she said. 'You can't possibly miss it, there's no need to worry.'

I realised she was right, that while for me the whole event had not yet taken place, in Claire's time it was something done and finished with, belonging to the past; the Moving Finger had already written what must happen.

But that knowledge, reassuring as it might be, didn't make me feel less nervous.

'Yes, but when—?' I left the question hanging, because just then one of the dogs raised its head and gave a shortened bark that brought the other dogs to quick attention, all their noses turned in the direction of the road.

Like them, I heard the footsteps on the gravel drive. Claire did, as well.

'Quite soon, I should imagine,' was her answer as she turned to greet our visitor as he came round the corner of the house. 'Good evening, Oliver.'

And in that single moment I knew everything she'd told me had been true.

Oliver came round the side of the house and glanced up at Claire's greeting.

'Hello,' he said, fending the happily leaping dogs off with one hand as I saw him both notice my gown and, with typical nonchalance, choose not to comment beyond a quick nod and a cheerful, 'Nice frock.' He stepped closer and flashed his endearing smile. 'I thought with everyone gone off to Southport, you might be in need of some company.'

Claire said, 'I see you've brought wine.'

There was something about how she said that, some note in her voice that reminded me this was a night she herself must have waited a very long time for – this night when she'd finally be able to sit down and talk, really talk, to the man who would become her friend and confidant; the man who would one day be Susan's husband, and the man whom she would meet again some sixty years from now, when he was old, and she was young.

She wouldn't know him then, of course, because for her it would be their first meeting, but Oliver would recognise *her*. On that day she walked into the pub, he would approach her, and he'd offer her the cottage, and he'd share with her the story of the Grey Lady he'd once seen disappear before his eyes, here at Trelowarth. Eventually, he'd tell her more.

He'd be as good a friend to her in her own time as he would be in this one, after they sat down and talked tonight, and I was pleased to know that by my leaving I was bringing them together.

'It does make a world of difference,' Claire had told me, 'having someone to confide in.'

She would have that soon, I thought.

But for the moment Oliver was still in total ignorance of what was yet to come.

He looked down at the bottle he was holding. 'Yes, it's only the one bottle, I'm afraid, but—'

'That will do,' Claire told him, 'for a start.'

'I'm sorry?'

She didn't explain. She only reached to take the bottle from him. 'Here, you'd better let me hold that, dear.'

And just in time. The air around me had already started changing, and the breeze had stopped, and at the edges of my vision all the colours of the landscape had begun to run, the honeysuckle vine washed grey against the stone walls of Trelowarth House.

I had the sense of movement to the side of me and, turning, I could see a shape that might have been a man approaching. Unaware of me at first, he nearly passed me by before he stopped, and I could see that it was Fergal now. I saw the quick flash of his grin as his head lifted slightly and, although I couldn't hear him, it appeared that he was calling out to someone in the house.

Oliver's voice seemed to come from a very great distance. 'My God,' he said. 'Eva . . .'

Claire calmed him, 'It's all right. She's fine.'

A sudden brightness flashed behind me and I turned instinctively towards it, blinking, watching it resolve itself into a shape I recognised: the warm light of the open doorway, with one shadowed figure framed within it.

Daniel.

Looking at him then I knew there was no need to wonder, any more, where I belonged. There lay my home, I thought, and all the comforts I could want, and come the spring when all the Duke of Ormonde's plans to raise a great rebellion in the west of England had been set aside for schemings of a newer sort, the *Sally* would raise anchor on the turning tide and sail towards the south, to Spain perhaps, or the Canary Isles, where no one would remark upon my accent and where Fergal could indulge his taste for sack and maybe find a Spanish woman who could match his wit and temper.

What did it matter that our lives would leave no mark upon Trelowarth? That the path through the woods which had led to the cliffs where the *Sally* lay moored would be needed no longer, and little by little the years would reclaim it, the trees growing over the trails of our feet until no one would know we had walked there at all?

I would know, and remember, and that was enough.

A breath of wind brushed past my face and brought the scent of woodsmoke with it from the kitchen hearth.

I looked back once at Oliver and Claire. Claire's cheeks were wet but she was smiling as she gave a nod and mouthed the word 'Goodbye.'

I thought I heard the words 'Come back' as well, but whether it was Oliver or Daniel who had spoken them I couldn't tell. My face by then was turning to the warm light of the open doorway and the man who stood within it, waiting for me.

Gaining substance by the second.

Wordlessly he stretched his hand towards me, and I saw his smile.

And with a smile, I went to him.

Author's Note

Polgelly is the Cornwall of my memory. But it bears a strong resemblance to the village of Polperro, as it was when I first saw it in the summer that remains the brightest bead in all my string of childhood memories. And Trelowarth owes its heritage to Landaviddy Manor, on the hill above Polperro, where my sister and I shared a room that looked towards the sea.

I've changed the names, in part because it *is* a work of memory, and in part because I've changed the landscape and the house to suit my story's needs: I've left The Hill exactly where it should be, but I've moved the cottage and the beach, and added in the Beacon and the Wild Wood and the gardens.

In my building of the latter, I'm indebted to the kind and generous help of Stewart and Rebecca Pocock, award-winning owners of both Pocock's Roses of Hampshire and The Cornish Rose Company of Mitchell, near Truro, who were constantly encouraging and patient with their guidance, as was Lara Crisp, my editor, who helped me prune the deadwood from my manuscript to let it take the shape that it was meant to be.

I'm thankful as well for the help of my friend, fellow writer Liz Fenwick, who from her Cornish home took time to help me get my details right.

The years stand still for no one, but I've always felt a magic in the crossing of the Tamar, and I like to think perhaps some future traveller to Polperro, having climbed The Hill, may hear a burst of laughter from the lawn of Landaviddy Manor, high above the sea, and glimpse the shadows of two sisters still at play there, in another time.

BY SUSANNA KEARSLEY

'Like something out of the pages of
Daphne du Maurier'
Daily Express

To order visit our website at
www.allisonandbusby.com
or call us on
020 7580 1080